BLOOD
IN THE
WATER

BLOOD IN THE WATER

JACK FLYNN

MINOTAUR BOOKS
New York

First published in the United States by Minotaur Books, an imprint of St. Martin's Publishing Group

www.minotaurbooks.com

The Library of Congress Cataloging-in-Publication Data is available upon request.

ISBN 978-1-250-09017-1 (hardcover)
ISBN 978-1-250-09018-8 (ebook)

First U.S. Edition: September 2019

10 9 8 7 6 5 4 3 2 1

ACKNOWLEDGMENTS

There are too many people to thank for all the help with this book, including all of my family and friends, as well as those who read manuscripts and provided thoughts and advice. In particular, I would like to thank my editors, Trisha Jackson and Peter Wolverton, for all their help and advice. Also, many thanks to the teams at Macmillan: In the United States, thanks to Hannah O'Grady, Hector DeJean, Joseph Brosnan, David Rotstein, Steven Seighman, Elizabeth Curione, Cathy Turiano, Kelley Ragland, and Andrew Martin. In the UK, thanks to Jayne Osborn, Natalie Young, Fraser Crichton, Liz Cowen, Philippa McEwan, Neil Lang, and Stuart Wilson. I would also like to thank all the wonderful people at the Aaron Priest Agency, including Aaron Priest, Lisa Erbach Vance, Lucy Childs, Mitch Hoffman, Eileen Priest, John Richmond, Juliana Nador, and Francis Jalet-Miller.

BLOOD
IN THE
WATER

ONE

Tuesday, January 1

He hummed as he worked.

An old folk tune he'd learned in El Calabozo as a child.

He couldn't remember the words, which was odd; as a rule, he remembered everything. Memories tortured Vincente Carpio, and his tortured mind gave him a special kind of madness. The leadership recognized it early on. That was why they'd sent him to America—because he was willing to do the things that others weren't. It was a decision many in the leadership now questioned. Now the madness seemed to have taken over.

He was sweating, and his bald, tattooed head was slick. This one was the eighth he'd done this way, and by far the hardest. He wouldn't have thought it to look at her. She was young and thin, shorter than him, with a punk haircut: shaved on one side and dyed multiple colors on the other. At first he'd thought she was probably a junkie; Cambridge had its fair share, a consequence of the ultra-liberal orthodoxy of the city that viewed tolerance of everything as an imperative.

He'd realized quickly that she wasn't. Junkies put up little resistance. They were so unhappy with their lives that they simply couldn't find a reason to fight. This girl, though, had been full of fight. She fought so hard he considered aborting the attack and moving on, but that wasn't a realistic option. If she'd escaped, the police would have combed through the area immediately, and there was little doubt that he would be found. He couldn't let that happen.

Eventually she had succumbed, as they all did in the end. Even now, though, she continued to resist in her own way. The sinew around her vertebrae was stringier and less cooperative than he had found with the others, forcing him to work harder, and his perspiration mixed with the blood on his hands, making the task all the more difficult. He found the work invigorating, though, and the blood sliding down the crosses adorning his wrists made him think of the graveyard in his home town—fields of crosses covered in blood.

He was surprised that he could sweat in the cold. Growing up, he'd thought that the winter in El Calabozo was frigid. The temperatures could sometimes dip into the fifties in January and February. He'd never experienced any cold like a New England winter. He'd left the upstairs windows in the little house open, mainly to keep the flesh refrigerated, and with the outside temperatures below zero, the house was an icebox.

And yet, still, he was sweating.

Finally, he finished with the knife and started with the ropes, tying her up the same way he'd done with the others. When he was done with that, he stepped back and examined his work.

He was satisfied.

He wondered how long it would take for his work to be found. Two days, he thought. Maybe three. The police were already looking for two of them. And he was a priority for the FBI and the other federal authorities. Even with the cold, the stench was overpowering in the basement. With the windows left open, it would not take long for one of the neighbors to decide that their civic tolerance ended with the smell of rotting flesh, and they would call the authorities. Then the real madness would begin. America would realize what it had wrought unto itself.

He walked to the basement sink and washed the blood and sweat from his arms and his face. He gave the place one last look. His fingerprints would be everywhere, as would other identifying evidence.

He didn't care. He wanted them to know it was him.

He needed them to know it was him.

TWO

Wednesday, January 16

The dream returned.

Her little boy had come back to her, with a smile that melted her heart and made her long for the chance to hold him just once more. They were by the shore, near the Nantasket motel south of Boston where they'd spent a week every summer of his life—just the three of them, the perfect young family.

She tried to run to him, but the ground slipped beneath her feet, like a great terrestrial treadmill. She called out to him, begged him to come to her, but he just smiled.

A foghorn blared in the background. She called to him again, pleading with him to say something—anything—to her. His lips were moving, but the foghorn grew louder, drowning him out. He was slipping away, and she could feel her panic growing. . . .

She opened her eyes. The dream was gone, but the foghorn droned on, beating in time to the dull throb in her skull until she reached over and grabbed her phone. She looked at the caller ID, recognized the number, and was instantly awake.

"Yeah, it's Steele." She listened for a moment, her heart rate climbing, the blood pumping through her body, clearing away the last of the dream-fog as anticipation took root. "OK, I'll be there."

She hung up and looked over at the body next to her—a silhouette draped in a sheet. For a moment it brought to mind all the crime scenes she'd worked over the years. She swung her legs off the bed, pulled on her underwear and jeans, a blouse and a jacket.

"Your tip panned out," she said. "I gotta go."

"So go," the body replied. She'd hoped he was asleep. It would have been easier.

"Thanks for last night. It was nice."

"Always is." He didn't turn to face her.

Kit Steele opened her mouth to say something, but could think of nothing appropriate. She grabbed her gun and her bag and headed out of the apartment.

THREE

Vincente crept along the pier, careful with every step to avoid a slip. The fall wouldn't kill him, but the water probably would. Not right away, but within a matter of minutes. Even in the dark he could see the chunks of ice floating in Boston Harbor, gathering at the edge of the shoreline as though conspiring to take over the waterway—choke it off, force it to grow still. Carpio had heard that it had happened once, a few years before, when the ice floats had become so large that ships had to be diverted, and the harbor had to be closed for two days as icebreakers were called in.

He was the hunted now. Every newscast flashed his picture and pleaded with the public to join the chase—to feed the police information regarding his whereabouts. The skulls tattooed over his entire head captured the imagination like a horror film, and he was regarded as a supernatural predator by all of Boston. It was understandable, given the carnage he'd brought down upon the surrounding area. What none of them understood was that everything up to now had been a prelude. He was growing stronger, and he would continue to take his revenge until he'd killed as many as he could.

He was looking for a new area in which to hunt. It was getting more difficult with his growing notoriety. It would be hard for anyone not to recognize him. Images of the dead and blood and bones and carnage covered his entire body. Even his eyeballs had ink in them—two crosses flanking both irises. He could keep his hood up, but that wouldn't work to hide his identity for long. He'd now taken to sleeping during the days and hunting at night in the deserted areas of Boston, where his work would attract less attention.

The pier ran along the side of the harbor, in what was known as the Seaport District. It was a patchwork of high-end developments at the edge of South Boston, just across Fort Point Channel from the Financial District and Downtown. Five years before it had been a wasteland of warehouses and parking lots, but now it was the hottest growth area in the city. A dozen high-rises were already up, with a mixture of office space and luxury condos nestled around the federal courthouse, which for a decade had been the area's lonely architectural sentinel. Seven more complexes were under construction and the shoreline was pocked with construction sites.

It was a perfect hunting ground. There was enough development to provide prey, but it was still new enough that there were few people who walked the streets at night. He'd had little luck on this night, though, and he decided to go down to the water to see whether there might be a drunk passed out by the shore. He'd gotten lucky in such ways before.

He'd been forced to hop a chain-link fence to climb onto the pier, which was nearby one of the newest developments. He saw the boat approaching and his hopes rose. If the vessel was pulling in, he might be able to overpower those on board. Perhaps his luck had changed.

Suddenly a spotlight on the front of the boat flashed so bright that it felt like an explosion. He was looking straight into it, and it blinded him, almost knocked him to the ground. He stumbled back into a piling, his hand defending his eyes as they adjusted and tried to make out shapes.

It was futile. A siren screamed, and the hands protecting his eyes flew to his ears. It continued for a few seconds, and then cut off abruptly. A voice came over a bullhorn. "Freeze!" It was a woman's voice, and he recognized it instantly. "FBI! You are under arrest!"

The voice spurred him to run. He had always known the risks of capture, but to be captured by *her* was too much to bear. He stumbled in the direction of the shore, still blinded, unable to see the rotted wood beneath him. It was only twenty yards from the edge of the pier to solid ground, but the pier was only ten feet wide, so there was precious little room for error. The odds were low that he would make it, but he was willing to take that chance.

On the lead boat, Kit held the megaphone. There were two other vessels in the group—all boats currently at the disposal of the joint task force through the Coast Guard and the Boston Police Department. Some of the brass had grumbled at the excess. There was a sense that it was overkill, but the tip indicated that Vincente Carpio was crawling the shoreline at night, looking for fresh meat. No one was willing to risk him slipping through their fingers once more. He was the most wanted man in the United States, and, of greater political importance, he had previously escaped from their custody. His escape had been an embarrassment that had tarnished every branch of law enforcement. No one wanted to be the one who called for fewer resources in the effort to bring him to justice, so Kit had gotten everything she'd asked for.

Now she had him again. She could see him running, his hands covering his bald, tattooed head, crashing into the fence by the edge of the pier, scurrying like a cockroach in the brightness of the spotlight. As the boat approached the pier she felt every muscle in her body tense, adrenaline driving through her veins. There was a special operations detail on land, closing in from the other side of the construction site, so there should be no way for Carpio to escape, but his elusiveness had taken law enforcement by surprise before, and she was unwilling to take chances. As the boat came within a few feet of the pier, Rich Alvarez, the Coast Guard commander captaining the vessel, cut the engine, and Steele dropped the megaphone, took three strong strides, and launched herself toward the pier.

"Shit!" Alvarez shouted. "Steele! What the hell are you doing?"

Bill McCaughey, a captain in the Boston Police Department also on board, barked angrily, "Get back here, missy!"

She ignored them both.

She could hear the commotion behind her as guardsmen lashed the boats to the pier, but she didn't look back. As soon as her feet hit the splintered wood she drove forward. Her gun was drawn, and she focused on the dark figure just now clearing the fence at the edge of the pier. She ran faster than she ever had before, possessed by the need to capture and to punish. She would not let him escape. She was no longer motivated by her job; she needed to fulfill a moral imperative, and as she pushed herself to the edge of her physical abilities, she knew that she had crossed a dangerous line where her perspective and her judgment had been compromised. Even that realization was not enough to stem her obsession, though, and she pushed on faster.

FOUR

Carpio's feet hit the hard, uneven ground on the other side of the fence. Earthmovers had spent the better part of two months on the site before the freeze set in, pushing giant mounds of dirt and rock from side to side, removing debris to be carted off, and their tracks had cut into the ground, leaving a checkerboard of pits and ridges in the frozen mud. He landed awkwardly on the edge of one of the ridges and heard a loud popping in his right ankle. He let out a muffled scream, but stifled it immediately. He rolled to his left and stood, taking most of his weight on his left leg as he hobbled forward.

The construction site was a maze of heavy equipment and materials and he ducked behind a tall pile of rebar, moving steadily toward the side of the site that bordered Northern Avenue. If he could get there, he might have a chance. It was a slim chance, but it was all he had at the moment.

He crept forward, ducked under a giant crane and around a temporary trailer that served as the nerve center for the construction site. He slid his back along the side of the trailer until he could see around the corner, and caught sight of the fence at the far side of the site. His spirits leaped at his good fortune when he saw that there was a gap in the gate, wide enough, he thought, that he might be able to squeeze through. His ankle throbbed, but there was hope if he could make it to the street.

He took a deep breath and felt the frozen air stinging his lungs as he started what was the closest to a sprint he could manage. He'd gotten only two strides from the trailer when the break in the fence widened, and a stream of police flooded through into the construction site. They were clad in full body armor and armed with military rifles. The sight brought him up short and he reversed course, diving back to the cover of the trailer.

He was trapped now. There was no question of escape—not for the moment, at least. He was resigned to that, and knew in his heart that he would eventually escape again. Revenge was his destiny. He still needed to play the part of the hunted, though. And if he was going to be captured, perhaps he could at least kill *her*.

He made his way back along the side of the trailer and slipped into the maze of rebar and construction equipment. As he hobbled forward, he tripped and went down, his hands grasping in front of his body to brace against the fall. His fingers touched metal, and he grasped a two-foot length of rebar that was lying on the ground. He picked it up and held it like a club, ducking into a dark recess in between two piles of gravel.

He could hear them as they spread out through the construction site. He could smell their fear and it made him feel powerful. He was but one man among all of them, and yet he was the one who was feared. It was further confirmation of the strength there was in terror, and that strength validated everything he had done. He wanted all of America to feel the terror he'd known his entire life. It was only fair, after all.

Crouched silently in the shadows, he could hear her now. She was approaching slowly from the water, breathing heavily. Her footsteps were muffled but unmistakable, and it made him angry to think that she believed that she could take him herself. The muscles in his arms tensed, and he gripped the length of rebar tightly in his hand, readying himself to strike.

Kit Steele could see the police special operations teams moving in from the street. They were spreading through the site, starting at the perimeter and working their way in toward the center. They worked in pairs, spaced in a military formation that allowed them to protect each other, providing cover and safety as they methodically searched the lot.

She should back off, she knew. There was no chance that Carpio could escape now, and the ops team was better equipped to root him out without bloodshed. They were appropriately armed and dressed in the best protective gear available. She, on the other hand, was in jeans and a windbreaker, and while the bright yellow "FBI" stencil on the back of the windbreaker might impress some civilians in the daylight, it wouldn't stop a bullet.

She couldn't back off, though. She needed to see his face when he was taken. She needed him to see her face, and know that she had caught him once more. This time she would make sure that he would never see freedom again.

The cold sliced through the windbreaker and her jacket underneath, and it felt as though her fingers were frozen to her 9mm Glock. She could have worn gloves, but she didn't trust the feel of a gun through the material. Even in the freezing cold, she was more comfortable with her skin against the weapon

She was picking her way through the giant piles of earth and construction material, alert to every sound and every movement, her heart pounding and her breath coming in desperate, shallow gulps she struggled to control.

As she came around a corner where two piles of gravel intersected, she sensed movement—feeling rather than seeing it—and spun and ducked at the same time, her two hands coming up with her gun, aiming it toward the gravel.

The pain was exquisite as the heavy metal connected with her forearm, and the gun went off as it was knocked from her hands. She could hear shouts from the tactical squad, and she knew they would be there to help in a matter of seconds, but it wasn't clear that she would survive those seconds. Carpio was raising the rebar above his head again, looking into her eyes, aiming for her forehead. He was moving forward awkwardly, as though unsteady on his feet, his own eyes cold and calculating. The thought to punch at him flashed through her mind, but she wasn't sure whether her arm was broken. It was too cold, and the pain was too acute to know. Instead she swept her left leg forward, aiming to take his feet out from under him. She hoped that he would lose his balance and that would disrupt his aim enough to prevent him from shattering her skull.

The impact, though, was far more effective than she anticipated. Her shin connected with his right ankle, and his cold, calculating eyes went wide with pain and fury. Carpio let out a scream like a wounded animal, and he swung the rebar wildly as he toppled over. He hit the ground just to the left of her, and she knew that her advantage would be short-lived. She lashed out with her left elbow, driving it into his face, satisfied with the dull crunching sound she heard as his nose snapped.

The shouts from the tactical team were close now, and she got to her feet. Her gun was a few feet away, and she grabbed it with her left hand. Carpio was on all fours, spitting blood into the ground, and she stepped to him and kicked him hard in the ribs, flipping him over. He looked up at her, and the hatred in his eyes was unmistakable. "Whore!" he screamed at her.

She kicked him again in the ribs and he coughed out blood. "You don't know me well enough to call me that," she said. With the dexterity of a seasoned professional, she grabbed one of his wrists and slapped a cuff tight to it. He grunted in pain, and that gave her some satisfaction. She pulled his other wrist behind his back and snapped on the other cuff. Then she grabbed him by the front of his jacket. "Get up," she ordered. He struggled to his feet, favoring his right side as she leaned him against a stack of rebar.

His face was a mess, his nose twisted, but his tattooed eyes had cleared and they stared at her with a malice she had seen before. She supposed it matched her own toward him.

The tactical team was there now, assault rifles out, body armor bulging, eyes vigilant. And as they regarded the scene—Carpio bloodied and cuffed and cowed—a few of them tittered.

"Nice job, Special Agent," one of them said. "Looks like we didn't need the heavy artillery, all we needed was a pissed-off chick with a badge." Several of the others laughed.

It was intended less as a compliment to her than as an insult to her prisoner. And it was clear that the slight had landed effectively. Carpio's bloodied face twisted in uncontrollable rage.

"You will all pay!" he screamed. "You will pay for what you have done to my people!"

One of the tactical guys shook his head. "Shit, he actually talks like that, huh?"

Kit nodded. "He does." She stepped forward, so that her face was less than a foot in front of Carpio's. "Sorry to spoil your plans, Vincente."

And then a strange thing happened. Carpio smiled.

"Don't worry, Special Agent," he said through a heavy accent. "You have not spoiled my plans. I can't be stopped. You should know that by now."

There was something about the look on his face that sent a fresh wave of rage and hatred through her. It was like she was losing her son all over again—as though no matter what she did to push back the tide of grief she had fought for half a decade, human trash like Carpio could bring it back, like a tsunami that washed away the emotional fortifications she had constructed to protect herself.

Before she realized what was happening, she brought her knee up hard and fast between Carpio's legs. His cheeks plumed and his face went a dark shade of purple. His right leg buckled, and he crumpled to the ground at her feet with a loud groan.

One of the tactical officers behind her laughed. "Jesus, Special Agent. Remind me not to get on your bad side."

FIVE

Friday, January 18

"Special Agent Steele, welcome to FMC Devens."

Warden Stevens was a soft, round man with prodigious jowls and sympathetic eyes. Kit could imagine no one better suited to put on a fake white beard and red suit and hand out gifts to children at an office Christmas party. She questioned, though, whether he was the right sort to guard truly hardened men.

The Federal Medical Center was forty minutes west of Boston, nestled in a suburban enclave where upper-middle-class families bustled through their lives without giving a thought to the criminals housed in their midst. Nor did the facility provide any real external reminders. The place was neat and clean, and there were no barbed-wire fences in view from the outside. It was split into two parts. One half housed a federal minimum security prison where tax cheats and Wall Street bandits played chess and made macramé hats for their hedge-fund friends, who would welcome them back to the financial world in six to eighteen months with *there-but-for-the-grace-of-God* nods and shrugs. The other half housed prisoners who required medical care or special attention. It had been designed to accommodate prisoners at every level of risk, from minimum security up through Supermax. Steele had read all of this on the FMC Devens website, which proudly advertised the humanity with which all prisoners were treated.

Warden Stevens led Steele through the administrative building, which looked more like an educational facility than a prison. "It's good of you to come all the way out here to check on Mr. Carpio. I understand you were the one who took him into custody?"

"That's right. Both times."

"The first time was on a raid, correct?"

Kit nodded. "I've been working to cut into MS-13 for the last three years."

"Yes, from what I understand, you have quite a reputation among the gang community. They even have a nickname for you. I'm told they call you the Hunter. Why is that?"

"I'm good at my job."

"Mr. Carpio certainly has a great deal of animosity toward you. How did you catch him the first time?"

"Dumb luck, really. We found one of their hangouts and raided it for drugs and weapons. He was there, and we picked him up. We didn't know at the time who he was. He had no papers, and he didn't show up in the system, so we handed him over to ICE. He was going to be deported."

"What happened?"

"Somebody screwed up."

Stevens frowned. "His escape was unfortunate."

"Particularly for the eight people he killed afterward. Since then, we've connected him to more than a dozen killings over the past few years."

Stevens nodded grimly. "As I say, it was unfortunate." His reassuring smile returned. "Of course, that had nothing to do with this facility, and such an escape could never happen here."

"No?"

"No. Here we have the most stringent Supermax medical containment protocols in existence, and the most modern incarceration equipment available. He is halfway through the orientation program, and throughout that, he is monitored constantly. There is a video feed to his cell, so that even when he is asleep, there is at least one guard who can monitor him at all times. There is no way that he could get out of here."

"Can anyone get in?"

"I'm not sure I understand your question, Special Agent Steele. Why would anyone want to get in?"

They were at his office now, and he led her in. It was neat and organized and the furniture was solid, though not ostentatious. It was an office that any high school principal or university provost would have found completely adequate.

"Vincente Carpio has a dedicated and inspired group of followers, Warden. He's an enforcer in MS-13's army. That means you need to consider the possibility that they will attack from the outside in an attempt to get him out of here."

Stevens waved a hand at her dismissively as he sat behind his desk. "They would have to be crazy to attempt such a thing." His eyes maintained a confident glint.

"They are crazy," Steele said. She reached into the satchel she'd brought with her and took out two manila folders. She opened one and put it in front of Stevens. It contained a series of color photographs from the crime scene where Carpio's most recent victims had been found. Steele pointed to the first picture. "This is from the last crime scene," she said. "There were eight of them. Their heads were found in another room."

In the image, the bodies were kneeling, their hands tied together behind their backs, the ropes tied to their ankles so the bodies would stay on their knees, hunched forward but upright nonetheless. The chests and backs were black with dried blood, and the stumps of their necks still looked damp. In the center of four of those stumps, vertebrae gleamed white.

"Jesus Christ," Stevens whispered.

"Christ had nothing to do with it, I can assure you." Steele pointed to one of the bodies. "By the time they were found, rigor had set it, so the bodies had to be transported in sacks. They wouldn't even stay on the coroner's gurney. We had to have the loved ones identify the clothing so we could match up the heads with the bodies. Even then, it wasn't easy. Have you ever seen a human head after the blood has been drained from it?"

Stevens shook his head, but didn't look up.

"It's hard to recognize. The skin sags and the features become muddled. Our coroners are good, but there were still a couple we had to use DNA with to make sure we weren't putting the heads with the wrong bodies." Steele walked over to the window and gazed out on the rolling grass in what would have seemed a suburban paradise, had she not had a complete understanding of the evil that was in the immediate vicinity. "You understand why I'm showing these pictures to you, don't you, Warden?"

Stevens still didn't pick up his head to look at her. "No," he whispered.

"Because you need to understand who we are dealing with. You have to understand *what* we are dealing with. We are dealing with pure evil. He's a psychopath. I've caught him twice, but he's escaped once. I'm not going to let that happen again. Do you understand?"

He finally looked up at her, and to her relief the confidence and reassurance was gone from his eyes. Their place had been taken by fear and revulsion. That made her feel better, and gave her some hope that he might have a grasp of the seriousness of his task. He nodded. "I understand."

"Good. Now, I'd like to go over your security procedures."

SIX

Thursday, January 31

Two weeks after the recapture of Vincente Carpio, the historic freeze still gripped Boston. The morning sun crawled into view over the waterfront. At six thirty, the thin light promised no respite from the New England winter. A slate sky met the ashen sea on the horizon as though in conspiracy to chill the bones of those who dared to make their living on the water. It was still dark enough that the inside light shone through the crack in the door from the small, run-down warehouse at the water's edge in East Boston where six men had gathered.

T'phong Soh studied the man across the table from him. The last few days' travel showed on the man's face; the lines were etched deep, the weariness apparent. The eyes were still sharp, though—sharp enough that Soh knew not to test him.

Physically, the two had nothing in common. Soh was small and thin, with a broad, shallow nose and pale Southeast Asian skin. His hair was cropped close, his scalp visible. His twenty-four-year-old face was hairless, the smooth skin marred only by the neck tattoos that strayed unevenly above the jawline.

Javier Carpio was well over six feet tall, heavyset, with hands the size of bear claws. His forehead fought a losing battle with the massive tangles of his long black hair, tinged with gray, that fell around an aquiline face that hinted at his Amerindian ancestry. His eyebrows were so thick they reminded Soh of the underbrush of some great jungle.

"Drink?" Soh offered.

"Yes," his guest said. "Tequila."

Soh nodded to one of his men.

Two shot glasses and a bottle were swiftly placed on the grooved table between them. Javier poured a single shot, picked it up and threw it down his throat. He put the shot glass back on the table and filled both his and Soh's. Soh picked his glass up, his eyes never leaving those of the man across the table. They both drank.

Javier Carpio stared at him for a long moment before he spoke again. "The routes are set," he said finally. "The supply is limitless. Two directions. One from our friends in Colombia to your people in California, the other from Afghanistan, across land to the Mediterranean, here to your port of Boston."

Soh glanced out through the grime-caked window toward the water. The warehouse that served as his headquarters sat by a small pier at the northern edge of East Boston. It was a convenient place from which to operate on a limited scale, but there was little doubt that a larger, more suitable location would have to be found if the plan were to move forward. "Price and quality?"

"As discussed." The man poured two more shots.

"And the leadership?"

They were both captains in MS-13, one of the most dangerous criminal gangs in the world. They knew that doing business behind the backs of their superiors was risky, and would result in death if discovered before they could finish their plans.

"They will be informed in good time," Javier said. "This is a deal that I offer to you as an individual. To strengthen you as well as the organization."

"We have a deal, then," Soh said.

The man shook his head. "Not yet. There is one thing that you must do before we are agreed."

Soh patiently folded his hands in front of him on the table. In his experience, people always wanted something more.

"My younger brother," Carpio said.

Soh frowned. "His situation is a great offense to you, no doubt."

"It is," Javier agreed. "It is a great offense to all of us, and it must be rectified. We are putting together a plan, and we need assistance along the shore. You are our representative here. Can you help us?"

"An escape?" Soh frowned. "It would be virtually impossible."

"Virtually, perhaps. But he is my brother. Besides, with the right weapons and the right plan, anything is possible."

Soh considered the request, and chose his words carefully. "There are those in the leadership who question your brother's sanity. I do not agree with them, of course. But an escape attempt would be violent and would bring the full anger of the police."

"It would," Carpio agreed. He stared at Soh without saying anything else.

Soh massaged his chin, considering the request. If he could close the deal that had been proposed, he would be one of the most powerful criminals in the country. He could take over Boston Harbor. "There is a man we would need to involve. He is not one of our people."

"Who?"

"A local who controls the harbor. If he finds out, and we have not included him, he will be a problem."

Carpio shook his head. "No, we cannot involve another."

"He has many eyes on the water," Soh said. "He will know."

"Will he cooperate?"

Soh shrugged. "There is no way to know with him. He follows a code from days that have passed. It makes him difficult to predict."

"Then he must not be told. This is too important. He must be removed."

Soh again chose his words carefully. "That will be difficult," he said. "What is the timing?"

"Two weeks, Wednesday."

"To remove this man so quickly," Soh said, shaking his head. "It will require great sacrifice."

"To sacrifice in the service of our cause is an honor," Carpio said. He poured two more shots and pushed one toward Soh. He lifted his in toast, to drive the point home. Soh sat motionless. "Do you not agree?"

Soh leveled his eyes at Javier Carpio. "We are no longer talking about *our* cause—as in the organization. We are talking about *our* cause—yours and mine. This is a dangerous discussion."

The man frowned. "And yet you are having it."

"I am. But there are those who are higher up who have reservations about your brother."

"He is a soldier!" Javier bellowed, slamming his huge fist on the table.

"He is," Soh agreed. "But he is also a psychopath." Soh leaned forward and put a hand on Javier's in a reassuring gesture. "For good reason, and I have no problem with his actions. But there are those in the organization who believe that he has gone too far. To free him without agreement from our superiors will be viewed as an act of disobedience. When you add that to the independent deal we are talking about, it will be viewed as revolt."

Javier put his glass back down on the table. "What do you propose?"

"The same terms as discussed, but my payment at ninety percent. That will ensure that I will have the funds to organize my men in case I am attacked by our superiors."

"And you will guarantee my brother's safety?"

"With my life."

Carpio raised his glass again. "Then our cause will truly be served." The two of them drank. "When will you move against this local boss?"

"Tonight."

Javier Carpio looked startled. "So soon? Do you not need to plan?"

Soh looked out the window again. Steam was coming off the frozen water, hovering low and fragile along the surface in the frigid air. "I have a plan," he said.

Soh could sense the realization dawning on his guest. "You were already moving against this man," the hirsute giant said in a tone of offense.

Soh nodded. "It will serve *our* cause under any circumstances."

"You deceived me."

"Perhaps," Soh agreed. "But in this case, that, too, was a service to our cause."

SEVEN

Diamond O'Connell sat at the table in her father's kitchen, staring at her hands. People had always remarked on her hands. Her fingers were long and delicate, her skin porcelain. When she was younger, people often assumed she was a pianist based on the grace with which she moved her fingers. Or maybe a dancer. She had such natural beauty and poise as a child, everyone always said she was destined for a brilliant career in some section of the entertainment industry.

Few made those assumptions anymore. Now, at nineteen, the tattoos started just above her wrists. Her hair, which had once been light when she was young, was dyed jet-black and cut in severe bangs that ended just beneath her eyebrows. Her clothes were dark and layered, and she wore heavy unlaced boots that came halfway up her calves.

Her beauty, though, was still undeniable. In some ways, her rejection of traditional fashion and makeup and other supposed hallmarks of attractiveness had made her more alluring. People saw strength in her nonconformity, and power in her refusal to bow to the expectations of others. And, she'd come to realize, men assumed her nontraditional appearance advertised promiscuity and a predilection toward sexual experimentation.

Men were idiots.

She'd always been willing to use that stupidity to her advantage. She'd been going to bars since before she could drive, and she couldn't remember ever having to pay for a drink. Notwithstanding her willingness to accept drinks and dinners, though, she was selective with men. She chose only the worst.

It wasn't deliberate—at least she didn't think it was. It was probably genetic. Given her parents, that would certainly make sense. They had hardly been decent role models. Their relationship had lacked any of the traditional hallmarks of stability. No rings, no vows, not even any cohabitation that lasted more than a few nights. And yet they had spent years drawn to each other with a passion that approached violence, crashing into each other's lives like two storms merging into one, wrecking anyone and anything that happened to have the misfortune of being nearby when the thunder and lightning really got going.

Diamond had spent her youth trying to stay in the eye of their storm.

Her mother had been a tempest unto herself, always searching in vain for brighter skies. Her few friends called her a dancer. Those who didn't know her called her a stripper. Many who were less kind called her a whore. She had lived out on the fringe, in a part of the world that polite society ignored, and many thought existed only in films. It was a dark, dangerous, alluring world; one that was never quite suited to raising a daughter. And so it hadn't surprised Diamond when one day she simply disappeared. It wasn't even "one day," really, it was more of a process. She had gone out for her shift at the club and hadn't returned that night, which wasn't unusual. Nor was it strange that she hadn't returned that day or the next two nights. It was a pattern Diamond was used to, and she was fine at the time taking care of herself. It took a week without any sign of her mother before she grew concerned and went down to the police station to ask what she should do. She was thirteen years old. After that, she'd been told that she would be living with her father.

Cormack O'Connell lived on an entirely different fringe. He worked down at the docks, but it was always clear to Diamond that there was more to his business than he let on. He knew too many people, and too many people were deferential to him to be explained by any role as a clerk or shipping manager. It was clear to her that he operated in the shadows of the law. She didn't care, and she'd learned enough to know when not to ask questions. Whatever his business was, it provided enough for her to be comfortable in the little clapboard house off L Street in the clean middle-class section of South Boston.

That was where she was now, in his house, at his kitchen table, uneaten eggs sitting on the plate in front of her, figuring out what to tell him when he got home.

She wondered how he would react, how he would feel, what he would say and do. Her timing was deliberate. He had not come home the night before, which had become a semi-regular occurrence in recent months. It was a sign, she assumed, that he was seeing a woman. She wondered whether he would introduce her to whoever was taking up his evenings. Probably not. It didn't seem likely that her father would be with someone he would feel was suitable to introduce to his precious daughter. He didn't travel in any circles where he would meet anyone he would think was good enough. Diamond respected his privacy. She knew enough of the world to understand that, even at his age, men and women have needs.

And in this instance, she supposed that played to her benefit. If he was out getting laid last night—and maybe even again this morning—he might be relaxed enough to deal with her request. Maybe it wouldn't make a difference. He was stoic and hard to read under the best of circumstances. How he would handle this was anyone's guess.

She glanced at her hands again. Maybe she could have been a musician. Or an actor. Or a ballerina. It's funny to think about what a person might have been if they'd grown up in a different fishbowl. She supposed it didn't matter. You make the most of what you have to work with. There was no shame in that.

She heard the lock turn in the front door.

Cormack O'Connell had been lost in thought on the drive home. It was a dangerous game he was playing, even for someone who had played the game for as long as he had. Boston was one of the largest ports in the country, and for years he'd controlled it with a certainty that was unchallenged. The world was changing, though, and he could feel others jockeying for position behind him. As a result, he'd started to cut some corners and seek help from people he never would have imagined working with before. He wondered whether his luck was running out.

As he stepped out of his Buick sedan in front of his house, he felt an ache in his back and his knees. Approaching fifty, he was no longer a young man, though he didn't quite feel old. He sometimes did feel tired, though—particularly after nights like this. He stretched his back as he closed the car door and looked around. It was a modest but pleasant life he'd created—certainly more modest than most in his position would have adopted. He'd never cared about flash. He cared about respect. And he had enough of that to be a burden.

As he turned the lock in the front door, he felt the familiar satisfaction of coming home. This was his sanctuary. It was the place where the rest of his life melted away and he could be normal. His daughter, Diamond, was a large part of that. He remembered the moment he'd been told that she would have to live with him, after her mother had gone missing. He'd never known real fear until that moment.

She had always been a part of his life, even before she'd come to live with him. He paid attention to birthdays and holidays, and spent time with her when it was possible. He probably could have contested paternity if he'd really wanted to. Her mother was no nun. But then again, he was no priest, so who was he to judge? And there was never any doubt that she was his daughter. She had his stunning bright blue eyes and his attractive angular features. He had looked at her the first time, when she was just a baby, and he knew. He'd paid more than required in child support, and kept tabs on her life to make sure she was generally doing all right.

But there was a big difference between being a part-time father and having full responsibility for raising a thirteen-year-old girl. The prospect had been enough to make him break out in a cold sweat. In those first few months, he'd probably slept less than a few hours a night, constantly worried that he was screwing something up.

That had passed, though. They had settled into a comfortable routine, and they had come to rely on each other in ways that he hadn't anticipated. She was willful and determined, but he liked that about her. He wasn't thrilled with the tattoos, but she was one of the smartest students in her school. She worked hard, and she had a good head on her shoulders and a solid heart, so he let things like that pass. It's not like she would ever be hanging out with the Daughters of the American Revolution up on Marlborough Street anyway. She was from Southie, and he liked her that way. He sometimes felt like he'd let her down—like she could have been so much more if given the chance. But then he'd look at her and see her smile and realize that she was exactly who she wanted to be.

That was enough. The time that he had with her, brief though it might be, was enough. He had to be at work in an hour or so, but even that temporary respite from the rest of his reality would help to serve as his touchstone.

He walked into the kitchen and saw her sitting at the table, and felt a wave of comfort roll over him. "Darlin'," he said with a smile. He'd never fully lost the Irish brogue from the land he'd left behind when he was twelve.

"Mack," she said. They'd struggled early on over what she should call him. Even as a young child, "Dad" just didn't fit, but he'd never been comfortable with his own daughter calling him "Cormack." It seemed too common and disrespectful. At some point they'd settled on "Mack." She was the only one who would have ever been able to get away with such informality.

"Good morning," she added.

"Morning." He moved to the counter and picked up the coffee pot, pulled a mug out of the cupboard and poured. "You're up early. Did you sleep well?"

"OK. You?"

He couldn't tell whether there was a hint of reproach in her voice. He supposed it didn't matter; she was entitled. Most parents didn't stay out all night with the regularity that he had for most of her life. "I grabbed a few winks at the shipyard office. It was a late night." He wondered whether she believed him.

"It's been busy a lot lately."

"Aye, it has. Not a bad thing for business, though."

"That's good, I guess."

"It is."

"Particularly because I have a favor to ask. I need to borrow five hundred dollars."

He was lifting his mug to his lips, and her request caused a hitch; he spilled some coffee on his hand.

Five hundred dollars, in the grand scheme of things, was a pittance, but he couldn't recall her asking for money before. She was not materialistic. She had worked from the time she was sixteen, and he generally provided enough spending money to meet whatever additional modest needs she had. "Five hundred," he said pensively. He licked the spilled coffee off his hand. "What's it for?"

"I'd rather not say."

He looked at her carefully. Reading people was a particular strength of his; he could not have succeeded in his line of work had it not been. And yet the one person he found hardest to read was his own daughter. "You want me to give you that kind of money without knowing what it's for?"

"I would, yeah."

"I'm not sure I can do that."

"You don't trust me?"

He thought about it for a moment. "I trust you more than I trust anyone else."

"That's not saying that much, is it?"

"Maybe not. What's the money for?"

He could see her struggle as she weighed whether to tell him or not. And then she took a deep breath and spoke the two words the father of every teenage daughter dreads most.

"I'm pregnant."

EIGHT

From the outside, Mariner Tavern looked like it had been condemned and abandoned. The two-story building listed to one side at the base of Pier Six in Charlestown's old naval yard, its few windows blacked out, the small sign over the door long darkened, lettering missing, clinging to the broken shingles in resignation.

Inside, the place was dim and poorly insulated. A draft swirled, seemingly from everywhere and nowhere at the same time, leading most of the patrons to keep their outerwear on. No one cared. They were seafaring men used to living in the same clothes—both outer and inner—for days at a time. They reeked of the sea and all that she brought to them and they brought to her: salt and sweat and fear and diesel and pain and the guts of the animals she nurtured and they hunted. Even if the stench could be borne by tourists, it was not a place outsiders would want to visit. It was a private place: a place of shared experience beyond the grasp of those who had never fought the loneliness of the sea and lost the battle against indifference.

Cookie Landrigan stood behind the bar, wiping down glasses and keeping an eye on the place. It could sometimes be a difficult task, but at ten o'clock on a Tuesday, business in the place was dying. It was an on-shift bar, frequented by the men who worked by day. Those on leave, with a week or more to blow the cash that slipped so easily into and out of their hands, found nicer places downtown where women were welcome and welcoming. The Mariner was for those who had to work the next day, and the days started early enough on the water that the nights were necessarily short.

In one corner, a group off a cargo tanker that had pulled in earlier in the day drank with raised Greek voices and tense good cheer. Cookie knew that rowdy celebration could easily turn sour among men who had been confined together for weeks at a time. He'd served for ten years, slinging hash aboard the USS *Warrington*, a navy destroyer that spent most of her time in the early seventies trolling off the shore of North Vietnam, bombing anything that moved along the trails at the edge of the jungle. He'd seen the stress of close quarters set best friends at each other's throats over trifles as simple as a misplaced cigarette. Men who had been together for too long were nitroglycerine—unstable and explosive. The Greeks seemed to be in control of themselves, though.

They'd better be, Cookie thought to himself. He'd always run a tight ship, and he had a heavy wooden club at the ready under the bar. Anyone stepping out of line at the Mariner was dealt with swiftly and in a manner that left a lasting impression. In that way, the Mariner was like most aspects of life along the waterfront.

The office above the bar at the Mariner was small but neat. There was a functional desk with a swivel chair behind it, and two mismatched chairs in front of it. The window behind the desk would have had a good view of the harbor if it hadn't been caked with twenty years' worth of diesel soot. There were two doors opposite the desk. One led to the narrow stairway down to the bar; the other led to a narrow hallway off which there was a bathroom and a tiny nook of a room with a cot and a small dresser.

Cormack sat in the swivel chair, rocking slowly, his hands folded on his lap. He wasn't a large man, but he was solid through the chest and shoulders, the way men who have spent a lifetime working the sea so often are. The dark beard that had framed his face for at least half of his nearly five decades was full and flecked with gray.

"We go back a ways, Jimmy," he said to the man sitting before him, the Celtic lilt ever-present in his baritone voice.

"We do," Jimmy responded. Cormack could hear the fear in Jimmy's throat.

"Long enough for you to know the rules."

"This was different," Jimmy started to say, but Cormack cut him off.

"Different, was it?" His smile was pure ice. "Well, if it was different, I guess the rules don't apply, do they?"

"That's not what I mean."

"Isn't it now?"

Jimmy's brow was slick, and he shifted in his seat. "It's not. But Cormack, you gotta understand the deal I was gettin' here, and I needed the help, y'know?"

"Oh, well, you were gettin' a deal, were you? I guess that's all I need to know. If you were gettin' a deal, then everything's set right, is that what you're saying?"

"I just thought—"

"You just thought I wouldn't find out." Cormack's voice was low and strong, and cut through the man before him. He stared until Jimmy lowered his eyes and looked at the floor. Only then did he relent even a little. He sighed. "What are my rules on this, Jimmy?"

"You get a cut of everything that comes or goes."

"Exactly. And you didn't give me my cut, did you?"

"I didn't, but I got it here." Jimmy pulled out a stack of bills and held it up for Cormack to see. "See, I kept it for you. I would have given it to you sooner, but I couldn't tell you."

"And you couldn't tell me because you were breaking one of my other rules, weren't you?" Jimmy didn't answer. "What's my other rule on this?"

Jimmy seemed to struggle as he answered. "No human cargo."

"That's right. And why is that?"

Jimmy's head went even lower. "The cops don't like human smuggling," he said.

At this, Cormack exploded. "For Christ's sake, Jimmy, it's not the cops, it's the fuckin' Feds!" He lowered his voice. "Immigration, FBI, Homeland Security, the U.S. Attorney's Office. Every single one of them has got fuckin' jurisdiction. And it's not that they don't like it—it's a fuckin' holy war for them! Do you remember when they found that cargo container full of dead Chinese in the nineties? They shut the whole fuckin' harbor up for a year. A few hundred kilos of coke—well, they find that, they make a few headlines and bust the people bringing it in, and then they go back to business as usual. But a cargo container full of dead chinks? That gets people really upset, and when people get really upset, the political types see opportunity."

"These weren't chinks," Jimmy said. "These were girls, Cormack! Russian girls, and at a thousand a head, I'm not gonna get cheaper pros."

"Slaves, you mean," Cormack growled. He leaned over the desk so that his face was close to Jimmy. "Understand me, Jimmy, I don't want you putting these girls to work. I hear that any of them are on their backs for you, you'll be gettin' a visit you don't want."

"What am I supposed to do with them?"

"How should I know? Buy them plane tickets back to Moscow. Or get them real jobs. I don't give a fuck."

"But that's a waste, Cormack," Jimmy protested. "I paid good money for these girls."

"Consider it a fine for breaking the rules, and be thankful we go back a ways. Anybody else, Jimmy, and I'd have one of my boys take you out fishing, you understand? I hear a Russian accent on any girl in your club, or in one of your houses, or I see a girl on the street with a short skirt who even looks Russian, and I may change my mind. Got it?"

"Shit, Cormack, half the girls I've already got working got accents."

"Then I'd get them elocution lessons if I were you, Jimmy."

"Electrocution lessons?" Jimmy shook his head in confusion. He stared at Cormack, and Cormack ran a hand over his face. "I don't get it."

"No, Jimmy, that's true, you don't." He looked down at the pile of work on his desk. Without looking up, he dismissed Jimmy with a flick of his wrist. "Leave the money on your way out."

Jimmy started to say something, but then held his tongue. Cormack O'Connell had made it clear that the meeting was over.

NINE

"Cormack still around?"

Cookie glared at Buddy Cavanaugh, a young stevedore sitting at the bar nursing a Guinness. Nate Chaplain, another novice cargo man, sat next to him.

"Who said anything about Cormack being here?" Cormack almost never stayed at the Mariner into the evening. It wasn't the sort of place he would want to be if something ugly transpired, as was often the case in the evening. And Cormack didn't often telegraph his plans to anyone. He was very careful about that.

"He called us," Buddy said, nodding at Nate. "He told us he might have some work for us tonight."

Cookie knew that Buddy moonlighted for Cormack, taking care of low-level muscle jobs, but his suspicion wouldn't let go easily. "Then maybe you should wait for him to call again."

"Sure. He said if it didn't happen by ten, it wasn't gonna happen. We've got an offload tomorrow. But I don't want to leave Cormack out in the lurch if he needs us is all. I just wanted to know if he was here."

"Greek freighter?"

"Yeah, I think so. It's the only one that's in right now, so it's gotta be, right?"

"What's the cargo?"

"I don't know, and I don't care. I know I'm not gettin' rich off whatever it is."

"No doubt," Nate grumbled.

Cookie glared at Nate. He didn't like the young man. There was something about his air of entitlement that set Cookie off. Cookie had been born just before the baby boom, and shared the attitude of the

Greatest Generation that had stood firm against the onslaught of both the Nazism of Germany and the Communism of the Soviets. Cookie took his first job when he was seven, sweeping up the floors at Old Man Murphy's shop out in Worcester, and he'd worked every day of his life since. He was loyal and trustworthy, and while he might fairly be described as taciturn at times, he'd never been heard to complain about his lot in life. Young men like Nate Chaplain, who felt that life owed them something, got under Cookie's skin. Men like that could never have beat back the Nazis.

"Could be worse," Buddy pointed out. "We got jobs at least."

"If you call it that," Nate said. "I was hoping to make some real coin tonight. Maybe not even have to show up tomorrow."

Buddy shook his head. "Showing up is half of it," he said. "Even if we had gotten some work tonight."

"Jesus, Buddy, live a little. You've never missed a goddamned day. I don't think there's anyone else who hasn't played hooky at least once."

"And you've missed more days than anyone. You miss another, they'll pull your union card."

Cookie looked at Buddy. He was all right, he decided after a moment. Buddy had his faults, no doubt. Like most young men he was a little too loud and a little too brash, and it was clear that he knew he was good looking. Vanity could be a dangerous vice, but it was a common sin. Even with his faults, though, it seemed as though Buddy had a decent work ethic, and that impressed Cookie. "Cormack's here," Cookie said quietly. "But it doesn't look like there's any work tonight."

"OK. Thanks." Buddy threw a ten on the bar. "Keep it, Cookie," he said. "Let's bail," he said to Nate.

Cookie watched the two of them amble across the barroom and out the door. A shiver ran through the entire place as they pushed out into the cold and an icy breeze blew in. Cookie supposed that Nate could be forgiven for wanting something better for himself; working the docks was a hard life, and during the winter months it was brutal and dangerous. It wasn't unreasonable for him to try to make a few bucks on the side, even if it wasn't strictly legal work. Still, he thought, there was something about the lad that didn't sit right with him. Cookie supposed it was not his concern. He kept out of everyone's business along the shore. That's how he'd survived for so long.

He glanced around the bar and saw that the only ones left were the Greeks in the far corner. It looked as though they were losing steam, and Cookie was guessing it would only be a half hour or so before he could lock up. Cormack might want him to stay later, but considering how slow the night had been, he would more likely tell him to head home. Cookie hoped so; the Bruins were playing the Canadiens, and he planned to catch the replay in the warmth of his shabby little apartment a few blocks away. A quiet life was all he'd ever wanted, and he had it now. He reflected on how lucky he was as he started to ring out the register.

Nate was pissed. He'd hoped that the work for Cormack would be lucrative enough to pay for a decent night out. "This is bullshit," he said under his breath as he and Buddy walked along the shore.

"There'll be other jobs," Buddy said. "As long as you don't piss people off."

"As long as I don't piss people off? What about when people piss me off? Why is it that I'm always the one who's gotta hold his tongue? That's bullshit."

"We're low men on the totem pole, but it won't always be that way, trust me."

Nate Chaplain wasn't so sure. It sure as hell felt like it would always be that way.

Buddy pulled his cell phone out of his pocket and dialed a number. "Hey." He paused. "No, I can't really talk right now." Another pause. "Yeah, he's still there."

Nate's mind began to wander. What would he have done with the money if the score had materialized tonight? It was pointless to think about. That was just torturing himself.

"OK, I don't know if I can tomorrow, but I'll think about it," Buddy said. He tapped the phone off and put it in his pocket.

“They say it’s gonna be even colder tomorrow,” Nate said, burying his hands deeper into his pockets. “You should really think about calling in sick. You’ve earned it, and tomorrow’s really gonna suck.”

Buddy nodded. “Tomorrow may suck,” he agreed. “But like I said, it won’t always be this way. Trust me.”

TEN

Cormack sat alone in the office over the bar, pouring over a large set of books that tracked all of the cargo traffic in and out of Boston Harbor. It was all he could do not to think about his daughter.

Pregnant.

He'd been tempted to ask who the asshole who'd knocked her up was, but he knew that would be counterproductive. He had tight rein over his emotions except when it came to Diamond, and it would do her no good if he did a long stint in the joint for killing her baby-daddy.

Normally he would never be at the decrepit bar at this hour, but after dismissing Jimmy he'd been waiting on a call about some cargo that had "fallen off" a freighter and might be available for purchase at a steep discount. Opportunities like that always interested Cormack, and he liked to know about everything that went on in his harbor. The call had come late, and it was clear that the opportunity wasn't worth the time, but he was still glad to have been given the option. It meant that he still had control over the waterfront, and that felt right.

He would have gone home after the call, but he wasn't sure he wanted to be there just now. His conversation with Diamond had been brief and tense. He hadn't given her the money, and hadn't asked again what it was for specifically—because he knew. He knew, and that was why he hadn't given it to her. Not yet. He had too much to digest before he could be a part of that. So staying at the Mariner to work seemed like the best way to occupy his mind at the moment.

He looked down at the paperwork in front of him to move his mind off the subject.

Detailed manifests from every ship that pulled into port were distributed in triplicate each day to the Customs and Border Patrol agency, to the harbormaster, and to the head of the CUPD—the Consolidated Union of Pilots and Dockworkers.

Customs needed the manifests nominally to track tariffs, collect duties, and prevent smuggling of any illegal material into the country—though with fewer than a half-dozen agents in Boston, there was no way that the agency could actually keep track of the contents of the more than two million shipping containers unloaded every year on the docks in and around the city. Everyone knew that the agency had more or less given up on any sort of effective monitoring.

Historically, the harbormaster oversaw all traffic patterns and dockage in the harbor, and needed the manifests to figure out when to schedule arrivals and departures, how to allocate dock space in port, and the best way to ensure that traffic lanes stayed open. In practice, however, as the ships became larger and fewer over time, the need for the kind of coordination required in the nineteenth and twentieth centuries no longer existed. The position of harbormaster had devolved into a patronage job controlled by the mayor's office, requiring little actual skill, knowledge, or competence. It was rumored that none of the past six harbormasters had ever been on a boat before taking office.

The only copy of the manifests that served a practical purpose was the one delivered to the head of the CUPD. The CUPD was the union to which all of the workers within the harbor system belonged. The system included the pilots of the tugboats that guided ships and barges all the way from the Atlantic, through the quirky passages of Boston's outer harbor, to the tight lanes of the inner harbor, to the docks. It included the deckhands who worked the tugs and who were responsible for ensuring a smooth transition for ships from sea run, to tug, to dock. It included the dockmasters who oversaw the operations onshore, and the stevedores who unloaded the ships, as well as all of the workers within the storage and holding facilities along the shoreline. The CUPD used the manifests to direct the human resources necessary to keep the blood of commerce coursing through the harbor's arteries in a reasonably efficient manner.

As a result, the president of the CUPD had an enormous amount of power, and endless opportunities to line his own pockets, as well as the pockets of others. Shipping companies were always willing to pay to have their cargo unloaded more quickly; importers were happy to pay to have their goods undercounted so that the tariffs they had to fork over to the government would be reduced; local politicians and power brokers were always looking to have sons or nephews of influential friends given their union cards and steady employment; and smugglers of everything from gray-market Asian goods to counterfeit products, to drugs, to people were always looking to strike a deal to make passage all the easier.

Cormack had been the president of the CUPD for twelve years, and he knew all of the ways money could be made, both legally and not. He had immigrated to the United States alone when he was twelve. He'd spent his youth on the docks, and learned quickly to fight for what he wanted. By the time he was eighteen, he was running the Charlestown offshoot of the Winter Hill Gang, the Irish mob that controlled most of Boston's illegal trade. When the Winter Hill Gang collapsed in the 1990s, Cormack took the opportunity to consolidate power along the waterfront. He had close connections to the men who worked the shoreline, and he had a reputation for getting things accomplished—no matter what the obstacle. By the turn of the millennium, Cormack had taken control of the union. A few years later, he was officially elected its president. Now he was the man who controlled the movement of every piece of cargo into and out of Boston. Along the waterfront there was no one with more power.

The position suited Cormack, who, in spite of his reputation for ruthlessness and brutality when required, was generally affable and treated people fairly. It was his belief that a certain amount of illegal activity like drug trafficking and smuggling was inevitable—healthy, even—in a port as large and central as Boston. The important thing was to ensure that it was managed and controlled. And if he and his men took a skim from the profits to make sure that control was maintained . . . well, they were serving the public good. Cormack kept the crazier criminal elements off the waterfront, and limited any violence to those who chose to play the game and break the rules.

Cormack always knew that he had the talent to handle the human aspect of controlling the union. He had a knack for balancing the ability to instill fear and the ability to inspire loyalty. What had surprised him was how much talent he also had for the administrative aspects of the job. He loved keeping track of the resources necessary to keep the harbor running smoothly—moving men around the piers and cargo around the shore, tracking units and tonnage and dollars. He handled almost all of it himself, with some help from Toby White, an assistant who'd been with him for years, and was always loyal. It was Cormack, though, who made it all fit together.

That was what he was doing when he heard Cookie call from the bar. "Skip!" Cookie yelled up the stairs.

"Yeah, Cookie?" Cormack called back.

"Down to the last few, here."

"You thinkin' 'bout last call, then?"

"I am, unless you're not."

"Nah, go ahead, Cook. Clear 'em out and clean 'er up. I have to touch base with Toby to schedule some men for tomorrow, but I've only got another half hour."

"Aye, Skip," Cookie called up. "Thanks."

Cormack picked his head up from the books on his desk and glanced at the clock on the wall. It was just after eleven thirty. It would be good for Cookie to get a break tonight—get home early and have a bit of a rest. He'd known the bartender for more than fifteen years, and the man was one of the hardest-working people he'd met. He'd never uttered a complaint and never asked for a raise. He didn't play the game, but he knew enough to keep his eyes and ears to himself, and Cormack had no doubt that if he ever needed to depend on someone, Cookie would be at the top of his list. He was the kind of a man who would gladly give up his own life for a friend. Men like that were few and far between, in Cormack's experience, and not to be taken for granted.

Cormack made a mental note to find a way to express his appreciation. He wasn't sure how to do that; after all, what do you get for a man who wants nothing? He was sure he could figure out something, though. He had time.

ELEVEN

T'phong Soh stood at the base of Pier Six, looking out at the Mariner. Juan Suarez, his chief lieutenant, stood beside him. A group of Greek infidels had just passed them coming from the bar, their voices raised, their gait unsteady. For a moment, as they passed, Soh thought they might be spoiling for a fight—a complication for which he had no contingency. One of the tall, fat Greek sailors looked at Soh with malevolence, and Soh could feel the man's desire for confrontation. Under other circumstances Soh would have welcomed the opportunity to make clear what a mistake it was to underestimate a smaller man. Soh's hand was in his pocket, and he rubbed his thumb lightly across the curved blade. It would have taken him less than two seconds to gut the Greek from pelvis to Adam's apple. He imagined with pleasure the look that would cross the man's face as his guts spilled across the pier. And yet it was not an option. Not tonight.

"He is still there?" Suarez asked in Spanish. He was from El Salvador, and therefore considered more loyal to the organization than Soh, who was thought of as a foreigner. He'd been sent by the MS-13 captains from his prior assignment in Los Angeles nearly two years ago to keep an eye on Soh for the organization. In less than six months, Soh had come to trust Suarez as much as he supposed he would ever trust anyone.

"That is what my informant has said."

Soh whistled, and could sense a shifting in the shadows around the pier. Eight more men emerged from different angles, converging on the base of the structure. With the ten of them walking toward the Mariner, anyone exiting would either have to go through them, or into the water. Boston's historic cold snap was hanging on, with Fahrenheit air temperatures reaching only into the high single digits at the warmest part of the day. The nights had dipped below zero for more than a week. Chunks of ice wandered the surface of the harbor, crashing into each other to form large ice floats, separating and heading off on their own again. Anyone going into the water wouldn't last more than a few moments before succumbing to the cold.

Soh made a hand gesture, and ten silhouettes started moving slowly toward the tavern.

Cookie had almost finished closing up the bar when they came in. He'd finished the last run of the dishwasher and hung the glasses; wiped the tables down and stacked the chairs; given the floors a cursory, though adequate, mopping; and counted out the register. The cash had been placed in the large plastic money pouch with a slip for the next morning's deposit. All he had to do was put out the creosote candles and wipe down the bar, and he was done for the night. He'd just glanced at his watch—it was eleven forty—and was looking forward to sitting and watching the hockey game. It would be just ending as he got home, but that didn't matter; he'd upgraded his cable account to add a state-of-the-art, unlimited storage DVR. It was not like him to splurge on technology, but the ease of recording and playback had changed his life in the short time he'd had the gadget.

The door opened, and Cookie felt the sharp bite of the winter air rushing at him from the entryway. He looked up from his musings. There were six of them, and they weren't regulars. From the look of them, Cookie was pretty sure they weren't even customers. They moved in silently, spreading out in formation. One of them headed to the far corner of the bar, one moved to the hallway that led to the toilets and the stairway to the upper floor, two stayed at the front door, and another headed to the hallway that led to the back door. The last of them just stood in the center of the bar, looking at Cookie. He was Southeast Asian, short and slight with a crew cut and tattoos covering his neck. He dominated the room without moving or speaking, standing expressionless, his cold eyes studying Cookie the way a Komodo dragon might. Cookie looked back at him without saying anything for a moment. This was bad, he knew instantly.

"Bar's closed," he said evenly. His hand went underneath the bar and took hold of the handle of the wooden club.

"We are not here to drink," the Southeast Asian man said in a thick accent, moving forward.

"We don't have a kitchen."

At this the man gave a slight smirk. "We are not hungry."

"What can I do for you, then?" Cookie had put the fat stacks of cash from Jimmy in the safe earlier in the evening, so he knew that was protected. He glanced over at the money pouch by the register. He'd just tallied it, so he knew there was just over seven hundred dollars in it, a mediocre haul for a Thursday night, and certainly not enough to get hurt over. Still, there was the principle of the matter, and Cookie was not ready to give up the cash without at least a brief fight. In the end, he knew that they would get the money, and he would probably take a beating, but beatings were just a part of life. His fingers tightened on the club.

"Are you alone?"

Cormack was still upstairs in the office, and he generally carried a gun. It might be helpful to involve him, although from the look of the intruders Cookie found it hard to believe that some of them weren't armed, and if this turned into a gunfight the odds of Cookie walking away from the situation alive would go down significantly. "Yeah, I'm alone," he said.

The man shook his head. "No, you are not."

Cookie frowned. "What is this about?"

"Where is he?"

Cookie looked around the room and saw that none of the men was looking at the register or the cash sitting next to it. They were shifting around, watching the corners, keeping an eye on the hallway. The realization swept Cookie away like a riptide.

"Cormack, get out!" he called at the top of his lungs.

All at once the room was in movement. The man in the corner closest to the bar rushed Cookie and was behind the bar faster than he would have thought possible. Cookie swung out with the heavy club. The man ducked and the blow glanced off his shoulder. The weight of the club and the force of the blow clearly took him by surprise, though, and he stumbled and lost his balance for a moment. That was all the time that Cookie needed, and he followed with two quick, expertly placed swings to the back of the man's head. Cookie saw the scalp split and the skull give in. The sound was sickening.

Cookie turned just in time to see another man coming over the bar at him. He raised his club, but the man was able to grab his arm before he could generate any momentum. A third man was on him now, pummeling him as they dragged him out from behind the bar.

"Get out! Cormack, get out!" Cookie shouted again. As he got the words out he was kicked in the stomach, and the air left his body. He choked and gasped as he was held by the shoulders. Someone grabbed his hair and yanked his head up. He was looking into the face of the Asian man, who was still standing in the center of the room.

"Where is he?" the man asked.

Cookie opened his mouth, but the wind was still knocked out of him, and all he could do was gulp for air. The man reached behind his back and pulled out a curved shoreman's knife, held it to Cookie's throat.

"I said, where is he?"

"G-gone," Cookie choked out.

The Asian man shook his head. "No, not gone. Otherwise you would not call to him."

"He was in the back," Cookie gasped. "He would have made it out already." Cookie nodded toward the hallway that led to the back door. The man's gaze followed the nod, then he shook his head.

"I have more men outside. We would have seen him. Where is he?" He pushed the knife hard enough into Cookie's throat that the bartender could feel blood running down his neck.

"He's—"

As Cookie began to speak, a shot rang out from the hallway back toward the bathrooms. The man standing in the hallway's entrance crumpled, his face disintegrating into meaty strings of blood and tissue, blown apart by a shot to the center of the back of his head.

That left four live intruders inside the bar. Two were holding Cookie up, one was holding a knife to his throat, and the other was now moving across the bar from the spot by the back door. The two men holding Cookie dropped him and he hit the floor hard. They pulled guns and started firing toward the stairs that led up to the office. Cookie was still doubled over from the beating he'd taken, but he started to get to his feet to add to the fight. As he did, though, he was grabbed from behind by the throat. He felt a knife pushed into his side, through the skin and just far enough to reach into his rib cage. He screamed out and his knees buckled, but he was caught and held on his feet by the man holding the knife inside him. Cookie was amazed at how strong the small Asian was.

"Do not struggle," the man said to Cookie. "Or I will push the knife into your heart and you will die."

Cookie screamed out in pain again, but fought to stay still.

"Move," the man said, and he and the other three headed for the staircase. The Asian stood behind Cookie, using him as a shield. "Cormack O'Connell!" he called up the stairs. With his accent it came out garbled, but Cookie had no doubt what he was saying. "I have your friend! I will kill him if you do not come down." Cookie had a good sense that the man was going to kill him in any event, but he wasn't in a very good position to say anything. "Come down, we can talk!"

The door at the top of the stairs swung open and the three men at the bottom of the stairs raised their guns, looking for something to shoot at. They moved in closer, their eyes straining. The Asian man kept Cookie in front of him.

Shots rang out again from the top of the stairs, and one of the three men went down. The other two started firing blindly, but there was still no visible human target. Another shot fired down, and one of the remaining men was hit. He stumbled back against the hallway's threshold, dropping his gun. Cookie thought it was a minor gunshot wound to the shoulder, but after a moment the man began grasping at his chest, his eyes going wild, and he began to choke. A mouthful of blood came up and landed with a loud splat near the Cookie's foot. The wounded man started reeling, his arms pinwheeling as he lurched out toward the bar, as though he'd be all right if he could make it out of the building. He managed only a few brief steps before he lost his balance and started to fall. His arms reached out, trying to grasp anything to keep upright. He hit a barstool and fell hard, his hand colliding with the top of the bar as he tried in vain to steady himself. His hand knocked against one of the creosote candles, turning it over.

Cookie had not finished cleaning, and there must have been some alcohol on the bar's surface, because the flame from the candle spread quickly across the top. The fire gathered and grew and advanced along the bar with alarming speed.

The Asian kept his knife in Cookie's ribs, crouching down, still using him as a shield. Cookie sensed some hesitation in his tormenter as he looked up at the top of the stairs. And then the indecision was gone. "We go!" he shouted to the last man remaining. "You die here, O'Connell!" he screamed at the empty landing at the top of the staircase.

Cookie could feel the heat from the fire as it spread from the bar to the stools to the floor. The place was old and wooden, and probably hadn't been through a legitimate inspection in more than a decade. It was clear that the entire building would be engulfed within a matter of minutes. Cookie felt a pang of guilt as he realized that the place would be destroyed on his watch. He wondered whether he would be able to live with that.

His concerns were brief, though. Once the Asian reached a spot beyond the hallway threshold where there was little risk that a shot from upstairs could reach him, he drove the knife hard all the way into Cookie's torso.

Cookie felt the warmth through his entire body. He was surprised that there was no pain. He'd been in agony when the knife was only an inch or so inside his chest, but when it penetrated his lungs and took the breath from him, he went numb. He couldn't tell whether he was breathing anymore, and he suspected that meant he no longer was. His head was swimming, and he felt his knees buckle. The Asian was yelling something, but Cookie could no longer make out the words. He was caught by the irony that he was a man who had spent much of his life on the sea, and now here he was, on dry land, drowning in his own blood.

The world tilted on its side, and a great wave swallowed all sound. Behind him Cookie could see the flicker of the fire as it spread, and it felt as though it would engulf him. He knew it wouldn't, though, at least not while he was alive.

He wouldn't last that long.

TWELVE

Cormack stood at the top of the stairs, looking down as the fire lapped at the railing. This was not good. He would have much preferred to face the guns than the fire. Guns were man-made, and somehow he'd always had the sense that anything created by mankind could be defeated. Fire, though, was sent by God, and when God wanted to take you . . . well, things were pretty much out of your hands then.

He moved slowly down the stairs, testing his resolve against the flames, gauging whether he might be able to run through them. It was no use, though, he realized quickly. It was thirty feet from the bottom of the stairs to the outside door, and the entire span was an inferno now. Even if he were able to make it, he was sure Soh would be outside with guns pointed at the door.

He knew it was Soh. He'd recognized the voice calling to him from downstairs. He'd been expecting a move by the young man. Soh had been chafing under O'Connell's restraint for months, looking to expand his smuggling operations in the harbor. Cormack had explained the way things had to work, but young men never see the wisdom in moderation. And so it was not a total surprise that Soh was looking to free himself from Cormack's bridle. But Cormack had not been expecting such a dramatic statement of Soh's resolve.

Cormack moved back up the stairs, to the second floor. The roar of the fire was growing, and he knew the building would not last long. He ran down the narrow hallway, toward his office. There was a short span of roof over the first floor just outside the office window. It would be about a fifteen-foot jump from there to the pier, and he wasn't looking forward to it. His legs had lost some of their spring in their fifth decade, and he was certain to break a bone. There was also still the danger that Soh would be waiting for him. At this point, though, he had few options.

He pushed the window up and stepped out onto the tar and asphalt shingles. They were slick with ice that had already started to melt from the heat of the fire, and he had to steady himself to keep from sliding off. Slowly he moved his way toward the edge of the roof, craning his neck to see how far a fall he had in store. As he did, a shot rang out and the clapboard behind him exploded. He whirled around, ducking and aiming his gun reflexively toward the shot. He fired twice and heard yelling on the pier. Glancing down, he saw three men now, and they were all taking aim. Cormack looked back up at the office window and considered climbing back inside, but the flames had already reached the second floor and were licking the sash, reaching out toward him. The roof ledge he was on was warm, and the building groaned. It occurred to him that he was at risk of falling through into the flames at any moment.

He was lost in indecision when the gunfire started in earnest. The three men on the pier were all firing at once, and the side of the building behind him was splintered as the cacophony of the gunfire competed with the angry growl of the fire to split Cormack's eardrums.

He was moving before he even realized it, running toward the side of the building that hung out over the water. The gunfire followed him, and he felt something rip into his left calf. The pain was sharp and clean, but his adrenaline was flowing and it didn't slow him down.

He hit the far edge of the narrow roof and hurled himself headfirst off the building. His arms whirled and spun and he lost his grip on his gun. The roof was fifteen feet above the pier, and the pier was at least another ten feet above the water, so the fall seemed endless. It was dark out, but the fire had fully overtaken the building, casting a bright orange reflection on the black water so that he could see it rushing up toward him.

At the last moment, he put his arms out, pointing his fingers to break the water. Nevertheless, he hit hard, the flat water driving into his chest, punching the air from his lungs. Great chunks of ice carved into his face, slicing the skin, the salt water invading the wounds. For a moment he thought he was dead. He'd contemplated Hell before, but his imagination had never conceived of any torment as cruel as the one he was experiencing. The water was so cold it burned through him, and his deflated lungs refused to expand. That might have saved him—if he'd been able to inhale immediately, his lungs would have filled with water, and he likely would have succumbed.

He fought to keep his wits and gain his bearings. The blaze spilling out from the Mariner lit up the surface of the water above him, and as he looked up and started to push himself toward the light, the water was pierced by a rapid succession of gunshots. Gritting his teeth against the pain, he forced his body along parallel to the surface, toward the giant wooden pilings that supported the pier. Only once he was able to touch one did he allow his body to float to the surface.

When his head cleared the water, the new pain made the previous few moments seem like paradise. He opened his mouth and the air rushed in, icy and biting, and his ribs shrieked as his chest expanded. For a moment he thought he was going to be sick—he probably would have been, but he forced himself to keep quiet, knowing that Soh and his men were still in the area, looking for him.

He was frozen through, and he wondered how long he could survive in the water. Not more than another few minutes, he estimated. He'd already lost feeling in his hands and feet, and he clung to the piling using his arms like giant fingerless chopsticks. Soon he would lose the feeling all the way to his shoulders. When that happened, he would lose his grip and slip back under the surface. And yet he was not anxious to face Soh's men.

The fire was almost directly above him, and he wondered whether it would spread from the building to the pier itself. If that happened, there would really be no saving him. Perhaps, he thought, it would be better to give up now and slip away beneath the water. He suddenly felt more tired than he ever had in his entire life. It was, he knew, a sign of extreme hypothermia, and yet somehow he didn't really care.

Just then he heard the sirens. They started like a distant, high-pitched moan from a forlorn animal, and grew quickly to a long, sustained shriek. They shook him back toward consciousness, and he forced himself to focus. He had very little time, he knew, and probably only one chance for survival. He could hear the firemen and police above him hollering to each other as they started to work to control the blaze. He let go of the piling and willed his leaden arms and legs to push him out away from the pier, where he might be seen. Then, with what little energy he had left, he filled his lungs with the frigid air, ignoring the pain, and called for help as loud as he could.

He could see firemen running along the pier, and one was close to the edge. When Cormack yelled, the fireman's head came up and he looked around, trying to locate the source of the noise. He was looking up at the building though, logically assuming that someone was trapped. Cormack summoned the last of his energy and took another breath.

"Help! In the water!"

This time the fireman turned toward the right way, and after a moment Cormack could see him raise his arm and point directly at him. "Man in the water!" the fireman called out to others. "Get a rescue team!"

Cormack felt some relief, but knew he was far from safety. He was rapidly losing the ability to move any of his extremities. He was only barely keeping his head above the water, and that battle was about to be lost. His head slipped under for a moment, and he caught a mouthful of water. Thrusting his useless arms down, he managed to get his lips to the surface and take one last breath. Then he was gone. The world faded through a liquid lens, and the harbor that had fed him and clothed him and provided his livelihood took him.

THIRTEEN

Friday, February 1

Kit remembered everything about that awful day, years before.

It was the day of her last law school exam. Her life was full of love and hope and promise. She'd done well at Harvard, and she was proud of that. Maybe too proud, but after all, how many people could be a good mother to a five-year-old boy and still manage to make excellent marks at one of the most prestigious institutions in the world? She couldn't have done it without Dillon, her husband and partner in everything that mattered. He was a schoolteacher in Everett, the town north of Boston along the Mystic River, where they lived.

They were looking forward to the summer. She would have to study for the bar exam, but after that, they would have six weeks when both she and Dillon were off. She would start work at one of the largest law firms in Boston in September at a salary she'd never even contemplated, but before that, she and Dillon could spend time with each other—and with Ollie.

Dillon was her soul mate, but Ollie was the true love of her life. Her son was a precocious boy with a round face and a laugh that could wrap itself around your heart. She loved that laugh. Sometimes, when he was lying on her chest, laughing, it felt like little puffs from his soul washing over her face, and she would breathe in every giggle. It was the greatest nourishment she'd ever experienced.

She went out for a few drinks after the exams let out that afternoon. It was more of an obligation than a celebration on her part. Most of her fellow students were a few years younger than her, and single. Almost none of them had children, so they were free, and the last day of law school exams was a time to let loose. She understood that, and she wanted to participate with those with whom she'd bonded over three years. But the real celebration would be saved for Dillon and Ollie later that evening. Dillon was making them dinner, and after Ollie had nodded off to sleep, the two of them would split a bottle of wine and make love until they had no energy left. Sometimes that could be hours.

Dillon had picked up Ollie at daycare after school. He was looking forward to the end of the school year with even more enthusiasm than she was. He taught at the high school, and by the time June rolled around, everyone was worn down. Nerves were frayed for both the kids and the teachers, and sometimes he said it was like they were just hanging on, trying to get everyone to the last day of classes. Just the week before, the tension had boiled over, and Dillon had had to step in to break up a fight between some of the students. He was ready for the summer to come.

Kit finished her second drink and headed home. It was a subway ride with a switch, followed by a bus. She usually drove, but she'd known that she would be having some drinks, so she'd left the car at home that day. It was fine with her. She was feeling free and relaxed, and looking forward to the evening.

She got off the bus and walked the four blocks to her perfect little house.

When she was a block away, though, she saw the lights. The police were there, and the ambulances. At first, she thought they were in front of a different house, but as she drew closer, she knew she was wrong. It was at that moment, as her perfect future stretched out before her, that everything changed.

She played the events of that day over in her head now as she stood in the central command center at FMC Devens, watching the monitor that displayed the constant video feed of Vincente Carpio in his cell. It was four in the morning. He sat motionless on his cot, eyes ahead, back straight, as though in meditation. Steele had visited the facility multiple times since her first meeting with the warden, learning everything she could about the security protocols that were being used to keep Carpio safely in custody. So far, she had been impressed, but not enough for her to give up on her quest to find the gap in the armor. She knew that Carpio's people would never stop searching for it, and that meant she had to find it first.

There was always one corrections officer in the command center, monitoring everything. Usually it was one of the junior officers, as it was at the moment. The warden had given them all instructions to cooperate with her.

"FBI, huh?" the screw on duty said to her. She could hear in his tone of voice a hint of admiration. Or was it flirtation?

"That's right," she said. She didn't look at him.

"Pretty cool. I'm taking the test to get into the Staties," he replied. "It's not the Feds or nothing, but it's still pretty hardcore."

"That right?"

"Fuckin' A." It was clear that he was trying to keep the conversation going. It was equally clear, though, that his conversational skills were limited. He stared at Carpio's image on the screen for a moment, then said with bravado, "He doesn't look so hardcore to me."

Steele finally looked at the young corrections officer. He sat to her left, at the center of the control panel, an array of forty-odd video monitors in front of him. He couldn't have been older than twenty-five, and he had a buzz cut and gym-fed muscles. He wore the gun off his hip like a second penis. Or maybe a first. She looked at the name tag on his chest.

"Officer Teadic, is it?"

"Yes, ma'am."

She hated being called *ma'am*. "What do you see when you look at him?" she asked.

The young man shrugged. He clearly hadn't expected to be challenged. "I don't know. I see an asshole. I see a coward."

"Look closer at the screen. Look at him. What do you see?"

Teadic leaned in toward the screen, squinting, almost as though he was looking for a hidden picture or taking a test. "I don't get it. What am I looking for? He's just sitting there."

"He's just sitting there," Steele agreed. "He hasn't moved in more than an hour. Not a muscle. I don't even know if he's blinked since I've been here. Do you see that? Do you see how still he is?"

"So what?"

"So, that's what patience looks like, Officer Teadic. That is what hatred looks like. That is what determination looks like. As he sits there, he's not spacing out or sleeping. His mind is formulating a plan. He's honing it, finding all the flaws in it, and fixing those flaws. It's fine to call him an asshole and a coward. It makes it easy to dismiss him, and it's safe to do that in here with the cameras and the steel doors and a dozen armed men just a phone call away. But don't ever underestimate him. He isn't some street thug. And no matter what you see on that camera, he is very dangerous. Understood?"

It looked like he'd swallowed a bug. "OK, yeah, I understand."

She went back to watching the screen.

Teadic cleared his throat several times, clearly trying to recapture the false confidence he'd displayed previously. "Speaking of street thugs, that's some story about the Mariner down in Charlestown, isn't it?"

He was back to making conversation, and it annoyed her. "What story?"

"Apparently there was some sort of gang war down at the old Mariner—that bar at the edge of the Charlestown piers. They burned the whole thing down. Heard it on my police scanner on the way in."

She didn't care about any gang war at the moment. Her mind had been too consumed with how to keep Carpio in prison. And yet, for some reason, perhaps habit, she asked the question. "Who burned it down?"

Teadic shrugged. "I don't think they know. Gangs, I guess. They found a bunch of them dead inside. Spics mainly, I guess. And some Mick union guy they fished out of the harbor."

Her intuition tingled. "What union guy?"

"I don't know. Just some guy who ran one of the unions. 'Mick' something or 'Mack' something. It's Boston. Who can keep that shit straight?"

"Cormack? Cormack O'Connell?"

"Yeah, that could be it."

"Was he alive or dead when they fished him out?"

"Dead. No fuckin' wonder. Cold as it's been out there? You go into the harbor in this kind of cold, you come out stiff. Literally."

Kit Steele stared at the monitor for a few seconds, her mind racing, her heart pounding. "I have to go," she said at last, struggling to keep her composure. "Keep an eye on him. Anything changes—he moves or talks or has any visitors, or anything—I want to know about it, got it?"

"Yeah, sure," Teadic replied, confusion in his voice.

As she walked to the door at the far end of the room she wondered whether Teadic had seen it on her face, sensed it from her demeanor. In the end it mattered little. Cormack O'Connell was dead, and the implications of his demise were too complicated for her to even comprehend.

FOURTEEN

Massachusetts General Hospital rose from landfill along the Charles River at the northwest edge of Beacon Hill—the "bad" side of the Hill, as it was known in the past, before every side of Beacon Hill teemed with luxury townhouses and condo complexes where one-bedrooms sold for more than a million dollars. Its location put Mass General a short trip across the river from the Charlestown Shipyard and Pier Six, which still smoldered in the wan early-morning light.

Cicero Andolini walked up the Causeway from the waterfront at ten in the morning, keeping his head down against the biting wind. It was snowing again, and the flakes stung his cheeks. He moved nimbly, his short, narrow frame cutting through the elements like a schooner through rough water. He wore a dark suit and narrow tie, covered by a cashmere-blend charcoal overcoat. A sharp-brimmed fedora clung improbably to his widow's-peaked forehead even as the gale tried to pry it loose. The elements were no match for Cicero's unyielding commitment to style.

He turned right onto Cambridge Street and slid down the hill toward the hospital. With his pale skin, sharp features, and dark clothes, the terminal patients might be forgiven for assuming he was an angel of death come to take them away. Truth be told, there were dozens of men over the years for whom Cicero had facilitated the transition from this life to the next. None of them had been ill, though.

He had read the news about Cormack O'Connell first thing that morning. It took him several minutes to digest the concept of a world without his old boss. Cicero hadn't seen Cormack in over a year, but for close to a decade he hadn't made a move without the Irishman's say-so. Boston's hardscrabble underworld was full of micks and spics and Russians. The FBI and Whitey Bulger's crew had run the Anguilo family and most of the other Italian gangsters out of the city in the eighties, and Boston could now be a difficult place for someone as Italian as Cicero, but Cormack had never discriminated. He recognized Cicero's abilities, and gave him a chance to thrive in the rackets, passing on information and opportunities that only someone in Cormack's position could provide. More than anyone else, Cicero owed Cormack O'Connell for his place in the world.

He turned into the drive that led to Mass General's entrance. The place was shielded from the wind by the horseshoe of buildings that ensured traffic flowed only one way to and from the front doors. It was desolate. There was no one on the street this early in the morning, and Cicero had an eerie feeling about the hospital. He'd left his gun at home, but he fished into his pocket and felt the stiletto that he had carried with him since he was nine. There was no reason that he would need it, he knew, and yet just feeling the shape of the handle gave him comfort.

He hated hospitals. They were weigh stations for the infirm. Cicero believed in his heart that men were not supposed to live forever, and odds being what they were, he was unlikely to live as long as most. He was fine with that. Immortality was never his aspiration. He had vowed, though, that he would never die in a hospital. When the angel of death came for him, he wanted to be on his feet with a weapon in his hand.

He paused only slightly at the front door, and took a deep breath as though if he held it for long enough he could keep all the disease and death and despair that seeped out of the building from invading his lungs.

The automatic doors slid open with a pneumatic whir, and slowly, reluctantly, he stepped inside.

FIFTEEN

Kit had arrived at Mass General by five in the morning, long before Cicero showed up. On the drive in from FMC Devens, she had made several calls to confirm the report. No one she knew was on duty at the Charlestown precinct, but they were able to confirm the basic facts. Cormack O'Connell had been pulled from the harbor, unresponsive, and was DOA at the hospital.

DOA.

Dead on arrival.

It didn't seem possible. Steele's mind spun. She took deep breaths as she drove, trying to sort through all it meant. She had to compartmentalize and deal with the practical issues first. Her personal feelings would have to wait.

She would have to tell her superiors. Maybe not all of it, but most of it. Enough to cover the people who could be most harmed. Enough to make sure that everything that had been put in place could be maintained.

She parked illegally in front of the hospital. The police license plate on the car would ensure that it was not towed, and she couldn't be bothered to find a spot in the garage.

The emergency room was a madhouse. Several firefighters had been injured battling the blaze, and there were two Latinos being treated for gunshot wounds. Cops crawled all over the area.

Steele caught the attention of a young detective and flashed her badge. "Where did they take O'Connell's body?" she asked, working to keep her voice even.

The detective motioned over his shoulder with his thumb. "Two doors down."

She went out into the hall and headed down the corridor. A small group of cops stood outside the door, talking quietly. They looked at her quizzically as she approached, but nodded when she showed her credentials.

"He's in there?" she asked.

One of them nodded but said nothing.

She pushed the door open and stepped in.

His body was on a cot, flat on its back, eyes closed. His skin was pale, his lips were pulled tight. There were cuts and abrasions on his face, and it looked as though he'd been through an ordeal before he'd died.

She walked over and looked down at him, trying to remember his face the last time she'd seen him. It was only two nights before, and yet now it seemed an eternity. The last time she'd felt something like this was years ago. Confronted once again with the reality of death, she felt wholly inadequate to the task.

Steele reached down and took his hand. It was cold.

She held it for a moment, trying to think of something to say. "I'm sorry," she said at last. She could feel a single tear run down her cheek. "I'll miss you."

It wasn't enough, she knew, but it was all she could manage. Her emotions had been closed off for more than half a decade. She shut her eyes for a moment, taking a final deep breath to clear her head.

When she opened them again, something had changed. It took a moment for her to realize what it was, but then she noticed that his eyes were open. Not fully, but enough that it appeared as though he was looking at her. She knew it was impossible, but it still made her gasp.

Then he spoke.

"You'll miss me, darlin'?" he said. "Are you going somewhere?"

SIXTEEN

Diamond walked along Congress at the northern end of Southie, her collar up against the relentless wind coming off the harbor. It was ten o'clock in the morning and the sun was bright and low in the winter sky, casting a flat light against the brick exteriors of the converted warehouses that were home to tech startups and fledgling advertising agencies and small law firms. The area was changing rapidly. When Diamond was growing up, it had been a wasteland of parking lots and abandoned buildings pocked with a few basement taverns stretching between the glass and steel towers of downtown Boston, and the bustling blue-collar enclave of South Boston. Back then, it had been a no-man's-land, where people might hide from the interest of the police; a rabbit's warren bubbling with the promise of what might be if you were brazen enough and had the right connections. The commercial development vultures, though, had swept in over the past decade and picked the bones of what was there, cleaning and subdividing the warehouses and clearing the parking lots for dozens of modern towers to be filled with luxury apartments and high-end business tenants.

Diamond missed the wasteland.

Her father had been out all night, which wasn't unusual. She understood. It would take him a little while to come to grips with the reality she had dropped in his lap. She could wait, and they would figure it out. Her father was nothing if not a practical man.

She headed south, away from the downtown area. It was so cold out that she had to get moving or freeze. The city seemed to have lost the ability to retain heat. Even the sunlight had a cold edge to it.

She had the day to herself. That was the blessing and curse of free time, she was beginning to realize. Her father was after her to go to college. She'd done well in high school, and she would have no problem getting into a good school, but she wanted time to herself before making that decision. She just wasn't sure yet that college was for her.

Now, though, after six months of working bars and tables, she was having internal doubts. She had thought she would enjoy her freedom more. Truth be told, she was finding more boredom than anything else in it, and she missed the structure of school and the challenges it provided. Perhaps she would consider applying for next year, but she couldn't yet. It would be an admission of error that she wasn't able to stomach.

She moved quickly, down into the heart of Southie, toward the projects and the public parks where the cold had chased away even the dealers and the junkies who normally stalked the place, preying on everyone and everything they could suck into their world. She walked with her head down, drawn more than driven, to the place where she'd spent so much of her youth. She'd given no thought to her intentions, but she knew where she was headed and why. Up ahead, on a dingy, narrow, time-darkened alley off Old Colony, next to a window front filled with roasted, skinless ducks twisting from their necks, the sign hung with all the subtlety of a Vegas streetwalker.

She didn't even look up, just passed under it as the neon threw rainbows off her jet-black hair, pulled open the heavy black door, and was greeted by the bass-laden dance rhythm pounding off the darkened stairway. The door sealed behind her with a pneumatic pucker that signaled a removal from the real world. She placed her foot firmly on the first step, paused for only a split second, and continued to the second floor of the building.

SEVENTEEN

"You're alive?"

Cormack turned his head. He looked weak and tired. "You don't sound relieved." It was a fair observation, but he had a wan smile as he said it. He pressed a button on the side of the bed and it raised him into a sitting position.

"No, I am," Steele stammered. "It's just . . . I'm surprised. They had you listed as DOA."

"And so I was, apparently. At least nearly so. The cold slowed down my body so much they couldn't find a pulse at first. The first ER doctor was an intern, just out of school. He called an official time of death and moved on to one of the wounded firemen. I was lucky, though. One of the other doctors took another look and realized I wasn't actually gone. By then, word of my demise was already out on the street."

"Jesus."

"They say that if hypothermia hadn't set in, I probably would have drowned. Thank God they got me out quickly."

Kit looked over her shoulder to make sure they were alone in the room, then reached out and took his hand. "You're still cold."

"You too."

"I'm trying to be sensitive."

He laughed. "Try harder, luv."

"I'm processing."

"Like a computer." He laughed again.

"I would have missed you, though. I would have."

"You would have missed the information."

There was some truth to that, she knew. "The information you give me helps me do my job and protects the country. You helped us stop that shipment of explosives last year that was headed for the crazy militia group in New Hampshire. Who knows what they planned to do with that? Without you, we never would have recaptured Vincente Carpio."

"I'm a patriot." His voice was thick with irony. "I'm glad you appreciate that."

If she didn't know him better, she would have thought his feelings were hurt. "I would have missed *you,* too, though. Not just the information." She gently squeezed his hand, but he pulled it away. "You're more than that to me."

"That's just physical," he said dismissively.

She withdrew her hand, took a deep breath. "Who was it?" she asked. "At the Mariner. Who came at you?"

"MS-13," Cormack responded. "Soh and his men. He killed Cookie."

She thought about this for a moment. "There's been cell traffic about Soh," she said pensively. "Drugs mainly. You think that's what it was about?"

Cormack shrugged. "I don't know. I don't care, really. Any way you look at it, I've got to respond. Something like this can't go unanswered."

Kit shook her head. "We have a deal. Nothing over the line. I can't protect you if you're active beyond the small stuff."

"I'm no use to you if people don't respect me. And people won't respect me if this isn't answered. You knew who I was when you reached out to me."

"Is that it?"

"No, that's not fuckin' it. He came into my bar. I owe it to Cookie."

She nodded in understanding. "I can't be a part of that," she said. "I understand, and I'll honor our agreement regarding everything in the past. That's all off limits. But going forward, I can't protect you, and I can't know about any of it. You'll be on your own."

He gave her a thin smile. "That's how I prefer it."

EIGHTEEN

The Naked Eye was a sad, stale place before noon on a weekday. The dancers—what few there were—strolled across the stage, their expressions blank, their movements disinterested. The patrons gave them obligatory attention, occasionally laying a bill on the bar, leaning back and looking on as the dancers bent over to pick it up. It was too early for lap dances or catcalls. The music seemed to pound with feigned enthusiasm, and even in the club's windowless world, daytime seemed to reveal the grit and grime and tragedy of the place that people were able to overlook late at night.

The daytime was how Diamond knew the place best. She'd been there at night as well, when the place came alive in a drunken, hormone-driven frenzy—when the crowd of sweaty, frothing men was three deep to the stage and bouncers paced like panthers on steroids, waiting for anyone to step out of line. She'd seen the women crawl over the men sprawled in the booths at the back of the place, naked and gyrating for twenty dollars a song, whispering whatever fantasies they thought might increase the tip or bring a request for one more dance. But in the daytime was how she *knew* the place. Sitting at the bar, doing what homework she could, as her mother served cocktails to the truly lost and desperate souls that found themselves there in the late mornings and early afternoons. This was what the Naked Eye looked like in the light of day, when the cracks in the facade couldn't be hidden.

Diamond looked around to see who was there, then slid into a seat at the corner of the bar, took off her coat and put it on the stool next to her, took off her hat and put it on top of her coat, stretched her neck and pulled her fingers through her hair in a halfhearted attempt to straighten it. Behind the bar, down at the other end, a woman pushing forty cast a glance down Diamond's way, and gave a sad, knowing smile. Diamond gave a halfhearted wave and looked away. The bartender made her way down.

"Hey, kid."

"Hey, Daisy Mae." As hard as it was to fathom, it was not a stage name. When she had danced regularly, she'd gone by "Chrystal." Her dancing days were, for the most part, behind her now. She would take an occasional turn on the stage late on a Saturday night, when the place was filled with men no longer capable of seeing the signs of age, whose desire for any flesh overcame the need for perfection. For Daisy Mae, those nights weren't about the money; they were about the attention. They were about feeling desirable—feeling powerful—for just that moment. As the years passed, there would be fewer and fewer of those nights, she knew, and it scared her. She spent most of her time now behind the bar, where she felt free to use her real name—one which, ironically, other girls might have chosen as a laughably obvious stage name. In that, she and Diamond O'Connell shared a bond.

"What are you doing here?"

Diamond thought long and hard about that. What was she doing here? "Can I get a whiskey?"

"No, you can't get a whiskey. You're nineteen."

Age seemed the least of the reasons Diamond shouldn't be drinking, but at that moment she didn't care. Everything seemed so lost, she just wanted a little escape. "Please?"

"You're underage."

Diamond glanced up at one of the blondes leaning against a pole on the stage, swaying unsteadily to the music. "Tiffany's a year younger than me, and she's so strung out on heroin she can't keep a beat."

"Only have to be eighteen to dance. And if she's strung out, at least I didn't give the shit to her."

"I'm not asking for drugs, Daisy Mae, I'm asking for a whiskey. Mom would've given it to me."

Daisy Mae frowned, wrestling with her best intentions. She reached under the bar and grabbed a highball glass, filled it from a plain-labeled bottle in the well, put it in front of Diamond. "One," she said. "That's it."

"Thanks."

"What are you doing here, anyway? You're living with Cormack. You don't need to be here anymore."

"This is where I grew up."

"Yeah, maybe. All the more reason to get out of the place. And get the place out of you."

"This is where I feel closest to her," Diamond said.

"Another reason not to come." Diamond could see the regret on Daisy Mae's face as soon as she'd said the words. "Sorry. I shouldn't have . . ." She took a deep breath. "She loved you."

"As much as she could."

"She was a good person."

"She was a fuckup," Diamond said. She sniffed the cheap whiskey, lost in indecision.

Daisy Mae poured a short glass, held it up. "Like the rest of us," she agreed, raising her glass. "A fuckup who did her best."

"A fuckup who did her best," Diamond allowed, touching her glass to Daisy Mae's. Daisy Mae threw hers down. Diamond sipped hers. Down at the other end of the bar, a man glanced impatiently down at Daisy Mae. "You've got a customer," Diamond said, nodding at the man.

"I do," she agreed, looking down the bar at the man. "He'll still be there in a minute. You OK, kid?"

"Not really, no."

"You ever need anything, you let me know, OK?"

"I will."

Daisy Mae started moving down the bar, then paused, looked back at Diamond with hesitation. "Tell your father the same goes for him, OK? If he needs anything . . ." Her voice trailed off.

"I'll let him know," Diamond said.

"He's one of the good ones."

"Sometimes," Diamond conceded.

"Sometimes is a hell of a lot better than most."

NINETEEN

T'phong Soh had learned at an early age that anger was the emotion of defeat. It grew from defeat and led to defeat. It clouded the mind, and caused mistakes. He had trained himself to avoid it at all costs. So the wave of rage that came over him when he learned that Cormack O'Connell was still alive took him by surprise.

He was sitting with Javier Carpio, planning out the raid that would take place within the next two weeks. Nautical maps showing Boston's inner harbor and the shoreline were spread over the table in front of them, and the men gestured toward different spots on the map, considering the options, using as few words as possible as they let the plan unfold organically, allowing the geography to guide them.

He could tell that something was wrong as soon as Juan Suarez came into the room. They had worked together less than two years, but in that time he had seen the man function under some of the most difficult conditions imaginable. They had literally faced down death too many times to count, and Juan Suarez had never blinked. He was as solid and steady a man as Soh had ever encountered. And yet, when Suarez entered the room, Soh could see the shadow on his face—a darkness he'd never seen before.

Suarez crossed the room and whispered the news into Soh's ear, and as the words slipped out, Soh felt his anger grow so quickly that his normal defenses against the emotion were ineffective. The beast of fury overtook him before he had time to compose himself, and he leaped out of his chair, knocking it backward, and grabbed Suarez by the shirt.

"That is not possible!" he shouted in his native Malay, pulling Suarez close to his face, snarling at the messenger like a lunatic. His hand went for the knife in his back pocket reflexively. Suarez saw the motion and, even though he understood no Malay, he recognized the danger. It was at that moment that Soh could feel Javier Carpio's eyes on him.

"Problem?" The giant didn't move. He just sat there, staring. Evaluating the situation.

Soh released Suarez and turned so that he faced away from everyone in the room. He needed a moment to compose himself. "No," he replied, a little too quickly to be believable. He turned back and looked at the giant El Salvadoran. "A setback, maybe. Not a problem."

The giant said nothing, but his eyes urged Soh on, demanding more information without using words.

"The Irishman is still alive," Soh said slowly, feeling the impact of each syllable, as though it hadn't been real until he spoke the truth out loud.

"How? You told me he was gone."

"He was," Soh said. "I saw him shot. I saw him in water, under the flames. He could not survive."

"And yet he has." There was a hint of judgment in the tone of the giant that brought Soh back to the reality of his situation.

"It is of no matter."

"No? You said that he needed to be removed. That will be harder now that he knows you are coming for him."

"Perhaps," Soh said. He wanted to lash out. If Carpio had not been there, he would have. If it had just been him and his men, one of them would have paid for his rage—given themselves up to assuage his anger. That was not an option, though. Outbursts like that would create an uneven foundation upon which to build a partnership with a man as dangerous as Javier Carpio. So he bit back his anger and forced himself to be calm, and to think. "We needed him out of the way because if he finds out what we are planning, he would be a problem."

"That is what you said," Javier agreed.

"But he will be of little worry if he is distracted," Soh pointed out.

"How do you intend to distract him?"

"We already have. He knows that we are at war. Now we need to make sure that he cannot focus on anything else." That was when the thought occurred to him, and he gave an evil smile. "And I know how we can make sure of that."

TWENTY

Diamond felt him approaching before she saw him. She'd been raised in this place, where the unwanted attention of men was a principal danger, so she'd developed a keen sense for it. He was harmless, she could tell as she glanced out of the side of her eye. Older, maybe early forties, sad and pathetic—he'd have to be to be in this place at this time of day—he walked toward her in a suit that hung loosely on his frame, suggesting perhaps he'd been a man of greater substance at some point in his life. His tie was askew, and judging from the hitch in his step, so was he. His drink, half empty, flirted with the lip of the glass as he carried it unsteadily on his ill-fated walk over in her direction.

"Hi," the suit said, as he sidled up to the bar next to her. Honestly, she'd heard worse openings in her life, but it wouldn't make a difference. She didn't reply, just sipped her drink and stared straight ahead. "You a dancer?"

She took a deep breath, turned her head, and looked him in the eye. "I'm having a drink," she said. "Alone."

It was clear from the look on his face that he misinterpreted her response as encouragement. "Yeah, I know what that's like," he said. "Nothing worse, is there? Drinks were meant to be shared. With friends." For just a moment he got a far-off look in his eyes. "Friends . . ." He said the word like it was a term he'd known once but had now forgotten. The silence drifted briefly before he pulled himself back. "Anyway, no need to drink alone, sweetheart. I could be your friend."

"No thanks. I'm not looking for a friend."

"No? What are you looking for?" His hand slipped under the bar and brushed her thigh. He leaned in toward her with the booze-soaked breath and heavy-lidded gaze of a lost soul. Diamond took a deep breath as she reached into her bag.

Buddy leaned back in his chair, fingering the glass resting on the edge of the counter that ringed the stage at the Naked Eye. He'd decided not to show up to offload the Greek freighter, after all. It was the first day he'd ever missed, but he knew he had more important things to do today.

Above him, a stripper tried to gain his attention, dancing with more enthusiasm than noon on a weekday deserved. Buddy was used to it. Women had always been drawn to him, particularly fallen angels searching for something to lift them up again. He'd never really understood it, but he never questioned it either. *Bad-boy looks and a good-boy smile.* That was how one girl tried to explain it once. He wasn't sure what that meant, but it sounded profound and he'd liked it enough at the time to stay in her bed with her for a few more hours, holding her and moving with her body in a way that would let her believe that there was something more between them than there really was. It was, he wanted to believe, a kindness that marked him as a decent soul. He would be more convinced of his decency, though, if he could remember her name.

He'd followed Diamond and saw when she entered the place and slid into the seat at the bar. He watched as she begged the drink from the bartender, wondered what they were talking about with such serious expressions. He was tempted to go right over to her, but he didn't. Instead he watched her, studying her face, trying to figure out what it was about her that transfixed him. She was good-looking, to be sure. But good-looking women were everywhere if you looked hard enough, Buddy had always found. There was something more about her—something dark and compelling.

He had to suppress a smile when the guy in the suit made his move. Buddy knew the man had no shot, with his rumpled jacket and tousled hair that screamed middle-management-midlife crisis. She would never be tempted by a man like that, he knew. Still, he was getting restless just sitting there, watching her. It was time.

Daisy Mae watched the scene unfold from the other end of the bar, far enough away that she couldn't hear what was being said, but close enough that she could intercede if necessary. Diamond's mother had been a royal pain in the ass. She was a junkie and sex addict who cared more about her next score and her next fuck than her own child. But she belonged to this place and this place belonged to her. She was one of Daisy Mae's people, for all her faults. And that was enough to give Daisy Mae reason to watch over Diamond to the extent that was possible with a nineteen-year-old girl who knew her own mind.

Daisy Mae began moving down toward Diamond and the suit when she saw his hand slip under the bar. She wasn't sure whom she was more likely to have to protect, her or him, but she knew there was no good outcome. She heard Diamond's voice.

"Take your hand off my leg." It was a growl. Not loud, but deep and threatening, with just a touch of pity. The suit was clearly too drunk and too horny to catch the tone.

"C'mon, sweetheart," he slurred, leaning in even closer to Diamond. "I got lotsa cash!"

Daisy Mae was hurrying down the bar, almost in front of them, but she feared she might be too late. "Is there a problem?" she asked loudly, hoping to distract them for long enough to defuse the situation. It was a foolish hope.

"What the fuck did you say to me?" Diamond hollered. The pity was now gone, and there was nothing but anger left.

"I said I got cash. We could be friends, you and me." The suit still hadn't caught on. He was pawing at her; the booze and testosterone had overpowered any good sense and judgment that might have ever existed in the man's brain.

The good-looking young man appeared as though from nowhere, like a Canadian Mountie in the midst of the swill of the strip club. He was standing behind the suit, a firm hand on his shoulder. "I think the lady would like to be left alone," he said. His tone was more amused than angry.

The suit turned to the young man, a confused look on his face. "I got cash," he said. He reached into his pocket and a roll of twenties tumbled to the floor. "See," he said as he bent down, fumbling to pick up the bills, "I got cash. I'm looking for a friend." He looked up at the young man. "Do I talk to you? Are you her . . ."

"Pimp?" A full smile broke over the young man's face. "How much you got?"

"Fuck you!" Diamond yelled at the young man. She stood up and grabbed her coat.

The suit held out the wad of cash to her, a pathetic, baffled look on his face. "How much?"

In one swift, clean motion, Diamond swung her fist hard into his soft belly, dropping him to the floor. He lay there, squirming in pain, moaning. She shot a look at the young man, and he took a step back and held his hands up. "Asshole!" she said.

She turned and walked toward the door.

Daisy Mae peered over the bar at the suit lying on the floor. He was still writhing, animal noises coming from his mouth. He rolled over, and she could see that he was still grasping the bills in his fist. He looked up at her in confusion. "But I got cash," he moaned, in a desperately wronged voice.

Daisy Mae almost felt sorry for him. Almost.

TWENTY-ONE

Cicero Andolini walked through the hospital corridor with his head held high, his shoulders pulled back, and his hand in his pocket grasping his switchblade. There were cops everywhere. He supposed that shouldn't be a surprise; the fire at the Mariner was the lead story on every local news program, and it was the story that caught the attention of politicians. When politicians get antsy, cops have to look busy.

He recognized several of the cops, and their posture stiffened as they saw him approach the room. One even stepped in front of him, blocking his path.

"Detective Paley," Cicero said with a cold smile. "It's good to see you, I'm sure." He held out his hand. The cop just stared at him. He was at least six inches taller that Cicero, but Cicero had never been intimidated by height.

"No?" Cicero said, letting his hand slip back into his pocket and onto the blade. "OK." He stepped to the side to get around the giant cop, but the bigger man cut him off.

"Get the fuck out of here, scumbag," Paley growled.

Cicero stared straight into Paley's eyes. "You need to work on your manners, Detective. I'm here to visit a friend."

"Not today. This is an investigation. You need to leave."

"An investigation? Led by you? I'm sure that will go well. You already decided who you want to go down?"

Paley reached out and grabbed Cicero by the lapel of his expensive overcoat. "You midget wop!" he yelled. It looked like the big man was about to hit him, but Cicero kept his hands at his sides. Two other cops grabbed Paley and pulled him away.

"He's not worth it," one of them said. He was young and plain faced.

Cicero didn't recognize him. He looked at Cicero. "You should go. He still blames you for his cousin's murder."

"You mean Sean Paley? It wasn't my till he was skimming from."

"I'll fucking kill you!" Paley hollered at Cicero, still struggling to get free.

"Maybe not. You need to leave anyway," the younger officer said firmly.

"Am I under arrest?" Cicero asked.

The officer shook his head. "No."

"Is Cormack O'Connell under arrest?"

The officer hesitated, but finally answered. "No, he's not."

Cicero gave them all a cold smile. "Good. Then I'm going in to visit with my friend. From what I heard, he's had a difficult night. I think he'll appreciate some support. Not that you all aren't doing everything you can to get to the bottom of this, I'm sure."

The sarcasm touched Paley off again. He lunged at Cicero, but he was still held back by his fellow officers. "Guinea cocksucker!" he yelled. "I swear I'm gonna fuckin' kill you!"

Cicero nodded at the giant, red-faced detective. "Detective Paley," he said. "You have my sympathies on your cousin's death. My father used to say that if you swim in the Devil's waters, you shouldn't be surprised when he reaches up and pulls you under. Your cousin should have kept that in mind. You should keep it in mind, too."

Cicero stepped around the remaining cops and headed down the hall toward Cormack's hospital room. Behind him he could hear the commotion as several officers struggled to restrain Detective Paley, who continued shouting obscenities and threats.

Cicero didn't look back.

"Thanks for coming."

Cormack was feeling better. "Better" being a relative term. Two of his ribs were badly bruised, and he had lacerations on his face and hands. Breathing was a journey through a thousand minor agonies. The gunshot wound in his calf oddly hurt least of his injuries. The bullet had passed through the muscle, missing the bones and tendons.

Cicero shrugged. "You called me. I came."

Cormack chuckled, and a wave of pain shot through his core. He grimaced. "Not everyone would have showed up. This was an act of war. Soh can't go back now; he has to take me out. By showing up, you've sent a message that you've chosen sides."

"Not much of a choice, in my book. Soh's a psychopath."

"The same has been said of you."

"That may not be totally wrong. But the last thing I need is some other psychopath running things around here. There's got to be someone providing some stability, otherwise everything goes to shit."

"Is that it?"

Cicero raised his eyebrows. "Loyalty?" He shook his head. "Look, I appreciate everything you did for me, but if I thought it would be better for me if you were out of the way, I'd put you down myself."

"That's comforting."

"It's honest. If we're in this together, we need to be honest with each other. I mean totally honest."

Cormack saw the question in Cicero's eyes. "What do you need to know?"

Cicero stared Cormack in the eyes. "Are you up for this?"

Cormack touched his ribs gingerly. "These will heal. The doctors say I'm lucky. All of my injuries are superficial. I'll be out of here today."

"I'm not talking about the ribs. Or the cuts, or the gunshot. I don't have any doubts about you physically."

"What, then?"

Cicero's gaze never left Cormack's. "It's been a while since you got your hands dirty." Cormack started to protest, but Cicero held up his hand and cut him off. "I'm not talking about taking a cut of the shit coming through the harbor. I'm talking about gettin' your hands really dirty. From what I've seen, you've been relying on your bark for quite some time now. It's been a while since anyone really saw your bite."

Cormack sat up straight, ignoring the pain that surged through his body. "I'll have to remedy that, then, won't I?"

"Yeah, you will."

"I'm good with that. Anything else?"

Cicero shook his head. "That's all I needed to hear. Where are we starting?"

"On the inside. My people," Cormack said. "There were only three people who knew I was at the Mariner last night. Cookie, Nate Chaplain and Buddy Cavanaugh. Cookie's above suspicion. Besides, he's in the morgue, downstairs."

"Where are the other two?"

"That's what I need you to find out."

"OK."

"Cicero, one other thing."

"Yeah, Boss?"

"Now that Soh's made his move, he won't just come after me, he'll come after Diamond, too. You need to make sure she's safe."

"Have you told her about last night yet?"

Cormack shook his head. "I was still getting my bearings, and I didn't want her to see me until there was a little more life back in me." He looked down at his hands. They were still white and he could see blue veins running over the bones and sinew. "She never asked me specifically about my work, but she knows some, I'm sure. When she sees me, I'm sure she'll have a lot of questions. I'm still thinking through how to answer those questions. Right now, I just want to make sure she's safe."

"I'll take care of it."

TWENTY-TWO

Toby White sat at his desk at the union office in Southie, looking out at Boston Harbor. This was his sanctuary—the only place where he felt normal and safe. Out in the world, he was a freak. People stared at his deformities in horror. In here, though—in this office—he was in control. He worked with Cormack to keep the harbor running smoothly. At Cormack's direction, he oversaw the movements of millions of tons of cargo, and hundreds of men. It was the closest to actual power he would ever come. When he heard about the events of the night before, he realized that he'd almost lost it all. The thought made him physically ill.

It was even colder today than it had been the days before, and the steam came off the harbor in thick white plumes. Toby wondered whether the cold would ever loosen its grip and whether the harbor would ever return to normal. Maybe the cold was so severe that the water would never come to life again. That was the way it felt to him.

The phone rang, and he looked at it for a moment before he answered.

"Union office," he said in his usual, flat tone.

"It's me." Cormack's voice came through the phone line as though everything was normal.

"I thought it would be," Toby said.

"You heard." It was a statement, not a question.

"Yeah, I heard. You OK?"

"I've had better mornings," Cormack said.

"Anything I can do?"

"Yeah, you can make sure everything there gets taken care of. I have other matters I have to attend to for a bit."

"I understand," Toby said.

"You tell everyone that when it comes to the traffic on the harbor, you speak for me, you got it?"

"Yeah, I got it Cormack."

"Don't take any shit from anyone. People may think that I'm not in control. They may look at you as being too soft because . . ." Cormack paused. He was the only person who seemed to be able to treat Toby as though he was a whole person.

"I understand," Toby said, letting Cormack off the hook.

"You're not soft, Toby. I know that. Make sure other people know it, too. That's all I'm saying."

The steam on the water seemed to have gotten thicker. Toby wasn't sure he could even see the water's surface anymore. He wasn't sure what to say, so he let the silence stretch out.

"Toby, there's one other thing I need you to do. It's about today's schedule." Cormack said.

"What is it?"

"I need you to reassign Nate Chaplain and Buddy Cavanaugh."

"They're supposed to be on the Greek freighter, right?"

"That's right. I have something else for them to do."

"OK, I can arrange that."

"Good. And Toby?"

"Yeah?"

"Keep this off the books. Understand?"

"Yeah, I understand."

The line went dead, and Toby put the phone back in its cradle. He looked out at the harbor again. A Down-easter was working the shore, pulling nets up and stripping them of any cod unlucky enough to have strayed into their reach. It didn't look like he was having much success. Toby wasn't surprised. After all, what could possibly live in water that cold?

He pushed his chair back from the desk and stood unsteadily on his deformed leg and made his way over to the log that contained the schedule of union workers for the day. He brought the ledger over and scanned it for the contact numbers. He found the information he needed, picked up the receiver. He took a deep breath, and dialed the first number.

TWENTY-THREE

Diamond could hear the footsteps behind her as she hurried along West Third Street, away from the Naked Eye. He was gaining ground on her, still twenty yards back but getting closer. Then fifteen yards, maybe less. "Wait!" the voice called. "Slow down!"

She had to find a place where she wouldn't be seen.

She saw it a moment later: a narrow alley off to the right, no more than five or six feet wide, cluttered with unwanted bedframes and discarded plastic chairs. "Stop!" the voice behind her called. She knew it was her only chance, and as she drew even with the alley, she darted to her right, through the gap, squeezing around a stack of trash cans and an old recliner that had lost an arm.

The alley seemed to go on forever—a deep obstacle course built of unwanted odds and ends; a grown-up, blue-collar version of the Island of Misfit Toys. She climbed through and around and over it all, moving quickly as she heard cursing behind her.

At last she came to a recessed doorway, partially hidden by a stained mattress, and she ducked into the cramped space. She tried the door, but it was locked, so she flattened herself against the cold steel and waited. Out of the wind the cold bit less, but small puffs of steam still drifted from her nostrils as she tried to control her heartbeat and her breathing. It was no use, she knew. She was sure that the world could hear the pounding in her chest as she waited there, helpless.

She heard the footsteps approaching; heard the breathing; felt the presence. And then she saw him passing the mattress. It was the young man from the strip club. He was looking the other way, confused and lost. It was her chance.

She sprang from the doorway, launching herself across the narrow space at him. She hit him hard, and he tumbled into the brick wall. He let out a light cry of surprise, and she pressed the attack, grabbing him by his jacket, pushing him up against the wall, keeping her weight against him. Her advantage wouldn't last long; she could feel the solid build under the jacket, and there was no question that he would recover his senses quickly. But for the moment, he was rubbing his head and getting his bearings.

She put her face up close to his, keeping her elbows on his chest, but pulling his face down so that their noses were only an inch or so apart. "You're an asshole!" she hissed at him, her eyes conveying the threat, her heart beating out of control.

He looked at her, still recovering from the shock, not yet able to assert himself. And then he gave her a crooked smile and raised his hands in surrender. "Guilty as charged," he said.

She looked at him for another moment, her eyes still hard, her fists still clenched against the fabric of his jacket collar. Then she pulled him even closer and put her lips on his and kissed him deeply, closing her eyes and slipping her arm into his jacket and around his body.

He kissed her back, and brought her body into his. For a few moments they stood there, lost in each other in the frigid alley hidden in heart of Southie. When the moment was over, he smiled at her. "I take it I'm forgiven."

"Why the hell would you tell me to meet you at the Eye? It's a strip club, and I know people there!"

"It's the only place I knew your father would never go," Buddy said.

"It would have been easier if we'd told him I was seeing you months ago."

He shook his head. "How do you think he'd react? You're his precious little girl. You're smart. You're gonna go to college eventually. I'm a two-bit dockworker who does jobs for him on the side, and not all of that on the up-and-up. I'm not exactly the kind of a guy he's gonna welcome to the family."

"Who's he to judge? He knocked my mother up and then left her because she was a drug addict. I know he's connected, that much is obvious. We're not exactly the Kennedys, for Christ's sake."

"All the more reason he won't want you hanging out with the likes of me. He knows you could make it out of here, if you wanted to."

"Maybe I don't want to. Maybe this is exactly where I want to be, and maybe he should know that."

He shook his head. "This isn't the life for you, and I'm not the man. You deserve better, and your father knows it. He can't find out about us."

Diamond thought about her father's face when she'd told him she was pregnant. She knew Buddy was right. "Then why were you calling out to me in the middle of the street? I had to slide into this dump of an alley, or we would have been making out on the street. If you really want this to be a secret, what the fuck were you thinking about?"

"I wasn't thinking," he said. "I was just worried that you were really pissed at me, and I couldn't stand it."

"I am really pissed at you. And trust me, I'll figure out a way to punish you." She grabbed him and kissed him again, sliding her hand down his tight stomach, over the front of his pants. He let out a low, guttural groan. "I suppose you earned some points, though, by taking the day off to spend it with me."

"I don't take that lightly," he said seriously. "I don't like not showing up. This is the first time I've ever done this."

"I know," she said. "What did you tell them?"

"Nothing yet." He rolled his eyes. "I couldn't think of anything. The union office has been calling me all morning, but I haven't picked up. I'll come up with something. They can't be too mad; I'm the only one on my crew who hasn't missed a day ever."

"So why'd you agree to play hooky today?"

"I don't know. You just sounded . . . sad. I didn't want you to feel sad, and I figured I might be able to cheer you up."

"Lucky me," Diamond said. "I get someone to play with for the day. Can we go to your apartment?"

"My apartment is a shithole."

"Your apartment is fine," she assured him. "Besides, I'd rather be in a shithole with you than a palace with someone else." She stuck out her lower lip. "Please?" She didn't need to plead, she knew. She could tell that her fingers had already been persuasive.

"I got a better idea," he said. "How about the Holiday Inn?"

She laughed. "They don't rent rooms by the hour, Buddy," she teased.

"I'm not talkin' about an hour," he said. "Let's get lost for a while. Stay the night. Shut out the rest of the world and pretend we're really together, for real, out in the open. We could treat it like a mini-vacation."

She smiled at him, even as her teeth began to chatter. "I don't care where we go, as long as we're together."

"OK," he said. "I'll go get the room. I'll wait for you by the elevators. Wait a couple minutes and then meet me there." He leaned in and kissed her quickly, then headed back out to the street.

She watched as he went, and she reflected on the truth in what she'd said. She would rather be with him than anyone on earth. It was so odd; she'd never been one for schoolgirl crushes or daydream fantasies. Her childhood had given her an early, brutal glimpse into the dark side of the ways in which men and women treated each other, and that was enough to crush the seed of romanticism before it could ever take root in her heart. And yet, here she was, standing in a ruined alleyway in the middle of winter, freezing her ass off, just so she could be with this perfect, beautiful young man. And she was happy about it. She would have waited there for hours, lost her fingers to frostbite, ruined her health and given over her sanity if it meant that she could be with him. For the first time, she wondered whether this might be love.

That question led to another. What would she do with his child? As much as she believed she loved Buddy, and that he might actually love her back, she had no illusions about any man's dependability when it came to long-term commitments. If she had the baby she had to assume it would be hers, not theirs. Could she handle it? Did she want to?

She wasn't even sure why she'd asked her father for the money. She wasn't sure she'd use it if he gave it to her. Maybe she wanted options. Or maybe she knew he would ask her what it was for, and as much as she was afraid to tell him, she needed him to know. For all his faults, Cormack had been the one person who had always been there for her, no matter what. Maybe she needed someone on her side.

She waited in the freezing alleyway for a few minutes, until she knew it was safe now to head to the Holiday Inn. It was hardly the Ritz, but she didn't care. She knew that she would be happy there, at least for a little while.

TWENTY-FOUR

Nate Chaplain let out a groan as he secured the line to the trap and pushed it into the icy water off the transomless stern of the *Sunny Day*. He could imagine no vessel less aptly named. She was a thirty-five-foot Maine lobster boat that had first touched water long before Nate's parents were old enough to copulate. She'd seen close to four decades of storms and showed the wear of each and every one of them in the grime and gunk caked to her hull and the scrapes and scratches etched in her deck. Like the men who had broken their backs and souls on her, pulling bottom feeders from the Boston waterways over the years, she was low and squat and steady in her pace. Nate Chaplain hated her, and hated even more the idea that he had been given the task of working her on such a frigid day. As he and two other men hauled the massive traps out of the ice-filled harbor, their heavy rubber gloves provided some protection from the ever-present risk of losing a finger on the gear but granted no warmth or comfort beyond that.

How the fuck did this become my life?

The thought rang in his ears over and over, so clear it could have been recorded digitally and laid down on a loop in his brain to play forever, or at least until he was back on land.

He should never have gone to work that morning. When he left the Mariner last night, he'd planned to take the day off, consequences be damned. Buddy Cavanaugh had warned against missing yet another day. Union membership had its privileges; it provided a steady stream of work, both legitimate and not. It couldn't be taken for granted, though. Enough slips, or offense given to the wrong person, and Nate's union card could easily be yanked, Buddy had reminded him as they parted ways. The point resonated with annoying accuracy, so Nate had pulled himself out of bed at an early hour and headed in to work to help unload the Greek cargo ship.

When he'd gotten to work, though, he'd been told that he would be filling in on the *Sunny Day* for a crew member who had broken an arm the day before. It wasn't the norm, but it wasn't unheard of. Many of the local fishing captains and lobster men paid tribute to Cormack to avoid hassles and so that everyone would look the other way when their holds were used to transport drugs. And, in any event, Nate had been told that the order came directly from O'Connell himself, so he knew not to ask questions.

Nate glanced at the other men on board. There were three of them, not counting Nate. Cap was the owner of the boat, a thick man with a long beard and heavy, gnarled hands that looked like they could break concrete. Peter was a deckhand, taller and thinner, with a patchy scruff covering both his head and his face. Spots of flesh shone through the hair both on his scalp and on his cheeks and neck, making it look as though moths had been gnawing on him. Nate guessed that tracks ran up his arms under the heavy rubber coat he was wearing. Cap and Peter directed Nate as the three of them worked the traps, pulling them from the water and cleaning the lobsters out, baiting the traps and sliding them back into the water.

The fourth man on the boat was a complete mystery. He hadn't spoken since Nate came on board. He stood next to the wheel up in the open pilot house, looking forward, calm and still. He was short and nattily dressed in a suit and topcoat, a fedora perched on his head. Nate had no idea what the man's face looked like because he had not turned around once. His presence on the vessel suggested to Nate that the day would not solely involve lobstering. He guessed that they would be receiving some illicit cargo at some point, and delivering it somewhere on shore. That certainly would explain the demand for Nate's presence, and the thought gave him some hope that the day would not be a total loss. If this was a drug run, Nate would be given a bonus on top of the day's wages.

"That's the last," Cap said, as one more of the giant traps disappeared into the dark, icy water.

"We're done?" Nate asked.

Cap shook his head grimly. "We gotta head out past the islands."

Nate nodded his head knowingly. If there was going to be a drug pickup, it would take place some distance from the harbor, where no one would see.

Cap trundled forward to the helm, had a quiet exchange with the mystery man who still hadn't moved, then eased the throttle forward and headed out toward the open ocean.

No one spoke as the seas grew rough and the water turned black as coal. After close to twenty minutes, Cap eased back on the throttle. Nate scanned the ocean, looking for a boat approaching, but there were no other vessels nearby. To the northwest he could see the shoreline, but it was a thin, undifferentiated line on the horizon.

Nate grew confused as he watched Cap nod to the mystery man and the two of them make their way to the stern. The man in the hat looked at Nate. He was even shorter than Nate had realized, and his clothes were impeccable, which made him seem wildly incongruous with his surroundings. His face was angular and his eyes were the dark, soulless eyes of a shark.

"Nate," the man said.

"Yeah?"

"I need to know where Soh is."

"Who?"

"Don't make this harder than it needs to be, son. It's going to be rough enough as it is."

"Who are you?"

"My name's Cicero Andolini."

Nate could feel the blood leave his face. "Fuck."

"That's right, son. This is as bad as you think it is. The only thing you need to decide is whether it gets better or worse. I need to know where Soh is."

"I swear, I don't know what you're talking about!" Nate's voice quavered. He glanced around him, but all he could see was the cold, relentless sea. As he brought his eyes back to Cicero Andolini, a man with one of the most vicious reputations in Boston, he saw a dull flash of metal as Andolini's brass knuckles shot up toward his jaw. His world exploded in a flash of light that faded quickly to darkness.

TWENTY-FIVE

Kit sat in her office on the nineteenth floor of the JFK Federal Building in downtown Boston. It was a plain office with a cold, government-issue steel desk and matching file cabinet. The chair was ancient, and creaked when she shifted in it. There were no pictures in the office, no mementos of loved ones or images of those she cared about. There was nothing but the implements of her work. She looked around the office, taking in its stark, utilitarian aura, and sighed. Was this all she was now?

She swiveled toward the window, the chair screeching as though it were being tortured, and looked out down the hill, across Congress Street and Haymarket, out toward the harbor. Cormack was out there somewhere. The police would have tried to keep him in the hospital, but she was sure he would have had none of that, and she knew from her sources that the police had no legitimate basis to hold him. So he was somewhere along the waterfront, planning a war that would rip Boston's underworld apart.

She'd had no illusions about Cormack when she first reached out to him. It was well known that he had a piece of all the illegal activity throughout Boston Harbor. The authorities had spent years trying to build a case to bring charges against him, but they'd never been able to gather enough concrete evidence for a successful prosecution. Eventually they gave up the effort. Truth be told, many in law enforcement recognized that Cormack did an effective job of keeping violence under control, and some level of illegal activity was inevitable. *Better the devil you know,* seemed to be the attitude that many took toward the corrupt union head.

That reality presented an interesting opportunity for her. She'd campaigned to be put in charge of a task force going after MS-13, which had grown in strength and influence in Boston and the surrounding towns since the turn of the millennium. It was a task she relished, not just because she wanted to fight crime, but for personal reasons as well. Her mission didn't necessarily conflict with Cormack's interests, and she knew that his eyes and ears along the shoreline could be an indispensable source of information.

She was straightforward with him the first time they met. She'd set a meeting to discuss the harbor's security concerns. It wasn't that unusual; his legitimate cover as the head of the largest union gave him an interest in maintaining harbor security. The pretense hadn't lasted long.

"I'm not interested in the information that comes to you through legitimate channels," she'd said directly. They were only five minutes into the meeting. He didn't reply; he just raised his eyebrow, and there was a hint of interest and amusement his eyes. It was the first time she'd felt the attraction to him. "I'm interested in the information you come by in connection with your more illicit activities," she continued.

"And what activities would those be?" he'd asked her. The smile was still in his eyes.

"Don't be coy, Mr. O'Connell," she'd said.

"Cormack. Please."

"Cormack. I'm aware that you direct—in one way or another—all, or at least almost all of the illegal activity in the harbor. From what I've heard, you do a hell of a job of it, too. No one gets too fat, no one gets out of control, and everyone is taken care of. You'd have made an impressive politician."

"Trust me, I *am* a politician," he'd replied. "Which is why I have little time to . . . How did you put it . . . *direct illegal activity*?" He shook his head. "I'm not even sure what that means, but I wouldn't have the time for that sort of responsibility. My job is too demanding."

"Really?" She'd feigned disappointment. "I must have been misinformed."

"That's the funny thing," he'd said. "It's tough to tell when information is accurate, and when it's not."

"That's supposed to be my job."

"You may need to find other employment." He smiled again.

"Maybe." She wasn't going to give up, but she'd needed a new strategy to gain his trust. "So why don't you tell me exactly what it is you do in your role as the head of the union, and I can figure out how we might be able to work together."

He'd laughed. It was a warm, inviting sound. "I'm afraid I couldn't begin to describe my responsibilities in such a short meeting."

"Perhaps we should have a longer meeting, then." She was looking directly into his eyes, and she'd felt as though there were two conversations taking place at the same time.

"Perhaps," he'd said. "Over dinner?"

She'd stood and picked up her briefcase. He'd looked confused, and fumbled a bit as he rose from his chair. She'd put out her hand and he'd shook it.

"It was an enlightening meeting," she'd said.

"Was it?"

She'd walked to the door and opened it. Just before she'd walked out, she'd turned and faced him. "I like seafood."

He'd nodded. "I know a place."

"I look forward to it."

The dinner had gone well a week later, and she knew not to push him. Not yet. She needed to gain his trust. That trust couldn't be gained over a dinner. Even after the first time they had sex together, she knew not to push. She lay in bed, listening to his breathing, wondering whether she would have allowed him to seduce her if she didn't have an ulterior motive. She was attracted to him, there was no denying that. And yet her focus had been so singular from the moment she'd lost her husband and her son that she no longer knew what it was like to truly feel anything other than the rage that kept her warm and drove her forward.

He came to her, as she knew he would. As she knew he had to. They had been sleeping together for nearly a month when he told her that there were explosives coming in through a dock in East Boston. He had been given his tribute, but he was concerned because the materials were destined for an offshoot of a militia group in New Hampshire. The explosives were sophisticated C4, easily hidden from detection, and not the sort of material used for traditional criminal endeavors.

She'd nodded when he gave her the information. She didn't thank him—to do so would have been an insult. His wasn't an act of charity or patriotism, it was an act of smart business. The information came with expectations of reciprocity; protection from the authorities when necessary, information on competitors when available. They both understood the nature of the exchange they were agreeing to, and in consummating the deal, they were committing to each other in a manner that was far more intimate than sex.

That bond was dissolved now, and she felt the separation in a way that was physical. She wondered whether her feelings were something resembling affection, but dismissed the thought quickly. This was still business, and her business was protecting Boston's population from MS-13, to make sure no one ever suffered the way she had. And if helping Cormack O'Connell advanced the goals of her business, then it was her responsibility to help him.

She picked up the phone and dialed. "Agent Martin," she said when the man on the other end of the line picked up. "I need anything new the local police have on T'phong Soh. He's Boston's head of MS-13. It's for the task force."

TWENTY-SIX

"Are the ropes tight?"

Cicero looked down at Nate Chaplain's unconscious body on the lobster boat's deck. He raised the lapels of his dark coat against the biting wind. They were farther out to sea than the small vessel was accustomed to being, and though the water was relatively calm, the swells pitched them up and down in a steady, maniacal rhythm. He hated being out on the water and longed to be back on dry land. Still, the ocean provided a convenient and private place to do what needed to be done.

"I know my knots," Cap replied. "They'll hold."

"Wake him up."

Cap broke a capsule of ammonia under Chaplain's nose, and Chaplain's body convulsed, his head shaking and pulling back from the noxious fumes. There was little he could do to get away, though, as his hands and feet were bound tight. Cap shoved the ammonia under his nose again, and Chaplain coughed hard and spat, his eyes finally opening and taking in the scene as best they could. The look of confusion quickly turned to fear, and then terror.

"Please!" he screamed. "Please . . . No!"

Cicero nodded to Cap, and the skipper kicked Chaplain in the ribs, quieting the young man by taking the breath out of him.

As Chaplain writhed on the deck, Cicero squatted next to him. "Listen carefully, Nate," he said. "You're only going to get one chance at this. Only three people knew that Cormack was at the Mariner last night. One of them was Cookie, the bartender. Good man. He's dead now. The others were you, and your pal Buddy Cavanaugh. It seems Buddy was smart enough to disappear. No one can find him. That leaves me with you. I'm going to need to know everything, understand?"

Nate Chaplain's convulsions had subsided, but he was still gasping for breath. A thick white line of saliva ran from his lips to the wood below him, and he struggled to talk. "I don't know anything, I swear!" he screamed.

"That's too bad," said Cicero. "It's going to make it less pleasant."

"No! Wait! Please! I'll tell you anything!"

"Did you talk to Soh?"

"No, I didn't! I swear it!"

"Where is Buddy?"

"He has an apartment. It's in the projects."

"We know that. He's not there. Where is he?"

"I don't know. I swear to God!" Chaplain was sobbing now, pulling desperately at the ropes. But Cap hadn't lied; he knew his knots.

Cicero nodded to Cap, and the large man with the gnarled hands moved up into the pilot house and started the engine. He pointed the boat into the wind and eased her forward. Then he locked the wheel so the boat would stay straight and came back to the stern. He and Peter picked Chaplain up under the armpits and dragged him to the open stern.

"Oh God! Please no! For the love of Christ!" Chaplain screamed as they threw him in.

The boat pulled away until the slack in the rope was expended and Chaplain's body was dragged through the frigid water by the feet. His hands were tied, so there was no way for him to keep his head above the water. Above them, seagulls circled.

"How long?" Cap asked.

"One minute," Cicero responded.

Cap looked at his watch as the second hand spun. Then he and Peter grabbed the rope that was tied to the cleat at the stern and began hauling Chaplain back on board.

TWENTY-SEVEN

The Holiday Inn in South Boston had seen better days. As Diamond lay in bed, listening to Buddy's even breathing, she looked around the room. The walls were taupe and matched the rug, except where the stains on the carpet provided some contrast. The headboard was screwed to the wall, and the flimsy bedframe squeaked, which she was sure had raised eyebrows among the passing cleaning staff in the halls in the mid-afternoon. At least the sheets seemed clean, if somewhat stiff and scratchy from repeated harsh washing to scrub each successive guest's secret sins away.

Like the headboard, the cheap flat screen was screwed into the table on which it rested. Securing the television made sense to her, but she wondered whether headboards were a popular target for petty thieves. On reflection, she thought it was probably to keep the headboard from banging off the wall as wives fucked their secret lovers, and bosses fucked their secretaries, and young men from the downtown skyscrapers fucked each other on the down-low on the seedy side of town where no one would know them or care.

She hadn't really looked at the place when she'd first arrived, so focused was her desire and so eager were the two of them to be with each other. As he'd kissed his way down her body she'd marveled at his skill and proficiency, and the thought that he must have practiced this a thousand times before with other women crossed her mind only briefly before the waves of physical pleasure chased all intelligible thought out of her mind. Her body succumbed fully to his ministrations three times in the hour they kissed and touched and gave themselves to each other; the last time was an explosion brought on by the furiousness of his rhythm as he climaxed and his muscles tightened, his entire body spasming in and around her.

He had drifted off to sleep shortly thereafter with his muscular arm draped over her, and she lay on her back, stroking his hair. Lying there, sated and warm, she wondered whether a normal life was too much to hope for. A small, clean apartment with a nice kitchen. A good-looking man who loved her and made love to her the way she wanted—with a passion that was based on his own need and desire, at the same time both selfish and giving.

It was probably too much to hope for, she knew, particularly with a man like Buddy. He was not a man who would be easily domesticated, and she suspected that if he was, she wouldn't find him attractive anymore. As she lay there, she imagined the cries of a baby from a nursery, and the babbling of a toddler amusing himself in the living room. By the time she conjured the playful patter of little feet on the floor in the kitchen, she could also hear his heavy work boots heading toward the door, and the finality with which that door would inevitably close.

He stirred and she kissed the back of his head. She let her fingers trail down through his hair and across his shoulders. They lingered there, enjoying the firmness of his muscles, before they continued down his back, touching his skin lightly . . . playfully. She could tell that he was awake now, though he hadn't moved or made a sound. There was something in his body that had changed. She could feel his muscles tighten without motion, ever so slightly, reacting with anticipation to her touch.

Her fingers trailed down to the small of his back, and then beyond, traipsing lightly over his taut, perfectly shaped ass. She slid her hand up, across his side and under his arm, finding his broad, solid chest. She could feel her excitement grow as she played with his nipples, pinching them firmly enough to at last draw a slight moan. She smiled in amusement as she slid her hand down his chest to his flat stomach. And then lower, and lower, until . . .

"I gotta take a leak."

She giggled. "That's so hot. I can see why you get all the ladies."

He rolled over and kissed her. "I'll be right back!"

He pulled back the covers and stood up. He stretched his arms high over his head, in all his splendor, and let out a loud yawn before he walked over to the bathroom door. He didn't close it, but stood with his back to her as he relieved himself. She smiled inwardly at the intimacy.

Before he got back into bed, he went to the window and peeked out through the heavy curtains. "It's snowing again," he said.

"Is it?"

"Jesus, I've never seen a winter like this before. Feels like the last time I saw a color other than white or gray was a fuckin' year ago."

"I can add a little color into your life," she teased.

"I bet you can."

He turned to look at her, lying in bed, partially covered by the sheet. He was hard, and she could feel her own excitement grow. Gazing at him, she was shocked at how beautiful she found him fully naked. She'd always been drawn to men, and she had been confident in her sexuality at an early age. She had enjoyed sex with the men she had dated, but she had never consciously been appreciative of the male member. For some strange reason, though, she was truly enamored with that particular part of Buddy's anatomy. As she stared at him, she blushed at her brazen desire. She wondered whether the pregnancy was pushing her hormones into overdrive. At the moment, though, she didn't really care. "Come here," she demanded.

"I should check my phone first." He came over to her and sat on the side of the bed, picked his phone off the bedside table.

"No," she said firmly. "We promised each other the phones stay off. This is our vacation, remember?"

"I should really—"

"No!" She grabbed the phone out of his hand. "I read an article that said that couples are losing interest in each other because they spend too much time on their phones. It's killing intimacy."

"Where'd you read that?"

"Some article that came up on my phone's newsfeed. See?" She put the phone back on the table. "Come back to bed." She grabbed his hand and pulled him toward her.

He smiled at her. "You've convinced me."

TWENTY-EIGHT

Nate went into the water twice. The second time he came out Cicero wasn't sure he was going to live, but after a few moments of coughing and spitting blood, he was able to talk. At that point, there wasn't anything that Chaplain wouldn't tell them to avoid going back into the water again.

He didn't have that much information, but it was enough. Buddy had been on the phone twice the night of the attack on the Mariner—once just before they went in, and once just as they left. Nate hadn't heard anything that was said on the first phone call, but as they came out of the bar, Buddy seemed in a hurry and was less careful. Nate heard Buddy clearly say, "He's still there." That was all that Chaplain could remember him saying, and then he'd put the phone back in his pocket. To Cicero, it was all the admission that was needed.

"What do we do with him now?" Cap asked, looking down at the crumpled, defeated figure that had only a short time before been Nate Chaplain.

"Cormack gave clear orders," Cicero replied.

Cap looked uncomfortable, and Peter rubbed the stubble on his chin nervously. "It don't seem right," Cap said.

Cicero took two steps over toward the boat's skipper, so that he was right in front of his face, so close he could smell the sardines he'd had for breakfast rotting in the teeth of the heavyset man. His hand was in his coat pocket, his fingers wrapped around the handle of his knife. "Cormack O'Connell decides what seems right on this waterfront," he said slowly and quietly. His eyes bore into Cap's face. "You understand that, you fat fuck?"

The blood was gone from Cap's face, and he nodded spasmodically. "Yeah, I got that."

Cicero stood there, inches from the other man, just long enough to make it clear that he wasn't moving until he wanted to. Then he looked down at Nate Chaplain. "Sorry, kid," he said. "Orders are orders."

TWENTY-NINE

Cormack stood at the large window of his union office, looking out at Boston Harbor. The office was on the corner on the second floor of a warehouse at the end of North Jetty, just off Fid Kennedy Avenue in South Boston. The warehouse jutted out at the tip of the shore, looking across an inlet at fifty acres of landfill piled high with shipping containers from all over the world. To the northeast, he could see the Boston skyline in the distance, separated from him by the revitalization of Southie's Waterfront District, with its brand-new skyscrapers and trendy restaurants. To the northeast, across the harbor, he could see Logan Airport and East Boston, just beginning the painful process of gentrification that would inevitably drive the immigrant population from one of its last strongholds within Boston's city limits. To the southeast, he could see Fort Independence, an enormous pentagonal military installation constructed of stone and earthwork rebuilt just before the Civil War. The original military fortification on that site had been built in 1634, and it had guarded the mouth of the harbor for the better part of four centuries.

That's how Cormack often thought of himself: the defender of the harbor. For all the graft he took from it, and all the illicit activity he sheltered, he gave back much more. He ran the place and maintained the delicate balance necessary to keep war from breaking out between the various underworld factions. He allowed the underground economy to exist, but he kept it in check. And at the same time, he protected the harbor and the city it fed from external threats. He was the first wall in a war that was being waged across the world on multiple fronts. He kept the schedules and made sure that ships were shepherded and docked and unloaded; he provided security when needed; he made sure that every boat in the harbor, from the smallest skiffs to the largest tankers, obeyed the rules and that commerce was served.

Even now, as he looked out at the harbor, he could see his hand in everything moving on the water. Near the city, a heavy tug pushed a barge full of scrap metal up toward the Mystic River for processing, its three-story pilothouse looking over its charge. A high-speed catamaran from Hingham was pulling into Rowes Wharf, serving the commuters who helped to drive the city's economy. Entering the harbor was a gigantic LNG tanker, over nine hundred feet long and ten stories tall, carrying more than thirty million gallons of liquefied natural gas up to a processing plant in Everett. An armada of police and Coast Guard attack boats surrounded the tanker.

And Cormack had had a hand in all of it. From the scheduling of the ferry runs to the timing of various ships' passages, he coordinated the manpower needed to make sure everything ran smoothly. He kept the traffic from being too great to be safe. So often he'd looked out at similar scenes and marveled at the role he played in keeping the city safe and running.

At the moment, though, he wasn't thinking about any of that. Right now, all he could think about was his daughter, and how he had failed to protect her.

"Any word?" he asked, as Cicero hung up from a call.

"Nothing yet," he said.

"What about her phone?"

Cicero shook his head. "It could just be that she's not picking up."

"Could be," Cormack agreed. His stomach was tighter than he could ever remember. He'd learned over the years to stay calm in the most difficult circumstance, but he'd never known the kind of fear he felt right now. "What about Buddy Cavanaugh?"

"He's disappeared as well."

"Find him."

"We'll get him. He can't stay hidden forever."

"I swear to God, Cicero, when he's found, I want him alive. Make sure everyone knows that he's mine. I need him talking, and then I'll decide how he goes. I'm pushing his button, too. No one else." Cormack felt the anger burning through him.

"I've given the word."

"Make sure."

Cicero changed the subject. "What do you want to do about Soh?"

"What are his numbers?"

"Tough to tell. We figure twenty core guys who are fully initiated into his crew. Maybe twice that number that he can use on a contract basis. They're less reliable, though."

"And we've got, what, fifteen?"

"A few more than that who I feel like we can count on. Maybe another twenty-five with less commitment."

Cormack considered the options. "Even odds. So a frontal assault would be risky, even if we knew where he was."

Cicero nodded.

"We need another way to get to him." Cormack looked out at the LNG tanker, with the Coast Guard and BPD gunboats zipping around like bees protecting a hive. He had no doubt that, wherever Soh was, there would be protection swarming around him in a similar way. There had to be a weakness in his defenses, though. He knew that he could formulate a plan if only he could focus. Right now, though, there was only one thing he could think about.

"Find her, Cicero," he said. "I need to know that she's alive."

Cicero stood up. "I know. I'll find her." He walked over to the office door and opened it. "I'll make sure she's OK."

THIRTY

Joshua Brooks passed through the security checkpoints at FMC Devens without incident. He carried with him an authorization that identified him as an attorney, and gave him authorization to consult with his client. His client was also named, and at each stage of the process, the guards raised their eyebrows and took a second look at Joshua's face, the expressions registering combinations of shock and disgust. His briefcase was searched for any contraband, and he was given a thorough pat down to make sure he wasn't carrying anything of use that could be passed to his client. Joshua wasn't concerned. He had spent a lifetime representing some of the most violent and hated men on the planet, and it had made him wealthy beyond his dreams. This would be no different.

At the final checkpoint, they took everything he had other than a notebook and a pencil. They even had him take off his white-gold Piaget Polo-S watch and put it in a bag with the rest of his belongings. It was a fifteen-thousand-dollar timepiece that a grateful hedge-fund manager had given him after an acquittal.

"I can't wear a watch?" Brooks asked the guard.

"Not with this guy," the guard responded. "Nothing that can be passed to him."

"What's he gonna do with a watch?"

The guard shrugged. "You're lucky you get to take in the pencil," he said. "I'm gonna check to make sure you've still got it when you come out, too."

"You're afraid he'll sketch his way out of here?"

"I got my orders."

"OK," Brooks said, turning and starting down the hallway to a lone steel door. Another guard accompanied him.

"We've got you on camera," the guard said. "You stay on your side of the table. Don't pass anything to him, and don't allow him to pass anything to you."

"The camera's going to be on?" Brooks shook his head. "I'm his lawyer. My conversation with him is privileged."

"The sound is turned off," the guard said. Brooks looked skeptical. "We won't hear anything," the guard assured him.

"I want the camera off," Brooks persisted.

"You can take that up with the warden," the guard said. "Given this guy's past, I think he's not gonna agree. Right now, I got my orders."

Brooks stared at the guard for a moment, and then decided to abandon the complaint for the moment. "Make sure the sound is off, and no recording is made," he said. "Otherwise, I will take it up with the judge, and you will find yourself in a world of hurt."

"Can I ask you something?"

Brooks knew what was coming. "Sure."

"How can you represent this guy? With what he did, with who he is, how do you do it?"

"Everyone is entitled to a lawyer," Brooks responded. "It's one of the great things about this country."

"And you get rich from it," the guard scoffed.

Brooks gave him a thin smile. "That's another one of the great things about this country."

The room was windowless and bare. Vincente Carpio sat motionless on the chair on the far side of the metal table, which was bolted to the floor. His hands were cuffed and folded on his lap. His shackled ankles were close together, his feet flat on the floor. Brooks was taken by how young he looked, even with the skulls tattooed all over his bald head.

Brooks walked over and put the pad and pencil on the table, pulled out the chair across from Carpio, and sat down. The two men regarded each other in silence for what seemed like a long time.

"You my lawyer?" Carpio said at last.

Brooks felt a small sense of victory that he'd not been the one to break the silence. "Your brother hired me."

"And you are willing to defend me?"

"Your brother was very persuasive."

"He paid you upfront."

"He did."

"What is your name?"

"Joshua Brooks."

Carpio looked closely at him. "You're Jewish."

"Is that a problem?"

Carpio considered the question for a moment. "No," he said at last. "Jews make good lawyers."

"You flatter me."

"I flatter no American," Carpio said. "I kill Americans."

"That won't be in my opening statement."

"You have no idea what your people have done to the world, do you? Like everyone else here, you sit in your safe homes and talk to the world about freedom while your country lets the violence go on far, far away. It spreads that violence. It pays for that violence."

"Is that why you do what you do?"

Carpio's gaze drifted past Brooks, into some distance that only he could see. "There are many reasons I do what I do," he said.

Vincente Carpio had never known a world without war. By his sixth birthday, civil war had ravaged El Salvador for more than a decade. His town of El Calabozo had seen the worst of the war nearly ten years before, when U.S.-backed government forces slaughtered more than two hundred people. Since that time, though, the war had only touched the town in indirect ways, siphoning off boys into various factions to fight in other towns and cities, coming back with the thousand-yard stare of those who saw the ghosts of those they'd killed looming in the distance of every field and forest.

Vincente's mother, Maria, had kept him safe by involving him in the local Catholic church. Javier, her older son, had already been recruited by the local insurgents, and been off at war for more than a year, but she had vowed that she would not let her youngest, who was more sensitive, fall prey to the same fate.

Maria was a devout follower and had dedicated herself to Christ since Vincente's father had been killed in the war four years before. There was no local school, so the church was the only place where he could be educated.

It was located at the top of the hill in the center of town, and Father Cardozo presided over the congregation. He was a young man, and handsome. Vincente occasionally wondered whether his mother's devotion to the church was in part driven by the fact that she was drawn to the charismatic priest. It wouldn't have bothered Vincente if a relationship developed between Father Cardozo and his mother. He could certainly understand—in his eyes she was the most beautiful woman that he could imagine. Who wouldn't be tempted? And the priest was already the closest thing he had to a father figure.

"Vincente," Father Cardozo said one day after Mass.

"Yes, Father," he replied automatically.

"How would you like to help put away the vestments today?"

"Yes, Father." Vincente knew that it was considered an honor to help Father Cardozo with the instruments of the faith, but truth be told, he would rather have had the opportunity to go outside and play with his friends. Jorge had found an old, beaten football in the local woods, and for once they would have a real ball to kick around during their weekly game. He obeyed anyway.

"Someday, my son, you may be an altar boy," Father Cardozo said. "Would you like that?"

"Yes, Father," the boy replied. He knew Father Cardozo was being kind. All Vincente could think about, though, was the delight in kicking an actual ball.

"Take this back to the cabinet, behind the altar."

He did as he was told. He could hear the small congregation chatting with the priest out in the church as he worked to put the vestments carefully away, as he'd been taught. His mother's voice rose above them, like a songbird's melody tickling his ears. He loved his mother's voice. He loved everything about her. She was his world.

The commotion started outside in the courtyard. There was shouting, and then a woman screamed. That was followed by the report of automatic gunfire and more screaming. Vincente was terrified. He'd heard the sound of gunfire before, but never so close. It was always in the hills, far off. Vincente, who had not been alive the last time the war had intruded upon the small town, could not imagine that the violence could really happen here. He'd always thought of his town as a safe haven.

He heard the shouting move into the church, and he poked his head around the corner of the church's little back room, where the vestments were kept.

There were a dozen armed men, all in the uniforms of the government's army. Most of them looked like ordinary soldiers, but one wore a uniform that stood out. It was a darker green than the rest, and he wore a peaked hat with a flat top. An ascot was tucked into his shirt. There was no doubt that he was in charge, and he was holding a revolver, shouting at Father Cardozo.

"You are the reason we are here!" he shouted. "You have been aiding the enemy!"

Father Cardozo remained calm, but there was something in his gaze that simmered under the surface. "I aid all mankind," he said. "I would aid you, if you would let me."

The soldier scoffed. "I don't need the aid of a peasant priest!" he shouted.

"Perhaps you do more than you know," Father Cardozo responded.

The soldier whipped his pistol across Father Cardozo's face, and a stream of blood erupted from a gash above the priest's cheekbone as he fell to the floor. The congregants pulled back in horror—all except Vincente's mother, Maria, who flew to him, her hands touching the handsome man's face gently, trying to stem the blood with the hem of her long skirt. There, in that moment, it seemed clear that this was not the first time his mother's hands had caressed his cheek.

"Do you deny that you aided two rebels who made their way here?" the soldier shouted at Father Cardozo, looming over him.

"I deny nothing," the Father said through Maria's skirt. "I do not ask men their affiliation when they seek the Lord's help."

"You lie!" the soldier said. He grabbed the priest by the shirt, and pulled him up on his feet. Blood continued to pour down the priest's face. "You took them back to their platoon. You administered the sacraments to the enemy!"

Father Cardozo said nothing. He just stared at the soldier, his head held high, even as he continued to bleed.

"Where are they hiding?" the soldier demanded.

Father Cardozo said nothing.

The soldier raised his pistol and pointed it at Cardozo's head. "Tell me." He cocked the gun.

"No!" Maria screamed. She lunged to try to place herself in front of the gun, but was restrained by one of the soldiers.

The man in charge seemed startled at first, but then an evil smile crept across his face. He looked back and forth between Maria and Cardozo, and the smile became more malevolent. "It looks as though Christ was right, Padre. We are all sinners, are we not?" He put his gun into his holster and pulled out a large knife. The smile never left his face as he walked to the broad, low alter at the front of the church. "Put her here," he ordered the soldier who had hold of her. She tried to struggle free, but two other soldiers grabbed her as well, and they dragged her up to the altar—really just a table at the front of the poor church. "Lay her down," the man in charge ordered.

As the three other men held her down on the table, the officer took his knife and cut off the peasant dress she was wearing, pulling and ripping at it until she was naked on the altar. The others in the congregation all looked away, but the officer nodded to his other men. "Make them watch," he ordered, and the soldiers raised their guns at those in the church.

"Please, no!" Cardozo begged.

"Tell me where they are!"

"I don't know, I swear it!"

The man in charge unbuckled his pants. He said to the congregation, "This is what your Jesus will bring you! This is what his priest allows!" Then he looked down at Maria and said, "Now I will have a taste of what the padre has been enjoying!"

Vincente wanted to go to her. He wanted to stop it, but he was scared. And just as he thought he'd summoned the courage to throw himself at the vile man, her eyes caught his as he peered from around the corner in the back room. Her eyes were full of tears and bravery and resignation, and she shook her head ever so slightly to tell him to stay where he was. It was as though she was telling him that it would all be over soon, and that she would be all right.

When it was over, the man in charge gave a satisfied grunt and pulled his pants back up. But it was clear that he was not truly satisfied. Not yet.

He walked behind the altar so that he was looking out at the congregation, Maria lying still and naked like some grotesque sacrifice. "You still will not tell me, Father?"

Cardozo's head was down now, and he was sobbing. "I do not know, I swear it!"

"I do not believe you." And with that, the man in charge took his large knife and swung it down as hard as he could. The blade sliced through her throat and traveled all the way down to the vertebrae before it stopped. The blood poured out over the altar like a deep red velvet cloth. "This is what your God brings these people, Father!" he shouted. "Death!"

"You will burn in hell!" Cardozo screamed. He lunged forward, but was cut down by automatic gunfire. The soldiers then turned their weapons on the congregation and mowed them down as they clambered to get away. Vincente watched the bodies dance and lunge as the gunfire tore them to shreds before it died away. The entire time, the man in charge was laughing maniacally.

When the shooting was over, the church looked like it had been painted in blood. Vincente sat there, in shock, unable to move. He watched the soldiers pick over the bodies, looking for anything of value that they might loot from the dead, until another man came in from outside.

"Holy fuck!" the man said. He was dressed in higher-grade military fatigues, and spoke Spanish with a distinctive accent. American. "Jesus holy fuck, what the fuck did you do?" he demanded of the man in charge.

"I sent a message."

The American looked appalled. "You can't do shit like this."

"This is what is needed," the man in charge said. "That is why you give us the weapons."

The American shook his head, but did nothing. "We gotta get out of here," he said. "When this is discovered, we need to be long gone."

The soldiers filed out of the church and disappeared into the hills.

Vincente never knew for how long he sat there, staring out at his mother's naked corpse, splayed out over the altar, her head nearly severed from her body. He was found by the first people on the scene, sometime later, his eyes still open. When asked his name, he didn't respond. In fact he didn't speak again for more than two years. Eventually his brother Javier was located, and he took Vincente away with him so that he could be trained as a soldier.

For years afterward, those who survived the massacre wondered what had gone on in the little boy's head as he witnessed such terror. He would never speak of it, but nor would he forget. And only he knew that as he witnessed the horrors, he made two promises to himself. He would never trust God again, and he would do everything he could to kill as many of those who had visited such horrors against his country from afar.

Brooks was speaking as Vincente Carpio's memories faded to the background. He was ticking through possible strategies for his defense. *There might be flaws in the evidence, or reasons to challenge the science that was used to tie Carpio to the crimes.* Vincente knew, though, that the science was sound. He'd been deliberate in letting the world know that he was responsible. *Maybe there were other suspects that they could offer up to a jury to sow the seeds of doubt.* That, too, was impossible. No one would mistake the deliberateness of Carpio's handiwork. *One final option was to plead insanity—the viciousness of the crimes themselves pointed to mental infirmity.* But Carpio would never allow himself to be labeled insane. There was nothing infirm about his mind; his intellect towered over those of all who sought to prosecute him, and in that intellect he would find salvation.

"My next court appearance is in two weeks, correct?" he asked, interrupting the lawyer.

Brooks looked startled. "Yes," he said. "Wednesday the thirteenth. You'll be formally charged."

"And you are my lawyer, so what I tell you, you cannot tell to the police?"

Brooks put his pencil down on the table and leaned back in his chair. Carpio saw him glance up at the camera in the corner of the room. "That's right," he said. "That would be a violation of my professional ethics."

"Can I communicate to my brother through you?"

Brooks rubbed his chin. "That's a little more complicated," he said. "Anything I tell your brother is not privileged." He paused. "And if I relayed anything related to illegal activity, I would be putting my law license in jeopardy. I would need a reason to do that."

"Money."

Brooks' eyes went to the camera again before coming back to Vincente's eyes. "It would have to be a lot of money."

"Are you trustworthy?"

Brooks' gaze now seemed to go inward, and he gave a dark smile. "I've never betrayed a paying client."

Carpio nodded. He closed his eyes. "Describe this process where I am formally charged."

"What do you want to know?"

"I want to know everything."

THIRTY-ONE

Saturday, February 2

"Where the hell have you been!"

The kitchen door had barely closed behind Diamond, the icy wind slamming it shut with a crash that seemed to rattle the entire house. Cormack was there, leaning against the kitchen counter, his arms crossed.

"I was out," she replied, not looking directly at him.

"That's all you have to say?"

"What else do you want me to say?"

Cormack fumed. "Did you get my messages?"

"My phone was off," she said. "I just listened to them now." It was the truth. She had listened to them while walking back from the Holiday Inn. He'd left several of them, each asking her to call him. None of them specified that there was anything wrong, but the tone in each had been progressively more worried. She felt a tinge of guilt for not having picked up the phone and for having been out of contact for so long, but fought that feeling down. After all, Cormack was known to disappear for days at a time as well. What was good for the goose . . .

"I was worried!" Cormack was almost shouting, and it caught Diamond off guard. She couldn't remember a time when she had ever seen him lose his temper. She looked at him, and her shock deepened.

"Oh my God!" she blurted out. "What happened to your face?" There was a bandage across his nose, and dark scabs covered his cheeks. The dark bruises under his eyes made it look like he'd lost a heavyweight title fight.

"I had an accident," Cormack said, looking down.

"Mack, that's not an accident," she said, shaking her head. "I'm not stupid."

He pried his eyes from the floor to meet hers. She could see the pain and fear in them more clearly than she'd seen it since her mother died. It wasn't a fear for himself, she knew; it was a fear for her. It was the fear, she supposed, that all parents feel when contemplating their child's future, and their own inadequacy in protecting them from all the evils of the world. Her hand went unconsciously to her abdomen.

"You're right," Cormack said. "You're not stupid. Far from it." The way he said the words sent shivers through her. She'd always known that her father's business wasn't entirely legitimate. There were too many people who showed him too much respect, and too many others who regarded him with palpable fear for him to operate entirely within the confines of the law. She realized that she'd always known that he wasn't just *involved* in the corruption that ran throughout the harbor; he ran the corruption. She'd just never wanted to admit it to herself. She loved him too much to think about him in that way. And yet, now, as she allowed herself to acknowledge what she had always known deep down, she still loved him.

"Are you in danger?"

He shrugged. "It's nothing I can't deal with."

She looked down at the phone in her hand and thought about the messages he had left for her, each one successively more desperate in tone. "Am I in danger?"

He shook his head. "Not if I have anything to say about it."

She could feel a tear running down her cheek. "What's going on?"

He uncrossed his arms, stepped forward, and wrapped them around her. She melted into the safety of her father's embrace, and it made her feel, at least for a moment, like things would be all right. "Don't worry," he said. "There are a few bad people who are unhappy with me. But I have the backing of the union, and this will all be taken care of."

She pushed away from him. "What the fuck does that mean? *The backing of the union?* Are they all involved in this?"

He crossed his arms again. "It means I'll take care of this. I'll make sure you're safe. Until this is done, though, I want you to stay here. I've got a man who will be here, too. Just to make sure nothing happens. He's with the union."

"The union?"

"It's for your own good." His phone rang and he took it out of his pocket. He held it up to his ear. "Yeah?" he said. "OK. I'll be there shortly." He put the phone back into his pocket. "I've got to go."

He started to walk out, and then paused. "The five hundred dollars you wanted . . ." he began. Then he stopped to regroup. "I'm sorry I haven't had a chance to talk to you about that."

"I don't want the money," Diamond said.

"You've made your decision, then?"

She nodded. It was true, she had. Without even realizing it, something clicked inside her brain or her heart, or whatever part of her that made the best decisions on instinct.

She saw Cormack allow himself a smile. She also saw that the smile was tinged with regret. She wondered what he was feeling.

"Who's the father?" he asked.

Diamond just stared at him, not answering.

He nodded. "OK. When you're ready. Does he know you're keeping it?"

She shook her head. "He doesn't even know I'm pregnant."

"How do you think he'll react?"

"How did you react when Mom told you about me?" The comment stung him, she could see, and she was instantly sorry she'd said it. "I didn't mean that," she said.

"No, it's a fair point," he allowed. "Who knows, maybe the world has changed since then. Maybe he's a better man than I was." She could tell that he wanted to say more. Finally, he asked, "Do you love him?"

She stared at her father for a moment, afraid of what she would say. Afraid of how he would react. Afraid of how she actually felt.

"More than I ever thought I'd love anyone," she said at last.

He held her eyes with his for a long pause. "Good," he said. "It may not make it work, but at least it makes it worth the try. I hope I get the chance to meet him soon."

"Yeah, me too."

He lingered for a moment, and then looked at his phone, and suddenly he was somewhere else. She saw the change in his face. He had been warm and tender and vulnerable talking to her, but now that was gone. Now he was rock steady, and all sense that he could have mercy or pity or love was gone from his expression. For the first time, she had an understanding of why so many seemed so afraid of him. "I've got to go," he said. "Don't leave the house until I say it's OK to."

She stared at him, not fully comprehending. "I'm just supposed to stay here?"

"For now." He nodded.

"I have a life!" she protested.

"Aye, you do," he said. "I intend to keep it that way." He nodded again and walked past her and out the kitchen door.

THIRTY-TWO

Cormack's hands gripped the steering wheel as he guided the car through the streets of Southie. He needed to focus. T'phong Soh was a worthy adversary—a dangerous, smart, ambitious young man with a solid cadre of men behind him and the will and ruthlessness to follow through on his plan to take over Boston Harbor. If Cormack wasn't mentally engaged, this young man would kill him, he knew.

And yet his focus was elsewhere right now. One simple phrase echoed in his mind, and he seemed unable to stop it.

I'm going to be a grandfather.

He wasn't sure exactly how he felt about that. He still thought of himself as too young to be a grandfather. Even with the ravages of age, and the injuries he'd sustained recently, he still felt young and strong and virile.

He was also concerned for Diamond. She was only nineteen, and while there were plenty of young girls in the neighborhood who got knocked up and had kids when they were young, he'd always hoped that Diamond would choose a different path—go to school, get a good job, become a professional. She was always at the top of her class, and she had more street sense than almost anyone he knew.

That was why, he knew, her child would be special. And that thought made his heart swell with pride. She would be a great mother, even at her young age, and she would love and protect her child better than anyone had ever protected her. He felt guilty as he thought back on how she had been forced to live her childhood—without any real stability or continuity. It was a miracle that she had turned out as well as she had. He blamed himself for all that she had gone through, and he vowed that his grandchild would never have to go through the same sorts of things.

In the end, he thought, maybe that was the answer. She was a smart, capable young woman, and she knew what was right for her. He had to trust her judgment, and make sure that she knew that he would be there to help her, whether the father of the child was there or not.

But in order to do that, Cormack had to make sure that he stayed alive. He'd be no good to Diamond or her child if he was dead, which meant—again—that he had to focus. He had to make sure that he got to Soh before Soh got to him. That was why he had to meet Kit Steele.

He'd been surprised when she called and told him that she had information for him. She knew he was going to war, and he could no longer abide by their original agreement that he would refrain from violence. She'd made clear at the hospital that she could no longer be involved with him if he was going back to his old ways. He wondered what had changed her mind.

Ultimately, he didn't care. He wanted to see her, more than he felt comfortable admitting. It was possible that she had information that would be truly useful to him. But even if not, he would still have gone to see her. She was the first person since Diamond's mother that he had felt real passion for, even if he refused to acknowledge it.

They met at the usual place—a small motel just over the Quincy border, past UMass. Boston on the McGrath highway. He could never go to her apartment or office, for obvious reasons. Nor could she ever be seen at his house or at the union. So this dingy spot with yellowing lace curtains and wood paneling had become their hideaway.

He paid for the room inside the office. The kid behind the counter didn't look at him; he just took the money and passed over the key. Cormack suspected he'd learned that his life would be easier if he could plausibly deny recognizing anyone who rented the rooms. It was not the kind of place where reputable businesspeople stayed, or where families vacationed. Cormack took the key without comment, and headed back out into the parking lot, down the row of doors to the one that matched the number on the key.

He was nervous, he realized with surprise, as he waited in the room. The curtains on the windows were drawn, the shades pulled down. He turned on the light, but all it could muster was an antique glow. He went to the bathroom and ran the water, splashed some on his face. He was running a towel over his cheeks when he heard the door open.

"Cormack?"

He put the towel in the sink and walked back into the bedroom. "I was surprised to hear from you," he said, standing in the bathroom doorway.

She nodded. "I was a little surprised I called," she admitted.

"You know our deal is off." Cormack didn't move. He just looked at her. She was a striking woman, but her eyes looked weary, and it made him sad for her. "There's nothing I can do about that. The war came to me; I didn't go looking for it."

"I know."

"What do we have to talk about, then?"

"Soh."

"What about him?"

Kit took a manila folder out of her bag and laid it on the bureau. "This is the latest intel we have on him. It's enlightening."

Cormack looked at the folder on the bureau, then back at Kit. "What does it say?"

"It says that he's branching out."

Cormack gave a grunt. "That's why he's coming after me."

She shook her head. "It's not just that he's expanding his control over the harbor," she said. "He's expanding worldwide. He's got connections in both Southeast Asia and in the Middle East. He's making a move to become the largest heroin importer on both coasts. His goal is to control the operations both here and in San Diego, where the drugs will be coming in."

"Ambitious."

"Very," Kit nodded.

"I can't imagine that Soh's superiors in MS-13 will be too happy to hear that his loyalties have been compromised. Pineda is supposed to run the organization throughout the U.S. Every cell has some autonomy, but they all pay the organization, and a move this big is going to upset the power structure."

"It's not clear that Pineda knows yet. And by the time he finds out, it may be too late for him to do anything about it. Soh may be too powerful by then. If he manages to get control of both harbors and the heroin starts flowing, he'll have enough money to control an army. A well-armed one at that."

"Better that Soh's stopped now, then," Cormack noted.

She nodded. "For everyone."

"That's why you're willing to keep feeding me information, even though you know what's coming?"

She shook her head. "It's not just that," she said.

"What, then?"

"There are rumors that Javier Carpio is in Boston, and that he's helping Soh. It makes me wonder."

Cormack let that sink in for a moment. "You think his brother's part of the deal?"

"It occurred to me," Kit said. "Why else would Javier come all this way from El Salvador?" She shook his head. "I think he's using Soh and his men to try to break Vincente out of prison." Her expression hardened. "I am not going to let that happen. I don't care what I have to do to make sure it doesn't."

"Is there anything in the file that will help me?"

She nodded. "You won't get to him right now, he's got too many people around him. But there's another you may be able to get to. Juan Suarez. He's Soh's right hand. All the information is in here. You get to him, and you'll find out what Soh is planning."

"So you'll turn a blind eye on my war against Soh as long as it means he can't help break Carpio out," Cormack said. "Federal agents have gone to jail for less."

Her gaze remained hard. "I'm not turning a blind eye toward anything. Both of my eyes are wide open and seeing fine. If I go to jail, then I go to jail, but I will not let Vincente Carpio loose on the American public again. I'd rather sit in a cell with a clean conscience than walk the streets with the knowledge that there was something I could have done and I didn't do it."

He held her stare for a long moment before he spoke again. "Keeping him in prison means that much to you?"

She dropped her eyes to the floor. "When my son and my husband . . ." she began, but her voice caught in her throat. "I promised that I would do anything I could to prevent anyone from ever going through what I went through. It's what I've dedicated my life to. And I've failed. I caught him once, and he escaped and eight more people died." She took a deep breath. "I went down to Nantasket beach yesterday and walked along the water. It's where we used to go every summer. I was so cold."

"Coldest winter in history so far," Cormack said.

"I'm not talking about the weather," Kit said. She looked back up at him. "I'm talking about me. It was our spot, so familiar to me it could be my home. But I couldn't feel anything. I couldn't feel him. The wind blew through me like I wasn't even there—like I didn't even fucking exist." A tear ran down her cheek. "That's what they took from me." She shook her head. "They took everything."

"What happened?"

She turned away from him. "I don't talk about it."

"Maybe you should."

She shook her head. "It's too much to think about."

"Maybe if you talk about it, you'll be able to let go of it finally."

"I'll never let go of it." She took a deep breath. "I remember the lights," she began. "They were swirling . . . red and blue and white . . . so bright. They were there, in front of the house, and I couldn't figure out what they could possibly be doing there. It didn't make sense. There were so many cars. So many lights."

"The police?"

She nodded. "And ambulances. I don't even know why they were there. Neither one of them was going to the hospital."

"What happened?"

"There had been a fight at the school a week before. One of the kids involved in the fight was being recruited by MS-13. Dillon pulled him off another kid, and held him back. The kid fought to get loose, but Dillon was a big, athletic guy, and he manhandled the kid pretty easily. He didn't hurt him—not really. Maybe a bruise or two from being held, but nothing serious. I guess the kid felt like he had been disrespected. He was in the final part of his initiation, and the last thing he had to do was carry out a murder. He chose Dillon."

Cormack leaned in, wordlessly encouraging her to go on.

"It was the day of my last law school exam. I was looking forward to a break with Dillon and Ollie, my son. He'd just turned six. We were going to go to the beach the next day. Everything was perfect."

"What happened?"

She shook her head, as though she might be able to dislodge the memories that crawled through her brain. "There were so many police cars and ambulances," she said. "It didn't make any sense, but I knew, somehow, that it was bad. It was written on the faces of the detectives. They weren't just dead. If they'd just been dead, their faces wouldn't have been so white—so drained of patience for the horrors that human beings are capable of. They wouldn't let me into the house. They said it was too terrible."

"Machetes," Cormack said quietly under his breath. It was the weapon of choice for MS-13 when carrying out revenge killings.

Kit nodded. She could feel the wave of memories cresting the parapets of her defenses. "They were hacked to death. The coroner estimated that it took at least a half hour for them to do the damage they did. I never even got to say goodbye to my son. There wasn't enough left to say goodbye to. I never got to see him. And I never went back into that house. There was nothing left for me. They arrested the kid, and sent him to prison, but there were others who had helped him. Others who held my husband down and made him watch as they hacked our boy to death."

"That's why you went into the FBI."

"I didn't have anything to care about after that. At least here, I feel like I'm helping to make sure no one else ever has to go through what I went through. It's the only point to my existence. And every time I put one of these assholes away, I think to myself, *Maybe this is one of the bastards who killed Ollie and Dillon.* It's not much, but it's all I have."

"How's that working for you?"

She shrugged. "Keeps me off the streets. Keeps me from putting a gun in my mouth."

"It's the brutality that's brought it all back," Cormack said. "Carpio's brutality—that's what you can't let go of."

"Maybe. I don't know. All I'm sure of is that I will not let him escape. I can't. He's never going to do what he's done to anyone else. I'll deal with the devil if I have to, but he's never going to taste freedom again."

Cormack stepped forward and put a hand on her shoulder. "Even if you keep Carpio locked up, it won't bring them back," he said.

She leaned against him, and he took her in his arms. She wrapped her arms around his back. "I want to feel something again," she said into his chest. Her voice was hoarse and muffled, but he could hear the pain in it.

He leaned his head down and found her cheek, kissed it softly. He could taste the saline in her tears. It was a new experience. She lifted her head and her lips met his, and the feeling was exquisite. He had work to do, and he should leave to get to it, he knew. And yet he couldn't bear the thought of leaving her so lost and empty.

He kissed her harder and knew that the work would have to wait just a bit.

THIRTY-THREE

"Does your father suspect anything?"

"About us?" Diamond held her phone tight to her ear, glancing furtively into the other room where her new bodyguard was sitting. She'd needed to talk to Buddy after her encounter with her father. Her decision was made now, and she knew there was no going back. The only thing left was to tell Buddy and see how he would react. "He's got other things on his mind," she said. That was another reason she'd needed to talk to Buddy. She'd always viewed her father as an indestructible force of nature. He was always in control of everything around him, and she'd never seem him nervous or concerned. It was clear, though, that he was now. The thought that anything could genuinely threaten Cormack made her question so much about her world. Talking to Buddy helped to restore some normalcy to her reality.

"That's good," Buddy said. "If he ever found out about me, he'd kill me."

"He's not that bad."

"No?" Buddy laughed. "I think you underestimate how protective he feels about you. Any way you look at it, it's better if he doesn't know."

"He has to find out at some point," she said, testing the waters.

"Why?"

It wasn't the response she was looking for. "Because I'm not going to creep around in the shadows for the rest of my life. If we're going to be together, we've got to figure out a way for him to be OK with it."

"Your father controls the entire harbor. He decides what he's OK with. You and me don't have any say in that."

She was frustrated that Buddy didn't seem to be budging. That frustration bred anger, but she knew that anger wouldn't advance the discussion. She decided to take a different approach. "Do you remember the first time?" she asked.

He was quiet for a second. "Yeah," he said at last. "Of course I do. I remember everything about that night."

"Where were we?"

"Is this a test?"

"Yeah," she said. "It's a test. You better not fail."

He gave a soft, low chuckle. "This summer. The last week of July. It was as hot then as it is cold now. It started at Lucky "O's," he said.

She gasped. "Oh, my God, you fucking failed! It was at the Horseman!"

He chuckled harder. "No, that was where we first met," he said. "It started at Lucky "O's."

"What are you talking about?"

"You were there with that friend of yours, the one with the bright red hair . . . what's her name?"

"That's Jess."

"Right, Jess. You were there with her before you went to the Horseman."

"Yeah, we were. It was lame there, though. Too crowded to move around. But you weren't there."

"I was. That was where I first saw you. You were leaning against the wall, swaying to the music with this look on your face. It was part boredom and part disgust. I remember guys kept coming up to you, and you kept blowing them off. But there was something about you that I couldn't stop staring at. I was with Nate and a couple of the other guys, and he couldn't figure out what had gotten into me. There were these three girls at the bar and we were hitting on them. Or maybe they were hitting on us, I don't know, but after I saw you, I couldn't keep the conversation going."

"You're lying."

"I'm not. And then you left. You and Jess nodded to each other, and you were out the door. I couldn't resist, so I followed you. You went over to the Horseman, and I went in after you. I stood at the far end of the bar, just watching you for a while. I was trying to figure out a way to meet you without coming off as a sleazeball. I'd almost given up when that other guy showed up."

"Chris," Diamond said, remembering. "My asshole ex-boyfriend."

"Chris, your asshole ex-boyfriend," Buddy agreed. "Thank God for Chris, your asshole ex-boyfriend."

"He was so drunk that night, and so pissed at me, he couldn't leave it alone. I wanted to kill him."

"He wanted to kill you, too, clearly. When he started screaming at you, I just reacted. I couldn't stand to see anyone treat you that way."

"You didn't know me."

"I know. It's weird, but it was just an impulse I couldn't resist. I didn't even think about it. I just moved across the bar and grabbed him."

"I thought you were going to start a brawl." Diamond could feel her heart beating fast as the memory overtook her.

"I thought I was, too."

"What stopped you?"

"I don't know. He was drunk. And it suddenly occurred to me how I'd feel if I ever lost someone who looked like you. I felt bad for him, so I just told him to back off and go to another bar."

"And he did. I think everyone there could see in your face not to mess with you. I've never seen Chris move as quickly as he did when he left that place. God, I was so turned on. I wanted you so badly, right then—right at that moment." She sighed. "But then you turned away. I remember, you looked at me, and all you said was, 'I'm sorry, are you OK?' And I said, 'Yes.' And then you walked back to the other side of the bar."

"I didn't know what else to say."

"You didn't even give me the chance to say thank you. That was when I knew I really wanted you. Anyone who could be that hardcore, and not expect anything in return . . . that was something I had never seen before. So I did two shots to get up my courage, and I went over to talk to you."

"You did," he agreed. "And the rest is history."

"I've never slept with a guy that quickly."

"I felt like the luckiest guy in Boston."

"Huh," she said. "I always thought I was the one who chased you."

He laughed. "You did. But it was only after I'd chased you."

"How do you feel now?" It was a sudden change of direction, but she needed to know.

"What do you mean?"

"I mean, how do you feel now? Do you still want to be with me? Do you feel like you made a mistake? Do you feel like you're done? What?"

"I'll always want to be with you," he said. Something in his tone made her believe it.

"Buddy, there's something I need to tell you."

"Yeah," he said. She couldn't find the words. "I'm listening," he said when she didn't respond.

"I'm . . ." Again the words wouldn't come.

"You're what?"

"I'm . . ." It was no use. It wasn't the sort of thing that she could possibly say over the phone. She needed to be able to see his face—to see how he would react. Besides, it wasn't fair to him to drop this kind of news on him over the phone. "I'm really glad we had yesterday together," she said. "It was wonderful."

"It was wonderful," he agreed. "Can I see you tonight?"

She thought about Cormack's demand that she remain in the house. He seemed scared, and he'd left one of his men with her. Even if she'd wanted to get away to see him, she suspected that she couldn't. "Not tonight, but soon," she said. "Are you working on Monday?"

"Yeah, but not until the afternoon," he replied. "There's a freighter that's scheduled to dock around one o'clock. We'll see how much trouble I'm in for missing yesterday."

"I'm sure it'll be fine. Like I said, it seems like he has other things on his mind."

"OK," Buddy said. "I'll talk to you soon?"

"You better."

She ended the call and put the phone on the table. She ran her hand over her abdomen. She so wanted her child to grow up with both parents. She so wanted to be with Buddy. She knew it wasn't likely to be, but she made a promise to herself and to her unborn child that she would try to make it happen.

THIRTY-FOUR

Sunday, February 3

Juan lay in his bed, looking up at the ceiling. There were cracks in the plaster running the length of the small room in the tumbledown apartment at the edge of the water in East Boston. He could hear the naked woman beside him breathing, a slight wet rumble in her chest from whatever she had found the night before to pack into her glass pipe and smoke. She had served her purpose then, but now her presence was an annoyance. He elbowed her in the back to get her to roll over in the hope that it would dislodge whatever was caught in her bronchia, but it was useless. If it weren't for the hassle of disposing of her body, he would simply slit her throat and roll her off the bed so that he could get more sleep, but that wasn't practical in this country.

As he lay there, he contemplated the strange and winding journey of his life. He remembered his childhood in the city of San Salvador, the orphan of a slaughter carried out by the Farabundo Martí National Liberation Front—the FMNLF—which invaded the city in 1989 and took control of the poorest quarters of the capital. Suarez still had no idea whether his parents were active participants on either side of the years-long brutal conflict; he was only three at the time. All he knew was that all of a sudden, their bodies lay before him, shredded by automatic gunfire, and there was no one left to care for him.

He survived in the war-torn country by begging and digging in trash for morsels of food until 1992, when the armistice was signed. The FMNLF members who killed his parents were pardoned, and the organization was christened as one of the country's major political parties. Only then did the government turn its attention to the plight of the children of the war. He was taken into an orphanage, which was only slightly better than the streets. Food was still scarce, and now his tormentors had legal custody and government sanction to do as they pleased with him. He would never speak of the manner in which he was abused in that place.

At the age of thirteen, he was released from the orphanage, coarsened by his experience and impervious to pain—both his pain and the pain of those around him. Crime became his occupation and his salvation. Even at that tender age he was an accomplished thief, and his willingness to dispatch victims with the flick of a knife at the first sign of resistance earned him a reputation for ruthlessness on the streets. It was that reputation that brought him to the attention of a group of former left-wing guerillas who had been forcefully repatriated from the United States when the war had ended and their amnesty was no longer recognized. In the United States, the guerillas had adapted their military skills to the gang wars that raged in Los Angeles. Confined to a small community in the violent city, they had banded together to protect the Salvadoran community from the black and Latino gangs, and to exploit that same community for the service. Because of their small numbers, they employed the most brutal tactics to instill fear in their rivals. That strategy had drawn the most sadistic members of the dispossessed to their ranks, and the group had grown dramatically in the 1990s and early 2000s. They took the name Mara Salvatrucha 13, or MS-13, for their gang—a nod to their native land and to the neighborhood where they started—and covered their bodies in tattoos as evidence of their lifelong commitment.

Those who had been deported identified Suarez as a young man who would be useful to what had now become an international criminal enterprise. They trained him, cultivated his brutality, and instilled their brand of loyalty. It was a loyalty born from desperation and fear, and any betrayal of that loyalty came with a sentence of death.

By the time Suarez was in his late teens, MS-13 had established an international network that formed the backbone for one of the world's largest criminal organizations, run from El Salvador and Los Angeles, but with a significant presence throughout Central America and the United

States. Their numbers were estimated at fifty thousand strong worldwide, and they were contracted by cartels in Mexico to transport drugs from Asia and Central America into the United States. The network smuggled Suarez into Southern California, and he was installed as the military leader of the largest faction in Los Angeles, moving steadily up the ranks, leaving a bloody trail of rivals and innocents behind him as he advanced.

Two years ago, his superiors in Los Angeles had sent him to Boston to keep an eye on T'phong Soh, a young MS-13 recruit from Malaysia who was consolidating power on the East Coast. The young man's rapid ascension had concerned the hierarchy in Los Angeles, and they wanted Suarez to learn the young man's nature and intentions, and dispatch him if necessary.

Suarez had come to Boston with every intention of killing T'phong Soh within weeks, but he didn't. He wasn't sure why, but he found himself fascinated by the diminutive Asian. He had all the ruthlessness of others in the organization—more, in fact. But his ruthlessness was more directed, and more effective. He also seemed to have an endless reservoir of followers who were willing to die for him. And Suarez soon realized that Soh's power over his followers was different from the dominion exercised by the other leaders in MS-13. The other leaders ruled by sheer force of terror and intimidation. Soh's presence struck fear into the hearts of many, but he also inspired true belief. He quickly became an acolyte of Soh's, and shortly thereafter the closest thing to a trusted adviser that Soh would ever have.

Now he and Soh were poised to reveal the full scope of Soh's power to the world.

The crack whore next to him continued to breathe, and the rattle in her chest grew louder and louder until the noise clogged his ears. His nostrils filled with the scent of her—a sickly sweet combination of burned chemicals and sweat and sex, until he couldn't stand it anymore.

He gave her body a tremendous shove toward the side of the bed. "Get out!" he yelled at her in Spanish.

She didn't move, and gave no sign of consciousness, which angered him even more. He twisted in the bed and kicked out furiously at her.

"Get out!" he screamed. "You fucking whore! Get out!" He kicked at her head and connected hard, sending her farther toward the side of the bed. She rolled over and opened her eyes. Her expression was one of resignation and acceptance, and he suspected that this was not the first time she had awoken to a beating. In all likelihood, it was more common than not in her experience. That reality made her even more repulsive to him, and he kicked her again, this time in her face, hoping to smash the expression into oblivion.

He connected well, and she tumbled off the bed and hit the wooden floor hard. She screamed out and crawled on her knees to the bedroom door, gathering up what few clothes she'd had on the night before when he picked her up.

"Get out, bitch!"

She reached the door and grasped for the knob. Blood was running down from her forehead and into her eyes, and it was making it difficult for her to see. Finally, she latched onto the knob, turned it, and fell into the hallway. He could hear her crying as she lay there, just outside the threshold.

"Close the fuckin' door!" he yelled.

She used an elbow to slide the door closed.

The room was quieter now, and he could think. There was much to do today. He picked up the prepaid burner phone he had purchased the day before. He swapped phones out twice a week: always prepaid and anonymous, no internet access or smartphone functionality, and he only used the text function.

There was a text from one of Suarez's local distributors to discuss the next batch of fentanyl he was due to deliver. The dealer wanted to meet late in the morning.

Suarez texted back a time and place, then swung his feet off the bed and onto the floor. The whore whom he'd kicked out of his bed had left a smear of blood on the bedroom wall, and he cursed her under his breath. He took two quick steps to the doorway and threw open the door to see whether she was still curled on the hallway floor, but the place was deserted.

He looked up and down the hallway, considering whether he should see if he could catch up with her to deliver another beating, but dismissed the idea after a moment. There was no point; it would not make him feel better for long, and it certainly wouldn't impart any lesson that she would retain.

Besides, he knew it would be foolish. Important events were unfolding rapidly, and he needed to avoid distractions that could derail the plans he had with Soh and the Carpio brothers. The world would soon come to understand the power that Soh had, and Suarez would become known as one of the most feared men in organized crime. He would do nothing to prevent that from happening.

THIRTY-FIVE

Cormack stood in a small clearing off one of the main paths that wound around Belle Isle Marsh Reservation in East Boston. The temperature was below zero again, and he had to clench his jaw to keep his teeth from chattering. The bruises from the attack on the Mariner days before were fading, but still added to his discomfort.

He regarded his companions in silence. John Hall was a giant of marginal intelligence who had worked for the union for years, and was as loyal to Cormack as he was cruel and evil. He was standing at the edge of the marsh, urinating into the Short Breach Creek, which ran along the edge of the spot. He seemed as oblivious to the cold as a man could be, and Cormack suspected that the generous layer of fat and a dearth of brain cells afforded his tolerance to the weather. Cicero was also with him, and stood looking out at the open path, his eyes sharp and his body still.

Belle Isle was a well-known spot among the Boston underworld for dumping bodies. It was a twenty-eight-acre park along the water at the northeasternmost edge of East Boston. It was less than a half mile across the Belle Isle Inlet from the eastern runways at Boston Logan International Airport. During the spring, summer, and fall, it was a popular place to jog along the extensive maze of trails, or bring dogs to frolic at the edge of the thick marshes of heavy reeds and bushes. At certain spots, long wooden piers extended far out over the marshes, providing sweeping views of the city. In other spots, the bushes and shrubs were so thick that they were impenetrable.

During the winter, the place was deserted. The marshes lay flat and lifeless, forming a thick white canopy of snow and ice with dark gray veins cutting through it where the eddies rose and fell with the Inlet's tides. Looking out toward the airport and the skyline beyond, Cormack was doubtful that any life could ever come back to this place after a winter so cold.

"You sure this is the spot?" Hall asked, zipping up his pants.

"I saw the text myself," Cicero replied. His voice carried with it a threat that made clear that he didn't like being questioned by someone like Hall.

Hall shook his head, squinting into the vast expanse of white and gray around them. "Seems like a strange place, is all."

Cicero turned slowly to glare at Hall, and the giant man turned away as though struck in the face. Cicero was perhaps the only man on earth other than Cormack who could intimidate John Hall.

"Just seems weird," he said. He took a step toward the marshes, and Cormack wondered whether the man might start running out along the frozen mud to escape Cicero's ire. At that moment, though, there came a rustling along the path, and the three of them moved quickly and quietly toward the mouth of the clearing, which blocked anyone walking along the path from seeing them.

They plastered themselves against a tree and a snow-covered bush at the edge of the clearing as they listened to the footfalls coming down the path. Cormack's heart started beating as he realized that there was more than one set of footfalls. It sounded like multiple people, and there was heavy breathing. He and Hall took the point, ready to attack.

"I thought it was just one guy," Hall hissed, and Cicero shot him a look that made him shut his mouth immediately.

"There could be more," Cicero said. "We take them all out, but keep the target alive."

The men on the path were close, now, and Cormack gripped the club he'd brought with him. Both Cicero and Hall had guns, but Cormack didn't want the man killed. The goal was to take their target alive. Information was the key.

The panting of the men on the path was loud. Cormack readied himself, and raised the club up to strike.

A figure passed by, but it wasn't a man. It was an older woman in a heavy coat. She held a leash, and at the end of the leash was a large, ancient dog of indeterminate breed. She spun as she sensed Cormack's presence, and he barely got his club down before she could see it. He turned to make sure both Hall and Andolini still had their guns in their pockets.

"Jesus, Mary, and Joseph!" The woman exclaimed. "I didn't see you there! You nearly scared the life out of me!"

"Sorry, ma'am," Cormack said. "I didn't mean to scare you."

"Well, you did," she said. She shook her head as though regaining her senses. The dog, out of breath and panting in the cold, lumbered over to give Cormack a disinterested sniff. "Charlie, no!" the woman barked at the dog, pulling on his leash to get him away from Cormack. The dog looked over his shoulder. The woman was too small to actually move the dog, but after a moment Charlie complied. "I thought I was the only person crazy enough to be out in this cold!" the woman continued.

Cormack gave her his most charming smile. "What cold?" he said.

She gave a nod at the attempted humor, but didn't smile. "Looks like you had a bit of an accident," she said, examining the cuts that were still healing on his face.

"My wife's got a temper," Cormack replied without missing a beat.

The woman nodded matter-of-factly. "And you got a wandering eye, I bet," she said.

Cormack shrugged.

"I walk Charlie here every day," the woman said. "No matter the weather. He likes it."

"I bet," Cormack said. He was praying that she would just move along. He had the sense that Cicero Andolini would have no qualms about killing her and Charlie and dragging their bodies out into the marsh. That would complicate matters. "We've got to get back to work," he said.

"What kind of work?" she asked, her eyes narrowing.

"Surveying," Cormack said, improvising as quickly as he could. "There's been some complaints about vagrancy here during the summer. We're trying to survey the land to see what effect cutting back some of the growth would have on the place. It might prevent the homeless from setting up camps." He turned to look at Hall and Andolini. Hall nodded sheepishly. Andolini just stared at the woman.

"Well," the woman said, "you just be sure that you don't cut back too much! Those of us who live around here like this park just the way it is. You cut back too much, and I promise you, you'll hear about it from not just me. Others, as well!"

With that, she turned and headed up the pathway, leaving them behind.

"Fuck," Hall said, taking his gun out of his pocket. "I thought we were gonna have to kill the bitch."

Cormack looked at Cicero Andolini. He was staring straight back into Cormack's eyes, and Cormack knew that Cicero was thinking the same thing. The old woman and giant dog had no idea how lucky they were that they were still breathing.

The synthetic opioid fentanyl, usually mass produced in Eastern Europe and Asia, is at the heart of the American opioid crisis—a crisis that claimed sixty-four thousand lives in 2016 alone. It's cheap to make and ten times more powerful than heroin. It's easy to cut with other more expensive drugs, like heroin and cocaine, as well as with prescription drugs like oxycodone. It can be mass produced in Asia and Latin America and made available on the black market at discount prices.

Despite the resultant crackdown on its importation by the authorities, all of this made it an ideal commodity for traffickers, and was why the Asian connections of Dr. Yee, Juan Suarez's fentanyl supplier, were important to him and T'phong Soh. Dr. Yee was a dentist with coke-bottle glasses who ran an import-export business on the side. He had always been reliable, and provided product of serviceable quality at cut-rate prices. The increased attention on the opioid crisis generally, and on the role of fentanyl in the drug trade specifically, was squeezing Dr. Yee and making shipments more dangerous. Dr. Yee had texted early in the morning that he needed to discuss the situation. Juan Suarez texted back and instructed Dr. Yee to meet him at the Belle Isle Marshes. His thought was that an outdoor meeting would ensure brevity; Suarez had a busy day ahead of him and didn't want to waste too much time with Dr. Yee.

Suarez pulled into the parking lot off Bennington Street in East Boston, at the edge of the marshes. The reservation was squeezed in between Eastie and Winthrop, so it was convenient for both Suarez and Dr. Yee, and with the weather as cold as it was, the place would be deserted.

There was one vehicle in the lot, a white rusted-out service van that looked as though it might have been abandoned rather than parked. Suarez got out of his car and looked around the area. A slight breeze drifted across the marshes, raising a soft rustle. Other than that, everything was quiet and still.

He headed up the main path to where it branched off into multiple smaller trails. He had instructed Dr. Yee to take the first two left trails and meet him by the bench that faced the airport. Suarez stuffed his hands into his pockets and watched the steam explode from his mouth as he breathed. He still had trouble fathoming the cold in this godforsaken place. Before coming to Boston, he had lived only in Central America and Los Angeles. His first Boston winter had been mild, though he had marveled at the freezing temperatures, and distrusted those who had said that it could get colder. This winter had proved them right, though, and he still could not believe that any place on earth could stay this cold for this long.

As he came to the spot in the trail where the second branch took him to the left, he was surprised to see an old woman walking toward him with a giant dog on a leash. He looked at her as she passed. She started to nod hello to him, but she stopped and a look of fear came across her face. He was used to it. The tattoos were hard to miss; they covered almost the entirety of his face. Ornate depictions of "MS-13" ran from his chin to his forehead. They sent a message to the world that he was a dangerous man who didn't care what anyone else felt about him.

The woman put her head down and her pace increased as much as the dog's languid trot would allow.

It was disconcerting to him that anyone would be out in this cold at all; only an insane New Englander would believe that it was reasonable to walk by the water in sub-zero temperatures. He would never understand the people who lived in this place. At least, though, her fear would prevent her from giving in to any curiosity, and there was no chance that she would return. He and Dr. Yee would not be disturbed.

At that moment, Dr. Yee was gathering his cash and belongings to leave the Boston area indefinitely. His involvement with Soh's men was in the FBI file given to Cormack by Kit Steele. Cormack had passed on that bit of information to Cicero, with instructions to use Dr. Yee's connections to get further information about Soh's whereabouts.

Cicero had visited Dr. Yee the night before with John Hall in tow. They found him alone at his dental office. Dr. Yee had been reluctant to give them any information about Soh or MS-13, even faced with Cicero's knife. Hall duct-taped Dr. Yee to one of his dental chairs, his head pulled all the way back, strapped to the headrest. Cicero began by removing two of the doctor's teeth. He then began methodically experimenting with each of the various dental instruments and power tools until Dr. Yee was begging to cooperate. After Dr. Yee had given them all the information he had, they instructed him to text his contact and tell him that he needed to talk. Cicero still had Dr. Yee's phone when Suarez texted the time and place to meet.

Dr. Yee knew he had to disappear as quickly as possible. Once MS-13 found out that he had given up information about Suarez, his time in the dental chair with Cicero would seem a pleasant memory.

As Cormack waited in the cold of the Belle Isle Marsh Reservation, he heard John Hall chuckle softly to himself.

"That fuckin' chink doctor last night . . ." Hall said, his laughter trailing away. "That was too fuckin' funny."

Cicero shot him a glare.

"What? It was." He looked at Cormack. "This guy was screaming so loud. In his own dentist's chair, for Christ's sake. And Mr. Andolini, here, was just workin' over the chink's teeth. It was the funniest fuckin' thing I seen." He chuckled again. "Payback for all the poor schlubs he worked over in that same chair, I guess. Only when he was doing it, the poor schlubs were payin' him for the pleasure. Too fuckin' funny."

The irony wasn't lost on Cormack, but he was trying to keep his attention on the trail. The old woman with the dog had thrown him off. He didn't think there was any chance that anyone else would be out in the cold. He had almost taken her head off, and that would have been more of a hassle than he could comprehend.

He heard footsteps on the path coming toward them, and he raised his hand to signal to Hall and Cicero to be ready.

The man passed the entrance to the clearing without seeing Cormack. This time O'Connell knew he had the right target. He could see the tattoos covering the man's neck and the side of his face that was visible. Cormack stepped out of the clearing and swung the club.

It connected solidly below the man's head, on the soft tissue between his shoulder and his neck. Cormack had been careful not to kill him with the blow, conscious of the need to gather information, but Suarez went down hard nonetheless. Cormack was on him immediately. There was no way to know what weapons, if any, the man might have on him. If he was able to get hold of a gun, the situation would quickly get out of control. Hall and Cicero were both on the path now, hanging back a step, pointing their guns at the man on the ground. Still, if Suarez managed to get off one lucky shot, it wouldn't be good for anyone.

Cormack swung the club again, this time into his ribs. Suarez seemed to give little resistance, and Cormack worried for a moment that he'd been too aggressive and that he was possibly unconscious. Without warning, though, Suarez turned quickly, and flipped on his side. His hand struck out, and Cormack saw the flash of metal in it, and ducked just in time.

Suarez didn't have a gun, but he had a knife. He was struggling to his knees, disoriented. He looked up and saw Hall and Cicero with their guns pointed at him. For a moment, Cormack thought that he would surrender without further resistance. Instead, he lunged at Cormack, aiming for his head. Cormack ducked again, and swung his club up hard. It connected with the man's skull, and blood poured down his face. Suarez looked at Cormack for a moment, and then his eyes rolled up into his head, and he fell face-first into the snow.

The blood spread out from his head in a semicircle, staining the white ground.

"Is he dead?" Hall asked.

"He better not be," Cormack said in a cold tone, cursing himself for being careless. "We need information. I'm not gonna be happy if he's dead."

Cormack moved forward, slowly. The knife had fallen inches from the man's hand, and he grabbed it and threw it into the marsh. He rolled the man over. There was snow in his mouth and nostrils, and Cormack cleared them. He bent down low and after a moment he could tell that Suarez was still breathing. He looked up at Cicero and nodded.

Cicero nodded back. "Good. Let's get him up and move him into the truck."

Hall stuck his gun back into his pocket and bent down. He took one arm and Cicero took the other and the two of them lifted the man up. They carried him down the path, his feet dragging in the snow, his head hanging down. Blood continued to drip, leaving a trail in the snow.

They got back to the white service van and opened the back door. Suarez was still limp as Cicero and Hall lifted him inside. Hall got in behind him and used duct tape to bind his hands and feet. Cormack closed the door and climbed into the driver's seat. Cicero slid into the passenger's seat.

Cormack started the engine and eased the van out of the parking spot. He pulled around and out toward the street. As the van neared the exit, he looked over and saw the old women with her dog standing near the park's entrance. Both she and the dog were staring at the van. The dog's gaze was disinterested, but the woman's mouth was gaping, and Cormack realized that she must have seen them carrying the man's body out of the park and putting him in the back. She was only twenty or thirty yards from where the van had been parked, and it would have been difficult for her to miss the commotion.

Cormack looked over at Cicero; he was staring at the woman as well. "Wait," Cicero said.

"No, there's no time."

"She saw us."

"Yeah, probably," Cormack conceded. "But we're too close to the street. If we kill her, someone else will see." He could see Cicero wrestling with the risks and probabilities. "She's from Eastie. She knows better than to talk to the cops anyway."

Cicero stared at the woman for another moment, perhaps trying to send a message to her. Then he turned his head and looked out the windshield toward the street. "It's a risk either way," he said. "It's your call."

Cormack stepped on the accelerator and eased the van onto Bennington Street.

THIRTY-SIX

Monday, February 4

The bleeding had started Sunday night. Diamond noticed it just before she went to bed, and had no idea how concerned she should be. She was able to put it out of her mind and go to sleep, hoping that it would stop by the morning.

When she awoke on Monday morning, though, she was still spotting. It was at that point that her heart started racing. The speed with which human emotions could swing awed her. Less than a week before, she probably would have welcomed a miscarriage. At that point, she was unsure that she wanted a child, but she was nominally a Catholic, and notwithstanding her lack of formal religious instruction, she still had an unyielding guilt at the idea of an abortion. A miscarriage would have taken the decision out of her hands and limited her sense of responsibility. Now, only a few days later, she had decided that she wanted the baby, and so the thought of a miscarriage was unbearable and struck terror into her very soul.

Cormack hadn't been home in two days and she couldn't talk to Buddy about her situation—she hadn't even told him about the pregnancy yet. She realized that she would need to deal with this on her own.

She called her doctor and made an emergency appointment. The nurse on the other end of the line was polite and reassuring, but Diamond could sense the disinterest in her voice. She supposed it was inevitable for someone who spent her entire life dealing with pregnant women. Diamond got dressed in sweats, slipping a maxi pad into her panties. Then she hurried downstairs.

Joe Konicki was sitting at the kitchen table, just where he'd been sitting when she went to bed. He was wearing the same clothes, and she wondered whether he'd slept at all.

He was older than Cormack—she was guessing in his mid-sixties—with a head of white hair and thick veins covering his nose. For his age, though, he looked like a powerful man, with a barrel chest and wrists like knotted ropes. She guessed that he had spent his entire lifetime on the waterfront, and it showed in every aspect of his appearance. He glanced up when she walked into the kitchen.

"How'd you sleep?" he asked. His voice was gravelly but kind.

"OK," she said. "You?"

He shrugged.

"I have to go out," she said. "I have an appointment I have to go to."

He stood, looking uncomfortable. "I'm not supposed to let you out of the house," he said, his voice uncertain.

"You can't actually keep me here against my will," Diamond said. "That'd be kidnapping."

"Cormack told me to do whatever I have to do to keep you from leaving," Joe said. It was a simple statement of fact, with little apology. "He was real clear about that. It's for your own safety."

Diamond realized that Joe was serious, and despite the kindness in his voice, she had little doubt that he would use whatever force necessary to keep her there. His determination and the apparent depth of her father's concern for her heightened her anxiety about what Cormack and Buddy were mixed up in. "But I don't have a choice," she stressed. "I have to see my doctor."

"A doctor?" Joe looked concerned at that. "Are you OK? Are you sick?"

"I'm not sick," she said. "Not exactly."

"I don't understand."

She sighed. "It's a woman issue," she said, drawing her shoulders up and crossing her arms. He was silent for a moment. "It's just—"

He held up his hands, mortified at the prospect of getting any more detail. "That's OK," he said quickly. "That's your business. I'm just not sure what to do. Cormack was real specific."

"I'll come right back after the appointment," Diamond said. "You could even drive me there and back." She could feel that the bleeding had not stopped, and she was growing more and more concerned. She could hear fear growing in her voice, and suspected Joe could hear it, too.

"How far?" he asked.

"Five minutes," she said. "It's over by UMass."

Joe was rubbing his chin. "How long will the appointment take?"

"Not too long, I hope," Diamond responded.

"OK," he said at last. "But I'm driving you, and we're just going there and back. OK?"

Diamond nodded. "Thank you." It was so odd. He was essentially keeping her hostage, and yet she felt a strong sense of gratitude toward him at that moment.

He shook his head as he stood up. "Don't tell Cormack, all right? He'd kill me if he found out I let you out of the house."

As she followed him out toward the car, she wondered how literally Joe meant that.

Kit was back at FMC Devens, staring at the screen that showed Vincente Carpio in his cell. She was trying to decipher some of the tattoos that covered his face and head. There were skulls, all of different sizes. They reminded her of the piles of skulls she'd seen in pictures from the aftermath of the Holocaust. There were other images as well, though. Just over his left ear, there was an American flag flying upside down, being carried by a skeleton with a military helmet on it. Over his right ear, there was an altar covered in flames. And on the top of his bald head, there was an image of what appeared to be an angel. Her wings were spread wide, her hair flowing. She was beautiful, except that where her face should have been, there was nothing but a black space ringed with blood.

Kit wondered at the hatred that could cause someone to have such images permanently inked into the face and head. She knew it existed—she'd seen it in the murder of Dillon and Ollie—so she supposed that it should not have surprised her. And yet it did. It always did.

Watching him, she could feel his determination, and she knew that if he managed to escape again, the odds of recapturing him again were low. And if that happened, the havoc he could wreak was difficult to estimate. Vincente had made clear that the madness had overtaken any other impulse he had, and his only goal was to kill as many Americans as possible. If he and his brother had partnered with Soh and Soh managed to take control of harbors on both coasts, there was no telling how Vincente might be able to spread that madness. Kit wouldn't let that happen.

"Where is he?"

There was no reproach in Javier Carpio's voice when he asked the question—no suggestion that anyone had done anything wrong. It was a question that, as a soldier, he asked to assess strategic realities, not to assign blame.

There was no blame to assign, Soh knew. Juan Suarez had never been late for an assignment. He was a careful soldier who believed in the process of extreme, targeted violence. He was good at his job; perhaps the best that Soh had ever encountered. And he was loyal. When Suarez did not show up on time for their meeting at the warehouse, he knew that Suarez had not sold him out. The situation was more serious than that.

"Where is he?" Javier Carpio asked again.

"Dead," Soh responded. "Or worse."

"Will this be a problem?"

Soh shook his head. "He knows what to do. He will not betray us."

"You seem sure."

Soh could detect a pinch of skepticism in Carpio's voice. "Do you have reason not to be?" He was not used to being questioned, and the notion that the El Salvadoran would doubt Suarez—one of Soh's men—annoyed him.

Carpio shrugged his enormous shoulders. "I was in the wars in El Salvador. I had a lieutenant under my command," he said. "A young, strong, brave man. The bravest anyone had ever known, and the most loyal. I taught him everything I could. I told him about our strategy for wearing the government soldiers down, for cutting their supplies. I told this young man where the best towns were to hide and how to blend into the crowd in those towns." Javier Carpio took a knife out of his pocket and used it to stab a hunk of cheese that was sitting on the table in the center of the warehouse. Soh couldn't help but marvel at the size of Carpio's hand. He slowly sliced the cheese into thin pieces and slid them into his mouth.

"One day," Javier continued, "this young lieutenant was out on a patrol, and he was captured. A week later, three of the towns where my soldiers were hiding were bombed to rubble. A week after that, I received a package in the mail. It contained the lieutenant's severed ear. It was wrapped in a note that read, 'He told us everything this ear ever heard.'" Carpio chewed a slice of cheese thoughtfully.

"What is your point?" Soh asked.

"I never had any reason to question this soldier's loyalty, but loyalty may not be in the front of a man's mind when his ear is being cut off his head."

Soh considered this for a moment. "Juan Suarez has already experienced tortures worse than most men can conceive of," he said. "He has his orders if he is captured, and I believe he will follow them."

"And if not?"

Soh picked up the last slice of cheese on the table in front of Carpio. "I have a contingency plan."

THIRTY-SEVEN

Joe Konicki didn't go into the doctor's office with Diamond. He had planned to, but when they pulled up to the medical building near the University of Massachusetts in South Boston, and he saw the sign with the doctors' names listing their specialties as "Obstetrics and Gynecology," he decided that she would probably be safe in the building; he preferred to wait outside.

He sat in his car in the parking lot fighting the urges for the first fifteen minutes. He was on his tenth day without a cigarette, and the withdrawal had him losing his mind. Some of it was physical—he knew that his addiction to the nicotine was a major part of his need—but he could temper that with nicotine patches and gum. As he sat in the car, he'd already powered through three pieces of the expensive chewables. But no amount of nicotine could wipe away the psychological addiction. His hands fumbled for something to do, and continually touched his face and mouth out of habit. The need to engage in the same repetitive motion that had comforted him for over fifty of his sixty-five years was overpowering, and in the end he gave into it.

He climbed out of the car, into the cold, and walked up the street to the nearest convenience store. A pack of Marlboro Lights was nearly ten dollars in Massachusetts because of all of the punitive state taxes that had been largely successful in reducing the number of smokers in the Commonwealth. He'd have gladly paid twice that at the moment, though, and he forked over the cash.

He opened the cigarettes in the convenience store and took a pack of matches from the counter. He knew he couldn't smoke in the car—his girlfriend Malinda was the reason he had tried to quit, and if she caught a whiff of smoke in there, he'd be on the couch for a week. So he ducked around the corner and leaned against the building, shivering as he sucked the smoke into his lungs. Who wanted to live forever anyways?

From the alleyway where he stood, around the corner from the parking lot, he could see the door to the doctor's office, so he knew that he wouldn't miss Diamond if she came out. The cigarette felt so good, and he wasn't sure when he would be able to sneak another one, so he smoked two as he stood there.

By the time he got back to the car, he was frozen through. He turned on the engine to get some heat going, and turned on the radio for company. The cigarettes had been so satisfying, he could feel his shoulders relaxing for the first time in a week and a half. He coughed up a small amount of phlegm, and there was something familiar and soothing about the loose rumble in his chest. Maybe the cigarettes would take a year or two off his life, but maybe they wouldn't. And in the end, life was short anyway, and there was no reason to live uncomfortably. He'd find a way to explain it to Malinda so she'd understand.

He took a deep breath and closed his eyes for a moment, giving into the sense of relaxation the cigarettes had given him.

He didn't even feel the blade slide across his throat. It was honed, and MS-13 soldiers were skilled with their knives. At first, all he felt was the warmth on his chest as the blood poured over him. It felt as though the car's heater had kicked in and was blasting hot air on him. Then, he realized that he couldn't breathe. He grabbed at his throat, and felt the blood cascading down his neck. Probing further, he felt the opening, and, to his horror, the slice clean through his esophagus. He tried to scream, but it was no use. He was starting to lose consciousness when he heard the back door of the sedan open and someone exit the car. He hadn't even thought to look in the back seat when he'd gotten in, and he knew now that someone had gotten in and waited for him to return. He survived only long enough to catch a glimpse of the tattooed man crossing in front of the car. The man didn't look back.

Ten minutes later Diamond O'Connell exited the doctor's office. She walked with an air of relief—the bleeding was normal, and the doctor had assured her that the baby was fine. All she needed was a little rest. She felt like a weight had been lifted from her; she couldn't remember ever having been as scared as she was before talking to the doctor.

As she turned toward the parking lot, a gray van pulled up alongside of her, and the door opened. At the same time, a man covered in tattoos came up from behind and grabbed her, pushing her toward the van. She started to protest, but the man with the tattoos flashed a knife in front of her face. It was covered in blood, and she instantly went silent.

The commotion was enough to catch the attention of some of the other people on the street, who yelled and looked around for a security guard or a police officer. One person even called 911, but by the time the police arrived, the gray van was gone. The two officers weren't sure how seriously to take the reports; people often think they see something wrong when there is actually a logical explanation short of foul play. As they stood in front of the medical office, debating next steps, they heard a panicked scream from the parking lot. They hurried over and found Joe Konicki slumped over the steering wheel of his car, covered in blood.

At that moment, they no longer questioned the seriousness of the kidnapping reports, and they called back to the station to alert the detective squad.

THIRTY-EIGHT

The effeminate man looked out of place in the dark and dingy warehouse. He was dressed in a suit that must have cost several thousand dollars. It was dark, but not black, and it had a subtle pattern to the fabric. A soft, white shirt that was so clean it seemed to glow was opened to the third button, revealing a hairless chest. His long hair had been lightened, and it was swept back in an elaborate coif.

Javier Carpio stood before him, slovenly and wrinkled. He didn't care; he could crush the man with one swing of his hand if necessary.

But such violence was unnecessary and unwise at the moment. Six larger men, also impeccably dressed and armed with assault rifles, surrounded the dapper man. Four of Javier's own men, not associated with T'Phong Soh, all also heavily armed, backed Carpio. If violence broke out here, it was likely that most of them would end up dead.

The man was Syrian, according to legend, though that seemed to be a matter of popular speculation rather than fact. His name was known only to a very few. Whatever his original nationality, he was said to have connections to all of the regimes in the Middle East. There were even rumors that he occasionally did business with the Israelis, though this, too, was more rumor than fact.

He gave a signal, and one of his men brought forward a large metal case. It was heavy, and the table that separated the two groups of armed men groaned as it bore the weight. The armed man stepped back, and the man in the expensive suit stepped forward. He unlatched the container and opened it.

Javier peered over the table and examined the weapon. "The FIM-92 Stinger," the man lisped.

"U.S. made?" Carpio asked.

The man shook his head. "It is the same model developed in the States by Raytheon, though." He had a soft voice with a slight accent that was indeed difficult to place. "It was manufactured in Turkey," he continued, "under a license between Raytheon and Roketsan. It has the same specifications as the U.S.-made models. And it is as effective."

"Range?"

"Five miles, give or take."

"Guidance?"

"It uses infrared guidance that tracks aircraft. Or, it can be adapted with laser painting for stationary targets."

"How many?"

"I have two now. Give me a month, and I can get two more."

Carpio grunted. "I do not have a month." He reached out and touched the missile launcher. If they'd had greater access to these types of weapons in El Salvador in the early days of the rebellion, they might have ended the war. "Cost?" he asked.

"Sixty thousand. American."

Carpio's eyes narrowed. "That seems high. I have heard of them sold for less in the past."

The man in the suit shrugged. "If you have someone who can deliver two almost immediately for less than sixty, I suggest you do business with them. They cost the American government forty. A fifty percent markup does not seem unreasonable."

Carpio nodded after a moment's calculation. "Agreed. And the boats?"

The dapper little man rubbed his chin. "Those were more difficult, but I have managed to find you two Coast Guard Defenders. Twenty-five feet, with artillery mounts both in the front and in the back."

"Armed?"

"I can outfit them with one mounted fifty-millimeter machine fore and two M-60s aft. They will be able to repel anything your rivals have."

"How much?"

"One hundred thousand."

"For both?"

The little man shook his head. "Each."

Javier was silent for a moment. It was more than he wanted to pay, but they both knew he had no bargaining position. He stuck out his hand and the man in the suit shook it.

"Good." The man nodded and one of his suited bodyguards closed the case and took the missile and launcher back. "We can arrange a place for the payment this week. Where would you like them delivered?" He gave a hint of a smile. "Based on your past, I would hazard a guess that they may be headed for El Salvador?"

Carpio shook his head. "I will take them when I pay."

The smile on the man's face disappeared, and it was replaced by a look of confusion. "I don't understand," he said. "Here?"

"Yes, here," Javier responded without hesitation.

The man frowned. "I can provide shipping," he said. "As I said, it is safer that way."

Carpio shook his head. "I will pick them up when I pay. I want them here."

The man's expression morphed again, and now he looked genuinely concerned. "If these were ever to be used in the United States and traced to me . . ."

"We have already made a deal," Carpio said.

"It is not worth the risk," the man repeated.

"You will take the risk." Carpio drew himself up to his full height, towering over every other man in the room. All of a sudden, his physical presence seemed even more of a threat than any of the firearms in the room. "I have paid men like you for years," he boomed in a deep baritone. "Men who supply the means of killing without ever accepting the risk that comes with that. We have a deal, and you will supply the missiles and the boats. Otherwise there will be consequences." He glared into the man's eyes, and even with armed guards behind him, Carpio could see the fear on the man's face. It was no longer a fear of what would happen if the missiles were traced back to him; now it was the fear of what might happen to him if he did not supply the giant standing before him with what he wanted.

"Seventy thousand for the missiles," the man said after a moment.

"And one hundred and twenty for the boats. If I am going to take the risk, I will charge more."

Carpio glared at the man. "Agreed," he said finally with a nod. "And if there is any more discussion or any issues with delivery, you will have a problem."

THIRTY-NINE

Agent George Martin greeted Kit Steele in the Belle Isle Marshs's parking lot. She had never met him before, though they had talked on the phone. He looked younger than she'd anticipated. He was assigned to a joint task force investigating gang activities that crossed state lines. MS-13 had become the focus of the task force's inquiries because it was the most active and coordinated gang in the United States. It was also the most dangerous. He and Kit Steele were ostensibly on the same team, but because they were on different task forces, there was an element of competition to their relationship.

Three police cruisers were in the lot, as well as two unmarked law enforcement vehicles. Two officers were talking to an older woman with a large dog.

Martin shook Kit's hand and dispensed with any pleasantries. She was OK with that; she preferred to get directly to business. "Special Agent Steele, you asked me for the file on T'phong Soh the other day," he said. "I thought you might want to know about this," he said.

"What happened?"

"Looks like we got a war brewing. The woman over there saw three guys grab an MS-13 soldier. She got a pretty clean look at all of them."

Steele thought about the file Martin had sent to her, which she had passed on to Cormack. The chances were high that the incident was the result of her having passed on the file. The information was sensitive, and if anyone found out what she'd done, it would likely end her career. She kept her expression impassive. "They took him in the parking lot?"

Agent Martin shook his head. "They grabbed him over here," he said. He led her down one of the trails until they came to a small clearing. A large patch of snow was stained a deep red. "We don't know if he was dead or not. If he wasn't dead, he was pretty badly injured."

"Who was it?"

"Based on the description of the tattoos on his face, the guy who got grabbed was Juan Suarez. He's Soh's number two. Out of El Salvador by way of Los Angeles. He's an up-and-comer. You read the file. From what we've heard, Soh's looking to take control over the harbor, and maybe even the whole MS-13 organization. If that's true, he's relying pretty heavily on Suarez, so the fact that Suarez was jumped is significant."

Steele squatted down, getting a better look at the bloody snow without touching anything that might be useful in the investigation. "Could be," she said noncommittally. "Of course, these MS-13 assholes are mixed up in a lot of different shit. There's no way to know this is the beginning of a war. It could be a one-off."

Martin frowned. "Not likely. The old lady saw the guys who took him. Two of them looked like longshoremen from central casting. Irish to the core."

"You just described half the people who live in Boston."

Martin's frown deepened. "You know about the attack on the Mariner the other day. Cormack O'Connell was almost killed, and the reports were that several heavily tattooed men were seen at the pier just before the place was lit up. You really think it's not all related?"

Kit Steele shrugged. "You said there were three guys. What did the third guy look like?"

"That's the clincher. He was a short Italian, in an expensive-looking overcoat and a fedora. Sound like anyone you know?"

Steele was silent for a moment. "Andolini," she said at last.

Martin nodded. "To the extent he's ever had any loyalty, it's always been with O'Connell."

Steele looked out over the marshes. "You asked me to come out here," she noted. "You could have called me."

Martin walked over and squatted next to Steele. "You and I have never met. I thought it might be useful to have a face-to-face."

She turned and looked at him. "Well, here's my face."

He looked uncomfortable for a brief moment, but recovered quickly. "What's your specific interest in all of this? You working an angle?" he asked.

"That's classified."

He gave her a wry, fed-up smile. "Bullshit," he said. "You reached out to me, I played ball. Now it's your turn."

He was right, she knew. There was a code among the federal law enforcement agencies. If you asked someone for cooperation, there was an expectation and understanding that information would flow in both directions. If she refused now, there would be no more information forthcoming, and that would make her job more difficult. She mulled her options silently.

"Vincente Carpio," she said after a moment.

"The serial killer?"

"We've heard in cross-chatter that Vincente's brother, Javier, may be working with Soh. I'm worried they may try to spring Vincente."

"Break him out of prison?" Martin mused. "How would they even do that? Seems a little far-fetched."

"He escaped once before."

"Yeah, but that was human error," Martin said. "And at the time, no one knew how dangerous he was. That's not gonna happen again."

"Not if I can help it," Steele agreed. "But you never know." She stood up. To the east, in the distance, she could see a plane headed toward them. It was huge; probably a 747, with two levels and six hundred passengers. It was sweeping in low and looked like it could crash into them. She looked to the west and saw one of Logan International Airport's runways just a few hundred yards across the marshes. Beyond that, the narrowest part of Boston Harbor separated East Boston from South Boston and the downtown skyscrapers. The federal courthouse was just visible across the harbor, its rounded glass facade reaching to the sky, reflecting the winter sun, low to the south. It was amazing to contemplate how closely everything was packed around what was a very narrow harbor.

As the 747 drew closer and lower, the noise from the engines became deafening. She looked up, and it felt as though she could reach up and touch it. It reminded her of the one trip that she took with Ollie before he was killed. She and Dillon had surprised him with a trip to Disney World in Florida. It was a discount package that they could barely afford, but it had been worth it. She couldn't remember ever seeing him as excited as he was when he first saw Mickey Mouse in person.

"You all right?" she heard Agent Martin ask.

She realized that her eyes were closed. She opened them, and she could see the 747 land safely. The squeal of the brakes was off in the distance.

Agent Martin's radio bleated. He took it off his belt and stepped away, talking low into it. She looked down at the blood sprayed on the snow and wondered what she had gotten herself into.

"It's a war," Martin said.

She looked at him, still slowly coming back to reality. "What?"

"They just found one of O'Connell's men slumped over in a car in the South End. His throat was slit ear to ear."

"MS-13," Steele said quietly.

"They're good with their knives."

Martin was right, she knew. It was a war. And it wouldn't end until one side won and the other side lost. If MS-13 and the Carpios won, the impact would be greater than she could even contemplate. It would increase the odds that Vincente Carpio would eventually make his way out of prison. If not in the immediate future, then maybe down the line, when other monsters and other mass killings had taken over the headlines, and no one could even remember who Vincente Carpio was.

But Steele would never forget him, and she would never allow that to happen. "Thanks," she said to Martin. "This is probably gonna get ugly. Any information you've got, it'd be helpful," she said.

He nodded. "As long as it goes both ways."

"It goes both ways," she lied. "You have my word on it."

FORTY

Cicero heard about Joe Konicki first. Cormack and his men had taken over the back rooms of one of the fisheries along the waterfront in South Boston. The place smelled so bad, Cicero had trouble breathing, but the owner was in Cormack's debt, and it was the sort of place they would not be disturbed. There were fifteen of them gathered, enduring the stench of fish guts as Cormack and Cicero mapped out a plan.

The call came in from a cop that Cicero had on his payroll. Cicero was in a room with Cormack and three others at the time, so he kept his half of the conversation short, asking one-word questions: Where? When? How? When he hung up, he told everyone other than Cormack to leave the room.

"I got some bad news, Boss," he said once he and Cormack were alone.

"What is it?"

"It's Joe Konicki," Cicero said. "Cops found him in a parking lot out by UMass."

"What the fuck are you talking about? Konicki's with Diamond. He's watching her."

Cicero shook his head. "Not anymore. He's dead." Cormack's face still registered his confusion, so Cicero continued. "He was in his car. They slit his throat."

"What the fuck was he doing out by UMass?"

Cicero shrugged. "The parking lot was by an office full of medical offices specializing in women's issues. Maybe he took Diamond there."

Cicero watched as the full range of implications dawned across Cormack's face. "Where is she?"

Cicero shook his head. "She wasn't with him in the car when they found him. Who knows, maybe this has got nothing to do with her. But maybe it does."

Cormack grabbed his phone and dialed his daughter's number. The phone rang four times. Then, just before it would normally go to voice mail, someone accepted the call. They said nothing, though.

Cormack held the phone to his ear, waiting for the person on the other end to say something. Finally, he couldn't help himself. "Diamond?" he said. "Is that you?"

The line stayed silent for another moment. Then a voice came over the line. It wasn't Diamond. It was a male voice, somewhat high pitched, with a thick accent. Cormack recognized it as Soh's voice immediately.

"Diamond can't come to the phone right now," he said. "Can I help you, Cormack O'Connell?"

Buddy walked along Allen Street, toward Boston Harbor. His hands were stuffed deep into his jacket pockets against the cold, his mind churning through the excuses he might offer to explain his absence the previous Friday. He had no family to speak of, but he could still claim that he'd had to attend to a sick relative. It seemed far-fetched, and he wasn't sure he could pull off the deception effectively. He tried to imagine some work-related task he might have been diverted by, but that would be too easy for the union officers to check up on.

It occurred to him that he might be best off telling a form of the truth—he missed work because he had the chance to get laid. That was an excuse that most of the rank and file would accept, perhaps even applaud. But it probably wouldn't be countenanced by the upper managers. Besides, he didn't want to answer the explicit and vulgar questions that would then be asked. It was odd, but that felt disrespectful to Diamond, and even though he was certain that it was a doomed relationship, he couldn't deceive himself that he wasn't in love with her. He shook his head at the absurdity of it.

He'd hoped that his absence wouldn't have been noted or remarked upon. It wasn't unusual for longshoremen to miss a shift or two. They could be, by nature and temperament, a transient and sometimes unreliable crew. It had occurred to him that perhaps no one would have even noticed.

He knew now, though, that wasn't the case. There had been two messages on his phone from Toby White, the gimp who assisted Cormack with harbor scheduling and administration. The first was a message indicating that Buddy and Nate had been reassigned to a lobster boat for the morning. The second was a call to make sure he'd gotten the first message.

This was bad news. If Nate and Buddy had been assigned to the offload of the Greek ship, he wouldn't have been missed. Dozens of workers would be crawling over the ship, working the giant cranes and moving the enormous shipping containers, and the absence of one man wouldn't have made much of a difference. But because he and Nate were supposed to have been on a small lobster boat, his absence would have caused a significant inconvenience. Buddy knew that was the cause of the annoyance in Toby's voice in the second message.

The union office was half a block away, and as nervous as he was about his weak excuses, he was eager to get inside. His jacket was old and poorly insulated, and the cold was cutting through him now. He could feel the steam in his nostrils freezing as he exhaled. He doubled his pace as he drew closer to the office door.

The union offices were on the second floor. The first floor was an open warehouse area that was sometimes used to hold union meetings. It was large and bare, with concrete floors and no windows. Folding chairs were stacked in one corner. It was often bustling with men in between shifts, waiting to go out to a job, or just shooting the shit. As Buddy stepped in, he saw that the room was nearly empty, which was odd. There were only four men milling around, and Buddy sensed nervous tension in the room. He recognized John Hall, one of Cormack's most loyal soldiers. They all seemed shocked to see him.

"Shit, Buddy Cavanaugh!" one of them exclaimed.

"Yeah," Buddy responded. "What's going on?"

Hall looked at Buddy like he was a ghost. "You showed up," he said. "Just like that?"

"There's a freighter coming in," Buddy said. "I'm scheduled to work the offload."

Hall looked at one of the other men and gave a laugh. "He thinks he's working today. You hear that?"

Buddy looked at the other man, confused. When he turned back to Hall, he saw the iron rod in the man's hand. Buddy didn't have the time to react before it connected hard on the back of his knees, buckling them, and driving him down onto the concrete.

"What the fuck!" he shouted.

The iron rod came down on his back, smashing into his ribs, driving the wind from his lungs. He gave a pained cough and fell over on his side, gasping for breath.

Hall was looking down at him. Buddy tried to talk, but there was no air in his lungs to work his voice. He wanted to ask what was happening—after all, he'd only missed one shift. He would have understood if he'd been given a reprimand, or even had his pay docked. But he never expected a beating. Finally, he regained his wind enough to squeak out a word. "Why?"

Hall just shook his head, raised his giant fist, and punched Buddy in the face. Buddy could feel the blood pour forth from his nose, and his eyes squeezed shut against the pain. As he gave himself up to unconsciousness, he heard Hall speak one last time.

"Call Cormack," he said. "He wanted to deal with this personally."

FORTY-ONE

Diamond had no idea where she was. She'd been blindfolded in the van when she was taken off the street. As near as she could tell, there had been three men in the van, but the man who had pushed her into the van hit her hard on the back of the head as soon as the door closed, and everything went black for a time.

When she woke, she was in a panic. Everything was dark, and she thought for a moment that the blow to her head had left her blind. As she thrashed, she felt coarse fabric scratching her face, and she realized that they had pulled a sack over her head. The knowledge that she still had her sight eased her fear, but only slightly. They had bound her wrists and ankles with duct tape, and she was unable to sit up or get her bearings. It was a utility vehicle with a gritty metal floor, and she slid back and forth, slamming into the sides with each turn.

She thought about trying to keep track of the turns so that she might be able to figure out where they were taking her, but she was so disoriented that it was no use. Besides, she had no idea how long she had been unconscious, so she had no starting reference even if she had been able to keep track.

She called out in fear once, begging to know what was happening, but one of the men kicked her hard in the leg. A moment later, he pulled the bag that covered her face up high enough to slap a length of duct tape over her mouth. Then he pulled the bag down again. She struggled to breathe through her nose, and had a moment when she thought she might actually suffocate right there on the floor of the van. She managed to calm herself down, though, and with a little focus was able to take in enough air to keep herself alive. All she could think about was protecting the baby she was carrying.

Eventually the van stopped on a rough, uneven surface, and the door opened. Two men pulled her out and carried her by her arms some distance. Her feet dragged on the gravel. They were speaking Spanish to each other, and she could hear the soft sound of water lapping on the shore. The gravel gave way to concrete, and then she was pulled onto a boat and pushed onto the floor of a cabin. She had spent most of her life on or around the water, and based on the wooden floor and the angle of the hull's roll, she guessed that she was on a commercial fishing boat. She could smell diesel fumes and the sickening stench of fish guts, and for a moment she thought that she was going to throw up. With her mouth taped, and her head covered by the bag, she knew she would have drowned in her own vomit within a matter of moments, and she fought to keep the bile down.

The engines gave a low rumble, and the boat pulled out away from the dock, rising and falling with the swells. The cold air cut through her clothes, even as she felt herself suffocating in the heat of the bag over her head. She thought she could still hear men talking, perhaps in English this time. The cadence of the discussion no longer seemed foreign, but the engines were humming now, drowning out any chance for her to catch specific words.

Time stretched out without measure, and she had no idea how long they'd been on the water. Maybe twenty minutes, maybe forty . . . maybe an hour.

Eventually, the engines quieted, and the boat slowed and swirled in a great arc that caused the hull to pitch back and forth in an uneven tempo. She could hear the voices again, now, some in English and some in Spanish. The English voice called out to grab hold of lines, and the Spanish voices chattered back and forth in response. Then she felt the boat bump into some hard object, bouncing twice off what she assumed was a dock before the lines held the hull still.

The door to the cabin opened, and men grabbed her and hoisted her up on their shoulders like a marlin—a trophy fish, landed after a long battle at sea. She was careful not to squirm like a fish, lest they drop her, or throw a shoulder into her abdomen, harming the baby.

They handed her up onto a stable surface, and two men took hold of her again, pulling her along by her shoulders, her feet dragging behind her. This time, it wasn't gravel or concrete. Instead, her feet beat out an uneven rhythm, ticking over the wood slats of what she assumed was a long pier. The pier gave way to stone, and then to grass and briars, up a hill. She thought her shoulders might dislocate as she was dragged, and she flexed her muscles to take some of the strain off the joints. If her shoulders gave out, her chances of escape would be severely limited.

Then they were back on concrete, clearly high up on a hill. The icy wind blew so hard, even her face was frozen under the bag. The condensation from her breath iced over, and the fabric fused to her face. She had to move her cheek against the bag to clear space to breathe.

That lasted only a few moments, though, as she heard a great steel door swing on heavy rusted hinges, and she was pulled into a shelter. It was cold and dank, but not nearly as much as the boat ride had been, and the break from the wind was a welcome relief.

They dragged her down what seemed like a long corridor, her feet sliding across a concrete floor covered in dirt and leaves. Once, in school, she'd been on a field trip to the crypts of the Old North Church in Boston, where eleven hundred settlers from colonial times had been buried. It was said that their souls inherited the ground underneath the church. The place she had been taken felt and smelled very much like those catacombs.

She had no idea for how long they dragged her, and it felt like they passed through several doors. At one point, they missed a door and her head slammed into the jamb. She let out a small cry of pain, and they pulled her harder, so that her head hit the wood again, and her neck snapped forward as she cleared the threshold.

After what seemed like an eternity, they stopped and tossed her into a corner. The floor was cold and hard, and the place smelled like stale sweat and gunpowder. Every sound echoed off the walls and it felt like she had been brought to a medieval dungeon.

Someone crouched down and spoke through the hood directly into her ear. He was so close, she could smell his foul breath, and his sweat was sickly sweet. He spoke with a heavy accent. "Do not talk," he said. "Do not say a word, understand? We will kill you, and send your body in pieces back to your father if you make a sound. Nod if you understand."

Diamond nodded. She could feel the tears running down her face.

"Good," the man said. Then he withdrew, and she was alone. At least, she felt alone. For all she knew, there was someone in the room with her, but if so, he remained silent.

She extended her arms so that she could feel the wall. It felt like it was made of cement, and it was cold and damp. She curled into a ball, facing the wall, protecting her abdomen. If they wanted to kick her now, at least it would start with her back or her extremities, and that might protect her baby.

As she lay there, fighting off the demons her imagination conjured, she knew now that her only hope was that Cormack was actually even more dangerous than the animals who had grabbed her.

FORTY-TWO

Cormack gripped the phone so tightly his hand began to hurt. He knew he had to remain calm. Soh was looking for him to get angry—to lose control and make a mistake. Now, more than ever, he had to make sure that he was rational and in control.

"Can I talk to her?"

"No," Soh replied.

"How do I know she's alive?"

"I have said she is alive. She will stay alive as long as you do what I say."

"What is it that you want?"

"You took one of my men. Is he alive?"

Cormack looked at Cicero, who shrugged. "Yes, he's still alive," Cormack confirmed.

"I want him back."

"Are you suggesting a swap?"

Soh laughed. It was a high-pitched cackle that pierced Cormack's eardrum, and he had to hold the phone away from his head. "Oh no, Cormack O'Connell, a daughter is worth much more than a single soldier. You will release Suarez by tomorrow. But that is just the beginning."

"What else?"

"You will give me control over the union. You will give me control over the harbor."

Cormack's head was swimming. "The union? You could never run the union."

"Not me," Soh said. "There is someone else I will put in your place who is capable. You will resign your position and appoint the person I will choose. Then you and your daughter will disappear."

"That's it? I give you control over the union, and I go . . . where?"

"That is up to you. As long as it is far away enough that I can be sure that you will not interfere ever again. Your time is over. It is best that you recognize that and retire. Most people in your position never get that chance. I am giving it to you so that you and I can avoid a war. You will get your daughter back, and you can live on. Do we have an agreement?"

Cormack was looking at Cicero. The man's expression was inscrutable. He took a breath before answering, to control his voice and keep it from breaking. "Yes, we have an agreement," he said at last.

"Good," Soh said. "I will call back to tell you where to drop Suarez. Then you and I will discuss how you will leave the union. Once you have resigned, I will release your daughter." The line went dead.

Cormack was still looking at Cicero. "Retirement," Cicero said. "Sounds nice." Cormack didn't respond. "Of course, you know it's a lie." Cicero folded his arms. "He can't leave you alive. There are too many people who owe you too many favors. There are too many men who are loyal to you. As long as you're breathing, you're a threat to him, and he knows it."

Cormack nodded. "I know."

"Who in the hell could he be putting in to run the union? Gotta mean he's got someone on the inside."

"Gotta be Buddy Cavanaugh, right?"

"The men wouldn't follow him," Cicero said with confidence. "Not after he betrayed you."

"Maybe. I've learned that loyalty often follows money and fear. If Soh controls everything along the shoreline, the men may not have a choice."

"So what are you going to do?"

"I haven't figured that out yet. I know that I've got to do whatever it takes to keep Diamond alive, though."

"The only chance you have to do that is to take him out. Even then . . ." Cicero's words trailed off as Cormack's eyes hardened.

"She stays alive," he said. "No matter what else happens. Did we get any information out of Suarez?"

"He's a hard man to break," Cicero said. "He's held out so far. You want me to speed the process up, increase the pressure? It's a little dangerous. We've been very persuasive already. Any more and he may not live through it."

"No. If he dies, Diamond dies. We need to make sure he's alive, at least until we get her back."

Cormack's phone rang. He looked at Cicero, and he could tell they were both wondering whether Soh was calling. Cormack looked at the caller ID and shook his head. "It's the office," he said. He held the phone up to his ear. "Yeah," he said. "When?" He could feel his jaw tighten as he heard the news. "OK, keep him there. He's mine, you understand?" He hung up and nodded to Cicero.

"We've got work to do," he said.

"What kind of work?" Cicero asked.

"They got Buddy Cavanaugh. He just showed up at the union office." Cormack stood up and headed out to the car.

"My favorite kind of work," Cicero said, following him out.

FORTY-THREE

Kit was back at her office. The war between Cormack and T'phong Soh was heating up, and there was no question where her loyalties lay. That fact alone, she knew, meant that her principles had been compromised. As a law enforcement officer, it wasn't her job to choose sides in a battle like this; it was her job to stop it, and to bring both sides to justice. But the danger posed by Soh and the Carpios was too great to ignore. She knew that Cormack had to prevail.

In order to prevail, though, he had to know where Soh was. Without knowing that, there was little that Cormack could do to bring the fight to his enemy. She was doing anything she could to get that information.

Her phone rang, and she picked up the call. "Steele here," she said.

"It's Damon." She recognized the voice of one of the agents on the task force. Kit knew that Soh was no longer using his warehouse in East Boston, but it was the only place she knew to start, so she had posted agents there to watch the place. So far, other than some traffic from low-level MS-13 soldiers, nothing had come of the surveillance.

"You got something?"

"Maybe," he said. "A van pulled up earlier. Three of Soh's men got out and headed right to a boat on the pier and out into the harbor. They were heavily armed."

"So?"

"So, they had someone with them."

"Who was it?"

"We don't know. It looked like a woman, but there was a bag over her head. They were dragging her. It all happened too fast for us to do anything."

"Where did they go?" she asked.

"Who knows? They were headed south, but we couldn't track them from our position."

Kit considered the possibilities. She couldn't think of why Soh would be taking a woman hostage, and she didn't know whether it had anything to do with his war with Cormack. "OK," she said. "Keep up the surveillance and let me know if you see anything else."

She hung up the phone and looked out the window, down toward the harbor. She wondered where Cormack was, and whether he was making better progress in getting information than she was.

Cormack stood over Buddy Cavanaugh. The young man was tied up, lying on the cement floor of the union offices. His face was bloodied, and he'd been hit in the ribs, but other than that, Cormack's men had left him alone. Looking down at him, Cormack felt nothing but the need for information. The lad was no longer human to him; he was a tool to be used to help win the war that Soh had started—the war that Buddy Cavanaugh had helped Soh start.

Cormack walked over and picked up one of the folding chairs that was leaned against the wall on the far side of the room, brought it over, and set it near Cavanaugh, a few feet from the cement wall.

"Pick him up," Cormack ordered.

Hall and one of the other men stepped up, grabbed Buddy under the arms, and pulled him to his feet. Cavanaugh gave a slight grunt of pain as his shoulders were pulled back.

"Put him in the chair."

The two men walked him over and set him in the chair. Buddy was hunched over, his head hanging down, and it took a moment for him to look into Cormack's eyes.

"Cicero, you stay here. Everyone else, head upstairs to the coffee room. Make sure the front door is bolted. We'll be up shortly."

Hall and the three other men filed slowly toward the front of the room, then up the staircase. They continually looked back, curious to witness Cavanaugh's ultimate demise.

Cormack walked back to the stack of chairs and pulled another one off the wall. He brought it over and set it down directly in front of Buddy Cavanaugh. He nodded for Cicero to stand behind Buddy, and then he sat down. The chairs were close enough that if Cormack leaned forward, his head would collide with Buddy's.

As soon as Cormack sat down, Buddy started trying to talk through the tape. His mouth was sealed shut, and blood had congealed in his nose, so the effort made him gasp and choke, and all that could be heard was a guttural sound from his throat.

Cormack put a hand on Buddy's shoulder and shook his head. "Don't try to talk, son," he said. "Not yet." He patted the shoulder gently. "The time to talk is coming, rest assured. First, it's my turn."

Cormack leaned back and took a deep breath. "It's not the betrayal itself that bothers me, Buddy," he began. "It's the nature of the betrayal. It's what you've betrayed me for. If you'd hooked up with another legitimate outfit and started to cut into my territory . . . well, I could understand that. It's the way our business works. I wasn't always the boss, which means that I had to remove others to get where I am. In some ways, that's to be respected."

Cormack leaned forward, so that he was talking almost directly into Buddy's ear. He spoke very quietly. "But you didn't do that," he said. "Instead, you sided with a sociopath. These MS-13 motherfuckers aren't like us, you understand? You remember what they did to that crippled girl out in Everett? They raped her and then cut her to pieces with machetes. You imagine that? You think that me, or Cicero, or any of those men upstairs would do something like that?"

Cormack shook his head and leaned back in the chair. "And Soh is the worst of them. He's not just MS-13, but now he's working with the Carpio brothers. You read about Vincente Carpio? The sick fuck who cut the heads off all those people? Well, Soh is working with his brother, Javier. He's now looking to take over the drug trade not just here, but on the West Coast. You really want to be in bed with these people?"

Cormack let the silence stretch out for a few minutes. Buddy Cavanaugh started to try to talk again, but Cormack shook his head. "Almost,

Buddy, almost. I just want you to have a minute to think about what you've done. Now, in a minute, I'm gonna take the tape off your face, and then you're gonna talk, OK? I'm gonna need to know everything you know. I'm gonna need to know when you were approached, and how. I'm gonna need to know where Soh is, and I'm gonna need to know everything you know about his organization. Cicero here—" Cormack nodded behind Buddy—"is gonna help jog your memory if it becomes necessary. But it's not gonna be necessary, OK? Just remember one thing, kid: you're not gonna live through the day, 'cause that wouldn't be right to Cookie, but we're not gonna cut your head off and leave it in your lap. And trust me, that's the direction you're headed right now."

Cormack leaned forward and pulled the tape off of Buddy's face in one clean tug. Buddy let out a shout of pain as it took hair and skin off his face. "OK," Cormack said. "What do you have to tell us?"

For a long moment, Buddy said nothing. His head was down, his hair hanging in his face. Then, at last, he picked his head up and looked directly into Cormack's eyes. "I can't tell you anything about Soh's organization," he said.

Cormack frowned. "Can't, or won't?"

"Can't," Buddy said. "I can't tell you because I don't know anything. I have no idea what's going on."

Cicero's fist slammed into Buddy's face from behind, and Buddy's head fell over to the side, almost taking him off the chair. He managed to straighten himself.

"You see, the problem with that story," Cormack said, "is that your friend Nate already ratted you out."

Cavanaugh looked confused. "Ratted me out how?"

"He said you called Soh as the two of you were leaving the Mariner. He said he heard you tell him, 'He's still there.' So you see why it's a problem now when you tell me you don't know anything?"

"I didn't call Soh," Cavanaugh said. "Where's Nate?"

"Don't worry," Cicero said. "You'll be seeing him very soon."

Even through the bruises and blood, Cormack could see Buddy Cavanaugh's face whiten. "It didn't take much to figure it out," Cormack said. "You and Nate knew I was there at the Mariner because I told you to meet me. Cookie knew I was there, but he's above suspicion. And besides, he's dead. No one else knew I was there. And then you made the phone call when you left. Two and two always makes four, you get it?"

"I swear to God, I didn't call Soh," Buddy pleaded. Cormack had been impressed with the kid's composure, but now it was beginning to crack. It was understandable, given the situation.

"No?" Cicero said. "The boys told us that when they were tying you up, you continued to tell them to tell Cormack you were sorry. Why's that, if you haven't done anything wrong?"

"When they first jumped me, I thought they were pissed because I skipped my shift," Cavanaugh explained.

"You've been here, what, three years?" Cormack asked. "More than a hundred men have missed shifts in the last three years. In all that time, you ever seen any one of them take a beating for it? It doesn't hold up. Why'd you keep telling them to give me your apology after the beating started?"

Buddy looked at the floor.

"You see what I'm sayin'?"

"I thought you were pissed about something else." He didn't raise his head.

Cormack looked Cicero. "Did they take his phone?"

"Yeah." Cicero reached into his jacket pocket and pulled out a cell phone. "I got it here." He handed it over to Cormack.

"If there's a record of a phone call from Thursday night right around the time that you left the Mariner, I'm going to have Mr. Andolini, here, get a little more persuasive."

"I didn't say I never called anyone, but I didn't call Soh!" Buddy screamed. Now there was real terror in his voice.

Cormack touched the phone screen. "What's the security code, Buddy?" he demanded.

"I swear to fuckin' God, I didn't call him! I've never talked to him! You got this wrong!"

"Only one way to find out, I guess," Cormack said. "What's the code?"

"You can't do this!"

Cormack nodded at Cicero, and he hit Buddy once in the face and once in the stomach. Buddy was hunched forward again, trying to get the wind back in his lungs. "Pick his head up," Cormack ordered.

Cicero took hold of Buddy's hair and pulled his head up and back hard. Buddy's body resisted involuntarily, still trying to double over in pain.

Cormack pulled a gun out of his jacket pocket and laid it casually on his knee, the barrel pointed loosely in Buddy's direction. "What's the code, Buddy?" he asked again in a low, threatening tone.

Buddy's head was back, his eyes wide with terror. Finally, he said, "It's ten, eleven, ninety-five."

Cormack gave a weak smile. "Your birthday, I presume?"

Buddy tried to nod, but Cicero was still holding his head back by the hair.

"Makes you a Libra, right? Me too. Libras are known for their fairness. I'm being as fair as I can be here, but my guess is your luck has run out, son." Cormack knew from the look on Cavanaugh's face that he understood he was a dead man. Cormack just hoped he could get some useful information out of him before he put the lad down.

He put in the security code and the phone's screen popped open, giving him access to all of Buddy Cavanaugh's phone records, texts, and social media. Cormack clicked on the phone icon and scrolled through the list of calls made in the past few days. There weren't many, and Cormack found what he was looking for almost immediately. It was an outgoing call made at 10:51 the previous Thursday to an unsaved number. It was a short call, lasting exactly eleven seconds. Cormack felt an odd sense of satisfaction at having been right. He turned the phone and showed the readout to Buddy. "There you go," he said. "That's the call."

The terror was still in Buddy's eyes, but there was something odd about it. He was looking at the phone with something that approached longing and sadness.

Cormack looked at the phone log again, trying to figure out whether he was missing something. All of a sudden, it struck him. The number on the phone screen was familiar to him. He frowned; he couldn't think of any reason he would be familiar with T'phong Soh's phone number. Was there any way that he had ever called the man? He didn't think so.

The realization dawned slowly and terribly. It wasn't Soh's number. He knew the number from somewhere else.

But it couldn't be . . .

His frown turned into a scowl, and he clicked on the phone screen to see Buddy's texts. The same phone number was there as well, with a long string of texts, some of them explicit in nature—too explicit for Cormack to keep reading. All of a sudden, the feeling of satisfaction turned into rage.

He took the gun in his hand and pointed it at Buddy Cavanaugh's head. The boy's expression turned from terror to resignation, and he closed his eyes, ready to accept his death. Cormack reached out and grabbed Buddy by his jacket, lifted him off the chair, and threw him into the wall. Cormack caught him by the throat and held him against the wall with his left hand, pointing his gun at his forehead with his right hand. Cicero raised his eyebrows in surprise, but knew enough not to speak or interfere.

"You're the bastard!" Cormack screamed at Buddy.

Buddy tried to raise his bound hands to his face to protect himself, but Cormack drove the gun into his gut, taking the wind out of him again. He gasped for breath for a moment before choking out, "I love her," in a barely audible tone.

Cormack held Buddy's neck, pushing him hard against the wall, his rage ebbing slightly, but not enough to overcome the urge to pull the trigger. "You're the father?"

The question caught Buddy Cavanaugh completely off guard. He frowned and tilted his head at Cormack, the confusion plain on his face. "Father?"

"Fuck. You stupid bastard," Cormack said.

Now the realization dawned on Buddy's face, and his expression conveyed a thousand different emotions. After a moment, all he could manage was to repeat himself with more vigor. "I love her."

Cormack stepped back slightly and considered Buddy's words and his expression. He wasn't convinced the young man was lying. He raised his gun to Buddy's forehead again. This time there was no resignation in his eyes. He met Cormack's hostile stare evenly.

Cormack pulled his fist back and punched Buddy in the face. The young man was out before he hit the ground. Cormack looked at him lying on the cement and considered his options. The thought of Buddy defiling his daughter kept running through his mind, and he wondered whether he would ever get past it. He aimed his gun twice toward Buddy's unconscious head before putting the gun away and turning around and heading back toward the staircase up to his office.

"You want me to take care of him, boss?" Cicero called after him.

Cormack paused. "No, Cicero. He's not working with Soh, and he didn't betray me. At least not in that way."

"You sure?"

"Yeah, I'm sure. Besides, I can't kill him. He's going to be the father of my grandchild—if we can get Diamond back. I've got to reach out to get some help." Cormack continued on, walking up the staircase without another word.

Cicero looked at Buddy Cavanaugh's unconscious body splayed out on the cement floor. "Fuck me," he said. Then he reached down to gather him up and try to revive him.

FORTY-FOUR

She met him on the boardwalk that ringed Pleasure Bay, just to the south of Castle Island, where generations of Boston's working class came to sun themselves during the summer. The beach carved a perfect semicircle from Fort Independence to UMass, Boston, and the waters were protected by the Harbor Islands. The James Curley Recreational Center and Bathhouse separated the boardwalk from the bustle of South Boston's residential neighborhood, only a few blocks from Cormack's home on L Street. It was huge, and ornate, and a testament to one of Boston's most popular and corrupt mayors from the last century. From June to September the place was awash with sunbathers and swimmers, and those who came down just to take in the sights or walk out to the fort.

On this day, though, there was no one else there. The bathhouse was locked tight, and the wind off the water made it feel like it was ten below.

Cormack couldn't feel the cold. He stood at the edge of the boardwalk, looking out at the water, seeing everything and nothing at the same time. The wind blew through him. Icicles formed on the tips of his beard and around his mouth as he exhaled. He thought about all that he had done in his lifetime—all the drugs he had helped smuggle, all the crime he'd tolerated, all the men he'd killed or had killed. There had always been a reason for it, he'd told himself: a reason beyond self-interest and individual profit. Crime existed. It was a fact. It was a reality that could never be overcome, particularly in places like this. Harbors, airports, border crossings . . . they were the funnels of international activity through which crime had to travel. The trick, he'd always told himself, was to make sure that crime was quarantined. His goal was to keep the crime from touching those who weren't a part of it. If he could do that, he always felt that he served the public good. And if he made a buck or two in return, he figured that was more than fair.

But now the consequences had been visited upon him. Worse, those consequences had been visited upon Diamond.

"What the hell is happening, Cormack?"

He'd known she was behind him. He'd heard the gate on the side of the bathhouse creak as Kit Steele came through from the street. Still, he was so deep in thought and self-torment that her shout startled him. She grabbed him by the shoulder and spun him toward her.

"Seriously, what the fuck is going on?"

"The war has started," Cormack responded quietly. "And it won't end until I'm gone or Soh is."

She took a step back and looked at him. His eyes seemed distant, and she wondered whether this was the same man she had known so intimately for months. "I know. I was over at the marshes," she said. "You gutted one of Soh's men."

He shook his head. "Not gutted," he said. "Captured."

She considered this for a moment. "Did you get anything helpful from him?"

Cormack shook his head. "He's well trained."

"And the guy over by UMass?"

"One of mine," Cormack replied.

"But they didn't capture him," she noted. "They weren't looking for information from him."

Cormack shook his head again, this time slowly.

"Why did they do it, then? What were they looking to get?"

"My daughter," Cormack said quietly. "He was guarding her."

Kit Steele gasped. "Oh my God!" she exclaimed. "Diamond!"

He was surprised by her reaction. She had never met his daughter, and while he was sure he had mentioned her in passing, he didn't think he had discussed her at length. That just wasn't his way. And yet, somehow she seemed to intuit the bond that he had with her, and her feelings toward him seemed to impart an empathy for his love for his daughter.

"They took her," Cormack said. "They're holding her as leverage."

Steele's face was serious and troubled. "My people saw her," she said. "My people saw them with her."

"What are you talking about?" Cormack demanded. "When? How? I don't understand."

She took a deep breath. "We've been watching Soh's warehouse in Eastie. We know he's involved with Vincente Carpio's brother and that he's planning something. My people saw them bring a woman in earlier today."

"How could they not do something?" Cormack shouted. He grabbed her by the arm and shook her. She pulled her arm away and looked at him.

"What were they supposed to do?" Steele pointed out. "We've just got a couple of men. It happened quickly, and Soh's men were heavily armed. They've had half a dozen men or more moving through there over the last day or so. My guys didn't know who it was or why they had her. Even I didn't know it was Diamond until you just told me. If they'd tried to do something at that point, Soh's men would have killed her rather than give her up."

Cormack considered that for a moment. "OK," he said at last. "Maybe you're right." He gave the matter more thought. "At least we know where she is," he said.

Steele shook her head. "We don't," she said. "They didn't take her into the warehouse. They loaded her right onto a boat and took her out."

"Out?" he yelled. "Out where?"

"We don't know," Steele said. "It happened too fast, and we didn't have anyone on the water."

Cormack turned away from her. "Then she's gone."

She tugged at his arm. "Have they contacted you yet?"

"They have."

"What do they want?"

"Me," Cormack said. "They want me to step down from the union. They want me out of the way."

Steele looked skeptical. "They know you'd never do that," she said. She waved her arm at the harbor. "This is all you know. They know it."

Cormack nodded. "They'll kill me. And they'll kill her." His mind was working furiously. "You said they have half a dozen men there?" he asked.

"Around that," she replied. "It changes from moment to moment."

He rubbed his beard and realized it was caked with ice, but he didn't care. "We figure he's got two dozen, maybe more, total. So if there are only a few at his warehouse . . ."

". . . He's moved his base to somewhere else," Steele finished the sentence. "You just need to know where. But how?"

"There was one other thing that he wanted," Cormack said.

"What was it?"

"He wants Suarez back."

"So?"

"Suarez is a strategist—his right hand," Cormack said. "That's what those files you gave me said. That's why he wants him back. He wants Suarez's help in figuring out how to take me out. That means that he's going to bring Suarez to his new base once he gets him back. I can't get any of my people close to his warehouse; they'd be spotted. But if your people are watching his place, and they let you know if and when they put Suarez on a boat, he can be tracked back to wherever Soh is now."

Steele looked skeptical. "I can't get the resources to follow them over the water without disclosing a lot more about what's going on between me and you," she said. "Obviously, I can't do that."

"That's all right," Cormack said. "Your people would probably be spotted on the water anyway. I have ways of tracking them as long as I know that we've got the right boat."

"Are you sure Diamond is with Soh?"

Cormack shrugged. "She's too valuable to him to let her out of his sight. I can't imagine he'd entrust her to anyone else." He looked out at the water and thought again about all the things that he had done that had brought him to this moment. He thought about the way he had put his daughter and his grandchild at risk. It made him want to throw himself into the harbor—just keep swimming out into the icy water, and let the sea take him this time. But he couldn't do that now, he knew.

Now he was her only chance to live. And he could only save her with Kit Steele's help. He looked at her. "Will you help me?" he asked.

She thought about it, but only for a moment. "If I do it, that means I'm in, all the way. I need to know everything that's happening."

"You sure?" he asked. "You won't have any plausible deniability if this goes sideways."

She gave a bitter laugh. "I lost plausible deniability a long time ago," she said. "All I want now is to stop these people from doing whatever it is they're planning. If I can do that, I'll happily go to jail."

FORTY-FIVE

Javier Carpio sat in a deserted warehouse in Chelsea. It was made of corrugated steel, without even the pretense of insulation, and the wind seemed to blow through it as though there were no walls at all. There was a kerosene heater that was lit, but kept low, so the temperature hovered just a few degrees above freezing—still some thirty degrees above the outdoor temperature.

There were five men with him. They were El Salvadoran, and while they'd all worked with MS-13, they were not associated with T'phong Soh. Nor did they truly owe their allegiance to the organization; the only loyalty they felt was to each other. They had fought together in the wars that plagued El Salvador long before MS-13 came into being. They had tattoos, but they were less prominent, and they contained imagery that only they truly understood. They stood behind him, spread out in a semicircle, staring at the table set up in the center of the warehouse.

The nattily dressed man with the blond dye-job had been good to his word. Before them, two FIM-92 Stinger shoulder launchers were laid out on the table. He hadn't shown up himself; he'd sent four of his muscle-bound, heavily armed clotheshorses to make the delivery. It was clear that he wanted as little as possible to do with whatever Javier was planning. Javier couldn't blame him; few would want to have any association with what was to come. The boats would be delivered later. He'd assured Javier of that.

Javier rose from the only chair in the warehouse and turned to face the men he'd bled with for more than three decades. "You know my brother," he said.

The men bowed their heads and murmured their unquestioning respect.

"You are the only men I trust. Only you understand what he went through—what we went through when our mothers and sisters and wives were killed. T'phong Soh is a capable leader, but we cannot fully trust him with this. I do not know whether he would be willing to use such weapons in his own harbor where he hopes to rule after we are finished. And so we must do what must be done."

"As always," one of Javier's comrades said.

"As always," Javier agreed.

"Are you committed?" Javier asked.

"You are our brother," another man answered. "That means that your brother is our brother."

"And if more Americans die," another man said, "all the better."

There was a murmur of agreement among the men.

It was enough, Javier knew. Men like this would never break their bond with him. Now, the real work would begin.

Diamond had been lying on the cold stone floor for hours. She couldn't be sure for exactly how many hours. Perhaps four or five, she figured, but if told it had been ten, she would have no way to doubt it. The door opened, great heavy steel shrieking on hinges that sounded ancient and sent shivers through her. She could hear footsteps coming closer. One set. She wasn't sure whether that was good or bad. They stopped when they were beside her, and there was silence for a long moment.

She wanted to scream. She was so terrified, she wanted to cry out, beg for mercy, beg for forgiveness—beg to be killed. Fear scattered her thoughts, and she fought to control her breathing.

She felt the person squat down beside her and grab her hands behind her back, and then she felt the cold steel of a knife on her wrist. She gasped and thought that she was going to bleed out, there on a cold concrete floor, until there was nothing left in her to feed the baby in her womb.

The knife pulled and tore, and then she felt the tape give way, and her hands were free.

She lay there, afraid to move at all. Finally, the person spoke. "I have water."

It was a high-pitched voice with a thick accent, and she wondered for a moment whether it was a man or a woman. "I have water, you can drink," the voice said again, and this time she believed it was a man, though she couldn't be positive.

She rolled over slowly and leaned against the wall. The cloth bag still covered her head, and her mouth was still duct-taped shut. She hesitated, afraid to reach up and remove the sack or pull the tape off. After a moment, her tormentor lifted the bag halfway up her head, so that her eyes were still covered, but her mouth and nose were exposed. Then she felt fingertips on her cheek, prying and pulling at the corner of the tape. All at once, the tape was ripped from her face. It felt as though half of the skin went with the adhesive.

The man took her hand and pulled it away from her body until her fingers touched a plastic cup. He pressed it into her hand, and she took it, unsure whether she should drink. She was desperate to—it had been hours since she'd had anything to drink, and she was severely dehydrated. Still, she worried that whatever was in the cup might be poisoned. Or, worse still, it could be drugged, and her unconscious body could then be raped and beaten.

She pulled the cup toward her face and sniffed at it. The liquid had the faint odor of plastic and chemicals, but then that could have been the cup itself. She was desperate to drink, but still unsure.

"Drink," the high-pitched voice said. "If I wanted to harm you, I would not need to do it through the water."

She realized that he was right. There seemed to be little reason for her captors to play games with her water. She was completely in their control. She had no idea where she was, and no reason to think anyone else did, either. Only a fool in her situation would hope to be saved. She'd never thought of herself as a fool before, but perhaps there was still time to learn.

She brought the cup to her lips and took a sip. It was water. Cold and crisp. She couldn't detect any chemicals, but it didn't matter in any event; her thirst took over and she gulped the water down so fast, she probably would never have been able to taste the liquid. She felt some of the water trickle down her cheeks, but she couldn't slow her consumption. When she was done, she wiped her mouth with her jacket sleeve, and held the cup out to her captor.

The cup was taken from her. "Is that better?"

"Yes, thank you," she said. The sound of her voice was enough to make her want to be sick. How could she thank this person who had kidnapped her? How could she express gratitude to a man who would allow her to be bound and kicked and brought to this cold, dank, disgusting place?

"You are welcome."

"Why am I here?" She thought it was a gentle way to start a conversation that might lead to information. She winced as she said the words, expecting to be hit for speaking without permission. She marveled at how easy it was to become a good prisoner, and how quickly the transformation could happen. She resolved to reverse the metamorphosis.

The man didn't hit her. "You are Cormack O'Connell's daughter," he said. "He is the reason you are here."

"I don't understand," she said.

"You don't need to," the man said. "He understands. That is all that matters."

She digested that. "Are you going to kill me?"

"No." The answer seemed definitive, and she wanted to take some comfort from that, but she knew to be skeptical. She figured that it wasn't in her captors' interests to have her lose hope. That would likely make her a more difficult prisoner. "At least, not if your father does what I have told him to."

"What did you tell him to do?"

The man didn't answer. "Do you need to use a bathroom?"

Diamond hadn't realized until just that moment that she needed a bathroom desperately. It seemed as though the water had flowed through her body from top to bottom like a raging river, and her bladder was now begging for relief. "Yes, please," she said. Again, the obsequiousness in her voice made her angry with herself.

All of a sudden, the bag was ripped fully off her head. Her hand flew to her eyes. Then, slowly, she lowered her hand slightly and peered through her fingers. The place was dimly lit. It was a small, cramped square room, with uneven cement on all sides. There was dirt on the floor and no windows. She couldn't fathom where she could be, unless she was underground in some sort of a mausoleum.

She looked up and almost screamed. The man was looking down at her. The only light was from some sort of electric lantern in the corner, so he was lit from below, giving him a ghostly appearance. He was Southeast Asian, short and slight, with large white teeth and close-cropped hair. Tattoos grew up from under his shirt, covering his neck like some sort of creeping infestation. She was partial to tattoos, and had many of her own, but somehow his were menacing in a way that scared her.

"The bathroom is this way," he said. "It is not what you are used to, but it is all that we have."

He smiled at her, and at that moment she knew that he had no intention of ever letting her live. He was too recognizable. If she thought that there was a chance that he was going to let her go, he would never have let her see his face. If she was going to live, she would have to escape, and she set her mind toward that goal. If not for herself, then at least for her baby.

His baby.

He was out there somewhere. Or she was. Buddy Cavanaugh didn't know and didn't care whether it was a boy or a girl. He cared that it was his. He cared that it was hers. He cared that it was theirs.

He touched the bruise Cormack's fist had left on his face. He didn't begrudge Cormack the punch. He supposed he'd react the same way if he had a daughter and someone got her pregnant. But Buddy hoped the punch was enough to purge Cormack of the worst of his ire. Now that it was out in the open—and now that Buddy knew that Diamond was pregnant—he was determined to be with her.

Buddy felt the burning need to talk to her, but Cormack still had his phone. He needed to get it back. The only way to make that happen, though, was to confront Cormack, and Cormack was in no mood to be confronted. The war had started, and it required all of Cormack's attention. He wouldn't like Buddy causing a distraction. Still, Buddy had no choice. Even if it meant that he would take another beating, he had to speak to Diamond before the true violence hit.

Cormack was in his office. His head was bowed over manifests and schedules, and he was studying them intently. Toby was hovering near him. "OK," Cormack was saying. "So these are the routes that all of our men are on today, throughout the morning?" Cormack was confirming with Toby. Buddy marveled at how Cormack could still care about and focus on the mundane details of his responsibilities as the head of the union with violence at his doorstep.

"Cormack, I need to talk to you," Buddy said. He filled his voice with confidence he didn't feel.

Cormack looked up at him the way he might look at a yipping little dog. "In a minute," he grunted. "I got that right?" he asked Toby again.

"That's the schedule through the afternoon," Toby confirmed.

"They know to have their radios on and tuned, right?"

"They always do," Toby said.

"OK." Cormack straightened up and let out a slight groan as he arched his back. "Gettin' too old for this," he said to no one in particular. He looked at Toby. "You head on home," he said. "You need to get some rest."

"I'd rather stay here," Toby said. "I could be useful."

Cormack shook his head. "You've been doing eighteen hours a day for more than a week. And the next couple weeks may be even worse, depending on how all this shakes out. I need you sharp and running the shop while I'm dealing with . . . other things."

"But—"

"No buts," Cormack said. There was a hint of annoyance in his voice at having his directions questioned. "Go home. Come back tonight."

"OK," Toby said. He hobbled over to his desk and grabbed his heavy winter jacket. "You need me for anything . . ." he said, pausing again.

"I'll let you know," Cormack barked. "Now go home!" Still annoyed, Cormack turned on Buddy. "What do you want?" he demanded.

For a moment, Buddy was tempted to leave at that moment and not confront Cormack. He could be a dangerous man when pushed, and he seemed to be at his limit. He held his ground, though. "I need my phone back," he said. "I need to talk to Diamond."

Storm clouds gathered across Cormack's face, but Buddy persisted.

"I know you don't like the fact that we fell for each other. I don't blame you. But I love her, and even if you won't let us be together, I still have to talk to her. I have to let her know that I know about the baby. You have to let me do that, at least."

Cormack exhaled heavily. "You can't talk to her," he said.

"I have to," Buddy responded. His resolve was unbreakable now. There was no going back.

Cormack shook his head, and it looked like he might lose his temper. "You can't," he repeated, and there was an incongruous note of anguish in his voice.

"Why not?"

It took a moment for Cormack to answer. He stared hard at Buddy, and it seemed as though he was trying to come to some judgment about the young man. "Soh has her," he said at last. The words seemed to deflate him slightly, but he stayed on his feet and it took him only a moment to regain a look of determination.

The news hit Buddy like a sledgehammer in the chest. It took him a few seconds to breathe. "What do you mean Soh has her?" he demanded at last.

"He kidnapped her," Cormack said. "I assigned Joe Konicki to guard her, keep her at the house. Apparently she had to go the doctor's office. Soh's men must have been watching them. They took Joe out and grabbed Diamond. He has her now."

Buddy felt like he was going to pass out. He stumbled to a chair and sat down, and took a few seconds to absorb what he'd been told. His disorientation didn't last long. "How do we get her back?" he asked.

"I'm working on it," Cormack said. "First I have to find out where they're keeping her. I think I've got a way to do that."

"Then what?"

"It depends on where she is. I'll have to come up with a plan on the fly. One way or another, I'm going to go get her."

Buddy nodded, deep in thought. "I'm coming with you."

Cormack shook his head. "I've got people with more experience in this sort of thing."

"How many of them stand to lose what I have to lose."

"What, exactly, do you think you stand to lose?" Cormack said pointedly.

"I stand to lose Diamond and a baby I just found out about."

"And you're going to be there for them? Not just in this, but afterward? You're not going to duck out—disappear when things get tough?"

"Never," Buddy said. "She's going to have to leave me, if it comes to that. I'll never leave her."

As he said the words, Buddy truly believed them.

Diamond's mind worked furiously. She was in a tiny bathroom down a short passageway from the room where she'd been kept. She couldn't figure out where they were. The entire place was cement—the walls, the ceiling, the floors. It looked as though the building had been deserted. There was trash and debris littering the passageways, and graffiti on many of the walls. The bathroom was disgusting. The toilet was steel and no longer functional. There was no toilet seat, and the waste from previous visitors covered the sides and bottom of the bowl. The stench was almost too terrible to endure.

She squatted, hovering over the receptacle, careful not to touch the metal. She looked around for anything that might help her. There was a matching metal sink that was also disgusting. It appeared that men had begun treating it as a urinal. Looking closely at the edge of the sink, she saw words etched into the steel. They were faint, and covered in dirt. She pulled the sleeve of her sweater over her hand and rubbed the metal until she could see the words.

UNITED STATES WAR DEPARTMENT.

She frowned. Abandoned military forts dotted the Harbor Islands—

relics from the days when the United States worried about an impending German invasion. Perhaps she was being held in one of them. If so, escape would be almost impossible. Even if she could escape from whatever building they were in, she would still need to find a way to get back to the mainland. The water was too cold to think of swimming, even if she'd been a better swimmer. She would have to hope to find some sort of a small rowboat, and even that seemed untenable. Her captors had large boats, and would undoubtedly track her down on the water before she could get to safety. Still, she had to try something. She knew in her heart that if she didn't escape, she would be killed.

The floor was covered with scraps of toilet paper and trash. After she'd finished relieving herself, she got down on her knees to search the floor for anything that could be useful to her in any way. There was nothing that seemed worthwhile. There were little empty nip bottles of cheap booze, some empty cigarette packs, and paper bags.

She looked more closely at one of the paper bags in the corner of the cramped space. It wasn't empty. There was a bottle in it. She pulled the bottle out and looked at it. It *was* empty. It had been a cheap brand of sweet whiskey, the kind she'd seen young derelicts drinking on street corners for as long as she could remember. It had a thin neck and a wide, flat body. She held it by the neck and swung it like a mini club. It wasn't much, but it might be something.

She slid the bottle into the inside pocket of her jacket. She stood in front of the sink, and started to reach in to wash her hands before she remembered where she was. She looked at her reflection in the steel mirror behind the sink. Her face and hair were a mess, and she looked older than her nineteen years.

"Stay alive," she said quietly to her reflection. "Stay alive and keep your head, and you'll be OK." The sound of her voice made her feel better, but only slightly. She knew that the odds were still against her survival.

FORTY-SIX

Tuesday, February 5

FBI Agent Roger Damon hated the water. He was born in Kansas, where the only water he saw as a child came out of the ground, up through a well. The closest lake was several hours' drive away. He didn't even envy the few people he knew growing up whose families had pools. To him, they were just wide wells in which to drown.

As a result, he was miserable in his current assignment. He was sitting in the hold of a large tugboat that was docked in East Boston, awaiting an overhaul that was scheduled for later in the month. The ship was awful, as far as Damon was concerned. It was old and decaying, and the galley, where he was situated, smelled of stale spam and tuna. Every time the ship lurched with the tide, his stomach lurched with it.

The only good thing about the tug was its location. It was tied up to a pier across a shallow inlet from the warehouse that T'phong Soh and his MS-13 crew had used as their headquarters for more than a year. It was the only place from which he could conduct surveillance and not be detected. The area on land around the warehouse was too congested for a surveillance van to go unnoticed. The roads were so narrow that any vehicle parked for more than an hour would become an obstruction that could not be overlooked.

From the tug, though, he had a clear view of the western side of the warehouse, which faced the harbor, as well as the southern side that faced the inlet. The only other side that had any doors was the eastern side, which bordered the alleyway from which vehicles accessed the place. He could only see part of the way around the corner there, but it was enough for him to at least know when a truck entered or exited. He had a camera with a telephoto lens that fit perfectly in the porthole window, and a long-range microphone that connected to his headphones had been fitted to the tug's navigation array topside, angled to catch as much sound from the outside of the warehouse as possible. The audio had proved relatively useless, though, so he only kept one of the headphones looped on his ear.

The door to the crew's compartment opened and slammed shut, and Damon's partner, Daniel Shift, climbed up the stairs into the galley. "Head's busted," he said.

"What's busted?"

"The head."

"Your head?" Damon pressed.

"*The* head," Shift responded. "Downstairs in the bathroom." It was clear that Damon still wasn't comprehending. "A toilet on a boat is called a *head*."

"Why?"

"How the fuck should I know?" Shift said. "But that's what it's called."

"That's stupid," Damon said.

"Maybe, but it's the reality. The more important reality is that this one is broken."

"Can you plunge it?" Damon asked.

Shift shook his head. "It doesn't work that way."

Damon paused. "Did you discover this before or after you went?"

"After."

"Shit."

"Bingo." Shift scratched his chin. It had been more than a week since he'd shaved. He and Damon were both dressed as longshoremen, and they had adopted a casual approach to grooming in order to fit in better with their surroundings. "Anything going on?"

"Not out there," Damon replied. "Been all quiet for hours. We got a ping from Steele, though."

"Yeah? What'd she say?"

"She says she wants us to pay really close attention to what's going on over there. She wants us to let her know if anything happens."

Shift scratched his beard a little faster. "Isn't that why we're here?"

"Yeah," Damon said. "But she wants to know as soon as *anything* happens, like immediately."

"Weird. She say why?"

Damon shook his head. "But I wouldn't want to get in her shithouse. She's a real ballbuster."

"Speaking of shithouses," Shift said, "I'm going to put in a call about the head. Then I'm going to go grab a coffee. You want one?"

Damon thought about it for a moment. "Better get the head fixed first."

Cormack sat at his desk, looking out of the great window toward the harbor. He could feel his stomach turning with each minute. If there was something he could do, he would feel better. The waiting was the worst.

His cell rang and he looked at the caller ID. It was Kit. He answered it and held it up to his ear. "Yeah?" he said.

"What's our timing?"

"Suarez is in a car. I told Soh he was on the way and he would be dropped off at the warehouse."

"Did Soh say anything?"

"He said that if anything happened to Suarez, or if he saw any of my men near the warehouse, he would kill my daughter."

"So keep your men away. I've got my men there."

"Do you trust them, and do they trust you?"

"Better. They're scared of me."

Cormack considered that for a moment. "Fear is a powerful management tool. Use it wisely."

"Will do. Did Soh say anything else?" Steele asked.

"He wanted to know whether I had submitted my resignation to the union yet."

"What did you say?"

"I said I was still drafting it. That seemed to confuse him, but he made clear that he wasn't going to release Diamond until I was gone, both from the job and from the city." Cormack took a deep breath. "Reading between the lines, he really just wants me separated from my people so he can take me out."

"That's logical."

"Call me as soon as your men see anything. If they're taking him to where Diamond is, they'll go by boat. I need to know what boat they're on so I can track them."

"How will you do that?"

"I have my ways." Cormack clicked off the phone. He'd sounded confident on the phone. That was something he'd always been good at—feigning confidence when he had little of it.

The call came a half hour later. "He was dropped off twenty minutes ago," Steele said. "He was inside the warehouse for around fifteen, then a boat pulled up out back and he got on it. They headed out into the harbor."

"What was the name of the boat?" Cormack asked.

"It was the *Lucy Dunovan III*."

"A trawler," Cormack said. He knew almost all the boats that spent any significant time in the harbor. "It's owned by an outfit out of Gloucester."

"MS-13 is making inroads up there. Maybe they've got a connection."

"They do," Cormack said. "It's a boat they use to run drugs."

"How do you know?"

"I get a tribute," he said matter-of-factly.

"Right," she said. She should have realized. "So what now?"

"I'll take it from here."

"Is there anything else I can do?"

"You've done more than you should have. I appreciate it." He started to click the phone off.

"Cormack," he heard her say.

"Yeah?"

There was silence on the line. "Let me know when you get back, OK?"

"You'll be the first."

When she hung up the phone, Kit Steele felt ill. She wondered whether she would ever see Cormack again, and figured it was even odds that she wouldn't. She recalled how she'd felt less than a week before, when she thought she'd lost him in the attack on the Mariner. She'd been surprised by the depths of her sorrow at the time. She'd believed before that moment that he was merely a part of her plan—a functionary in her quest to gather and use information that might help combat the likes of Vincente Carpio. It was a worthy mission, she believed, and one that at times justified questionable tactics. Cormack played an important role in her being able to carry out that mission.

But somewhere along the way, the lines got blurred without her even realizing it. Somehow he had touched something in her that had been dead for more than a half a decade. Letting someone back in that way made her uncomfortable. It scared her. She didn't know whether she could survive another loss.

FORTY-SEVEN

Juan Suarez stood on the bridge of the *Lucy Dunovan III,* looking out at Boston Harbor as the boat pulled away from the pier behind the East Boston warehouse where he'd been dropped off by Cormack O'Connell's lackey. His head ached. His chest ached. He had so many contusions that every movement caused pain. He was alive, though, and that was no small miracle. He had assumed as O'Connell's men were beating him that his life was over. His only goal was not to break—not to give them any information. It was a point of pride for him. He'd had a strict code of loyalty beaten into him from a tender age, and he was determined to live up to that code until someone put a bullet in his head.

The bullet had never come, though. Without explanation, the beatings had stopped and he was left alone. Someone had come to look at him, apparently to make sure that none of his wounds was life-threatening. He was left alone for close to a day, and then he was put in a car, driven to the warehouse, and left at the entrance. He had no idea why he was still alive until he spoke to one of the MS-13 soldiers in the warehouse.

"We took a girl," was all he'd said, but that was enough. Suarez knew that O'Connell had a daughter. It would make sense for Soh to go after her—having control over her would create a weakness in O'Connell and give them a strategic advantage. It was what Suarez would have done. It was what he'd learned over time: threaten a man's life, and he will often comply; threaten a man's family, and he will always comply.

"How long?" he asked the man driving the boat.

"Fifteen minutes," the man responded. "Maybe twenty."

Suarez nodded. As the boat pitched, his body rocked in pain. He welcomed the pain, though. Reveled in it, even. From the time that he was young, he'd been taught that there was only one certainty he could count on . . . dead men don't feel pain.

Tommy Breslin ran a tug out of Chelsea, and that morning he was piloting a barge full of scrap metal from the South Shore up to Everett. He was headed north past the airport when he passed the *Lucy Dunovan III.* He gave a tip of his cap to the skipper of the other boat, as was the custom. Then he picked up the handset to the radio.

"Cormack, you on?"

"Yeah, Tommy," the voice came back.

"I just passed them. Headed south just off Logan."

"How many?"

"I could see two in the pilothouse. There could be more, but that's all I saw."

"OK. Thanks Tommy."

"Let me know if there's anything else you need," Tommy said. The line went dead. Tommy gave a look in his mirror at the *Lucy Dunovan,* powering in the other direction. He wondered what Cormack's interest in the boat was, but quickly put the question out of his head. Whatever the interest was, it was none of his business. Cormack had radioed earlier and asked him to keep an eye out for the vessel, but beyond that, he had no desire to be mixed up in anything that might be illegal or dangerous. He was aware of a lot of the illicit activity that went on around the harbor, but he kept his nose clean and did his work. He had two kids in college, and he was focused on paying for their education. He didn't want any trouble.

"They're headed south," Cormack said. Buddy and Cicero were in the office with him, and he looked out the window. Off in the distance, he could see a trawler headed past Deer Island, just south of the airport. "That must be them," he said, pointing. It was a nondescript boat, but at the moment, it was the only thing on the water of any interest to Cormack. They would have a visual for another minute or two, but then the boat would round the corner at Castle Island and be gone. He had to know where the boat was going.

"You have others out there?" Cicero asked.

Cormack nodded. "I've got a network at the ready that can see them wherever they go without attracting attention."

"Who's up next?"

"Based on where they're headed, they should be off Spectacle Island in a moment. I've got Romero out there working on the pilings off the south pier." He picked up the radio handset on the desk and tuned it to a particular frequency. "Romero, you there?"

The answer was instantaneous. "Yeah, Boss," Sal Romero's voice came through the radio.

"The *Lucy Dunovan* is headed your way. I need eyes on her."

"You got it, Boss."

"Let me know when you've got contact."

"Will do."

Cormack put the radio down. "If they get to Quincy Bay, Mel Costa's there. He's got lobster traps lined up all the way down to Hull, so he can keep an eye on them without looking suspicious. If they head east toward the outer islands, I've got two boats running supplies out to Little Brewster. Between those, I think we should have him covered."

"Should," Buddy said quietly.

"It's the best we can do. Soh was clear that if he sees anyone following him or his men, he'll kill her. I'm not letting that happen. Any eyes we have on that boat have to stay low and look normal."

"What if it's not enough? What if your people lose sight of that boat?"

"We'll figure that out if that happens. Right now, this is our best option."

The radio crackled. "Cormack, it's Romero, you there?"

Cormack grabbed the radio handset. "Yeah, Romero, I'm here. You got something?"

"Yeah, the *Lucy Dunovan* just passed me."

"She still headed south?"

"It's not clear. She wrapped around the southern tip of Spectacle and she might be headed out toward the Atlantic."

"Outer islands?" Cicero asked.

"Don't know," Cormack responded. "Was she running full steam?" he asked Romero.

"Tough to tell, but she wasn't idling. I've still got a good look at her. I'll keep watching until I can't see her anymore." There was a pause for a moment, then Romero spoke again. There was an edge of excitement in his voice. "Hold on," he said. "It looks like she's slowing down."

"In the middle of the harbor?" Cormack asked. "Is it possible that they made you?" He couldn't understand why else the *Lucy Dunovan* would be slowing down.

"She's turning due south again," Romero reported. "Looks like they're pulling in to Long Island."

Cormack frowned. "East side or west side?" he asked.

"East side," Romero replied. "The pier on the northeast end. They're definitely pulling in now. I've got two getting off the boat, walking toward the land. Looks like they're leaving the boat on the pier."

"OK, thanks Romero. Stay there and let me know if anyone comes or goes, you got it?"

"Yeah, Cormack, I got it."

Cormack put the radio handset down and looked at the chart in front of him, zeroing in on Long Island.

"They shut the island down a couple years ago," Cicero commented. "Tore down the bridge and left everything there to rot."

"They did," Cormack agreed. "That's why it makes sense. There's no one to bother them." Cormack pulled out another chart that showed Long Island in more detail. He pointed to the northeast end. "Fort Strong," he said. "It was abandoned in the seventies, and there's only a couple of ways in. That's where they are if they let him off on the east end."

"Tough place to attack," Cicero commented.

"That's why they chose it."

"So what now?" Buddy asked.

"Now we come up with a plan," Cormack said. "We'll have to go in at night. It would be suicide to try to go in when it's daylight."

"Seems like it'll be suicide either way," Cicero pointed out.

"Maybe," Cormack said.

"I'm going," Buddy said.

Cormack nodded, knowing that there was no chance the young man would agree to stay behind. He looked at Cicero. "You can beg off if you want. You'll get no argument from me. Like you said, it may be suicide no matter when we go."

Cicero shook his head. "If Soh takes control of the harbor, *that's* suicide for me. I won't survive in that world. Besides, I like bucking the odds."

FORTY-EIGHT

Kit Steele sat across the table from Vincente Carpio, staring into his cold, dark eyes, absorbing the hatred from them, and returning it in kind. Joshua Brooks was in the room as well, sitting next to his client. "You asked for this meeting," he said in a bored voice. "What is it that you wanted to talk about?"

Kit Steele didn't look at Brooks. She continued to stare at Carpio. "I wanted to know why he does it."

"OK, we're done," Brooks said. He stood up and tapped his client on the shoulder. It took a moment to realize that the chains had to be unlocked before his client could stand up. "Guard!" he called.

Carpio didn't move. He continued to stare back at Steele.

"What is it that you hope to accomplish?" Steele continued. "I just want to understand."

"Enough," Brooks said. "You think this kind of stunt is cute? I have other clients and other business. I don't need to make the trip all the way out here for this kind of shit, Agent Steele."

"Do you enjoy it?" Steele asked Carpio. "When you kill them, does it bring you pleasure? Joy, even?"

"Don't answer that!" Brooks barked at his client. Carpio's gaze seemed to intensify, and the shadow of a smile crossed his lips.

"You must take some satisfaction from it, right?" she said. "You've done it often enough."

"Would you take joy from killing me?" Carpio asked.

It was a fair question, she supposed. She considered it for a moment. "I don't know," she said. "Probably," she admitted after a second thought. "But that's not the way we do things. We have systems in place to protect the accused. We have punishments that are more humane. We try to rehabilitate criminals here."

"You live in a dream world, Special Agent," Brooks said. "Come on, we're done here. Guard!" Again, though, Carpio made no move to suggest that he was interested in leaving.

Steele took out a folder and lined the images of the dead up on the table. There were seventeen of them in all. Each one displayed in some grotesque fashion. Carpio had acquired greater skill and creativity as he'd progressed from killing to killing, and it showed in the images. He looked at the pictures without any change in his expression.

"What was it like the first time?" Steele asked. She pointed to one of the pictures. "It was this one, wasn't it?"

"You think these are the first people I have killed?" For a moment, she thought he might actually smile at the notion.

"Don't say another word!" Brooks hollered.

"In my country, death and killing is everywhere," Carpio said with quiet intensity.

"That was war," Steele pointed out.

"This is war. It is the same war. America can pretend that it is not, but that does not change the facts."

"Agent Steele, I am ordering you to end this interrogation!" Brooks demanded.

"I'm not forcing him to talk to me," Steele said. She looked back at Carpio. "I think he wants to talk to me. I think he needs to talk to me."

"This is not a war that we started," Carpio continued. "It is a war that you started. My people only wanted to live in peace. America came to El Salvador. So I came to America. You should understand that more than anyone. You are the hunter. Why do you hunt?"

"We're done now," Brooks said. He put a hand under Carpio's armpit and tried to lift him up, but the chains held.

"You will never get out of here," Steele said. "I promise you that."

Carpio stopped even as Brooks tried to pull him along. He stared evenly at Steele, his red-tattooed eyes boring into her. "Agent Steele, you should stop making promises you can't keep."

FORTY-NINE

Wednesday, February 6

Long Island was a narrow spit of land in the middle of Boston Harbor, roughly a mile and a half long and a quarter mile wide at its widest spot. It ran south to north and had once been connected to the mainland by a rickety two-lane steel bridge that traversed the half-mile of harbor between its southern tip and the northern end of Moon Island.

The island was owned by the City of Boston, and the southern two-thirds had been used for nearly a century as a dumping ground for society's less desirable elements. Beginning in the 1820s, the city constructed an almshouse and shipped its poorest and most helpless residents out to work a small farm on the island in exchange for a bed and enough food to sustain themselves.

Over time, the public offenses warranting removal from the public's dismay to Long Island swayed with the mores of the day. The facilities were used, over the course of the nineteenth and twentieth centuries, as housing for unwed mothers, as a chronic disease hospital, and as an orphanage. By the early twenty-first century, the island's facilities, which included one thousand beds, were used primarily to house a combination of drug addicts and homeless men. In 2014, however, the city's Corps of Engineers condemned the bridge that connected Long Island to the mainland, and residents were given three hours to gather their belongings so that they could be bused one last time off the island. The bridge was subsequently demolished, and the island was left deserted.

The northern third of Long Island had been given back to nature much earlier. Beginning in the nineteenth century, the bulbous northern outcropping had housed Fort Strong, an installation dedicated to the defense of Boston Harbor. The twenty-five-acre area, separated from the rest of the island by a low, narrow strip of beach and field, had been commandeered by the federal government in the 1880s, and a major construction project was begun to create an elaborate warren of cement caves and rooms in the hillside. By the 1950s, the fort was home to a Nike Missile system, a massive post–World War II air-defense project involving line-of-sight antiaircraft missiles developed by Bell Labs.

By the late 1960s, though, the threat of nuclear annihilation had eclipsed any fear of an air-to-ground attack, and Fort Strong was decommissioned. In the half-century since the fort was abandoned, the cement compound had been swallowed by vegetation. The gun blocks were still visible from the air, but from the water and from the land it was difficult to discern the outlines of the man-made fortress.

It was after two o'clock in the morning as the *Citacea* idled by the northern end of Long Island. She was a Viking sport-fishing rig, fifty-two feet in length with a flying bridge and a carbon fiber composite hull sharpened at the bow to cut through rough seas. She had a luxurious salon and three staterooms to keep her inhabitants swaddled in comfort when not manning the heavy rods.

The time of day for the journey was not unusual—serious sport fishermen often headed out east in the wee hours to be fishing by early morning off the outer limits of Stellwagen Bank, a kidney-shaped underwater plateau between Cape Ann and Cape Cod where the waters teemed with marine life. The time of year might raise an eyebrow, particularly in the current cold snap, but there were enough wealthy dilettantes of questionable sanity who would relish the tales to tell of big-game fishing in the most inhospitable conditions. Enough to dampen the suspicions of anyone who might take notice as the boat turned toward the northeast and headed out to sea.

The *Citacea* was piloted by Skip Olney, a charter captain who was forever in Cormack O'Connell's debt. Two years before, Skip's twenty-year-old son had been caught running ten kilograms of cocaine into Chelsea, and Cormack had interceded to keep the lad out of prison.

Cormack, Cicero, and Buddy searched Long Island's northern shore as the boat passed by. It was a bright, clear night, and a full moon cast enough light to make out the pier and the lighthouse built into the hillside.

"There," Cormack said. "Just to the left of the lighthouse." The other men strained to see a dim rectangular outline partially obscured by the snow-covered trees. "That's the northern entrance." For a moment, he thought he could see the flicker of light around twenty yards to the west of the entryway.

"Not the way we want to go in," Cicero commented.

"No," Cormack agreed. "There's another entrance on the east side of the hill."

"Won't they be watching there as well?" Buddy asked.

"Maybe," Cormack said. "But it's less likely. The fort was separated into two sections. Two different artillery groups operated independently. The two sides are connected, but if we're lucky Soh and his men are only using the northern section."

"What if we're not lucky?" Buddy asked. No one answered.

Skip Olney steered the boat out past Lovells Island so that if anyone was watching them from Fort Strong, they would assume they were headed out to sea. Then he swung the bow around and to the south, around Lovells and Georges Island, then headed back to the west so that the boat could approach Long Island from the southeast, protected from sight by the northern hill.

Olney cut the engines and the *Citacea* idled in toward the shallow inlet formed by the low, narrow run of beach and field that separated Fort Strong from the rest of the island. He kept a sharp eye on the depth finder. The boat was his life, and notwithstanding the debt he would always owe Cormack, he wasn't eager to risk running aground. Besides, they needed the boat to remain seaworthy—it was their only way off the island in the unlikely event that they were able to get in and get out without getting themselves killed.

"That's as far as she'll go," Olney said, shifting into neutral and working the controls to maintain the boat's position. Cormack nodded, and he, Cicero, and Buddy left the bridge and headed out to the stern.

The ten-foot inflatable was loaded with three tactical vests, rope, and the weapons they had gathered for the assault. Cormack wished they'd had more time so that he could have found more weapons, but there was no option to wait. As a result, they were going in with two guns and multiple clips each. In addition, Cormack had been able to scrounge up three flash-bangs that had been left at the union office after the last raid police had been carried out on a tip from Cormack. They wouldn't kill anyone, but they could stun people, particularly in close quarters, and Cormack thought they might prove useful.

They slipped the small vessel over the transom and into the water. The three of them were dressed all in black waterproof SD Combat wet/dry suits, with black neoprene hoods and gloves to help protect them from the cold, but even the high-tech gear could not really keep them warm. They slid from the *Citacea*'s stern into the inflatable and paddled the twenty yards into shore. The entire way, Cormack scanned the hill on the back side of Fort Strong, expecting at any minute to be engulfed in a hail of gunfire.

The bullets never came, though, and within a matter of minutes, the three men were pulling the inflatable up onto the beach and lashing it to a large boulder to prevent the incoming tide from taking it out to sea.

They silently emptied their small raft of the weapons and slipped them into the vests covering their foul-weather suits. Cormack motioned for them to follow him as he crept along the beach, toward the northern end of the island.

It took only two minutes for them to reach the spot at which the southeastern side of the hill met the shoreline. Cormack pointed up the hill, and in the moonlight Cicero and Buddy could see the dim outline of a concrete rectangle, roughly ten feet wide by six feet high, identical to the entryway they had seen from the *Citacea* on the northern side of the fort. Cormack nodded at them and started up the hill, through the heavy vegetation.

The progress was slow, as they tried to make as little noise as possible.

It was rough going, and the cold cut through their gear, leaving their extremities near frozen. They made their way inexorably up until they were on a small cement ledge outside of the concrete entryway. A heavy metal door clung to its hinges, but there were no locks, and the latch had fallen away. Cormack looked from Cicero to Buddy and back. Then he reached into his vest and pulled out a Glock 9mm semiautomatic pistol. Buddy followed Cormack's lead, and pulled out an identical gun. Cicero pulled out his knife, and motioned for Cormack and Buddy to position themselves so that they could shoot in at the entryway. Cicero then took hold of the door and gave it a pull. It creaked softly, but to the three men it sounded like a screech. The door swung outward on its hinges, and Cormack and Buddy pointed their guns into the dark abyss beyond the entryway, ready to shoot if they sensed any movement.

They stood there for a moment, barely breathing, listening intently for any indication that someone inside had heard the door open and Soh and his men were coming to cut them down, but there was no noise, and once enough time had passed for them to feel encouraged, Cormack lowered his pistol slightly and stepped through the opening and into the darkness.

"He will not give up the union and the harbor," Soh said quietly. He was sitting on a rusted metal chair in a windowless concrete room roughly ten feet wide by twenty feet long. He guessed that this had been the operations center of the artillery unit that had run the Nike missile installation on the northern end of the island. It was by far the largest room in the maze of low corridors and small side rooms. The military had left behind a few items—metal chairs and tables, and a stack of metal pikes, the operational purpose of which escaped Soh's imagination.

"Even if he does, will you be able to keep control?" Juan Suarez asked.

"What do you mean?"

Juan Suarez shrugged. "Even if O'Connell is removed, much of what he has put in place will remain. His men. His connections. There will be others who will try to take control, and even if they cannot, I wonder whether we will be able to insert ourselves into a system that has been built around one man and one way of doing things."

Soh frowned. The thought had occurred to him, but he'd been unwilling to admit the risk of failure to himself. He didn't like being confronted by reality, but he appreciated Suarez's keen mind. "What options do we have?" he asked.

"Perhaps none," Suarez said. "It may very well be that we have to kill many more, even if O'Connell is gone. We will have to find a way to wipe out the old system and build a new one around you."

"You may be right," Soh said. "But first we have to deal with O'Connell. He will have to leave, or he will have to give up his daughter."

Soh had welcomed Suarez back with a nod and nothing more. Suarez understood. They were soldiers, after all. There was no need for any acknowledgment of Suarez's ordeal, or of Soh's efforts to have him released. They would remain, as always, focused on their objective; maudlin feelings had no place in their world. If Suarez had been killed by O'Connell's men, Soh would have missed the tactical advantage that Suarez's presence gave him, but there would have been no further emotion. It was one of the things that Suarez respected about Soh.

Suarez shook his head. "He will never do that."

"What possibility does that leave?" Soh asked.

"He will try to get her back with force," Suarez said after a moment.

Soh gave a derisive grunt. "It would be impossible," he said. "We are too heavily defended here. There is nothing he can do."

"Perhaps," Suarez conceded. "But he will try. We must be ready for him to try."

Soh nodded. "Agreed. But if he does, his daughter will die instantly. And he will follow almost as quickly."

It took them twenty minutes to make their way through the southeastern section of Fort Strong and reach the door leading to the long corridor that connected to the northern section of the fort. Cormack was well acquainted with the interior layout; the place was often used by smugglers as a temporary storage area for various contraband. He had described the place to Buddy and Cicero so that they would have a good idea of where they were and what they could expect. If Cormack was correct in his assumption, Soh and his men would likely be utilizing the northern section. It was the larger area, and there was plenty of space for two dozen men, which was the size of the force Cormack estimated that Soh had.

So far Cormack's assumptions had been borne out. But that was little comfort. He knew that in order to get into the northern section of the fort, they would have to first open the steel door on their side of the corridor. In all likelihood, the noise from that would be enough to alert Soh's men that they were there. They then had to make their way down the fifty-foot-long, low concrete passageway. If Soh and his men were alerted to their presence, all they would have to do was crack the door at their end of the corridor open and shoot blindly through the opening. The concrete walls, floor, and ceiling would guarantee an endless ricochet and there would be no way that Cormack and his men would escape being carved to ribbons.

Even if they made it down the corridor and managed to get the door on the other end open, they would still be forced to fight their way through anywhere between fifteen and twenty well-armed, highly motivated MS-13 soldiers who accepted that their lives were by definition likely to end early.

As Cormack stared at the door to the corridor, the hopelessness of the situation fully dawned on him, and he realized that he would likely never see his daughter again. After a moment's thought, he motioned for Cicero and Buddy to follow him back out toward the eastern entrance.

"It's no good," Cormack whispered once they were back out near the entryway. "It won't work. It'll get us killed, and it'll get Diamond killed." He could tell from the looks on the other men's faces that they knew he was right.

"What now, then?" Buddy asked. "I'm not leaving her here."

"I'm not either," Cormack said. "But there might be a better way."

"I'm all ears," Cicero whispered. "This is your show."

"You two head back to the corridor. Wait there. As soon as you hear a commotion, you hit the hallway as hard and as fast as you can. Get to Diamond before they do, and get her out."

Cicero frowned. "What commotion?" he asked.

"Trust me," Cormack said. "I know how to make a commotion when I want to."

FIFTY

Cormack climbed out of the entryway on the southeastern side of Fort Strong and moved as quickly as he could through the trees, down to the waterline. He didn't like being out in the open, but he could move much more quickly around to the northern tip of the island picking his way around the rocks at the edge of the shore. Besides, the vegetation that had reclaimed the exterior of the fort was so thick he couldn't have moved through it without making such a racket that he would have been announcing his approach to any guards stationed outside the northern entrance. He stayed close to the trees on the shoreline in the hope that they would provide some cover and prevent anyone higher up on the hill from spotting him.

The cold bit through the neoprene, and his feet felt like chunks of lead in his lightweight boots. They were supposed to be waterproof, but the ice stuck to them and Cormack could not feel his toes anymore. He put that out of his mind, though, and continued his trek as quickly and quietly as he could. He had to step carefully, as the rocks were also covered in ice, and one wrong step could send him crashing into the shallow water, alerting anyone keeping watch from the fort's northern entrance.

He was surprised at how quickly he was able to round the northeastern corner of the island. Now, he knew, he was more exposed. The trees still provided some cover, but it was more likely that there would be guards in spots where they could see through the snow-covered brambles. He slowed his pace and kept his eyes on the hill above him, searching for the entryway.

He saw it through a break in the trees a few moments later. It was around twenty yards to his west, and about twenty yards up the hill. He froze when he saw it because he could clearly make out three armed men milling around the cement ledge outside of the entryway. They were lookouts, clearly, though Cormack suspected that the cold had sapped much of their attention. They stood close together, whispering quietly, shuffling their feet back and forth. They were carrying what looked like assault weapons, though, and even in their inattentive state Cormack recognized that they posed a significant threat. One idle glance in his direction, and they would have a clear shot at him.

He pulled back slowly from the break in the trees, so that he could no longer see the guards, and they would no longer be able to see him. He took a moment to assess the terrain as he debated the best approach. He felt through his vest and found the three flash-bangs. He also had his two loaded pistols and two spare clips.

If it were up to him, he would have preferred to attack from where he was, as that would not risk making any noise that would alert Soh's men, but he knew he needed to get closer in order for his plan to be effective. It would also be helpful, he knew, if he could attack from above them on the hill, though he suspected that might be pushing his luck.

He tucked his weapons back into his vest and started carefully picking his way up the hillside, parallel to the fort's entryway and the guards stationed there. Now the going was extremely slow. A few times he slid through narrow openings between tree branches and the tree rustled, snow coming down on his head from the branches above. Each time, he assumed that he would be discovered, and he held his breath, his hand going to his vest, searching for a weapon. Each time, though, there was no attack from the guards, and no indication that he'd been sighted.

He made it up to a spot that was roughly even with the entryway on the hill, and then he encountered a small clearing and a solid wall of rock. The surface had some crags and ledges, and under other circumstances, he could probably have scaled the cliff and put himself in the perfect vantage point from which to attack those guarding the entryway. He couldn't feel his feet at that instance, though, and he was wearing neoprene gloves that had iced over. He figured that the odds of him making it to the top of the ledge without falling were low, and such a fall would put an end to his life—not to mention Diamond's. After a moment, he concluded that his position in the clearing was the best he was going to be able to do.

Cormack dropped to a knee and took out his weapons and ammunition again, making sure that they were ready and accessible. He had to hit the entryway as hard and as quickly as he could. His goal was to create such a commotion that Soh and his men inside would assume that there was a full-scale assault coming from the north. With luck, that would lure them to the front, by the entryway, and away from the corridor connecting the north side of the underground fort to the eastern side.

From where he was, he could just make out the entryway, twenty yards or so due west. It had been a long time since he'd thrown anything any significant distance, and he wondered whether he would be able to be accurate enough to be effective. It was his only chance—and Diamond's only chance as well.

He held one of his pistols in his left hand, and placed the other on the ground, where it would be easy to grab. Then he picked up one of the flash-bangs, pulled the pin, and threw it as far as he could toward the entryway. As the concussive was in the air, he reached down and grabbed his second gun and aimed both weapons at the entryway, waiting for the explosion.

Diamond was sitting against the wall in the tiny room toward the back half of the northern section of Fort Strong, her knees pulled up to her chest, her arms wrapped around her knees, trying to keep her belly as warm as possible. The cold had overtaken her at that point, and she wondered whether the baby could survive the night. She was aware of how fragile a pregnancy could be in the first three months under the best of circumstances. And these were, most certainly, not the best of circumstances. The doctor had said the spotting was totally normal, but fear still haunted her. If the baby was strong enough to live through this ordeal, it would be strong enough to live through anything once born, she believed.

She could hear two voices outside the room, talking in low, tired tones in Spanish. Neither was the Asian man who had let her use the bathroom; their voices were too deep, and it was clear that they were men for whom Spanish was their native tongue. She looked at the door to the room where she was being kept. She was pretty sure it wasn't locked—the place they were in had been deserted and in disrepair for a very long time, and it seemed likely that even if there had been a working lock at some point, it wouldn't work now. Of course, the fact that her room wasn't locked was hardly cause for optimism. If she opened the door, she guessed she would be confronted by more than a dozen men. She still had the bottle hidden in her jacket, but that would be useless against so many men with so many weapons.

The explosion shook the entire fort. For a moment, Diamond thought that it had come from inside, the noise was so loud. Perhaps they had accidentally detonated some sort of a bomb in the room where all the men were loitering around. Quickly, though, she realized that the explosion had come from outside. She heard the men inside yelling and rushing somewhere, presumably toward the entrance.

Then the gunfire started. Diamond was sure that her young life was about to come to a very violent, premature end—and she lamented the possibility that she would never get to see her child.

Soh was lying on the ground in a side room, alone, trying to get some rest. It wasn't comfortable, but he'd had far worse accommodations at various points in his life. Rest was not coming easily to him; he was too preoccupied with the plans for Vincente Carpio's escape in mere days. When the explosion hit, Soh thought, like Diamond, that one of his men had dropped one of the grenades that they had with them. The entire complex shuddered, and dirt and rocks shook free from some of the fractures in the cement ceilings. After a moment, though, he heard the gunfire, and he knew that it was not an accident; it was an assault.

He leaped up and rushed through a short corridor to the main room where most of his men were congregated. "What is it?" he yelled.

"It's an attack!" one of his men shouted. "They're at the entryway!"

Soh caught the eye of Juan Suarez, and the two acknowledged each other. Suarez had been correct; O'Connell was not leaving the union, and he wasn't waiting. He was making a full frontal attack. It seemed like suicide—Soh and his men could hold out for hours in the stone bunker, and once the light came up, O'Connell would have to call off the assault. Soh shook his head—O'Connell's fool-headedness had just sealed his daughter's fate.

Soh's men were rushing toward the entryway, guns drawn. Soh grabbed one of them, though, and redirected him. "Get the girl!" he shouted. "Bring her here to me!"

The man headed off to the rear of the bunker. Soh headed toward the front of the bunker to direct his men. Fighting off an attack would not be terribly difficult, but if they could inflict heavy casualties on O'Connell's men, it would bring the war to a close even faster. If they could kill O'Connell himself, the war would be over.

It seemed to Cormack like the flash-bang was in the air for an unusual amount of time, and he wondered briefly whether perhaps it was a dud, but then it went off with a tremendous explosion, and he saw the three men at the entryway double over, covering their eyes and ears, momentarily disoriented by the device.

Cormack immediately began shooting with both guns. He aimed halfheartedly, directing the shots toward the entryway. His focus was not necessarily to hit anyone; rather he wanted to shoot as quickly as possible to give the impression that there were numerous men engaging in the attack. It took less than thirty seconds for him to empty the guns—twenty-two shots in all. By then, the three guards had regained some of their faculties and were struggling to get back into the bunker. It looked as though, even without aiming carefully, Cormack might have hit one of the guards in the shoulder, but he couldn't be sure. As Cormack ran out of bullets in his first set of clips, he reached down and picked up another flash-bang. He pulled the pin and threw it, looking to hit the ledge just outside the entryway. His aim was off, though, and the flash-bang hit the cement above and to the left of the entryway.

Cormack swapped out the two empty clips in his guns for two new ones, and resumed shooting as quickly as he could. Again, it took less than thirty seconds to unload both guns, and there was no one visible outside of the fort's entrance at that point, but Cormack didn't care. He needed to keep up the attack and commotion. It was the only chance.

Once the second set of clips were exhausted, Cormack reached down for the third flash-bang—the last of his weapons. At this point, there was a steady volley of gunfire shooting blindly out from the entryway, and he hoped that Soh's men would mistake their own gunshots for a combination of assault and defense. He pulled the pin on the flashbang and threw it toward the cement entryway. It went off, and the shooting from the entryway quieted briefly, and then picked up again in earnest.

He took a last look at the stone passage, gunshots firing out from the breach in the metal door. His assault had lasted for less than two minutes. It was the best he could muster, though. He prayed that it would be enough.

Cormack knew that Soh and his men would realize quickly that there was no more shooting, and he had little doubt that they would emerge from the fortress quickly to give chase. There would be several of them coming after him, and he no longer had any weapons to fight back with. The odds of him making it to the boat before Soh's men had a line of sight on him were low, but he had to try. With any luck, Diamond was already out of the bunker and headed to the boat with Cicero and Buddy, but he knew the odds that the plan had been successful were also low.

He threw off the assault vest to give himself a little more mobility and started down toward the water. He was no longer concerned with maintaining silence. Speed was all he cared about.

FIFTY-ONE

Buddy and Cicero heard the explosion, and there was no mistaking Cormack's misdirection. They were in motion as soon as they felt the fort shake. They threw open the door and paused for just a second to make sure that gunfire was not coming down the corridor in their direction, but it seemed that Cormack's diversion was, at least for the moment, keeping Soh and his men occupied.

Buddy was the first into the passageway. The ceiling was low—just over six feet, and he had to keep his head down as he ran to avoid it scraping against the cement. Cicero was able to run without bending, and he overtook Buddy midway down the corridor. He reached the door at the far end first and gave Buddy a quick glance, just to make sure that he was ready for an attack. Then he turned the latch.

Buddy felt a wave of relief when he saw the latch actually turn. It was possible, he'd thought, that it might be rusted beyond opening. It was even more likely that it was locked. In either event, Buddy had no idea how they would get through the doorway. They could try shooting at the latch and hope that it would give way, but it was far more likely that the ricochet off the metal and cement would kill one or both of them. The fact that the latch turned seemed a miracle, but Buddy was willing to believe in miracles at that point.

Cicero gave a nod and pushed the door open.

It swung in about six inches, and then stopped. Cicero frowned and pushed harder, but the door wouldn't budge. "There's something blocking it," he said.

Buddy's heart sank. If they didn't make it through the door, it was a virtual certainty that he would never see Diamond again—both she and his unborn child would be killed. "Move away!" he hissed.

Buddy lowered his shoulder and charged at the door. He connected hard, and his shoulder shot pain throughout his body, but he felt the impediment give slightly. The door was close to a foot open now, and he was able to stick his head through. There was a large table with supplies pushed up against it. There was no one in the room, though, and Buddy assumed that anyone who had been there had been drawn to the northern entrance by Cormack's attack.

"We can move it!" Buddy said. "Help me push!"

Buddy and Cicero threw all their weight and effort into the door, pushing as hard as they could. The table moved, tipping up on two legs. Buddy was able to get his hand inside the doorway and give the table one hard, direct shove, and it upended, crashing to the floor, spilling the supplies over the cement.

There was no chance now that the breach would go unnoticed; the table hitting the cement had been too loud. Both men knew that they had only seconds before Soh's men would descend on them, and they would die in a hail of bullets.

They pushed the door open and ran through, into the rear portion of the northern section of the fort.

The man sent by Soh to bring the girl to him was standing outside the room where she was kept hostage when he and the two guards heard the table crash to the ground at the far end of the complex. They exchanged a look, and the most junior of them headed down the passageway to check out what had caused the noise. The other two opened the door to the girl's room and stepped inside.

They found her cowering in a corner, her back turned toward them. One of them went over to her and grabbed her by the arm. "*Levantate!*" he shouted, telling her to get up. The girl pulled her arm back hard, though, and it slipped through his fingers. "*Perra!*" he yelled at her, pulling her hair this time to get her on her feet. "*Levantate!*" he yelled again.

He had nearly pulled her to her feet when he heard his partner make a noise behind him, and he turned to see what was happening. It was a terrible miscalculation on his part.

The younger MS-13 soldier hurried down the passageway toward the storeroom at the very rear of the northern half of Fort Strong. He had his gun drawn, but he was inexperienced and nervous. He had never seen close combat; he was a street soldier, and had been involved in drive-by shootings and had killed defenseless enemies, but he had never experienced true face-to-face fighting.

As he rounded the corner, he could see the table tipped on its side, the supplies covering the floor. Behind the table, he could see an opened door and a long passage. He'd never noticed the door before—the table had been backed up and covering it since the first time he had been in the fort, and he wondered whether anyone on Soh's team knew that there were additional entryways.

The wonder was short-lived, though. As he stood there, looking down the newly discovered corridor, he lost his breath. At first he wasn't sure what was happening, but then he felt the pain shoot through his torso, and a hand on his throat. The knife was withdrawn from his back and then plunged into his rib cage again.

He heard his gun fall to the floor and clatter into the corner. Then he was on his knees, looking up at two men dressed in black tactical gear. One was tall and the other short. He wondered what was happening, but he realized it was not his concern anymore. The blood was filling his chest, and he was gasping for air, and he knew that he would never see another sunrise.

Diamond saw the man pulling her hair turn his head toward the doorway. It was probably her only chance, she knew. She was almost fully standing, and he wasn't looking at her at that moment. As she heard him call to his partner, she raised the empty bottle and brought it down on the back of his head.

She'd never hit someone with a bottle before, and she had no idea what to expect. In the movies, the bad guys always seemed to collapse instantly when hit on the head. As the bottle connected, the glass shattered, and the man faltered forward. He let go of her hair and seemed to wobble, and for a moment she thought that perhaps the movies were right, and he would go down. He steadied himself, though, and turned to face her.

His expression was a tangle of rage and hatred, and he raised a pistol at her. She moved quickly, taking two steps forward and swinging her fist. She was still holding the jagged neck of the shattered bottle, and the sharp edges dug into his abdomen. He doubled over and dropped his gun as his hands went to his stomach, grabbing hold of her wrist as she dug the broken glass farther into him.

The man's expression intensified. The rage and hatred were still there, but now there was fear as well—an animal panic driving him to do anything necessary to survive.

Diamond could feel the man's hands on her wrist, trying to force the glass backward, out of his body. She summoned every ounce of strength that she had to keep the broken bottle digging into his flesh, but he was too strong, and he slowly managed to push it back far enough that it was no longer slashing into him. There was a look of victory on his face—she thought perhaps there was even the hint of a smile—as he twisted her wrist back and lifted her hand above her head. She could feel his blood running down the bottle and onto her hand. Then he gave a tremendous twist and wrenched the bottle out of her hand.

She was knocked off her feet, and she was looking up at the man coming after her. There was a deep, bloody gash in his belly, but that didn't seem to be slowing him down. He had the broken bottle raised high above his head, and a maniacal look in his eyes. He took a step toward her and raised the bottle up even higher, ready to strike at her.

All of a sudden, his chest seemed to explode. His blood splattered her face and the wall behind her. The man hovered above her for just a moment and then collapsed inches from her knees. Behind him, there was the figure of a man, a gun in his hand aimed at the body on the floor. He was dressed in what looked like a fitted high-tech scuba suit with a vest and a foul-weather hood that covered most of his head and most of his face. He was looking at her in an odd, familiar way, and she wondered what was going on. The shock of watching her tormentor's chest explode, and the taste of his blood in her mouth, had sent her into shock, and she was no longer processing information logically. Then the man reached up and pulled his mask off.

It was Buddy, and she immediately started sobbing. She wasn't even sure why, but the tears started streaming uncontrollably down her face and sobs racked her chest. He came over, pulled her to her feet, and put his arms around her, but only briefly.

"We've gotta get out of here," he said.

The thought of having him there with her inspired a strength that she thought had left her. The tears stopped flowing and she caught her breath. "OK," she said. "Let's go."

FIFTY-TWO

Soh realized quickly that something was wrong. The attack had been abrupt and intense, with deafening explosions and a hail of gunfire. Then, as quickly as the assault had started, it ended. It took a moment for him to realize it—his men were continuing to fire their weapons out of the small entryway, into the frigid night, and the gunfire in the fort was disorienting. But after a moment, it seemed that the fight was entirely one-sided.

"Wait!" Soh screamed at his men. "Stop firing!"

It took a moment, but the gunfire died away from inside the fort. All that was left was silence. Soh made a motion to one of the MS-13 gang members closest to the entryway, and he pushed the door all the way open and crawled out. A moment later he called back into the fort.

"They're gone!" he yelled. "I can hear them running!"

"Move!" Soh screamed at his men. "After them!" Suddenly a bolt of panic went through his body. He turned and looked back toward the inner recesses of Fort Strong.

Suarez was a few feet behind him, and he saw the look in Soh's eyes. "The girl," Suarez said.

Soh nodded, and the two of them were moving instantly. Several of Soh's men followed them out of instinct. It took them less than a minute to make their way back toward the room where Cormack O'Connell's daughter was being held. Soh knew the situation was worse than he'd thought when he saw one of his men slumped in the doorway. There was a bullet hole in his forehead, and his lifeless eyes stared out at Soh as if to mock him.

Soh looked into the room and saw another body. This one was lying face up, his body mangled and twisted. Soh could see a hole in his chest and a great bloody tear in his stomach.

The girl was gone, that much was clear. But where had she gone? She couldn't have slipped past the men at the entryway. Even in all the commotion, there was no way to get by. Then the realization hit Soh—it hadn't been an attack. Not a real one, anyway. It had been a diversion. Which meant that there must be another way into the fort that Soh was unaware of.

He motioned for his men to follow him, and they headed toward the room farther back where they'd stored many of their supplies. The third soldier was lying facedown just inside the doorway. Blood covered the back of his shirt. The supplies had been strewn around the floor, and the table that had rested against the wall was overturned. At that moment, Soh saw the door for the first time.

He let out a bloodcurdling scream. "No!" he yelled. "Cormack O'Connell! I will kill you!"

He stormed over the supplies and the overturned table and through the door. He could not allow O'Connell to escape. He could not allow him to have his daughter back. There was still a good chance he could chase him down before they could get off the island. And if there was any way he could get to him, Soh would make sure he took full advantage of that chance.

At that moment, Cormack was slogging along the shoreline. The night had clouded over, depriving him of the ability to see the rocks and ground before him. He was in the shallow water at the edge of the shore, moving as quickly as he could, but his feet were leaden, and he slipped repeatedly on the ice-covered rocks. He could hear Soh's men crashing through the frozen vegetation on the side of the hill, gaining on him every second.

He stepped over a large rock, and his foot came down on a slick spot. He lost his balance and went down facefirst into the shallows. The icy water jolted his system, and his breath caught in his chest. His beard was covered in ice, and his hands were numb. He wondered whether he'd be able to make it to his feet.

Just then, he heard a gunshot and there was an explosion in the water next to him. He glanced back over his shoulder, and he could see Soh's men fifty yards back, up on the hill. It was a long way for a good shot, but they had a clear line of sight on him, and it was obvious that if he stayed where he was, they would eventually get lucky even from that distance.

He hauled himself onto his feet. His frozen legs felt like they would no longer obey his brain's commands, and he was reminded of dreams in which he would struggle to move his extremities. Slowly, though, he moved himself forward as more shots splattered the water around him.

Another twenty yards along the shore, he rounded the corner to the little inlet where the *Citacea* was anchored. He could see the inflatable raft on the water, headed out toward the large boat, and after a moment he could make out three people on the raft. His heart was filled with relief, even as Soh's men continued to pepper the water around him.

The tide had come in, and the *Citacea* was in six feet of water, around thirty yards offshore. He would have to swim for it, he knew. He didn't know whether he had the strength left to make it, but he decided that it was worth a try. In any event, he preferred the prospect of drowning over capture by Soh's men.

He eased out into the water, and began the long swim.

"Did Cormack make it back?"

Cicero shouted the question to Skip Olney as he and Buddy helped Diamond onto the *Citacea*.

"Where is he?" Cicero demanded again as he and Buddy climbed aboard.

"Isn't he with you?" Olney asked, confused.

Cicero shook his head. "He went around to the north to draw their attention. He's supposed to meet us here!"

"He's not here yet," Olney said. "We can't stay here. We're completely exposed."

Olney had barely finished the sentence when they heard shouting from the shore. Looking back up toward the southeast entrance, they could see a steady stream of men burst out onto the hill. They were shouting and running toward the shore—toward the *Citacea*—guns drawn.

"Shit!" Olney yelled. "We've got to get out of here!"

Buddy looked north and saw additional MS-13 soldiers running along the edge of the water. They were shooting, and at first Buddy thought they were targeting the boat, but then he saw the splashes where the bullets were hitting the water, halfway between the shore to the north and the *Citacea*. He searched the water until he saw him.

"There he is!" Buddy shouted.

The other three on the boat looked out and saw the dark spot in the water, like the hump of the Loch Ness Monster, arms laboriously slapping the surface in an attempt to swim.

The first shots hit the bow a moment later. The hull shuddered, and Buddy wondered whether the rounds could pierce the carbon fiber and sink them.

"We've got to leave!" Olney shouted, scrambling to the flying bridge.

"We're not leaving my father!" Diamond yelled. They were the first words she'd managed since the cell.

"Too late, we gotta go!" Olney shouted. More gunshots rang out, and Olney revved the *Citacea*'s engines. Cicero scrambled up to the flying bridge. From there, he had a good look at the two groups of Soh's men on the shore; one shooting at the *Citacea,* and the other taking aim at Cormack.

"We're going to pick him up!" Cicero shouted at Olney.

Olney shook his head. "We can't do it!" he said. "We draw five feet, and the water he's in is too shallow! We'll run aground!"

"We're going to pick him up," Cicero said again. "I don't care how shallow the water is." He pushed Olney aside and took control of the boat. Olney considered pushing back, but realized to do so would put him in graver danger than dealing with the gunshots coming from the shore. "Get down on the deck and help pull him in!" Cicero ordered. Olney paused for only a second before he headed back down the ladder.

"This is insane," he said to Buddy and Diamond.

"We're not leaving my father," Diamond repeated simply.

Gunshots rang out again, and the three of them fell to their knees to take shelter. "We're gonna be killed!" Olney shouted.

"Maybe," Buddy agreed. "But they're right, we're not leaving Cormack behind." He poked his head up above the side of the boat. "He's about twenty yards to port!" he shouted up to Cicero at the helm.

"I've got him!" Cicero responded. "They're getting closer to him! I'm gonna swing in between him and the shore to cut them off! Get to the stern and get ready to pull him on board!"

Cicero gunned the engines, and the *Citacea* shot forward. Buddy scrambled to the rear of the boat, keeping his eyes on Cormack.

The *Citacea* closed the distance quickly, which was fortunate. Cicero could see that two of the MS-13 soldiers had left the land and were moving quickly into the water to try to catch Cormack. He steered the boat in between the men and Cormack.

They hit the rocks when they were still ten yards from him. Both sets of Soh's men were now firing at the boat, and the vessel lurched and groaned as it scraped over the harbor's bottom.

"You're gonna sink us!" Olney screamed. It was to no effect. Cicero leaned on the throttle, pushing the boat forward over the rocks.

"He's here!" Buddy shouted. He reached over the starboard gunwale and grabbed Cormack's arm. Bullets pelted the port side of the boat, which faced the shoreline. Olney reached over with Buddy and the two of them hauled him on board. "We got him!" Buddy hollered. "Get us out of here!"

The two who had entered the water to try to catch Cormack were almost at the *Citacea*. They swam around the stern to try to get on board just as Cicero threw the throttle into reverse. The boat lurched and bucked, hung up on the rocks, struggling to free itself.

"You're gonna rip the hull apart!" Olney screamed.

Cicero floored the engine in reverse and the *Citacea* gave one great lurch and then bumped backward over the shallows. Soh's men were floundering behind the boat, and they screamed in unison as the propellers shredded them, leaving them as chum in the water.

The gunfire continued, and Buddy, Diamond, Cormack, and Olney lay flat on the stern deck. Cormack slid his body over toward Diamond. "Are you OK?" he asked her through chattering teeth. "Did they hurt you?"

She shook her head. "Are you OK?" she asked back.

He nodded.

"Are you shot?" Buddy asked him.

"I don't think so," Cormack responded. "But I can't feel much at the moment, so we'll have to wait and see."

Cicero had pulled the *Citacea* free from the harbor floor, and had turned the boat around. He pushed the throttle forward again, and the boat picked up speed as it pulled away from Long Island. There was still gunfire behind them, but fewer and fewer shots came anywhere near the boat.

Olney hurried up the ladder to the flying bridge. "Let me take over," he said to Cicero. Cicero relented. Olney handed him a flashlight. "Downstairs, in the hallway between the staterooms, there's a hatch that gives access to the hull. Go take a look," Olney instructed him. "We need to see whether the hull's been breached. If so, she could go down quickly, and we're all fucked." Cicero gave Olney an angry look, but headed down.

Buddy and Diamond were helping Cormack down into the salon, where it was warm. Diamond stripped off his gloves and worked to untie his boots. They were caked with ice, and it took a few minutes to make progress. Cicero went down the stairs toward the staterooms. He found the hatch and pulled it up. He switched the flashlight on and aimed it around the hold below the hatch. He could see the interior of the hull and couldn't see any water in there.

He pulled his head out, closed the hatch and headed back up to the salon. "Doesn't look like we're going to sink," he said to Cormack. "You should get out of these clothes."

"In a minute," Cormack said. "Go back up and tell Skip to head south as fast as he can."

"South?"

"Soh's got a boat on the northwest side of Long Island. If we come around the tip and head back north toward the city, he may be able to cut us off. If we head south to Weymouth, we can make it there before Soh could find us on the water. The harbormaster there can give us a covered slip. He'll get us a car, too. It's the safest way."

Cicero nodded. "I'll let him know. You need to get out of that suit, though. Hypothermia will set in, if it hasn't already."

Cormack nodded. "I'll go down and get changed."

"There's a mirror," Cicero said. "Make sure you haven't been shot."

"I think I'd feel it by now," Cormack said.

"Maybe. Just make sure."

Cormack struggled to his feet and made his way to the stairs that led down to the staterooms. He took hold of the railing, but turned before he headed down. He looked at his daughter and gave her a weak smile. "The next time I tell you to stay at home, you better goddamned listen."

She nodded as a tear ran down her cheek. "I had to go to the doctor."

She looked hesitantly at Buddy. Cormack understood, and said, "You two have some things to discuss. I'll be downstairs." He nodded at his daughter. "When you're ready, we've got a fresh change of clothes for you, too, down here." He went down the stairs, leaving Buddy and Diamond alone.

"I have something I need to tell you," Diamond started, hesitantly.

"I know," Buddy said. "Your father already told me."

Diamond just looked at him, as though frightened to say anything. She was sitting on a chair, her arms pulled around her, still fighting off the cold. Buddy went over and knelt in front of her. He put his arms around her.

"I'm not asking for anything from you," Diamond said. The tears were flowing freely now. "This is my decision. So it's my responsibility. You're not on the hook."

"Don't worry," Buddy said, stroking her hair gently. "It will all be OK."

She buried her face in his chest. "Will it?"

He forced a smile. "It will. I promise."

She didn't smile back. He took her in his arms and kissed her, and she reciprocated. After a moment, she pulled away. "What's wrong?"

"You're suit's wet," she said. "And I feel gross."

"Go get changed. I'll be down in a second."

She nodded and stood up, rubbing her fingers through his hair as she separated from him. He stayed there on his knees for a moment, in silent prayer—for what, exactly, he wasn't entirely sure. Then he got to his feet and opened the door at the rear of the salon. He stepped back out onto the deck and watched the mainland shoreline stream by as the boat sped south.

A moment later Cormack stepped out onto the deck with him. "Things OK with the two of you?" he asked.

Buddy shrugged. "I think things are going to be all right, eventually. Better than all right, maybe. I hope." He looked at Cormack. "Are you good with that?"

Cormack shrugged. "It's not for me to judge. Besides, I've got bigger things to worry about."

"This thing with Soh isn't over, is it?" Buddy said.

"It's barely started," Cormack said.

Buddy looked uncomfortable. "You're gonna need help."

Cormack looked at him, frowning. He needed all the men he could get, he knew. Even one more might make the difference. "You've got responsibilities now."

Buddy nodded. "I do. But she's not gonna be safe if this thing isn't taken care of. Our child isn't gonna be safe."

"It's gonna get uglier. Are you prepared for that?"

"I did all right back out there, on the island."

"That's true, you did." Cormack sighed. He knew Buddy was right, but he also knew the risks. "If you fight this thing, and you die, Diamond will never forgive me."

"If I don't fight this thing, and you die, she'll never forgive *me,*" Buddy responded. "Your daughter could never love a coward." The boat was pulling into Weymouth Harbor, and Olney eased off the throttle. "Once we're through this, I'll make sure they're safe," Buddy said. "I can promise you that."

The boat slowed and eased its way forward. Cormack breathed in the cold air. "I understand how hard you'll try to keep that promise," he said. "But it's been my experience that there's no way to keep bad things from happening to the ones we love. In the end, that's up to God."

FIFTY-THREE

Special Agent Kit Steele was sitting at her desk at eight o'clock in the morning when her cell phone rang. She'd tried to sleep the night before, but it had been a futile exercise. She came into the office to keep busy and to try to quell her imagination. She was reading through all the information she had on Vincente Carpio, looking for anything she might have missed in the past. The attempt at distracting herself was only partially successful, though. Imaginations aren't always easy to silence, she'd learned over the years.

She picked up her cell phone, her heart racing as the caller ID registered. It was his number. She clicked on the call and waited.

"It's me," he said. She recognized Cormack O'Connell's voice, and she took a deep, grateful breath.

"How did it go?" she asked. They kept their phone conversations general as a precaution.

"I've had better nights," he said. "But I've had worse nights, too, so I guess it went as well as I could have expected."

"How's Diamond?"

"She's safe for now. That's all that matters."

"Just for now?"

"It's still a dangerous world out there," he said. "That hasn't changed."

"Too bad," she said.

"It is."

"Can we meet?"

"That might be difficult. Do you have information?"

"Nothing useful. It would still be good to meet, though." Steele kept her voice even, but she couldn't deny her need to see him again.

"OK," he said. "I'll try to figure something out. I'll let you know."

The line went dead, but she kept the phone to her ear for a moment, a part of her hoping to hear his voice again. Finally she put the phone back on top of her desk.

Her office phone rang, and she picked it up. "Steele here."

"It's Martin."

"Special Agent Martin," she said. "To what do I owe the pleasure?"

"I wish it was a pleasure," he said. "You told me that information would go both ways. It doesn't feel like that's a promise you're living up to."

"If I have information to give, my first phone call will be to you," she lied. "That's the best I can do."

"You sure about that?"

"You have my word." She marveled at how easily she was able to betray others in law enforcement at this point. It was for the greater good, though, she told herself.

"There was a war out on the harbor last night," Martin said. "You know anything about that?"

"No," she said. "What happened?"

"No one knows for sure. There was a series of explosions and gunfire out around Long Island. From our reports, it lasted for ten minutes or so. But it was late, and there were no boats at the ready, so it took a couple hours to get people over there to check it out. By then it was light, and everything was gone. It looks like someone was using Fort Strong as some sort of a hideout. No one's talking along the waterfront, though. You sure you haven't heard anything?"

"Like I said," Kit reassured him, "if I hear anything, you'll be the first to know."

"I hope so," Martin said. "This feels like it's getting out of control." Steele remained silent. "When is Carpio due in court?"

"Next Wednesday," Kit said. The word seemed to stick in her throat.

"One week," Martin said. "Not much time."

"Not much time," Kit agreed.

"OK," Martin relented. "If you need any help making sure you've got all the bases covered, let me know."

"Will do," Kit said. Martin hung up, and Kit lingered with the phone against her ear. In her heart she knew that one week wasn't nearly enough time to make sure all the bases were covered, no matter how much help she had.

FIFTY-FOUR

Saturday, February 9

"The police will bring him in through here."

Javier Carpio was leaning over a table in the back room of a garage near the harbor in Charlestown, speaking to T'phong Soh and his men. The room was far more cramped than the space at the Eastie warehouse, but Soh was determined to move to a new location every day. Cormack O'Connell's successful raid at Fort Strong served as a reminder that the Irishman's information network along the water could not be challenged. Soh had been overconfident. He'd been stupid. He'd had the advantage, and now he'd lost it. He was angry, but there was nothing to do about it. Now he had to focus on the plan to help Vincente Carpio escape from custody. Javier and his brother had offered Soh the opportunity to take over a large portion of the drug trade in the United States. If they were able to break Carpio free, they would conclude their bargain and Cormack O'Connell would no longer be an issue—Soh would be able to crush him in a matter of months, and then he could start the process of putting in place his own power base in the harbor. He would have unlimited funds and nearly unlimited power—as long as he could keep O'Connell from interfering in the next few days. The union head's network was still tied in, and he could still pose a threat to the plans to spring Vincente Carpio—Javier had made it clear that there would be no agreement as long as his brother was in the hands of the American authorities.

There were a dozen men around the table, and they were looking at maps of the waterfront. As Soh considered the strategic options, he realized that he might have been overly optimistic in his ability to break Vincente Carpio from U.S. custody. In reality, the chances of getting through the security at the courthouse were extremely low.

"Courthouse Way," Soh said, following Carpio's finger on the map. It was a one block dead-end lane that led to the back of the courthouse and the edge of Boston Harbor. "They'll have the courthouse surrounded," he pointed out.

Javier nodded. "They will. But the lawyer says they will focus on the area along Northern Avenue, where the cars will turn onto Courthouse Way, and where there will most likely be crowds of people."

"Once he is through that point, it will be impossible to get him away. Even if we could get to him, we would have to fight back out Courthouse Way to Northern Avenue, where most of the police will be," Soh pointed out. "We have to get to him before that." He looked at the map and considered the streets leading to the courthouse. "Does the lawyer know which direction they will come down Northern Avenue? From the north or the south?"

Javier nodded. "From the north."

"Do we know what time they will bring him?" Soh asked.

"The hearing is scheduled for two o'clock. The lawyer says that they will arrive at the courthouse before noon."

Soh examined the maps, looking for a weakness—a flaw in the defenses that they could exploit—but he could see nothing.

It was Javier who stated the obvious. "We must attack on Northern Avenue. In front of the courthouse, as they slow down to turn."

Soh considered that for a moment before shaking his head. "It will be suicide."

"There will be a crowd. We can use them as a distraction," Javier persisted.

That was true, but Soh wasn't convinced. "I still don't like it," he said.

"Do you have a better plan?" Javier asked.

Soh did not, and they both knew it.

"We will need men," Javier continued. "They will need to be armed. Can you see to it?"

Soh nodded. He saw no other option. He wanted to point out that a plan to try to free Vincente Carpio was madness, but the lure of the riches the Carpios could provide if they were successful was too tempting to pass up. More than that, Soh knew that if he backed off now, Cormack O'Connell would come for him—and without the riches that the drug routes would provide, it was more than likely that Soh would be dead in a matter of weeks. "I will make sure we are prepared," he said.

Javier nodded and left the room. In dribs and drabs Soh's men drifted away, until Soh was left only with Juan Suarez standing by his side, looking over the maps on the table. They could both sense the trepidation in their men as they melted into the larger spaces of the garage.

"You are troubled," the loyal lieutenant noted.

Soh nodded slowly.

"But there is no better plan."

Soh nodded again. "Not one that we can see. But Javier Carpio must know that this plan is suicide. And he would not sacrifice his brother."

"I don't understand," Suarez admitted.

"There is something that he is keeping from us. Some part of the plan that he is keeping to himself."

Suarez considered this for a moment. "That is not all that is troubling you, is it?"

Soh shook his head.

"What else?"

Soh looked at Suarez. The bruises from the man's mistreatment at the hands of Cormack O'Connell's men were still prominent on his face. "I have heard rumors about arms being brought to harbor," Soh said. "Very dangerous arms. I must find out whether there is anything to them."

FIFTY-FIVE

Diamond O'Connell lay in her bed in Cormack's house, curled up on her side. Buddy was wrapped around her, one arm tucked under her head, the other heavy on her shoulder and arm. It felt good. Not good enough to wipe away the terror of the past few days, but better than she ever thought she'd be able to feel again.

His arm moved, and she felt his hand caress down her chest toward her abdomen. At first she thought he was trying to entice her. That would have been his style, she thought. He had always been driven by his sexual attraction to her. Truth be told, she had always been the same with him, so she had trouble faulting him—though she also knew that she wasn't ready yet. Not after what she'd been through.

She was about to warn him off, gently, when his hand's southerly journey stopped. He rested his palm on her belly, rubbing gently in a circle. The gentleness of his touch felt wonderfully intimate, and it took a moment before she realized what he was doing.

He's rubbing the baby.

The thought made her heart throb. Could it be that he was genuinely happy about the prospect of being a father? It seemed almost impossible. She'd known that he was a certain type of man when she had taken up with him, and she was too streetwise to believe that people change. Not really.

And yet there was always a chance, she was beginning to think, that she'd been wrong about him. That possibility brought with it a flood of contradictory emotions. She was thrilled at the notion that she might actually have a love and a partner in her life, but the thought of relying on someone—counting on them as she set expectations for what her life would be—terrified her. She had spent her life relying solely on herself, never expecting anything from anyone else. She loved Mack, and they had developed a comfortable level of interaction and trust, but it had never risen to the level of reliance on her part, and she suspected it never would. Particularly now that she had a better understanding of how dangerous and illicit his business was, she would never put her future in his hands.

Now, for just a moment, she felt as though there might be something more to life than a lonely existence of self-protection. And the rational, protective part of her brain rebelled against such a notion.

She rolled over and looked Buddy in the eyes. They were so close together that his face was a blur.

"What?" he asked.

"You're going to help my father, aren't you," she said. It wasn't a question, and she could see how uncomfortable he was with the fact that she knew his mind so well.

"I have to," he said. "It's the only way I can be sure that you'll be safe. That the baby will be safe."

"And when this is over?" she asked. "If you survive, where do we go then?"

It was clear that he hadn't really thought that far ahead, and the question took him by surprise. "I don't understand," he said.

"I mean, what do we do after? Are you going to get a real job? I mean a legitimate job. Are you going to settle down and get out of the game? That won't happen if you're working at the harbor."

He sat up in bed, and looked down at her. "I don't know," he said. "I've always been a hustler. I'll always be yours, though."

"That's it?" she asked. "That's all you can promise? You can't at least sit there and tell me that you'll try to get out, that you'll try to make a normal life for me and our baby?"

He thought about that for a moment. "No," he said at last. "I can't tell you that. The reality is that I like the life. I like the risk and I like the excitement. It's a part of who I am."

"Good," she said.

"Good?"

"Yeah, good." She could see the confusion on his face. "I'd rather have you be honest with me," she told him. "Maybe I've got too much of my mother and my father in me, but I like the excitement, too. It's just as much a part of me as it is of you."

"Even after the past few days?" he asked.

"The past few days were awful," she admitted. "I was afraid for my own life and the baby's life. I knew if I made it through that and the baby survived, this was meant to be. Besides, how many girls get to have the man of their dreams come to their rescue the way you did? I've never wanted to change you. I just need to know that you're not walking away from me."

He leaned over and kissed her, passionately. "I'll never walk away from you," he said. "Like I said, I love you."

"I love you, too." She hugged him tightly.

FIFTY-SIX

Sunday, February 10

Javier Carpio stood before the men he'd fought with in wars that went back further in time than any of them cared to admit. They were in the deserted Chelsea warehouse. He'd laid out the plan, and they'd followed the logic, but they knew that the likelihood that they would all walk away from the mission alive was low. Still, that had been true of every military operation they'd undertaken, and yet they were still alive. Enemies and comrades had fallen in numbers that were too great to comprehend, but Javier and his close cadre were still breathing. It gave them a sense of invulnerability.

The two Stinger missiles were laid out on the table in front of them. Only two of the men would be handling them, but they all trained with them, so that if one went down there would be another to step up and take his place.

"There will be chaos," one of the men commented.

Javier nodded. "That is what we need. Without it, there is no way that Vincente will be able to get to us."

"Our inside man is trustworthy?"

"As trustworthy as a man can be who is betraying who he is supposed to be."

That seemed to be enough for the men. They continued to go over the plan for another half hour, and then the five soldiers left the warehouse, one at a time, staggered to avoid attracting attention.

Javier was now alone, sitting at the table, staring at the missile launchers before him. He thought back to the time when he'd taken responsibility for his younger brother. Javier himself had only been in his teens, and yet he'd already been hardened by war. He'd taught Vincente to survive, and trained him well. His brother hadn't spoken for more than two years after witnessing their mother's murder, but he'd made a quick study of the art of killing. Javier wondered whether his brother would have turned out differently if he hadn't brought him into the war. Probably. But there was nothing he could do about that now. Now all he could do was make sure Vincente didn't spend the rest of his life in an American jail cell. He couldn't let that happen. They would both rather be dead.

His eyes were closed when he heard the door open behind him. At first he assumed that one of the soldiers had forgotten something. They each locked the door as they left, and only they had keys. He turned to find out which of his men had come back and why.

T'phong Soh stood just inside the door, looking at Javier with sharp eyes. Those eyes went from Javier's face to the Stinger missile launcher on the table. "I heard rumors about such weapons in Boston," Soh said.

Javier looked at the launchers on the table and cursed himself for not putting them away. He looked back at Soh, staying silent.

"I find it strange that you have not mentioned that you had these weapons," Soh continued.

"Have I not?" Javier asked, as though it could simply have been an oversight.

"No, you have not," Soh said. He pulled his hand out of his pocket and Javier saw that he was holding a knife.

Javier stood up. He towered over the diminutive Malaysian. He took a step toward him, his fists clenched like sledgehammers. "You come here with a knife as though you can threaten me?" Javier said, the threat clear in his voice.

"I am not threatening you," Soh said. "I came only to get information. What is it that you are planning? Are you going to sacrifice me and my men?"

"My plans for these weapons is not your concern," Javier said.

"No?" Soh circled wide, holding his knife casually at his side. "I have also heard about the sale of military boats. The rumor is that those were sold as a package with missiles like these. I suppose that is also not my concern?"

"Idle gossip should never be a concern," Javier said.

"I will not help you if you do not tell me what you are planning. All of it," Soh said.

"Then our agreement is off," Javier said. "And you will not have control over the shipments my people can arrange."

"And your brother will die in an American prison."

Javier knew it was true, and the thought enraged him. He screamed in anger and took two steps toward Soh, swinging his fist. His anger made him careless, though, and the smaller man easily ducked the blow. Javier felt the blade slide across his side. Soh moved away, out of range, and Javier put a hand to the wound. He blood ran warm over his fingers, but he could tell it was superficial.

"I do not want to kill you," Soh said. "I want to help you. But I cannot do that if I do not know what the full plan is."

Javier weighed his options. There seemed to be few. "How do I know that I can trust you?" he asked.

"How do you know you cannot?"

Javier thought about this for a moment. "You saw the men who were here before you came in?" he asked.

"I did."

"They have the devil in them. As I do. As my brother does. As do many of us who fought and bled together in my country. They cannot be killed. And if you betray me, they will come for you. Do you understand?"

Soh nodded.

"A frontal attack will not work. There is no way for my brother to escape—nowhere for him to go." He nodded toward the missiles. "But if the attack is violent enough, it may provide enough of a distraction. Then there might be another way."

"Tell me."

"You will help me? No matter what? Even if it means sacrificing some of your men?"

"My men are expendable," Soh said. "I will help you."

In the end, though, Javier knew that Soh would only help himself. If that meant advancing the Carpios' plans, he would be all right with that. But Javier had no illusions about Soh's self-interest. If they aligned with those of the Carpios, that was fine; if not, he would make other arrangements. "Then I will tell you my entire plan," Carpio said.

When Carpio was finished laying out what he was intending, Soh had to admit that it made sense, and it might just work. He realized, though, that there was a piece missing. "There is one thing that you have not considered," he said to Carpio.

"What is that?"

"Cormack O'Connell is still alive. It is likely that he will hear rumors of this plan, and he could still ruin our efforts."

"Then he must be killed."

Soh shook his head. "He is waiting for a direct attack. He is expecting that."

"How can we keep him from causing a problem, then?"

Soh considered the options silently for a moment. "There is a rumor that O'Connell has worked with the FBI in the past. A woman. We call her the Hunter. She is in charge of the efforts to disrupt our organization. Perhaps she can help us?"

"Why would she?"

"If she believes that she is acting to prevent your brother from escaping, she will do almost anything. We may be able to use that to occupy O'Connell and create misdirection at the same time."

"Do you think that will work?"

Soh shrugged. "She is obsessed with keeping your brother in prison. If we can convince her that she will accomplish that, it may work."

"Where is he?"

Cormack asked the question, though it wasn't clear to whom it was directed. There were a dozen men in the room at the back of the fish market. Cicero Andolini offered the obvious answer. "He's disappeared."

“He can’t just fuckin’ disappear,” Cormack stormed. “He’s not a goddamned ghost.”

“No, he’s not,” Cicero agreed. “But he’s doing a good impression of one. We’ve got men shaking the bushes all along the waterfront, and they ain’t finding any sign of him. He’s not using any of his usual spots. I even sent one of my guys back to Fort Strong, but they must’ve cleared out of there as soon as we hit the place.”

“The place in Eastie . . . ?”

Cicero shook his head. “Picked clean. Nothing there.”

“What about Suarez?”

“He’s gone, too. I’ve got someone looking in on the rooming house he stays at, but he hasn’t been back there.”

“What the fuck are they up to?” Cormack wondered aloud.

“One thing it doesn’t look like they’re up to,” Cicero commented, “is coming after us. No one’s heard a peep. It looks like they’ve got other things on their minds.”

“That’s what makes me worried. If they’re done mucking around with us, it means they’ve got something serious that they’re planning. We’ve got to find them and take them out.”

Cicero nodded. “Just as soon as we figure out where they are. What do you want to do now, Boss?”

“We need to find a way to draw him out,” Cormack answered.

“Easy enough said,” Cicero pointed out. “Who are you gonna use for bait?”

“I’m the only one he’s really interested in,” Cormack said. “I’m the only one he’d stick his head up for.”

Cicero raised his eyebrows. “You sure you wanna do that, Boss? You know that there’s no way we can guarantee your safety. We might be able to get him, but it might be after you’re already dead.”

“I know,” Cormack said. “You got any better plan?”

FIFTY-SEVEN

Monday, February 11

Joshua Brooks was grateful that he wasn't a religious man. A religious man would fear for his salvation. This wasn't the first time he had bent the rules or advanced the interests of an individual he knew to be evil. In many ways, that was the role of a defense lawyer. He'd always been able to rationalize it. He was a necessary component of what he regarded as the greatest system of justice in the world. Defense lawyers have the duty to protect their clients, not to judge them. And Brooks knew that police and prosecutors didn't always play by the rules either. If the system was to be truly fair, defendants needed lawyers on their side who would fight as hard as the prosecutors did. It was, he'd often told himself, a sacred trust he owed to those he represented.

Except that now, he found himself questioning whether he'd bent the rules too far in this case. Vincente Carpio wasn't just some drug dealer or gang kingpin trying to game the system. He was a psychopath who wanted to kill for the sake of killing—and that was difficult to justify, even for a defense lawyer.

He'd told Javier to meet him at a rest area on the northbound side of Interstate 195. Vincente's arraignment was only a few days away, and the younger Carpio had made clear that Brooks had to pass one last message on to Javier. Brooks had no idea what the messages meant, but he had little doubt that the information was illicit, and probably put people in danger.

He saw Javier parked in a spot at the far end of the parking lot at the rest area. He pulled alongside and rolled down his window. The cold invaded the car.

"Your brother sends his greetings," he said after Javier had rolled down his window.

"What else does he send?"

"A message. He says he is ready." Brooks paused, considering for a moment the possibility that he would not deliver the message faithfully. He knew that he had no choice, though.

Javier nodded. "You delivered my message?" he asked. "You told him our eastern friend is with us?"

Brooks nodded. He didn't understand the code, but he didn't like the sound of any of it. "I gave him that message," Brooks said. "He said he understands."

Javier stared into Brooks's eyes for a moment, as though searching for some sign of deception. He wouldn't find any, though, Brooks knew. He was relaying the messages faithfully. It might cost him his soul, but he had memorized the phrasing and delivered the words with precision.

Javier rolled up his window, backed out of his parking spot, and pulled out of the rest area.

Brooks sat in his car for a moment, wondering what series of events he had just set in motion; wondering whether people would die as a result, and whether he would be able to live with himself if they did. The window was still rolled down, and it was colder outside than he could ever remember. And yet, as he caught his reflection in the rearview mirror, he saw sweat trickling down his temple.

It was nearing midnight as Kit pulled to the curb in the heart of East Boston's Latino neighborhood. During the summer, the place would have been alive with passion. The outdoor music and revelry would have been deafening, but at the moment the place was frozen solid, like the rest of Boston. It was as though the cold had slowed the blood in everyone's veins, and movement itself had become difficult. Everything felt thick and sluggish.

It was foolish of her to be there, she knew. No, not foolish. Foolish didn't capture it. It was asinine for her to be there. It was dangerous for her to be there. It was possibly criminal for her to be there. She'd considered calling someone for backup. She could have reached out to Agent Martin, but she couldn't trust him. It wasn't because she thought he was bent, it was that she was confident that he wasn't—and she was. As a result, she couldn't involve him without risking all of her transgressions coming to light. She didn't care about being caught, but she couldn't live with the possibility that her work would be undone, and that Vincente Carpio might slip through their fingers again.

She walked into the Colombian restaurant on the narrow corner where Bennington Street intersected with Chelsea Street. The cold wind blew in with her, and everyone in the place turned to look. None of the faces were friendly. They regarded her with suspicion and hostility. She stood there, looking at them. After a moment, they went back to their business, but quietly. There was an interloper among them now, and the talk came in whispers. She could hear numerous languages being spoken, none of them English. Spanish was dominant, but she could hear Vietnamese and Eastern European cadences as well.

A young man approached her. His skin had the tan glow of a South American, and his hair was unruly. He had an elaborate tattoo of a cross on his forehead. A snake wound around the cross as though to strangle it. Two "13"s were incorporated into jewels at the top and the bottom of the cross. His eyes seemed dead as they regarded her.

"In back," he said to her.

"I sent word, only in a public place," she responded.

The young man's eyes turned angry and confused. He started to sputter in Spanish and gesture for her to move to the back of the restaurant, toward a door.

"I said only in public," she repeated, more forcefully this time. He didn't speak English, though, and her intransigence was angering him.

He began to push her, and leaned in close to her face as he jabbered at her in Spanish. She whiffed the chemical stench given off by meth addicts, and she could see the gaps in the young man's mouth where teeth should have been. His voice was raised, and the patrons in the restaurant had grown quiet at the commotion. Steele noticed that none of them looked directly at her. They looked straight down at their drinks and their food, and they refused to acknowledge what was happening.

Her hand was in her bag, touching her gun. The wise move would have been to leave right then. She was still close to the door, and there was no question that she could have been out of the place and speeding away before anyone could react. That was what she should have done.

But she couldn't bring herself to take the wise path. She'd been promised information, and she couldn't pass on the possibility that it was a genuine offer. Besides, they would have to be crazy to kill a federal agent, wouldn't they?

She slipped her hand off her gun and out of her bag as she allowed herself to be pushed toward the door at the back of the restaurant. As she made her way through the tables, not one patron looked up at her.

Something was wrong.

Cormack could feel it deep down in his marrow as he sat in his office, looking out at the harbor. Events had not played out as they were supposed to. For the best part of two days he'd telegraphed where he was going to be at various times. He made sure that there were plausible reasons for his whereabouts to become known throughout the waterfront community. He'd had Toby set up a union meeting, where the rank and file needed to be reassured that he was still in control. That would have been a prime opportunity for Soh to try something.

At that meeting, he'd let it be known that he would be visiting the Customs Office later that afternoon to press for reforms that would ease the workload for stevedores who were charged with keeping count of containers and tonnage removed from ships in the harbor. It was the view of the union that there should be a separate position for such monitoring. This would result in less work and more jobs controlled by the union. Again, when he visited the Customs Office, he'd been as exposed as he would ever be.

And yet Soh never took the bait.

It was possible that Soh had suspected that each opportunity was a trap—which they were, though imperfect traps that still left Cormack vulnerable. Cormack could have as many eyes as he wanted watching him, but a single bullet would still end his life, and make Soh's path to power free from any impediment. It was hard to believe that Soh had resisted the urge to have Cormack taken out, particularly when he'd already taken greater risks to do just that. It didn't make sense.

"Maybe one of his own men killed him," Cicero proffered an answer to the silent questions he knew Cormack was asking.

Cormack shook his head. "If someone had killed him, they'd make it be known. They'd be feeling around for a reward of some kind from me if they'd done me that sort of favor."

"Maybe he's given up on his ambition."

Cormack shot Cicero a look. They both knew that wasn't a possibility. "There's only one answer," Cormack said.

"Which is?"

"He doesn't think I matter anymore. He thinks he's found a better way to neutralize me and make sure I don't fuck up his plans."

"How can he neutralize you without killing you?"

It was eleven forty-five, and Cormack stared out at the dark harbor. No ships were moving; the water was still. Ice caps congregated along the shoreline, and the city skyline had dimmed. "I don't know," he said. "But I need to find out."

FIFTY-EIGHT

The room was behind the kitchen. It was hot, and the smell from the cooking was overwhelming. Chicken and beef and chorizo simmered and the aromas made Kit Steele feel light-headed.

She'd seen pictures of T'phong Soh before, but she'd never met him in person. She was struck by how small he was. It wasn't just that he was short, but he was slight as well. He was wearing a sweatshirt that seemed to swallow him whole. And yet she could see the veins under the tattoos on his arms.

He regarded her the way a lion regards prey—sizing her up with an evaluative eye and a touch of indifference. She had no sense that he felt she was a threat to him in any way. It seemed as though he was trying to decide whether she was worth his time.

"Thank you," he said after a moment.

She frowned. "For what?"

"For agreeing to see me." His English was perfect, but his accent was so thick it was a challenge to understand him.

There were three others in the room. Kit recognized Juan Suarez from pictures in the FBI's files on MS-13, though it looked like he'd had a rough week. The bruises on his face were deep purple, and the cut on his forehead was prominent. The other two were unknown to her, but they were covered with similar tattoos that adorned Soh up to his chin, and they both held automatic assault rifles.

"I was told you had information regarding Javier Carpio and an attempt that he will make to free his brother."

"I do," Soh said simply. "Would you like that information?"

"If it's accurate."

"My information is always accurate."

"How can you be sure?"

Soh hesitated for only a moment. "Because he has asked me to help him with the plan." He continued to look at her, gauging her reaction, and she wondered what he could see in her face. She'd always been a good poker player, and she prided herself on the ability to keep her emotions to herself, but she could feel her heart beating faster at the prospect of turning Soh into an asset, and making sure that Vincente Carpio never saw freedom again.

"Why would he ask you for that kind of help?" she asked, feigning doubt. She knew that Soh had been working with the Carpios, and there was no question in her mind that they would have involved Soh in any escape attempt. The only question was whether his offer to provide her with information was genuine.

"He has offered me certain . . . contacts that could be profitable for me in exchange for my help," Soh said slowly. He spoke slowly, so that Steele would understand him, even through his accent. "I admit that I have been tempted by his offer."

Tempted was an understatement, she knew. The intel on Soh made clear that he was active in the drug trade. There was no question that contacts from Javier Carpio would be priceless to Soh. "But . . . ?" Steele prodded him to continue.

"But I am not comfortable with these men," Soh said. "Vincente Carpio is not sane. And Javier is not trustworthy."

"No?" Steele took a step backward and leaned against the wall. The heat and the dense aroma from the kitchen were overwhelming. She was tempted to take off her jacket, but to do so would involve putting her bag down, and she wanted to make sure that her gun was readily available. She knew that it was pointless—there was no doubt that if violence erupted, her pistol would be of no use against the automatic weapons held by Soh's men. Still, she couldn't bear the notion of being completely unarmed. "I thought there was a code of honor among those in MS-13."

Soh smiled at this, and she could see that most of his teeth were gold. "I am committed to the organization, as long as it is committed to me," he said. "The Carpios are committed only to themselves." He took a step toward her. He seemed to get larger, and the room smaller. She leaned back farther into the wall behind her. "They are willing to put their interests ahead of my interests, as well as those of the organization."

"Just as you put your interests above theirs and those of your organization?"

He smiled again. "I believe that the organization needs to adapt. I believe that the organization needs allies—including allies in law enforcement."

"So you would give me this information out of the goodness of your heart?" she asked, and tilted her head. "That seems very generous of you."

The menacing smile remained on his face, and the gleam from his teeth was dizzying. "Not out of the goodness in my heart," he said. The way he said it made Kit wonder whether there *was* any goodness in the man's heart. "I would give you this information in exchange for your help."

"How could I help you?"

"There are rumors that Cormack O'Connell is protected by someone in the federal police," he said. "Have you heard these rumors?"

Kit shook her head slowly.

"No?" Soh tilted his head at her and she could feel his gaze crawling across her face, examining her, probing her for the truth. "You know that it has happened in the past, though?"

"It has," she admitted. The FBI's protection of Whitey Bulger and the Winter Hill Gang was well known.

"Perhaps it could happen again. You and I could have a partnership that could help both of us. I could give you information about people like Vincente Carpio, and you could give me information about police activities that might be important to me. Would that be something you would consider?"

Kit looked around the room. The two men with the automatic weapons shifted, and she wondered whether they understood English. They could kill her instantly if she refused, she knew. It would be risky for Soh to so brazenly kill a federal officer, but he struck Steele as a man who was not afraid of taking significant risks.

"You say that the Carpios are planning an escape?" she asked. Ultimately, that was the main question on her mind. No matter what, she would not allow him to be free again.

"Does that mean that you agree?"

"If you have information like that, then we may be able to work together."

That was it. For her, it was like a thunderclap. She'd crossed the threshold, and there was no going back now. She'd lost her innocence a long time ago, and she'd never deceived herself about that. But until now, she could fool herself that she was only a little corrupt. If she worked with Soh, she could no longer pretend to be that. She could only hope that the information Soh had was worth it. If it kept Carpio from escaping, in her mind it was.

"There is one more thing," Soh said.

"Yes?"

"Cormack O'Connell," he said.

"What about him?"

"He is a thorn in my side. If I am to help you with the Carpios, I will need you to keep him from interfering. He wants to kill me, and I cannot help you if he is successful."

"What is it, exactly, that you want me to do?"

"I leave that to you," Soh said. "But if we are to have an agreement, you will have to choose between me and him. That is the only way this can work."

She knew he was right. She knew that she had to make a choice. Her heart told her that trusting this man was a mistake. She also couldn't stomach the notion of betraying Cormack. They had been through so much together. They'd helped each other, and she'd begun to feel things that she hadn't felt in a long time.

And yet Cormack couldn't help her ensure that Vincente Carpio would stay behind bars, and this little Malaysian man could. He was still looking at her as she considered his offer. His gaze was intense, and the thought occurred to her again that if she rejected his offer, he might have her killed on the spot. Perhaps that would be the easiest way out.

Perhaps that would end her pain once and for all, and reunite her with her husband and son. She opened her mouth, still not entirely sure what she was going to say.

"I can take care of O'Connell," was what came out. She could hardly believe the words, even as she said them.

FIFTY-NINE

Tuesday, February 12

Diamond stood over the stove in her father's kitchen, staring at the egg in her hand and the pan heating up on the burner, wondering whether she could bring herself to do it. She needed to eat; she was famished. She'd put almost nothing in her stomach since she'd been freed from Fort Strong, and she was starting to feel weak. And yet, as she stood there, looking at the egg, the thought of cracking it and watching it cook made her feel nauseous.

Some of it was morning sickness. She'd already vomited twice that morning. It was a singularly unpleasant experience for her, particularly because there was nothing in her stomach, so the process was more of a forced pantomime. She'd knelt over the toilet, mouth stretched open, convulsing as a thin trickle of spit ran to the edge of the bowl.

She was also worried about Buddy and Cormack. She understood that they were locked in a battle against T'phong Soh and his crew, and Diamond had witnessed firsthand the brutality with which Soh operated. Buddy hadn't tried to minimize the dangers, and the reality that their lives were at risk petrified her.

She was so lost in her thoughts, she didn't hear her father enter the room. It startled her when he touched her shoulder. She gave a sharp gasp and pulled away instinctively.

"I'm sorry," he said. He seemed almost as startled as she'd been. "I didn't mean to scare you."

She shook her head. "No, it's OK," she said. "I was just a little preoccupied. I didn't hear you come in."

"You've got a lot on your mind, I'm sure."

"You too, I'm guessing."

"Did I hear Buddy leaving your room this morning?" Diamond shot him a look but said nothing. "None of my business. I suppose I'll just have to get used to that. He's actually not a bad kid, from what I can tell."

"Are you giving me your blessing?"

He shook his head. "It's not my place to bless anything. I'm just saying if you really love him, you could do worse." He nodded, and held his hand out to take the egg from her. "Here, let me do that for you."

"I can do it," she protested. She didn't like the idea of relying on anyone—for anything.

"No, you can't."

"What does that mean?" she demanded.

He gave an amused laugh. "I'm not challenging your right to make breakfast," he said. "But you won't be able to eat anything you cook right now. Your mother was the same way when she was first pregnant with you. Hungry all the time, but the act of cooking made her sick. She was in the bathroom so often, I thought she was using again. We had fights about that."

"Oh." Suddenly the thought of someone cooking for her was enticing. "I didn't know that. Thanks." She relinquished her grip on the egg and took a seat at the kitchen table. She watched him deftly prepare scrambled eggs. He didn't stop with the one she had—he cracked an additional three and added milk, whipped them up, and added some onions and cheese. She was amazed at his domesticity. Her nausea eased. "I forgot you liked to cook," she said.

"I used to cook for you," he reminded her.

"You did," she admitted. "I remember that now. I remember because Mom never did, so when I moved in with you, that was a new experience." She leaned back in her chair, and felt more relaxed than she had in what felt like a millennium. "You haven't done it in a while, though."

He looked over his shoulder at her. "You haven't been around during the evenings in a while."

Was there reproach in his tone? "Neither have you," she parried.

"Fair enough," he conceded.

She decided it was best to leave it there. As she sat at the table, the aroma of the onions frying with the eggs smelled delicious. She wondered whether this might be the last time that they would enjoy a simple meal like this. "What was it that didn't work between you and her?" she asked. Her mother was a topic they most often avoided, but it occurred to her that she might never have the opportunity to ask these kinds of questions again.

He grunted. "You were the only thing that worked with us. And even that was a struggle."

"I'm serious."

"I am, too." Cormack scooped the eggs onto two plates and gave the plate with the larger portion to Diamond. He sat down next to her as she started eating. "I loved your mother, but she made it hard. She was a free spirit. She drank, she did drugs, she wouldn't let anyone tie her down."

"Would you have let her tie you down if she'd been willing?"

He smiled at the prescience of his daughter's question. "I don't know," he said. "Probably not. I'm not saying I was an easy man to love either. I might have run if she'd been willing to slow down. I never got the chance to find out, though."

Diamond looked down and realized that she'd nearly finished the eggs. They were so good, she couldn't believe it, and her nausea was now completely gone. Cormack shoveled the remaining eggs from his plate onto hers. She gave him an embarrassed smile. "Thanks, they're really good." She tucked into the rest of them. "I can't believe how much I'm eating."

"You're eating for two, now," Cormack pointed out. "And I haven't seen you eat anything of substance in days." He took his plate to the sink and rinsed it off.

"What happened to her?" Diamond asked. Cormack had his back to her, but she could see his shoulders stiffen.

"She disappeared," he replied. His voice was tight.

"That's really all you know? You never found out more?"

He was silent for a moment. All she could hear was the sound of the water running in the sink. "Nothing that you need to hear," he said at last.

She put her fork down. All of a sudden she was no longer hungry. "So there's more," she said. "And you never told me."

He turned and looked at her. "You were a kid. Hell, you still are a kid, or would be in a rational world."

"We've never lived in a rational world," she pointed out.

"No," he agreed. "No, we haven't. But I still wanted you to have something to hold on to. I wanted you to have something left of your childhood."

She took a deep breath. "What happened to her?"

He lowered his head. "They found her," he said. "Two days after you reported her missing."

"Where was she?"

"She was in a motel. In Revere."

"Alive?"

Cormack shook his head.

"I want to know everything."

"No, you don't."

"Tell me."

"She was on the bathroom floor. There was a needle sticking out of her arm."

"What else?"

Cormack was silent.

"What else?" Diamond persisted.

"She'd been with men," Cormack whispered. "Multiple men. She had no clothes on, and they left her there, on the bathroom floor. She'd been there for days when they found her. The place was crawling with bugs. The police called me when they found her, to have me come down to identify her. They could have waited until she was down at the morgue, but they wanted me to see her there."

"Why?"

"Spite," Cormack said. "They'd been trying to find something they could arrest me for forever, but they'd never been able to make a case. They knew I was in love with her. They figured if they couldn't arrest me and make anything stick, they'd find another way to punish me. This was it."

Diamond took all of that in, turned it around in her mind. "The police hate you that much?"

He shrugged. "Only some of them. I actually work well with others, but for some of them the hatred goes deep."

"Is it deserved? The hatred?"

He lifted his head up and looked at her. "I guess that depends on your point of view. I'm not going to justify everything I've done in my life. I'm not going to apologize for it, either. I've tried to keep anything over the line limited to the people who have decided that they want to be a part of the game, and I think I've done a pretty good job at that. That's not an excuse, though. I'm not in the business of making excuses."

"And now?"

His brow furrowed. "Now?"

"How ugly is this going to get?"

He breathed in deep and exhaled. "There's no way to know. It's not going to be good, though, you should know that."

She nodded. "Will you look out for Buddy?"

"As best I can, but I can't make any promises."

"I know," she acknowledged. "I don't believe in promises anyway."

"Smart girl."

She stood up, leaned over, and kissed him on the cheek. "OK," she said. "Thanks for the eggs. I feel better."

She picked up her plate and took it over to the sink, rinsed it off, and put it in the dishwasher. She went back up to her room. Cormack didn't move, and she could tell that he was still recovering from having had to sift through one of his worst memories. She felt badly about that for him, but not sorry. She'd needed to know, and he'd needed to tell her.

"You're sure they know how to operate the missiles?"

T'phong Soh and Javier Carpio stood in the warehouse in Chelsea. The Stinger missiles were laid out on the table before them. Soh was calm, but he couldn't ignore the sense of power that the weapons gave him, and he couldn't escape the implications of what the Carpios had planned.

"They have drilled for a week, and they have more experience than all of your men combined," Javier said. "Perhaps all but you."

Soh nodded. It was true. Soh felt as though he'd been fighting gang wars his entire life, and he longed to have enough power to insulate himself from it. He supposed, though, that it was impossible. War would always rage. Particularly after tomorrow.

"You met with this policewoman and offered to turn on me?" Javier asked.

"I did."

"Were you convincing?"

"I believe I was."

"She will take care of O'Connell, so that he cannot interfere?"

"She will."

"And she still doesn't know the truth of our plan?"

Soh shook his head. "She still believes that our attack on the front of the courthouse will be the main assault rather than a diversion. She has no idea what is really planned. And she knows nothing of our inside man."

"Good," Javier said. "If the police believe that is where we will attack from, we will be successful—as long as we can control the traffic in the harbor. Can you guarantee that as well?"

"I can," Soh said. "I have a man who will make sure that the harbor will be clear. He is monitoring the situation, and if anything changes, he will notify me, and he will make sure that the situation is set right."

"Who is this man?" Javier asked. "And how does he have so much power?"

"Under normal circumstances, he would be a man of no consequence. It is just fortune that has made him instrumental to our plan."

"And you trust him?"

"I trust that he fears me. He has allowed himself to be used before, and that has made him vulnerable. And I have made promises to him, in exchange for his help. Promises a man like him cannot ignore."

"Does he understand the power that he has over the lives of so many?"

Soh shook his head. "He knows nothing, other than that he must do as he is told, and that he will be rewarded for it. That is all he needs to know."

It was evening when the call came in. Toby looked at the number on the caller ID screen and braced himself. His heart was beating so fast, he thought he might throw up. He was never cut out for the kind of deception he had been forced to practice in recent weeks, and he wasn't sure whether he would be able to pull it off one more time.

He took a deep breath and picked up the receiver. "Yeah."

It was Cormack. "I'm just checking in," he said. "Everything OK there?"

"Yeah, Boss, everything's good."

"You got all the allocations done for tomorrow's harbor traffic?"

"Yeah, it's done. We're all good."

"OK, good." Cormack sounded weary—lost, even. Responsibility could do that to a man, Toby was just discovering. It wasn't, as Toby had always suspected, freeing. "Listen, Toby," Cormack continued. "I want to let you know, you've done a good job. Things are crazy right now, but hopefully it'll be back to normal soon. In the meantime, you should know that the way you've stepped up to keep the harbor running hasn't gone unnoticed, OK?"

"Yeah, OK, thanks, Boss," Toby said. The praise made him uncomfortable. "You coming in tonight?" he asked. "You could look over the books for tomorrow."

"I would, but I can't," Cormack said.

"You got a date?" It was meant as a joke, but Toby could hear it fall flat. "Sorry, I didn't mean . . ."

"No worries, Toby. I've gotta see someone. Depending on how things go, I may or may not be in tomorrow, OK?"

"Sure, I can keep things running either way."

"OK. Thanks again Toby."

The line went dead. Toby placed the receiver back on its cradle. For a moment he thought he was going to throw up, but he managed to get hold of his fear and keep his stomach down. It would be over tomorrow. That was what he'd been told, and after that . . . well, he'd just have to see how things played out.

SIXTY

The address she'd given him was at the terminal end of Kneeland Street, at the edge of Chinatown, in the no-man's-land in between Downtown, the South End, and the Back Bay. It was the spot where Boston's two major highways intersected, with Interstate 93 splitting north toward New Hampshire and south toward Cape Cod, and the Massachusetts Turnpike springing west toward the wealthy suburbs and on to Worcester and Springfield. All around, the surface roads yielded to hideous on-ramps, rising from the earth like unholy cement monuments, and gave way to dark, cavernous tunnel openings. As Cormack guided his car to a parking spot outside a former industrial warehouse, the surroundings seemed a testament to the ugliness that human progress sometimes left in its wake.

The elevator in the building hadn't been replaced when the place had been converted to lofts, so Cormack had to pull the metal fencing at the front closed before pushing the button to the fifth floor. The elevator rose through the heart of the building, until it stopped at his destination and he pulled the gate open.

Kit Steele's loft was at the end of the dark, barren hallway. It was a corner unit—probably twelve hundred square feet of open space—with industrial wood floors that, if properly refurbished, would have been considered trendy. She opened the door almost immediately when he knocked, as though she had been waiting at the threshold, anticipating his arrival.

"Hello," she said. Her voice was reedy. She stepped back to allow him in.

He looked around. "So this is your place," he said, taking it in. It had potential she'd neglected to fulfill. The corner windows looked southeast, over the highways to South Boston and the harbor beyond, with its endless construction along the shore in the waterfront district. It was early evening, but already dark outside, and the lights twinkled in the city stretched out toward the water. The ceilings seemed impossibly high, with exposed wood beams and pipes painted off-white. The interior corner was a kitchen area, with a large sink and oversized appliances. An old butcher-block island separated it from the rest of the loft. There was a nondescript sofa set along the windows with a coffee table in front of it, and mismatched chairs on either side. There was no dining area he could see. At the far end of the loft, there was a partial wall that rose halfway toward the ceiling, blocking off what he assumed was a bedroom nook. "It's nice," he lied.

She looked around at the place as though she'd never really seen it before. "It needs some work," she conceded. He wondered whether she was talking to him or to herself. "I'll get around to it at some point. I guess I've been too busy."

"I'm surprised you asked me to come here," Cormack said. "It's risky."

"Compared to what I've already done?" she asked. There was more life in her voice now, and it made him feel better. "Besides, I needed to see you before I could believe you were really alive, after the last few days," she joked.

He held his arms out at his sides, as though ready for inspection. "Well, here you are," he said. "See for yourself, still breathing and only a few extra dents."

"I'm glad."

"Me too," he admitted. "Are you?"

"Am I what, glad?" she asked.

"No, are you OK?"

She shrugged. "I don't know." She stepped toward him, reaching out and touching his chest. Before he could move, she was leaning forward, kissing him—gently at first, and then harder, with unmistakable urgency.

He kissed her back, and for some reason it felt like the first time. It was odd; they had been intimate for seven months, and their physical relationship had always been active and fulfilling, and yet it had always been just that—physical. This felt like something new, something different. After a moment she broke off the embrace. She looked at him, and it seemed that she was as surprised as he was.

"What was that?" he asked.

"I'm not really sure," she admitted. "Was it weird?"

"It was different."

"Different good, or different bad?"

"Good, I think."

They stood there, looking at each. He moved forward and took her in his arms. They kissed, and this time there was no hesitation for either of them.

Later, they were lying in her bed. Cormack looked at the beams overhead, wondering what had happened between them. There was no question that the stress of the preceding weeks had taken its toll on him. He'd lived a life on the edge for as long as he could remember, but he couldn't recall a time when he'd escaped near certain death in the way he had twice in a short period of time. And the guilt he felt at the thought that he'd put his daughter in danger was more profound than he could comprehend. Maybe that stress was breaking down his walls.

"What are you thinking about?" she asked him.

"Soh," he responded. It was only a partial lie. He had been thinking about everything that had transpired recently, and Soh was a central player in those events.

"Do you know where he is now?" she asked. For a moment, it felt as though she was pumping him for information the way she had in the past. The moment passed, though, and he let himself accept the possibility that they had moved beyond that stage in their relationship.

He shook his head. "He's gone to ground."

"He's getting ready," Kit said.

"For what?"

"To try to spring Vincente Carpio," she said.

He frowned. "You really think he's that crazy?"

"I think he's that ambitious," she said. "The Carpios can give him the keys to the castle. If he has access to their supply and control over ports on both coasts, he'll be one of the most powerful gang bosses in the world. He may even take over MS-13. And I can't even imagine what could happen if Carpio escapes. He's determined to kill as many people as he can. If he's given another chance, there's no telling what he's capable of."

"But how can Soh seriously think he could free Carpio? I assume he's in Supermax?"

"He is. At Devens."

"There's no way to get into a place like that," he pointed out.

"Probably not," she agreed. "But he has to appear in court tomorrow. That may be his opportunity."

"He'd never try," Cormack said. "It would be suicide."

"He will try," Kit replied. "I've got sources. It's planned. We're ready for him, though."

"I'm sure it seems that way," Cormack said after a moment. "You must have an army guarding Carpio. Soh's got men, but not enough to take on an army."

"No? How many men does he have?"

"Near as I can tell, between fifteen and twenty," he said.

"How do you know?"

"I have sources. Like you." The feeling that she was treating him like an informant again crept back into the corner of his mind. Was it possible she was still using him? "Who are your sources?"

"Who are yours?" She waited a beat before saying, "See? Neither one of us is willing to give the other that kind of information." She rolled over and put her head on his chest. "I want you to do me a favor," she said. He held his breath. Maybe this was all an elaborate setup, and the other shoe was about to drop. "I want you to stay out of this for now," she said.

"What?" He didn't understand.

"I want you to lay low and let my people handle Soh and the Carpios. I've figured out a guaranteed way to make sure he never escapes, and I need you to stay clear."

"There's nothing in this world that's guaranteed."

"You're probably right," she agreed. "Then let's just say I don't want you in the line of fire. You've risked enough already."

"I'm already in the line of fire," Cormack pointed out. "Soh's going to come after me. If not now, then later."

"Maybe," Kit said. "But he can't come after you if he doesn't know where you are. And he's not going to want to split his resources. If he's going to try something at the courthouse, he's probably going to keep all of his focus there."

"Even so," Cormack said, "my men and I might be useful."

"I'm sure," Kit said. "But I can't take on that responsibility." She picked her head up and kissed him. "Not anymore." She got out of bed and put on her clothes.

He sat there in bed, his head swimming. He had too many questions rushing at him all at once. "This doesn't make any sense," he said. "You need all the help you can get. And I need all the help I can get. We're on the same team."

She looked at him, and the intimacy that he thought he'd detected earlier seemed to be gone. "We're not on the same team. Not really," she said. "Everything I've done with you has been illegal. I've never had authorization for any of it. You know that."

"I know that," he conceded. "But it's been in everyone's best interests."

"Has it?" she asked. "Maybe it has. I don't know anymore. All I know is that I've taken care of this," she said. "I need you to not interfere tomorrow."

"That's it?"

"For now," she said. "Not forever." She leaned over the bed and kissed him. There was none of the warmth that there had been before. "I have to leave, I have somewhere I need to be. You can let yourself out."

She walked around the half-wall that served to cordon off the bedroom area. In the large open space he could hear her shoes clack over the wooden floors. He heard the front door open and then slam shut.

SIXTY-ONE

Kit had George Martin run the meeting. Boston's law enforcement community was still an old boys' club at the higher echelons, and she knew that she had a tendency to antagonize those within the establishment. Having Agent Martin run the meeting would also appear to put distance between herself and the information she'd received from Soh. She'd told Martin that she had an informant, and after some convincing, he'd accepted the accuracy of the information without knowing the specific source. The two of them had discussed the plan at length. Now he was relaying that plan to the other men in charge of security for the next day's hearing at the court.

There were three of them who needed to coordinate. Kit and the FBI had already taken over the role of overseeing the federal corrections force that was responsible for transferring Vincente Carpio from Devens to the courthouse. Marshal Troy Kingman was in command of the Federal Marshal's Office, which was in charge of security at the courthouse itself. Bill McCaughey was the Boston police captain tasked with providing street security, manpower for crowd control, and SWAT support.

"They'll attack the caravan on Northern Avenue," Martin said. "Just as the vehicles make the turn onto Courthouse."

"How can we be sure?" McCaughey demanded.

"We have an informant," Martin said. "Besides, it makes sense. Once the vans are onto Courthouse Way, there's nowhere for them to go. Even if they could get Carpio out of the van, they're up against the harbor. They have to strike before that."

"If we know all this, why the hell is the hearing still on for tomorrow? Why not change the date?" McCaughey asked.

"That's just delaying the inevitable," Kit said. "Besides, with the information we've got, we can keep Carpio in custody and also put a dent in MS-13 in Boston."

"Which means it's on us to make sure this goes right," Martin said. "We've got the manpower. As long as we have them positioned right on Northern, we should be fine. So let's go through the plan one more time."

The meeting broke up an hour later, and the participants headed out to brief their teams and make the necessary arrangements. It was late in the evening, and Martin and Kit Steele were left alone.

"Can I ask you something?" he said.

"It's a free country."

"What is it with you and this guy?"

"Who?"

"Carpio. I get that he's a psycho, but you've got an obsession."

She felt the past welling up inside of her, but she pushed it back. "These people took everything from me."

"How so?"

She shook her head. "I shared my informant's information," she said. "You don't get my personal information. Understand?"

He nodded. "Yeah, I get it. You're sure your information is good on this?" he asked.

"I am," she said. She felt sure, though she knew no information was one hundred percent perfect. The kernel of doubt nagged at her.

"Good," he said. "Because if you're wrong and Carpio gets free, the shitstorm is going to swallow all of us whole."

"If I'm wrong, and Carpio gets free," Steele said, "I'll be dead. I'm not leaving his side. If they want to get to him, no matter where they're coming from, they're going to have to go through me."

"I want all eyes on the shoreline open tomorrow."

Cormack O'Connell was leaning against the bar at Lucky's Lounge. It was a dark, step-down hole-in-the-wall with scarlet Naugahyde bar stools and matching booths on the south side of Fort Point Channel, just inland from the expanding waterfront district. For decades, when the area had been surrounded by warehouses and parking lots, it had been a favorite of the Southie scruff crowd—a place where crooks and street runners felt comfortable, and where few questions were asked. Since the first office buildings and luxury apartments had been built, though, it had been overrun with Millennials who seemed determined to seek out every "authentic" place they could find and ruin the very authenticity they sought. At ten o'clock on a Tuesday night, though, the place was quiet, and Cormack could pretend that the world hadn't changed in the ways that depressed him. He lifted his Tullamore to his lips and took a sip. One was all he would allow himself on this evening. He needed to be sharp in the morning.

"And I want you and Buddy at the courthouse. Vincente Carpio's got a court appearance, and there's a chance Soh and his men will try something there."

"We'll be there. I've got all my people on alert," Cicero said.

"This whole city's on edge," Cormack said. "It's the cold. Everyone in this city's been cooped up inside for more than a month. It's unnatural, and it's got people ready to let loose."

"They say the cold snap is ending soon. Maybe that'll bring things back into line."

"Yeah, maybe," Cormack said. "But you know what happens when you freeze something solid and then heat it up too fast."

Cicero nodded. "It shatters."

"It does," Cormack said. "Into a thousand pieces." He took another sip of his whiskey. "Make sure everybody's ready for anything."

"I love you."

Steam wafted off her lips as she said the words. It was like they had a physical presence, but the steam faded after a moment. She and Buddy were standing on the widow's walk on the top of Cormack's house. Leaning against the railing, they could see all the way down to the harbor and out toward the Atlantic.

"I love you, too," Buddy said, looking down at her.

She pulled at his jacket sleeve. "I mean it," she said. "I need you to know."

He turned to face her. "Are you worried about something?"

"Tomorrow."

"What about it?"

"I have a bad feeling. I can't explain it, but it feels like something is going to go terribly wrong." He took her in his arms and she pressed her face into his chest. "I don't want to lose you. For the first time in my life, I feel like I might have a future. I don't want to raise our baby alone."

He hugged her tight. "You won't have to. I'll be fine. I'm sure nothing's gonna happen tomorrow. I'm going down to the courthouse so I'm there when they bring Vincente Carpio in, but Soh would be insane to try anything with all the cops and marshals around. You'll see."

"If nothing's gonna happen, then why do you need to be there?" she asked.

He shrugged. "Cormack wants me and Cicero down there just in case. But if Soh does try something, we probably won't even be involved. Maybe the cops will win this war for us."

She pulled her face out of his chest. Over his shoulder she could see an eerie glow along the horizon on the water out to the east—a faint yellow-orange line that looked as though it was just out of their grasp. "What is that?" she asked.

He looked out at the water. "Weird," he said. "Never seen that before."

"They say it's gonna get warmer tomorrow. Maybe that's some sort of a sign."

"Maybe," he said. "It feels like a lifetime since it wasn't freezing. It'd be nice to be warm again."

"It would be," she agree. "Promise me one thing?"

"Anything."

"Promise me you'll be careful?"

He gave a resigned laugh. "I'll be as careful as I can be. That's all I can promise."

SIXTY-TWO

Historical cemeteries blanket Boston. Tourist excursions include stops at the Grannery Burying Ground on Tremont Street in the shadow of the State House, and Central Burying Ground on Boston Common, among others. Those seeking a supernatural thrill can touch the headstones of famous historical figures and patriots like Paul Revere, Samuel Adams, and John Hancock. The corpses of lesser known but still notable figures like Mary Chilton, the first European woman to set foot in New England, and Crispus Attucks, a freeman of African descent who was the first to be killed in the Revolutionary War at the Boston Massacre, lay in repose under the soil throughout the city.

The Bennington Street Burying Ground in East Boston, while on the Historic Registry, is not a place tourists would visit. The most famous remains at the small patch of grass near the deserted strip along the northeastern edge of Logan Airport belong to Red Woodhead, a professional baseball player who died in 1881 at the age of thirty after three and a half seasons of unremarkable play in the long-defunct International Association.

Special Agent George Martin leaned against a gravestone at the far southern corner of the cemetery. He glanced at his watch—an old Seiko that he was tired of looking at, not just because it was a reminder that his contact was late, but because it reminded him of how he had to scrape and scrimp and save just to buy the most basic essentials. He knew people he'd gone to law school with who wore watches that cost more than he made in a year. For a long time, he'd been OK with that. They led empty lives, he told himself, working for bloodless corporations and hedge funds, so they had to console themselves with the trappings of success. He, on the other hand, was doing good work—work that helped protect the American people and put bad guys in jail where they could no longer do anyone any harm.

It was a lie, though, and he could no longer breathe enough enthusiasm into it to get himself to believe it. His second divorce had cost him what little savings he'd been able to amass, and now he was paying alimony and child support to two women who hated his guts. His daughter was looking at colleges, and he didn't know how he was going to be able to tell her that he wouldn't be able to pay for her to attend anywhere but a state school. He'd gone to Yale Law School, for Christ's sake, and now he was on the verge of bankruptcy. He wondered how it had come to this.

He heard the footsteps in the snow even before the figure appeared. Martin was expecting him to come from the north, where the cemetery met Bennington Street, so that he would be able to watch him approach and steel himself against the fear and revulsion at his own betrayal, but the man came from behind him, out of the thin shrubs that bordered the airport.

Martin turned, and his breath caught in his chest, the way it had the first time he'd beheld Javier Carpio. Martin never thought of himself as small—he was a little under six feet tall, and his once athletic build, while softer than it had been in his youth, made him feel adequate in most circumstances. Looking up at Javier Carpio, though, made him feel Lilliputian. With the airport lights shining from behind Carpio, all Martin could see was a giant black silhouette against the white snow that seemed to have claimed a permanent right to blanket the city. Standing there in the cemetery, surrounded by the rotting remains of men and women who'd passed more than two centuries before, Martin couldn't help feeling as though he'd entered a Stephen King novel.

"Does she believe Soh's information?" Carpio asked.

"She does," Martin responded.

"And the plans?"

"They'll have all the firepower lined up along Northern Avenue, many of them in plainclothes. They'll be waiting for the attack there."

Carpio pulled a satchel from behind his back. "There is one more thing you must do," he said.

A shiver ran up Martin's spine, and it wasn't from the cold breeze blowing through the cemetery. "I've done what you asked."

"And you have been paid."

"You still owe me another fifty thousand."

"There is one hundred thousand in this bag," Carpio said, holding the satchel up.

Martin's mind raced. There was no way to say no. And the allure of an additional fifty thousand dollars was too great to ignore. "What do you want me to do?"

"In the confusion that we create, someone still needs to take my brother's chains off."

Martin shook his head. "Can't do it," he said. "Someone will see me, and what's the point of the money if I'm in jail?"

"You will do it," Carpio insisted. "No one will see you because they will be running for their own lives. And jail is not the fate you should be most concerned about at this moment." He threw the bag of money at Martin's feet. It landed softly in the snow, and Martin stared at it with terror, as though it was filled with snakes rather than cash. He'd feared that it would come to something like this when he took the first payment, but there was nothing he could do now. He was caught, and he was addicted. He needed the money now, like a junkie needed his fix.

"Even if he makes it to the boats, there's no way for you to escape in the harbor," Martin said. "The cops will have our boats out there in a matter of minutes, and there's no place to hide on the open water."

"Who said the water will be open?" Carpio responded. And with that, he turned and walked back toward the airport. Martin watched him go and wondered what he meant. After a moment, he gave a labored sigh and picked up the bag. At this point, none of the choices he had were his own anymore.

Kit was at Devens before midnight. She wouldn't leave now. From this point on, she would be near Vincente Carpio wherever he went.

She'd spent some time monitoring him from the control room. He was awake, and he sat as still as ever—just staring ahead, the tattoos covering his skull shining like some rubber mask. She wondered whether it was sweat, but she couldn't tell from the camera. "I'm going down to see him," she told the young corrections officer who was in the control room.

"You're going where?" he asked, shocked.

"I'm going down to see him," she repeated.

"I don't think that's allowed," the guard responded. "We gotta notify his lawyer, and we gotta set up an interview room. You don't just go down there—"

"I'm going down there," she repeated. "If you need to call someone, go ahead. I won't be long. But I'm in charge of his transfer tomorrow. I'm the special agent in charge of the MS-13 task force. I am going down." She flashed her badge as though the shield was real and could prevent him from doing anything. Then she stood up and walked to the door. She turned around and shot him a glare, and he reluctantly pressed a button that allowed her into the holding area. She needed him to pass her through two more checkpoints, but she was sure that he would do it. In the hierarchy of law enforcement, she was so far above him that there was little else that he could do.

Carpio's cell was clean and sparse. It was cement on three sides. There were no bars—just a Plexiglas barrier four inches thick on the front of the cell with an automatic door operated from the control room and holes that allowed for communication, but that were too small to pass anything through. As Kit walked down the corridor toward his cell, she picked up a folding chair that was sitting in front of another cell and brought it with her. She placed it in front of Carpio's door and sat facing him.

At first his expression barely changed. But slowly, an evil smile crawled across his lips. "You cannot stay away," he said.

"I wanted you to know that I am here," she said. "I won't allow you out of my sight. I wanted you to know that all hope is lost for you. That was important to me."

"Why?"

She frowned. It was a question that she wasn't expecting. "Because, you're evil," she responded. It was all she could think to say.

"But you know what made me evil. Your country made me evil. What put the darkness in your heart that you feel the need to be here?"

He was still smiling at her, and she wanted to wipe the smile off his face. "Your people did," she said. "Your people created me."

"How?" he asked. "How did my people create you?"

The full force of what had happened years before swept over her like a wave, and for a moment it felt as though she might drown. She fought to the surface of her grief, though, and kept her face hard so that he would never see the depths of her pain. "Your people killed my son," she said. Her voice was steady, even as her heart pounded so hard she could barely breathe. "Your people killed Ollie, and your people killed my husband Dillon."

Carpio shrugged. "Maybe," he said. "We killed many people, just as your people killed many in my country. But how can you be sure?"

"They caught one of them," Kit said. "He was just a boy. A student in my husband's high school class. But your people had recruited him, and convinced him that this was something that he had to do. They couldn't catch all of you, but they caught him, so we know. That is what made me who I am."

Carpio's eyes grew wide, and a look of shock came across his face. He leaned forward and looked at her in earnest, with new interest. "Everett," he said.

His response confused her, and she thought perhaps she had misheard him. "What?"

"Everett," he repeated. "Your husband was a teacher in Everett, no?"

It felt like she had had all of her insides ripped out, and she struggled to maintain her composure. "How would you know that?" she demanded.

The look of shock was gone from his face, and now the smile was back, but it was wider—almost gleeful from what she could tell. "I was there," he said. "In charge of bringing that young man into our organization. They sent me here, because I was willing to do what it takes. I instructed him on how to kill your husband."

"You?" Kit couldn't breathe. She thought she might throw up. "I don't believe you!"

"It was a small house," Carpio said. "By American standards. In the village where your soldiers massacred my mother and others, it would have been a palace. Your husband fought to save your son, but we could leave no witnesses." He shrugged again. "We had no choice. And as for the brutality—we need to train our future soldiers. Again, we had no choice."

Kit's heart was beating so hard in her ears, it was difficult to hear anything. She was aware that her hand was on her gun. She was looking at the Plexiglas, trying to figure out whether a bullet would penetrate it, but she knew that it had been designed specifically to prevent something like that from happening.

"Special Agent!"

She barely heard the shouting from down the hall, as she considered firing her weapon anyway, just in case the glass had been poorly fitted.

"Special Agent!"

She looked down the corridor and saw two guards rushing toward her. She took her hand off her gun and stared at Carpio. The guards had reached her, and there was nothing she could do now. "At least they caught the boy who murdered my husband and son," she said. "That's one soldier you won't have in your army," she spat. It was weak, but it was all she had.

"Oh no," Carpio said. "The young soldier killed your husband. He did a very thorough job, as I instructed." The smile grew even wider. "But I killed your son," he said. Kit tried again to reach for her gun, but the guards grabbed her.

"You're going to die!" Kit screamed. "I swear to god, I will make sure that you face justice, and you get what you deserve!"

SIXTY-THREE

Wednesday, February 13

Boston's record cold snap surrendered early on Wednesday morning. The polar vortex that had pushed as far south as New York and trapped New Englanders in a deep freeze for more than six weeks retreated to Canada, chased northward by a shift in the jet stream that brought unseasonably warm temperatures from Texas up through the Mid-Atlantic. Within three hours, the temperature on Boston Common rose forty degrees, climbing above freezing for the first time since December. By nine o'clock, it was in the forties, and winter-weary residents poked their noses out of their doors and windows with an uneasy mixture of skepticism and relief. It felt as though a siege had been lifted from the city, and, as the reality took hold, the warmth was greeted by Bostonians like a liberating force. The shift was so drastic that stir-crazy children went to school in shorts and sweatshirts, oblivious to the fact that it would still be months before the temperature in the city would cross the fifty-degree mark. It mattered little to them. As far as they were concerned the worst was over. There was a sense of shared survival among the citizenry. They had taken the worst that Old Man Winter could throw at them, and they had endured and overcome. Now was a time to celebrate.

The sudden thaw caused some mild mayhem in the urban infrastructure. Water pipes that had cracked during the cold snap but had gone undiscovered because the water remained frozen, burst, flooding homes and businesses. Ice dams formed on peaked roofs, trapping two months' worth of melting snow, causing leaks and several collapses. Giant icicles that had formed on high-rises snapped free, falling forty stories to the sidewalks below, killing two pedestrians and injuring dozens of others. Still, the break in the cold was viewed as heaven-sent by those who escaped the collateral damage from the thaw.

From his office on the sixth floor of the John Joseph Moakley Federal Courthouse, Judge F. Barton Baylor could sense the warm front advancing from the south, up through Boston Harbor. The weather had started to change even before he rolled into the garage at five thirty that morning, but now the thaw was spreading in earnest, and it seemed that the waters were waging an open war against the ice floats that had choked the waterways.

Barton was one of the few Bostonians who didn't welcome the change in the weather. He was eighty-five years old, and hated change. The break brought with it the certainty that the construction and development that was overwhelming the waterfront district would gather speed. The machinery that had lain silent since Christmas would roar to life again, the joints in the backhoes and cranes and earthmovers stiff from the cold, but eager to continue to remake his city in the image of some modern nightmare. And the Millennials would come . . . and come . . . and come.

He sighed. Perhaps, he thought, it was time for him to climb down from the bench. Many of his judicial colleagues, even many much younger than he, had taken their pensions and retreated to homes in New Hampshire or Arizona or Florida. He'd heard their justifications when they took off their robes for the last time. They were tired. They had given all that they could give, and made what small contribution they could make, but the realization that they could not stem the tide of lawlessness and greed that seemed to advance every year notwithstanding their best efforts to hold it back was too much to bear. Baylor understood their feelings. He'd fought those feelings for the better part of three decades. He'd lost his idealism over the job early in his judicial career, and many of those who had departed the judiciary had asked what kept him on the bench. To that question, he had only one answer:

If not I, then who?

Days like today justified that conceited obstinacy. Today he would stand as the protector of the greatest judicial system ever created. In his heart, he knew that Vincente Carpio was guilty and deserved the harshest punishment available to a civil society. In his head, though, he knew that it was not his job to take sides. It was his job to hold the prosecutors to their burden, and to ensure that any verdict reached was the product of a fair and balanced process that protected every man or woman accused of a crime, even the most heinous crimes—*especially* the most heinous crimes.

Baylor looked out his window, across a construction site out toward the water. It was nearly eight o'clock, and six stories below, he could see two workers climbing over their rigs. They were dressed in bright yellow sweatshirts with the name of their construction company stenciled on the chest, and hardhats decorated with decades of stickers. They were talking and laughing with each other as they inspected their machinery to make sure that it hadn't been damaged by the cold. Safety—as always in this new world run by insurance companies and plaintiffs' lawyers—was priority one. And the insurance companies and plaintiffs' lawyers would make sure that the workers were safe as they constructed the next great gaudy monument to the ego of some rich developer.

He sighed again. He would never hold back the progress of a world that refused to recognize the importance of tradition. He would, however, do his part to keep some of those traditions alive in a world that seemed determined to desert them.

He'd heard many in the courthouse whisper, often with a tinge of malevolence, that F. Barton Baylor was sure to die with his robe on. They might be right, he secretly conceded. And perhaps that would not be a bad thing. He could imagine many worse ways to die than from a massive coronary or stroke as he presided over the courtroom he loved so much. But he had no intention of allowing that to happen before he saw that the judicial system's treatment of Vincente Carpio lived up to all that it promised to the world.

Until he made sure that was the case, he believed nothing could kill him.

Javier Carpio looked at the other two men. They were in a small warehouse just off Clipper Ship Drive in East Boston. There was a construction site next to them, where new condos were going up. It seemed as though there was no area of Boston that was immune to the creep of gentrification. Fortunately, though, the site was not active—the impact of the cold snap was still being felt across the city, and it would be days after the thaw before much of the construction began again in earnest. The attack boats had been delivered and were tied to the dock near the warehouse, covered in tarps to avoid attention.

T'phong Soh and Juan Suarez were going over the plan once more. This would be the last time they would see each other before their mission. Soh and Suarez would go from here to meet their men and then set out for the courthouse.

"Call me as soon as my brother arrives outside of the courthouse," Carpio continued. "Even with the traffic on the water, it should take us no longer than five minutes to cross the harbor, and that should be just enough time." He looked at Suarez. "You and your men are in charge of the distraction at the front of the courthouse. That will keep the attention of the police focused there. It will also make them overconfident when they are able to turn off Northern Avenue and onto Courthouse Drive."

Suarez nodded grimly. "The police will be violent in chasing those of us in the front of the courthouse," he said. "We will lose some of our men."

Soh frowned. "We will make sure those who carry out the main part of the plan are dependable," he said. "Even if they have to be sacrificed."

Suarez said nothing. Soh knew he would carry out his orders, though, no matter how unhappy he was about them. He was a good soldier.

"You may have the most important role," Carpio said to Soh. "We will be firing the missiles from the water, and the targeting must be precise." He handed Soh a device that looked a little like a large garage door opener. There was a button at the top of it, and when he pushed it, a red beam came from the clear portion at the top. "This will paint the target and allow the missiles to strike where we need them to."

"I understand," Soh said, slipping the device into his pocket.

"Do you have a place identified where you have line of sight?"

Soh nodded. "Bond Drive is right off Courthouse Way, and it has a view of the garages. They will have some security to keep cars and the crowd from the courthouse, but there will be fewer, and they will not shut down the street some distance from the building itself. I will have a clear line of sight."

"Good." Carpio seemed satisfied for the moment.

"What happens after the missiles hit?" Suarez asked.

Carpio and Soh looked at each other for a moment, and then Carpio shrugged, giving Soh permission to share the rest of the plan.

"We have a man on the inside who will free Vincente," he said. "All he has to do is make it to the shore and Javier and his men will be there to pick him up."

"What then, though?" Suarez pushed. "How will you escape on the water? They will be able to follow you."

"We have arranged for there to be enough traffic on the water to make it impossible to keep us in sight. And we will have another boat in the harbor that we will be able to transfer to once we are lost on the water, so that by the time the police locate our attack boats, we will be gone."

Suarez raised his eyebrows. "That seems risky," he said.

"It is," Javier agreed. "But it is the only way. And he is my brother. If you both do your jobs, there will be such chaos on the shore that the likelihood that the police will have a boat on the water in time to catch us is very low. If they do manage it, we will fight our way through."

Soh nodded. "We will do our jobs. And when this is over, you will make good on your end of the bargain."

Javier Carpio nodded. "I am always true to my word," he said. "You will control the harbor."

Toby White sat at the desk in the union office overlooking Boston Harbor. He had watched, over the years, as Cormack O'Connell sat in this very spot, looking out at the ships and the shore as though he owned all he could see. And in a sense he had owned it all—at least a piece of all of it. Everything that moved on the shoreline or flowed up through the harbor's waters owed something to Cormack.

Now, though, it would be Toby's. Soh had promised him that. Soh had offered him the world, and Toby had taken it, abandoning the loyalty he had once pledged to Cormack for the chance to be boss.

Toby had thought that would make him whole. If he was the boss, it would be as though all of his physical weakness would fade away. No one would see him as a cripple anymore. He would be respected and feared, and the power would flow through him, healing his deformities if not literally, at least figuratively.

And yet, as he sat there, looking out at all that he had been promised and would soon receive, he knew it was an illusion. He could already feel that what he had been promised was a lie. No one would respect him, and to the extent that he would be feared, it would only be because of Soh's backing, and the threat of what he and his men might do. But Soh's support could be withdrawn at any time, and if that happened, as it inevitably would, he would be thrown to the sharks without hesitation, and there was no question in his heart that the sharks would devour him. He would never rule over this domain in the way that Cormack had, and it suddenly occurred to him that it wasn't his physical weakness that would hold him back; his true infirmity ran deeper than flesh and bone. The true defect lay in his soul.

His cell phone buzzed on the desk in front of him, and he looked at it with dread. He considered not answering it. Perhaps he should avoid the illusion and simply walk away from the pretense of power before that pretense was exposed. He wouldn't, though. The defect in his soul was too powerful.

He picked up the phone. "This is Toby," he said.

"This is the day." Soh's voice was clear and commanding.

"I know." Toby could hear the contrasting weakness in his own voice. He hated it.

"Everything is set?" Soh asked. "There have been no changes?"

"No changes," Toby confirmed. "The schedule is still the same."

"Good," Soh said. "And O'Connell knows nothing of this?"

"Nothing," Toby said. "He hasn't been in the office for days. I can't guarantee that he won't be in later today, though. And if he does stop by, there isn't anything I can do to keep him from seeing what's happening."

"I understand," Soh said. "There is nothing that he will be able to do at that point."

The line went dead. If there had ever been any question in Toby's mind who was in charge, that question had been answered. Toby looked out at the harbor. The traffic was already starting to choke the waterways. Shipping had slowed during the cold spell, and once shippers understood that the worst of the weather was over, the number of ships seeking entry had grown exponentially. Normally, Cormack and Toby would have facilitated an orderly process that kept traffic on the water manageable. Instead, Toby had scheduled all of the ships to arrive in a two-hour period. It was already causing confusion and anger among the captains. The radio on the desk blared continually with skippers seeking clarification.

Toby had betrayed them all, he knew. He opened a drawer and pulled out a hammer. He looked at the radio and slammed the hammer down on it, cracking it. He took three more swings until it lay in pieces. It was just as well, he thought. At least he wouldn't be tempted to bring order to the situation.

SIXTY-FOUR

Soh pulled Juan Suarez aside after the meeting with Javier Carpio was over. "There is something you need to do," he said.

"After the attack is over?" Suarez asked.

"No, now."

Suarez looked confused. "But we are headed to the courthouse now. I am in charge of those with the backpacks."

"I will oversee the boys with the backpacks," Soh said. "That is not a problem. I can see to that and still make sure that the courthouse is targeted. There is something that is even more important that I need you to do."

"What is it?"

"I am concerned," Soh said. "Even after we are successful, it will take weeks before the shipments from Carpio's contacts begin to arrive. And it will be weeks after that before we have the kind of money that we truly need to make sure that no one can challenge us along the water. If Cormack O'Connell is still operating during that time—still fighting—we are not assured of what we need."

Suarez still seemed doubtful, and Soh understood why. It was true that Soh was concerned about O'Connell. But he was also concerned about Suarez. He saw the man's face when the full plan was laid out, and saw his resistance to deliberately sacrificing his men in the cause. Soh knew Suarez was an excellent soldier, but Soh was an excellent leader. And sometimes the most important skill in being an excellent leader was knowing how far men could be pushed. He thought, perhaps, Suarez had reached his limit.

"What is it that you want me to do?"

"There is only one true way to get to O'Connell. Do you understand?"

Suarez considered this for a moment before nodding slowly.

"Good. Then take care of it. That way, O'Connell will cease to be the problem he otherwise might be."

By ten o'clock, the crowds in front of the courthouse were as thick as Cicero Andolini could remember ever seeing on a Boston sidewalk. It was like the 1970s, when residents of South Boston were confronted with the prospect of school busing. There were signs and chants, almost all demanding justice—an accounting for the lives taken by the butcher Vincente Carpio. There were a few social justice warriors in attendance, protesting the potential imposition of the death penalty under federal law, but they were drowned out by those calling for blood.

The authorities, in their various incarnations, were out in force as well. Uniformed officers tried to hold a security line, keeping the crush of humanity at bay. What success they were having looked like it had more to do with the wariness with which the crowd regarded the federal officers clad in full combat armor with assault weapons. Cicero could also pick the plainclothes cops out of the crowd with ease. It was clear that the security forces had not anticipated the size of the crowds, and Cicero could sense their frustration at having their attention turned from their primary task of protecting the courthouse.

Cicero and Buddy Cavanaugh were down at the courthouse to be Cormack's eyes and ears. Cormack had intimated that something was likely to happen when Carpio was brought in, but he hadn't been able to say what, exactly. Cormack was off working his sources for more information, but wanted to know what was happening at the scene as events unfolded. Cicero and Buddy had found a spot leaning up against a bank window across the street from the courthouse's main entrance, right where Courthouse Way sprouted from Northern Avenue. From there, they could observe everything.

"Christ," Buddy said. "I didn't expect this many people."

"It's as close to a public hanging as most of these people will ever come. How could they resist?"

"You think people want to see that?"

"You think they don't?"

"So, what are we supposed to do now?"

"Not sure," Cicero said. "Cormack wanted a report about what's going on down here. So I guess I'll report." He took his phone out of his pocket and dialed Cormack's number.

Cormack was at his house, sitting in the kitchen. He'd spent the morning working the phone, contacting anyone he could think of to get any information possible about T'phong Soh's whereabouts. He'd talked to local cops he'd worked with over the years, and many of the men who ran aspects of Boston's illicit businesses. No one had any useful information. He was frustrated, and he was thinking of heading into the union office for no particular reason other than to keep himself from going stir-crazy.

His phone buzzed and he picked it up, recognizing Cicero's number. "What's the situation down there?" he asked.

"It's not pretty," Cicero said. "I think the police may have underestimated the emotion Carpio generates among the good people of Boston."

"How many?"

"Hundreds, at least. And growing, from the looks of it. Things could get out of hand very easily."

"I'm sure that's what Soh is counting on," Cormack said. "The more out of hand things get, the more likely it is that he'll be able to use the confusion to his advantage. I take it they haven't brought Carpio in yet?"

"If they have, they did it very quietly, which would probably be for the best. But I suspect they didn't have that degree of foresight."

"OK," Cormack said. "Let me know if things get worse or anything happens."

"Will do." Cicero ended the call and Cormack placed the phone back on the kitchen table. His brow furrowed, and he ran his fingers through his beard. He couldn't recall a time when he'd felt this helpless and uninformed about events unfolding along the harbor. It made him angry, and that anger made him feel reckless. He needed to do something, but he had no idea what that something would be.

His phone buzzed again, and he picked it up. The display indicated that it was a blocked number. His brow furrowed more deeply and he answered the call. "Yeah," he said simply.

"Is this Cormack O'Connell?" The man's voice was soft and somewhat effeminate, with a slight lisp and an accent that could have been from somewhere in the Middle East.

"Who's asking?"

"Someone with information that you will be interested in," the man said.

"I'm always interested in information," Cormack said. "What does this information concern?"

"It concerns violence that I believe is going to unfold in your city today."

Cormack paused, contemplating what to say next. "What do you want in exchange for this information?"

"Absolution," the man said. "I know that you exact a tribute from those who do a certain kind of business in this city. I have done that kind of business, and I have not paid you that tribute. I offer this information as an alternative payment."

"What makes you think I would accept information in lieu of cash?"

"I believe that you will find this information more valuable. It concerns the brother of Vincente Carpio."

"So, tell me," Cormack said.

"Not on the phone. I will be at the far southern end of the Conley Terminal facility at eleven o'clock this morning, just across from Fort Independence. If you are interested, you will meet me there, alone. If you are not there, you will not hear from me again."

"That's a secure facility," Cormack pointed out. "How do you intend to gain access?"

"I have my ways," the man said. The line went dead.

Cormack was unsure exactly what to make of the call. His instincts had been honed over forty years of illicit activity, and they had kept him alive against all odds through that time. He could tell that the man on the call had been serious, and should be taken seriously. But he also knew it would be foolish to accede to a request for a meeting like this one; for all he knew, the man could be setting him up for T'phong Soh. For some reason, though, he didn't think he was.

He stared at his phone, debating whether to dial the number he had in his head. She had asked him to stay out of everything going on, but he simply couldn't. He scrolled through his recent calls list, found hers, and dialed.

Kit was in Warden Stevens's office, going through the protocols for Vincente Carpio's transfer one last time. Her head was buzzing, and she was having trouble concentrating. She'd had almost no sleep, and her exhaustion made her feel disassociated from everything around her. She'd lain down on a cot at around three o'clock that morning and closed her eyes for a bit. Sleep lasted only for a brief period, and it was punctuated by a series of vivid, disturbing dreams.

The one that stood out most, and had stayed with her after she was fully awake, was one that started out the same as the dream that she had been having for years. She was at Nantasket Beach again. She could see Ollie up ahead of her, and she tried to run to him. At first, as always, her feet slipped beneath her, and she was able to make no headway. This time, though, her feet gained traction, and she was able to catch him. His back was to her, and when she reached him, she threw her arms around him, sobbing. She was so relieved and happy to finally be able to touch him again that it took a moment for her to notice how skinny he was. He'd always been a cherubic, healthy child, but now he was nothing more than skin and bones.

As she hugged him tighter, she could feel him grow skinnier and skinnier, until all she could feel through his clothes was brittle bone and sinew. She turned him toward her, and screamed in horror when she saw his face. She could tell it was him, but there was nothing left but a skull with patches of gray skin. He had no eyes, and the flesh of his nose had decomposed so badly that she could see the bones around his nasal cavity.

And then he spoke to her. His voice was reedy and distant, and it sounded like he was speaking to her through a long metal pipe. "The water," he said. "It's warm today."

She shook her head, not comprehending. Her head and her heart were still clouded by the horror of what had become of the little boy who was the greatest love she had ever known.

"I think I'll go in the water today," he said. She thought he might be smiling, but she couldn't tell. There wasn't enough flesh around his mouth to be sure.

"No," she said.

"You have to let me go," he said, and now his voice sounded even more distant.

"Why?" she demanded.

"There's nothing left," he said. "I think I'll go for a swim. I'll be careful in the waves."

He turned away from her and began to walk toward the water.

"No!" she screamed. She reached out to grab hold of him once more, but as she touched his arm, the bone turned to ash. "No!" she screamed again. She panicked and tried to wrap her arms around his chest, but as she did, his rib cage disintegrated and fell through her arms. She kept trying to hold him until every part of him vanished, and all that was left was a tattered shirt. In her head, she could hear Vincente Carpio's maniacal cackle.

She'd come back to consciousness with a start, drenched in sweat, her pulse beating so fast she wondered whether she was having a heart attack. It had taken fifteen minutes for her to compose herself enough to sit up on the cot, and she still wasn't sure that she'd really recovered from the dream now. Nor had she recovered from the revelation that Carpio was the one who had killed Ollie. There were too many thoughts and emotions swirling for her to think clearly.

"Special Agent Steele?"

It was Warden Stevens speaking to her, and she realized that she had been lost in her remembrance of the awful dream. There were other members of the transfer detail in the room, and they were all looking at her curiously. She didn't know what to say; she had no idea what aspect of the process they'd been discussing. Her mind raced, looking for something to say to inspire confidence, or at least allay any fear that she might have lost her mind.

Just then her phone buzzed. She pulled it out and looked at the caller ID.

"Sorry, I need to take this," she said. It was weak, but it at least allowed her to escape further scrutiny for a moment. She stepped out of the room.

"What are you doing calling me?" she demanded as she answered.

"I needed to talk to you," Cormack said. There was no apology or defensiveness in his tone. "I got a call. Someone offering me information about Carpio's brother."

"I told you, I need you to stay out of this."

"I know," he said. "I didn't say that I would, though."

"I need you to say it now. I have this under control. I have all the information I need."

"No one has all the information they need," Cormack said. "You can always have more."

"Cormack, listen to me," Kit said. "It's a trap. Soh wants you dead. I know that for a fact. This would be one way to accomplish that. Please don't go. Just stay wherever you are until this is all over."

"I'm not sure I can do that."

"You have to. For me. I . . ." She almost said the words.

"You what?" He'd heard it in her voice, she could tell, and that scared her almost as much as the dream about Ollie had. "You what?" he asked again.

"I want you to be safe."

She could hear him breathing on the other end of the line. "That's it?"

"What do you mean?"

"I thought you were going to say something else," he said.

"You were wrong."

“Was I?”

She could feel her pulse racing the way it had when she’d woken from the dream. She could feel the sweat forming on her brow. For a moment she thought she might collapse, but she took a deep breath and steadied herself. Then she spoke to him with all the control she could manage. “Don’t call me again,” she said.

She ended the call, and stood in the hallway for a moment, trying once again to compose herself. And then, once she’d felt the shaking subside to the point where she thought it might not be noticeable, she walked back into the room.

“OK,” she said to the men gathered in the office. “Let’s go through this one more time.”

SIXTY-FIVE

Soh watched the boy carry the backpack toward the front of the crowd that had gathered at the federal courthouse. He was one of his best soldiers, in spite of his age. Suarez had recruited him himself. He recognized the alienation in the boy's face. He had been separated from his mother at the border after making the months-long trek from El Salvador to the United States. His mother had been detained, and he had been taken into protective custody. He hadn't seen her or spoken to her since the night they were picked up by the Border Patrol a mile inside the country more than two years ago. He was transferred to a holding facility in Massachusetts while she was deported. Eventually, he was settled with an El Salvadoran family in Lynn. Suarez trolled the schools, looking for kids like him who were searching for someone to give them purpose.

His name was Pedro. He was fourteen years old, and he had taken to gang life like he'd been born to it. His anger was potent, and he was vicious when convinced that his viciousness was in protection of his new gang family. He was also unquestioning in his loyalty. When asked to perform any task, he carried it out without hesitation or question. So it was not surprising that he never asked Soh why he was being asked to put on a backpack and walk into the heart of the protesters.

There were two other boys wearing similar backpacks, but Pedro was the only one whom Soh was sure Suarez would miss. But he also knew that he would get over it. He had sent more people to their deaths than he could count in his lifetime. Any guilt that he believed he might have would be short-lived.

* * *

Suarez kept his hood up to conceal his tattoos. He had strolled along L Street for a half hour, passing the modest house on the corner twice. There were two cars out front. One was a tiny, beat-up Honda—the sort that a nineteen-year-old girl might drive. The other, though, was a newer Mustang with tinted windows and a spoiler on the rear. This was the kind of car that a younger man would drive. Suarez knew that Buddy Cavanaugh didn't have the means to drive a car like that, and O'Connell drove an older sedan, which meant only one thing: O'Connell had left a man—maybe more than one—to guard his daughter.

Suarez wasn't surprised. O'Connell was smart enough to know that his daughter was still a target in the war. It was the reason Soh had sent Suarez here now. She represented a pressure point for O'Connell like none other. The fact that Suarez would have to get through those protecting Diamond O'Connell would make his task more complicated, but not impossible. Few of O'Connell's men had real experience with war and killing the way that Suarez did.

And Suarez had the element of surprise on his side.

The Conley Terminal Facility was the largest cargo holding facility in Boston. It was directly across the Reserve Channel from the union office, and spread out for nearly a mile from South Boston toward Fort Independence. Vast cargo containers were stacked in endless rows, like some giant child's building blocks.

Cormack O'Connell steered his Buick up L Street from his house and turned right onto East First Street. The entrance to the terminal was at the corner of East First and Farragut. It was a secure facility, surrounded by tall barbed-wire fences. At the terminal entrance, Cormack was required to show a series of passes and identifications to get through, but his position as head of the union permitted him full access.

Once through the gate, he drove down a series of pathways between the cargo containers stacked thirty feet high. Off to his left he could see the giant cranes that were used to load and unload the containers from cargo ships.

It took a few minutes for him to make it all the way to the far end of the facility, but eventually the stacks of cargo containers grew smaller and sparser, until there was a clear space a few hundred feet from the water. Cormack pulled his car to the side of the last container and parked it. He sat there for a moment, wondering what would happen next. It was just a few minutes before eleven.

He got out of his car and walked into the middle of the small clearing. He kept his hand on a gun he had hidden in his pocket, and he looked furtively for any spot from which someone might hide to take a shot at him.

He looked at his watch again, and saw that it was now just after eleven. For a moment he thought that the call had been some sort of a diversion, and it was likely that no one would show up. Just then, though, he heard an unmistakable rhythmic beating above him. He looked up and saw the helicopter coming in low and fast. It pulled up short and landed at the very far end of the clearing.

Three men got out of the helicopter. One was small and slight, carefully attired in a perfectly tailored suit. The other two were also well dressed, though in suits that were not as well tailored, and they towered over the first man. Both of the larger men held automatic pistols and were pointing them in Cormack's direction. They approached Cormack, and the smaller man smoothed out his blond hair, which had been disrupted by the helicopter's blades.

"It's convenient transportation, but it doesn't do much for one's personal presentation," the man said by way of introduction, straightening his suit.

"It's also fairly conspicuous. You may draw the attention of the police," Cormack pointed out.

"It seems the authorities have all their attention trained a mile north of here, at the courthouse," the man said. "Besides, we will be gone before the police would be able to get here to investigate. You are Cormack O'Connell. We've never had the pleasure." He didn't hold his hand out. Cormack still couldn't place the accent that adorned his high-pitched voice.

"You know who I am," Cormack said. "I don't know who you are."

"Nor do you need to. I have never done business here before, nor am I likely to again."

"What sort of business do you do?"

"I sell arms, Mr. O'Connell."

"Guns?"

The prim little man gave a chuckle, as though Cormack were too naïve to truly understand the way the real world works. "Guns only in large quantity. Most of my business involves heavy artillery. Tanks. Missiles. Even the occasional aircraft."

"Interesting," Cormack responded. "What brings you to Boston?"

"A peculiar order. One which I fulfilled, but about which I have reservations. For obvious reasons, I can't go to the authorities. From my inquiries, I was informed that you are the authority that those who can't go to the police deal with."

Cormack digested this. "What was the order?"

"It was an order placed by a man named Javier Carpio."

"For?"

"Two Stinger missiles and two thirty-three-foot transportable port security boats, each armed with one mounted fifty-caliber machine gun and two M60s." The man let that information sink in. "Javier Carpio is well known to me by reputation from his work in El Salvador. He was a leader of the resistance against the American-backed government forces. When he placed the order, I assumed, naturally, that they would be delivered there. I was unnerved when he indicated that the delivery was to be here. Had I known that that was the intention, I would never have become involved in the transaction."

"You're afraid that they will be used to kill Americans," Cormack noted.

The man shrugged. "If a school is bombed in a place like El Salvador, or a plane is shot down in Malaysia, there is a momentary outcry, and then people move on with their lives. The governments in those countries do not have the resources to interfere with my business, and the American government does not generally get involved beyond minimal cooperation." He paused. "But if Americans are killed—particularly on American soil—well, then your government brings its full force to bear. I would not want to be implicated in that."

"So, what do you want me to do about it?"

"I have heard that you have connections with the federal authorities. You have the information now, and you can pass it on."

Cormack shook his head. "Why would I want to get involved?" he asked.

"Because, Mr. O'Connell, you are already involved. If those missiles are used against Americans, the authorities are likely to learn of my involvement and come after me. If I am caught, I will, of course, tell them that I gave you this information. It may buy me some leniency. And you will have to answer for not having done anything with this information."

Cormack didn't bother thinking the implications through. It was irrelevant. There was no question that he would relay the information to Kit Steele.

"One more thing," the man said.

"What?"

"Your organization has a leak. There is someone working against you. You need to understand that."

Cormack frowned. It was a concern that had nagged at him.

The diminutive man nodded and he and his bodyguards walked back to the helicopter and climbed aboard. He was gone as quickly as he had arrived, and Cormack stood in the middle of the clearing, looking out toward the outer harbor, his mind racing. As he looked out, he suddenly noticed that there were more commercial ships in the harbor than he'd ever seen before—far more than was authorized or would be safe. It was as though someone had scheduled all of the traffic for one moment of the day.

And suddenly it all made sense.

Soh had moved to Bond Drive, a quarter block from the garage entrance at the back of the courthouse. The end of the street, where it ran into Courthouse Way, was blocked off by a contingent of Boston's finest, outfitted in riot gear, standing behind flimsy wooden barricades. The crowd on Bond was thinner and less agitated than the crowd in the front of the courthouse itself, but it was still a solid contingent, and he could sense the tension in the way the officers regarded those staring down the small street toward the portal through which Vincente Carpio would be driven. That was fine with Soh; it made it less likely that they would wander out into the crowd to create a problem.

He regarded the fifteen-foot garage doors, currently pulled closed. The doors were made of solid steel, and it was unlikely that any common firearms would be able to breach them. Javier Carpio had been very specific—he wanted Soh to paint an area five feet above the door through which Vincente Carpio's van would travel.

All Soh could focus on was the power he would have if the plan was successful. He felt in his pocket for the large laser pointer, and leaned against the building, hood up, trying not to be noticed.

SIXTY-SIX

Kit Steele's phone buzzed, and she saw Cormack's number on the caller ID. She turned her ringer off and put the phone back in her pocket. She couldn't afford to be distracted now, and Cormack was unquestionably a distraction.

She was in the transport van with Vincente Carpio, headed into the city. There were four heavily armed and armored security squad members with them, alternately watching Carpio and checking outside the van for anything unusual. There were three other federal vehicles in their convoy, each with a complement of armed guards from a combination of federal and local law enforcement agencies. It seemed that while no single agency wanted responsibility, none of them wanted to be accused of failing to supply support.

Carpio had been loaded onto the van more than an hour before. She had watched him in his cell on the video monitor, and he had spent almost the entire morning on his knees. She thought perhaps he was asking God to help with his escape, but she knew that he had lost all faith long ago. In any event, she was sure that no deity could help set him free now. She knew what his plan was, and she knew that she would stop him.

To Diamond, the thaw felt like a new beginning. It seemed to signal, somehow, that the nightmare of the previous weeks was at an end. She knew that it wasn't, though. Cormack had left two men downstairs in the house to guard her, and that was reminder enough that the danger remained. These two were younger and bigger than Joe Konicki had been, and that gave her some sense of comfort.

She'd slept late that morning. It felt good. She needed her sleep. Pregnancy wasn't fully agreeing with her, though it wasn't nearly as bad as she'd heard. She'd had some morning sickness, but that seemed to pass, and now all she had was a little nausea every morning until she got some food in her. The baby seemed to have come through the ordeal on Long Island strong. Strong and hungry, she thought with a smile. Like Buddy. Maybe that meant it was a boy. It didn't matter to her one way or another; all she wanted was a healthy baby.

She slid out of bed and put on some jeans. They were feeling tighter, and she realized that she would soon have to start wearing bigger pants. The thought made her laugh to herself. She'd always been thin, and she wondered what it would be like to gain weight.

The stairs creaked as she went down to the first floor. "Mike?" she called. She was pretty sure one of the men whom Cormack had left to guard her was named Mike, though she could be wrong. It could have been Mark. She couldn't remember even being introduced to the other young man. "Mike?" she called again, muddling the name a little, so that if his name was Mark, he might somehow not notice.

No one answered, which she thought was odd. Perhaps it meant that she was wrong about the name. "Mark?" she called as she came off the stairs and walked through the living room toward the kitchen. She was feeling the twinge of nausea that she'd come to expect in the morning, and she knew she had to get something in her stomach to chase the feeling away. "Mark? Are you in here?"

She pushed the kitchen door open and walked in. She heard the door swing shut behind her. She nearly vomited as she beheld the scene. There was blood everywhere. It covered the counters and the floor. She could hear the sound of a man coughing over near the door to the outside, around the corner by the small entryway. She stepped gingerly in that direction. "Mark?"

An arm suddenly clawed its way over the threshold from the entryway to the kitchen. The man's head followed. It was Mark. Or Mike—she still wasn't sure. He was covered in blood, and he was gagging and coughing. She could see a monstrous cut in his throat. His eyes were bulging out, pleading with her for help. And then, just as suddenly, he was pulled back into the entryway, and there was a grunt of finality.

She was frozen, just standing there, looking toward the wall behind which her protector had just disappeared. "Mark?" she said faintly.

A man stepped from the entryway into the kitchen. She recognized him from Fort Strong. He had tattoos covering his face, and he was covered in blood and holding a long knife. "You are the daughter," he said. He stepped toward her. "I am here for you."

At that moment, Cormack stormed into the union offices at the edge of Boston Harbor, at the end of Black Falcon Avenue, "Get the harbor traffic cleared, now!" he shouted at Toby White, who was sitting at the desk overlooking the inconceivable traffic on the water. It seemed as though a person could walk across the harbor stepping on boats and not get his feet wet.

Toby White didn't move.

"I said now!" Cormack shouted again. "We need to get this cleared! Carpio's using it to attack the courthouse!"

"I can't," Toby said at last. He'd pulled himself up almost into a ball on his chair, his crooked legs tucked unevenly under his body. "The radio's busted."

"What are you talking about?" Cormack demanded. "What happened to it?"

Toby shrugged.

"What do you mean busted?" Cormack strode over to the desk and looked at the wreckage of the radio. The realization dawned on him. "Oh, fuck," he said. "It was you, Toby."

Toby looked away, unable to meet Cormack's eyes. Cormack lifted him out of the chair and threw him into the wall, holding him by his shirt.

"It was you. You knew that I was at the Mariner the night it burned. You told Soh I was there. You're the one who has been feeding Soh information from the start."

"I didn't want to," Toby said weakly. "I didn't know what I was getting myself into."

Cormack pulled his fist back, ready to hit Toby in the face. He couldn't bring himself to do it, though. He stood there, suspended. His legs felt weak. He loosened his grip on Toby's shirt and let him slide to the floor. "You didn't know what you were getting all of us into," he said. He pointed out the window. "Do you see that traffic out there, Toby?" Toby refused to look, so Cormack grabbed him by the shoulders and forced him to. "Do you see it?" he spat.

"I see it," Toby whimpered.

"That's how they're going to break Carpio out! They have boats! They're going to use the traffic to get lost and outrun anyone chasing them!"

Toby was curled into a ball.

"If they get Carpio out, Soh will take over! He'll be one of the most powerful gangsters in the country! You think he'll protect you? You think he'll honor whatever promises he's made to you?" He shook his head in disgust. Then he took his phone out of his pocket and dialed Kit Steele's number again, but it went straight to voice mail. "Goddammit, Kit!" he screamed. He tried dialing the number of other cops he had in his phone, but no one picked up. Then a thought occurred to him, and he dialed Cicero Andolini's number.

"It's a fuckin' madhouse down here," Cicero said as he answered the phone. "I swear to God, I don't know what's gonna happen. Everyone's lined up along Northern Avenue. It could be a riot. That may be what Soh and Carpio are counting on."

"It's not!" Cormack interrupted him. "It's what they want the cops to believe, but it's fake. It's a diversion!"

"I don't understand," Cicero responded. "What's a diversion?"

"The madness in front of the courthouse! They're going to break Carpio out of custody from the water, not from the street! They have attack boats and Stinger missiles! They're going to create a diversion out front and then try to break him out from the water!"

"Shit. Is there any way to stop it?"

"I don't know," Cormack admitted. "We need to get word to the Feds. We need to get to Kit Steele. I can't reach them. You've got to get to them on the scene!"

"I don't have the best credibility with law enforcement personnel," Cicero pointed out. "I don't think they'll take my word for it."

"You've gotta try," Cormack implored. "I'll figure out some way to get out on that water." He hung up and ran to the pile of manifests. "Toby, are there any boats we've got that aren't being used?" Toby hadn't moved. He was still curled up on the floor. "Toby!" Cormack picked the smaller man up, pulling him out of his fetal position.

Toby struggled, putting his hands up over his face, as though protecting himself from an imminent blow. "There's a MEP boat they just finished working on in the dry dock!" he whined defensively. "I think that's it!"

Cormack let him drop again and headed toward the door.

"You don't really think you can do anything, do you?" Toby asked.

"I don't know," Cormack said. "But I'm going to try. If Carpio escapes and Soh takes over the harbor, we're all fucked. He'll control everything."

SIXTY-SEVEN

The crowds outside the federal courthouse had continued to grow throughout the morning, and they were now spilling into the street. News crews were set up along the sidewalks, their satellite links extending upward from their vans, temporary monuments to the sacred twenty-four-hour news cycle. Reporters—both the bleached-blond bombshells from the national networks and their less glittering local colleagues—jostled for room to deliver their stand-ups from positions that gave their viewers the most intimate view of the chaos. The police and federal marshals fought against the tide of bodies, trying in vain to keep it back from the brick edifice.

Buddy made his way across Courthouse Way, fighting through the crush of people calling for Carpio's head on a stick. He wondered what the people who had come to protest the arraignment did for a living, and how they could take a day from their lives to show up to a circus like this.

He and Cicero had concluded that it made little sense for Cicero to attempt to pass Cormack's message on to law enforcement; he was too well known and recognizable to gain any traction. He might even be arrested. So it fell to Buddy to try to get someone's attention. They also realized that reporting the information to a member of the Boston Police Department was likely to provide little value. The cops tended to have blinders on and focused solely on whatever task they had most recently been directed to accomplish. A cop tasked with crowd control wouldn't listen to anyone trying to distract him—Buddy would be dismissed as a crackpot. Instead, he had to make his way to a federal marshal. It might still be useless, but it seemed that they were more likely to pay attention.

The masses were most concentrated in front of the main entrance to the courthouse, so Buddy made his way along the side of the courthouse, down Courthouse Way. The ratio of protesters to law enforcement fell off dramatically as he approached the entrance to the garage. There were several police vehicles there, set up as barricades to prevent any unauthorized vehicles from passing. Buddy was still twenty yards from the garage when he was stopped by a police line.

"This area is restricted. Please move back, sir," a BPD officer informed Buddy firmly. There were no marshals nearby that Buddy could see, but a few yards behind the cop stood a young man in a blue windbreaker with "FBI" stenciled in large yellow lettering.

"Of course," Buddy said. "I just have a message to deliver to that man." Buddy pointed to the FBI agent.

"Sorry, sir, you'll have to do that later. We're busy at the moment."

"It's important, officer."

"Yeah, I'm sure it is," the cop said with derision.

"Please, it's a message for Kit Steele."

"Who?"

"Special Agent Kit Steele. She's the one in charge of Vincente Carpio's detention."

The cop glanced down the street at the mayhem that was unfolding. "Figures there's a woman in charge of this shit show." He turned and shouted to the FBI agent. "Hey! Agent Capshaw!" The FBI agent turned. "You know who's in charge of all this?"

"The MS-13 Task Force," Capshaw responded.

"You know the agent?"

"Special Agent Steele."

The cop looked at Buddy with slightly less skepticism. Then he called back to Agent Capshaw. "This guy says he has an important message to deliver to her."

Capshaw made his way over to the police line. He looked at Buddy, clearly unimpressed with his appearance. "Yeah, what is it?"

"You heard of Cormack O'Connell?"

The agent frowned and there was an air of hostility in his gaze now. "The union guy, right? He's a crook."

Buddy didn't see the point in arguing. "Yeah, that's him. He's apparently had some dealings with Special Agent Steele in the past. He needs to get a message to her."

Capshaw looked unimpressed but reluctant to refuse to at least hear the message. "So, what is it?"

"He says this is all a diversion."

"What is?"

"All this out in front of the courthouse. Carpio's people are going to attack from the water instead."

"What the fuck are you talking about?"

"Walk down the street and look in the harbor. You'll see all the traffic. They have boats and they're coming in from there."

The agent still looked doubtful, but there was an air of concern about him as well. "How does he know this?"

"I don't know," Buddy said. "All I know is that everyone here is in danger. I was just sent to deliver the message."

The agent seemed to debate his options for a moment. Just then, though, there was a commotion out toward the front of the courthouse. The security convoy carrying Vincente Carpio was arriving. Because of the size of the crowd spilling into the street, they were having trouble getting through, and a few overly enthusiastic protesters had rushed the van to bang on the windows. That brought a forceful response from the police, which only seemed to encourage others in the mob. Soon, the entire law enforcement contingent was rushing toward the front of the courthouse.

"Clear out of here!" the cop standing next to Agent Capshaw shouted at Buddy.

Buddy looked at the FBI agent, trying to reinforce the seriousness of his message. He couldn't tell whether he'd been successful.

A moment later, the agent joined in the chorus of law enforcement.

"You need to clear out, sir!"

Suarez stared at the girl. Killing the two men had seemed simple; they'd been stupid. They thought their assignment was an easy one—who in their right mind would try again to get to Cormack O'Connell's daughter?

But then, Suarez had never been in his right mind. Not really. All it took was an innocuous noise outside the kitchen door to draw the first man in. Suarez's blade sliced through his throat before he could make a sound. The second man had put up more of a fight, and had then run to the kitchen, where Suarez carved him up effectively. He'd thought he was dead as he dragged his body back toward the door, but the man had more life in him than Suarez had anticipated. That was easily rectified.

Now he was standing before the girl, covered in blood. She was staring back at him, her eyes wide with terror. His orders were simple. "Come with me," he said. "Come with me, or you will die now."

She was shaking her head, babbling something, perhaps begging him to leave her alone. He couldn't make out the words, and his English had never been perfect anyway. He hoped she would see reason and come with him. Soh would kill her eventually, but at least that way Suarez wouldn't be the one putting her under the blade. He'd started to wonder what all the killing was for. Soh was in the process of sacrificing the boys Suarez had recruited with promises of brotherhood and family. He'd always known that it was overblown, but a part of him believed it. He believed that the organization was giving these boys something they would never find anywhere else. Now it seemed that it was all a lie, and that realization had dimmed his desire for killing.

"Come with me," he repeated.

She was still babbling, backed up against the kitchen counter. It was foolish of her, and Suarez knew he couldn't waste any more time there. He should just kill her and be done with it, but he thought, perhaps, if he gave one pull on her shoulder, she would overcome her shock and fear.

He stepped toward her and pulled on her sweatshirt. "Come! Now!" he ordered. He was looking into her eyes, and something about them literally took his breath away. He wondered what it was. And then he looked down.

The large kitchen knife was sticking deep into his chest. Her hand was still on the blade. It seemed impossible, and it took a moment for him to comprehend what had happened. If he'd come to his senses before that, he might have lashed out with his own blade and finished his last job, but by the time that impulse came to him, his strength was gone. He tried to raise his knife, but she pushed him, and he slipped on the blood-covered floor. He fell hard, and now he was staring up at her. She still held the knife, and he looked down at his chest and the blood pouring out of him.

"Get the fuck out of my house!" she screamed. Of course, it was an absurd order. He would never make it off the floor alive, much less out of the house. She stared at him for another moment, and then ran out of the house, stepping over the body in the doorway.

The last thing Juan Suarez heard was the old, beat-up Honda starting and pulling out of the driveway of the modest little house on L Street.

"No luck," Cicero reported back to Cormack by cell phone. "Buddy relayed the message to one of the Feds, but it doesn't seem like they took it seriously. The convoy just arrived and things are really starting to get out of control now. What do you want us to do?"

Cormack was in a near-sprint toward the dry docks, lugging a sack with all of the weaponry that remained in the union office. It wasn't much—a couple of handguns, two rifles, and a shotgun—but it would have to do.

"Get out of there and get over to the pier at the far end of the World Trade Center!" he shouted.

"What do you want me to do there?" Cicero asked.

"Wait for me! I'll pick you up!"

"Pick me up?"

Cormack heard the incredulity in Cicero's voice, but he ignored it, turned off the phone, and shoved it in his pocket. He had other issues to worry about at the moment.

Jim Jackson was a junior at the Massachusetts Maritime Academy, a college on Cape Cod that prepared students for careers in maritime and emergency services professions. He had an internship at the Boston dry docks, where he was supposed to be learning high-level engineering and repair skills. As he'd learned early on in the internship, though, he was assigned primarily menial tasks associated with ship repair work.

At the moment, he was at work sanding down some patchwork in the metal hull of a twenty-two-foot boat used for patrols by the Massachusetts Environmental Police. The boat had struck a rock during a rescue a few months previously, and had been awaiting the final preparation to go back into the water since the deep freeze had arrived six weeks before. It was suspended over the pier by a small crane that could swing out over the dry dock to lower the boat easily into the water once the repair work was completed.

Jackson was lying on his back, under the boat, when he saw a man carrying what appeared to be a heavy canvas sack enter the repair area.

"You can't be here, sir," Jackson called out. "It's a restricted area."

"Put the boat in the water," the man said.

"What?" It was such an odd order that Jackson didn't even look up. He assumed it was a joke.

"Put the fuckin' boat in the fuckin' water!" This time there was no mistaking the tone for humor. Jackson slid half his body out from under the boat, and faced the barrel of an assault rifle. "You hear me?" the man said. He was of average height, around fifty, with a salt-and-pepper beard and an Irish lilt in his angry voice.

"Holy shit!" Jackson thought he might soil his work pants. He put his hands up to his face, as though they might defend him against a bullet. "Holy shit, don't shoot!"

"I'm not gonna shoot you," the man said, though there was still urgency in his voice, and Jackson wasn't fully convinced. "You're gonna put that goddamned boat in the fuckin' water, and I'll be on my way."

Jackson was on his feet now, working the crane to get the boat in the water. He looked at the canvas bag and saw that it was filled with guns of various sizes. Jackson gasped, and worked faster. The boat was hanging a foot or so over the water now. The man reached over Jackson's shoulder and hit the switch that released the suspension cords from the crane and the boat fell to the water below with a loud splash. He threw the canvas bag into the boat. "Keys," he said, looking at Jackson.

"In the ignition."

The man jumped down into the boat and started the engines. He hit the throttle hard, and the boat shot forward.

"That epoxy hasn't been sanded yet!" Jackson called after him. "It may not hold at speed!"

The man didn't even acknowledge him. It seemed that sinking in the small patrol boat was the least of his worries.

SIXTY-EIGHT

Kit couldn't believe the size of the crowds. She'd anticipated some level of public interest—after all, Vincente Carpio was one of the most reviled criminals in American history. He was, to many, a combination of Jeffrey Dahmer and Osama Bin Laden. His crimes were both grotesque and anti-American, and inspired a mix of hate and curiosity that many found irresistible.

And yet the number of people who had turned out to scream obscenities was shocking. There were so many that the van had difficulty passing down Northern Avenue once it got near the courthouse. The mob had spilled into the street, and the police and federal forces seemed powerless to control them.

It took only a moment before some in the crowd realized that the convoy was carrying the object of their venom. At first, they simply shouted at the van and its accompanying vehicles. Quickly, though, the crowd pushed forward until it was up against the van on all sides. The police were fighting to keep people back, but it seemed hopeless. The van started rocking as protestors pushed back and forth on the sides. They were stalled, with crowds in front of them now.

Steele was sitting in the front seat and she looked back at Carpio. For the entire ride, she'd been tempted to take out her gun and shoot him right there. He was so close, she could touch him, and it would take almost no effort to blow his head off. It would be just, in her view. He'd killed Ollie. He'd killed so many more. No one could say that it wasn't just.

But it wasn't justice.

That was what she couldn't let go of. Even in all of her hatred and grief, she couldn't let go of her sense of justice. And justice could only happen with a trial and a jury, and a process that ensured fairness.

He sat there, staring straight ahead, his face impassive. He didn't look to either side, and he didn't acknowledge the hate that was directed at him from the crowd. And then just for a moment, Steele thought she detected the shadow of a smile on his lips.

She looked out at the crowds again, and she noticed a group of men with hooded sweatshirts and backpacks, the hoods pulled up over their heads. They weren't chanting with the crowd, and they seemed not to be paying attention to the convoy at all. As one of them turned his head to scan the crowd, Steele caught a fleeting glimpse of his face, and was sure that it was covered with tattoos.

"Move forward!" she ordered the driver.

"There are people blocking us, ma'am," the driver responded.

"They'll get out of the way if you move forward!"

"How do you know?"

"Just drive! Go slowly and blow the horn."

The driver grimaced as he leaned on the horn. The blare seemed to startle those at the front of the van, and they pulled back reflexively. That created a sliver of space for the van to move. The driver eased forward. For a moment it seemed as though the crowd might push back, but when the people saw the van moving, they cleared away even more.

The van gained some momentum, and the crack in the mob's resolve allowed the police to move in and shoulder people away from the convoy. As the van neared the turn onto Courthouse Way, Kit Steele thought they were home free.

At that moment, all hell broke loose.

Buddy saw the boy explode. He was standing near the corner of Northern Avenue and Courthouse Way, watching as the federal corrections vans fought their way through the angry mob. The boy was across the street, up toward the courthouse entryway, standing near the police barricades that were set up to keep the crowds at bay. He stood out because he was the only one in the crowd who wasn't paying attention to the vans that were transporting Vincente Carpio. Instead, he was milling about, head down, seemingly oblivious to the world around him. The backpack seemed heavy on his slight shoulders, and he looked out of place to Buddy.

And then, all of a sudden, he was gone. The explosion rocked the area, and Buddy was thrown back into the building behind him. For a moment, it seemed as though the world went quiet and time slowed. Buddy watched as shrapnel tore through those standing in the crowd, and the wooden barricades rose into the air in slow motion.

The second explosion was farther down on the other side of the street, and it seemed to bring the world back to reality. Buddy didn't see that one, but he felt it, and it buckled his legs. All at once everyone was in motion, and the screams pierced the air. The crowd dispersed, running in every direction. The vans pulled forward, crawling around the corner onto Courthouse Way. Two armed federal marshals sprinted toward the vans and began pulling the injured out of the way to allow the vehicles to pass.

Buddy gripped the gun in his pocket as his head cleared and he tried to focus on what all this could mean. Cormack had said that Soh and his men were planning to break Vincente Carpio out of custody. It appeared that his information was accurate, and the attack was now under way. That meant that Soh might very well appear at any second. Buddy decided to keep his attention trained on the vans. They would be the focus of any further attack, he reasoned, and if he could take out Soh and a few of his men, that might end the war with MS-13 for control of the harbor. He thought about Soh kidnapping Diamond—taking her when she was carrying his child—and the rage grew in him. For him, this wasn't about business anymore. It wasn't about control over the harbor or the power dynamics in the Boston underworld; it was personal. If there was any way he could take Soh out, he was determined to do it.

Diamond was almost at the courthouse when the explosions rocked the Seaport District. She needed to find Buddy. She didn't know where else to go. Given all that was happening, calling the police didn't seem an option, and she had no idea where Cormack was, but she knew that

Buddy was somewhere around the courthouse. He was the only one she felt she could trust at this point. As she drove, she looked down at the blood on her hand. She couldn't think clearly, but she forced herself to take a deep breath to try to compose herself.

The crowds were so heavy along Northern Avenue that she'd detoured a block before and headed down Fan Pier Boulevard so that she could come up Bond Drive, where the crowds were much thinner. She pulled her car to the side of the street when it was clear that she couldn't get any closer to the building. She was still a block or so away, and she got out and started running. She didn't even know why—she didn't know exactly where Buddy was.

The explosions made her stumble, and all of a sudden everyone in the crowd was rushing toward her, headed away from the courthouse and the explosions.

"Oh God, Buddy!" she said under her breath. She knew that he was there—sent to take out Soh if he and his men showed up to free Vincente Carpio. She instantly feared that he was dead, and the thought deepened her disorientation.

The crowd streamed past her, screaming in terror. Diamond saw a young woman carrying a small child. They were both bleeding, and Diamond wondered what could have possessed the young woman to bring a child to this kind of a scene. Then again, she realized, she was pregnant and yet was there herself. But she was there because there was no other place she could think to go.

Moving forward, against the flow of those fleeing the scene, was a struggle. It seemed that everyone was trying to escape. As she moved north toward the courthouse, though, she bumped into a slight man in a hooded sweatshirt who seemed to be the only person unfazed by the mayhem. He was holding something in his hand, pointing it toward the courthouse's garage doors.

Diamond stepped around him, still headed forward into the madness. She continually slammed into people streaming in the other direction. She was nearing Courthouse Way when she felt a strong hand grab her from behind. She turned, hoping against hope that it was Buddy.

It wasn't. Instead she was staring into the face of the Asian man from Fort Strong. He was staring at her as though he'd seen a ghost.

"Diamond O'Connell," he said. "You shouldn't be here."

Javier Carpio and his men were in the boats. The traffic on the water was crazy, and they had to weave in and out of the commercial ships that crowded the inner harbor. He could see the shocked expressions of those on the ships as they passed in the attack boats with guns mounted fore and aft.

They were ready and waiting, and pulled out as soon as they heard the first explosion. Javier had given instructions for Soh to detonate the backpacks when the caravan carrying his brother was approaching the turn onto Courthouse Way. In the ensuing confusion, he estimated that it would take the vehicles another two minutes to make it to the courthouse garage. That gave them enough time to get more than halfway across the harbor before letting loose the missiles. As long as Soh was accurately painting the area above the garage doors, they should have a chance. Men on the ships they passed watched them closely, and Carpio wondered whether one of them might alert the authorities. It was a risk, but a small one. In light of the explosions near the courthouse, no one would be surprised to see Coast Guard attack boats headed toward the scene.

Even from out on the water, Javier and his men could hear the screaming coming from the area around the courthouse. The sounds of civilian terror brought Javier back to his days in El Salvador, when every day brought violence and bloodshed to the people of his small country. He had contributed to that bloodshed, there was no doubt, but that had not been by choice. He had been forced into that life by the American-backed government forces. At least that was the way he remembered it. At some point he probably could have gotten out of that life, but by then it was all he knew. And it was all his brother knew. Their involvement in MS-13 was just an extension of their long-standing guerilla warfare.

The screams grew louder as they crossed the harbor, and Javier nodded to his men. One of his soldiers hoisted the missile launcher onto his shoulder. Over on the second boat, another of his men did the same.

SIXTY-NINE

The explosions at the front of the courthouse rocked the van carrying Kit Steele and Vincente Carpio. The attack was under way, she knew. Fortunately, they were ready for it. She was immediately on her radio giving orders, instructing all the manpower of the BPD, the FBI and the federal marshals to converge on Northern Avenue. Soh had said that that's where all of Javier Carpio's soldiers would be, and that was where the authorities had focused their planning. The first priority was to make sure that the van with Vincente Carpio in it made it safely to the courthouse garage. The second priority was to capture or kill as many of Javier Carpio's men as possible. Steele had given Soh her assurances that he would not be intentionally targeted, but if he was accidentally killed, that would be fine with Steele. Ultimately, she had already decided that she would never honor her bargain with anyone as evil as T'phong Soh. If that meant she would go to jail, she could live with it.

As the van inched forward, several federal marshals swarmed them, moving injured and panicked members of the public out of the way so that the vans could pass. Kit was focused on identifying any possible threat, but even as she kept her mind on the mission, she could not help but see all those who had been killed or badly injured in the crowd. It was heart-wrenching. She could see people bloodied and unconscious, some of them unrecognizable as complete human beings. She felt the rage well up within her, and she hoped the task force would be able to take out as many of the MS-13 contingent as possible. It wouldn't make up for the death and destruction they had caused, but at least it would be something she could cling to so that she might be able to go on without feeling useless.

It took only a moment for the caravan to complete the turn onto

Courthouse Way. There, they passed through the barricades formed by a phalanx of police cars and vans. Once through the gap, they were out of the crowds and safe, it seemed.

Steele looked back at Carpio. "Your brother has failed," she said. "Did you think I would let you escape? Did you think I wouldn't be prepared?"

Carpio stared darkly at her. "Many people have underestimated my brother," he said. "You are just the latest."

"Let's get this asshole into the courthouse and in front of the judge!" Kit ordered.

The garage was only a hundred yards ahead of them. There was no doubt that they would make it now.

The water in the harbor was flat and calm. The soldier carrying the launcher steadied himself, and with the aid of one of the other men managed to fire the weapon in the direction of the federal courthouse. Because the missile would be targeted by laser, all he had to do was send it in the general direction of its target. Computers would do the rest. A second later the second missile flew from the other boat.

The missiles circled up into the sky, seemingly directionless, searching, but after a few seconds it was as though they made a decision, and they honed in on the courthouse with a sense of purpose.

"They've got the target," one of Javier's men said.

"Yes," Javier said. "Let us just hope that it is the right target."

Buddy was shadowing the caravan moving toward the garage at the federal courthouse. He was moving east along Courthouse Way, toward Bond Drive. Cormack had said that the real attack would be coming from the harbor, up ahead, so he kept his eyes moving between the vans and the shoreline. As he moved along Courthouse Way, though, a commotion halfway up the block on Bond Street caught his eye. A man and a woman seemed to be struggling with each other. The man had a hood pulled up over his head and he was holding the woman with one hand while pointing something at the courthouse with his other hand. She seemed to be struggling to get away.

He recognized Diamond instantly, and it took only a second more for him to recognize the man as T'phong Soh. Buddy broke into a sprint toward them. Any thought of Vincente Carpio and the implications of an escape attempt fled his mind. All he could focus on was protecting the woman he loved.

"Diamond!" he called out. Soh recognized that Buddy was intent on attacking. A look of consternation came over his face, and he threw Diamond to the sidewalk. As he did, she lashed out and knocked something out of the hand that he had been pointing toward the courthouse. Just then, Buddy heard the deafening roar of what seemed like rockets echoing off the building as they flew up Courthouse Way.

"No!" Soh screamed, diving for the object he'd dropped.

"Diamond! Stay down!" Buddy screamed. It was instinctive, but he knew that whatever was about to happen wasn't going to be good. If he could have, he would have thrown himself over her, but he wasn't close enough. And then, all of a sudden, there was an explosion that made the attack at the front of the courthouse seem like firecrackers.

SEVENTY

Cormack had pushed the MEP patrol boat to its limits. He had no idea how much time he had. The police radio on the center console was already blaring with reports of the initial explosions at the front of the courthouse. Every emergency responder from every unit of every police, fire, and rescue force in Boston and any nearby town seemed to be headed for the area to help, and to catch whoever was responsible. But Cormack knew they had no assets on the water. He was the only hope to keep Carpio and his brother from escaping into the harbor, and from there to safety.

He barely slowed the boat down as he pulled into the pier by the World Trade Center, a quarter of a mile from the courthouse, to allow Cicero Andolini to jump on. He'd considered pushing the attack on his own—he was worried that even a slight delay in getting to the scene would allow Carpio to escape—but he knew that would be foolish. He couldn't drive the boat and shoot at the same time, and he knew Carpio's brother had two well-armed Coast Guard attack boats. Alone, he'd be useless. With Cicero he might not be much better, but at least one of them could drive and the other could shoot. That would give them a glimmer of hope.

"What's going on, Boss?" Cicero shouted as he landed on the deck. Cormack floored the engines again, and Cicero was momentarily thrown off balance.

"Carpio's brother's got attack boats!" Cormack shouted back. "They're going to try to break him out from the water!" He pointed to the sack on the deck. "There's guns in there. I don't know which are loaded, but take your pick!" He was weaving around a cargo ship, and they were fast approaching the pier in front of the courthouse.

"You're kidding, right?"

"We've got no choice, gotta fight with what we've got."

"We'll be outgunned," Cicero pointed out, pulling out an assault rifle.

Just then, they saw the missiles go up from the two boats in the harbor, off the shore near the courthouse. They wandered aimlessly for a moment before acquiring their target and heading toward land with purpose.

"That looks like an understatement," Cormack replied.

Javier Carpio had instructed T'phong Soh to target the area roughly five feet above the garage doors so that the explosion would block the entrance and take out many of the police and federal marshals nearby without coming too close to the vans. He wanted to make sure that his brother wasn't harmed in the explosions. Diamond O'Connell had knocked the laser guidance out of Soh's hands seconds before the missiles hit, though. Without specific target acquisition, the missiles' momentum carried them lower and slightly off course, hitting the area to the left of the garage doors, around five feet above the sidewalk. The van carrying Vincente Carpio and Kit Steele, as well as a driver and two other security personnel, was almost to the garage when the missiles struck the courthouse. As a result, the explosion had far greater impact on them than intended.

The first explosion rocked the van and shattered the windshield and windows. For a moment, Steele thought that they had been hit directly by some sort of a bomb, but when she looked out, she could see the destruction to the side of the building. At least she seemed to be uninjured. She glanced behind her, and Vincente Carpio was still in custody. One of the security guards had been hit by some sort of shrapnel, and it looked as though half his head had been taken off. The other guard was alive, but unconscious.

The far left door to the courthouse garage was destroyed, but the middle door was intact and open. "Get into the garage!" Kit screamed at the driver. She looked over, and could see that he had lacerations across his face from the glass.

"I can't see!" the driver screamed back.

"Just hit the gas!"

The driver was trying to clear the blood from his eyes as he jammed his foot down onto the gas pedal. The van shot forward, but it wasn't aligned, so it careened into the side of the door and Steele was thrown forward into the dashboard.

Her head hit first, and she felt herself losing consciousness. She looked back briefly, and through the wire screen separating the front seat from the prisoner, she could see Carpio staring at her. He was smiling.

George Martin was in the second of the vans, and he saw the missiles strike the courthouse. His heart was racing. There were injured police officers and law enforcement personnel all around him. The scope of the destruction was breathtaking, and he knew that he was responsible. No one could ever find out.

Worse, his betrayal wasn't complete. He still had to free Vincente Carpio. How, exactly, to do that without people finding out that he had sold himself to the devil was still a mystery. Then he saw the lead van slam into the side of the garage door. He jumped out of his vehicle. "Secure the perimeter!" he shouted to the corrections officers in the van with him. "I'm getting Carpio inside!"

As he hit the sidewalk, the entire area was in chaos. Nearly all the federal marshals who had been manning the barricades by the garage, waiting for Carpio to arrive, were dead or injured. Most of them were covered in dust and debris. It was, Martin thought, like a mini version of the scenes from the World Trade Center on September eleventh; some people were screaming and running, others wandered aimlessly with vacant eyes.

Martin ran to the lead van. Surveying the situation, he could see that one of the two guards in the back was dead, and the other was incapacitated. In the front, the driver and Kit Steele were both unconscious. That was good luck for him. He unlocked the door to the prisoners' compartment. Vincente Carpio seemed to be the only one in the van who remained unscathed. He looked at Martin with malevolence.

Martin leaned over the seat and took the key off the dead guard in the back. "Your brother," he said simply to Carpio. The tattooed man nodded in understanding. Martin unlocked Carpio's wrists and unshackled his legs. "You're on your own from here," Martin said. "No one can know." He handed his gun to Carpio. "If anything happens to you—if you get caught—tell them you overpowered me, understand?" He could live with people thinking he was incompetent, but not with people knowing he was dirty. Besides, with the money he had and his retirement, he could live a good life. He'd put in his twenty and he had a fat pension waiting for him.

He turned around to make sure no one was watching the scene unfold. It looked as though he was going to get away with it. No one was paying attention—everything was in a state of chaos.

When he turned back, he saw that Carpio was smiling at him. The gun was raised, and Martin was looking down its barrel. At first, he thought Carpio was merely playing his part, pantomiming the act of overpowering Martin. Then he saw the glint of pure evil in Carpio's eyes. "No, wait!" Martin cried.

Carpio pulled the trigger.

The explosion from the missiles knocked Buddy off his feet, and his head slammed into the pavement. When he opened his eyes, he had no idea for how long he'd been unconscious. It couldn't have been for long, as smoke and ash still rained down from the explosion's aftermath. He was groggy, and it took him a moment to get his bearings. He remembered a feeling of panic, and a sense that someone was in danger, but it took a moment for him to put the pieces together.

Vincente Carpio was being brought to the courthouse . . .

Buddy was there to try to stop Soh . . .

He'd been watching the van, watching the waterfront . . .

Soh was there . . .

Missiles overhead . . .

Diamond!

It all came flooding back to him. He was on his feet, unsteadily at first. He felt like his skull had been split, but he fought through the pain, shading his eyes against the sun, which now seemed brighter than he could ever remember. He looked up the street, toward where he'd seen her fall as the missiles flew overhead.

She was no longer there . . .

And neither was Soh.

SEVENTY-ONE

Kit Steele felt someone moving her. She was in the front seat of the corrections van, her head was leaning against the dashboard. Her forehead was sticky from the blood that had run from the gash in her scalp, covering her face. The blood congealed in her eyes, making it difficult to see. At least, she thought, someone had reached her and was providing assistance. More important, it meant that they had also gotten to Vincente Carpio, and they were undoubtedly taking him into the courthouse now. Ultimately all she cared about was that he would be held to account for what he'd done, and he would never be allowed to prey on others again.

The first responder was rough with her as he pulled her from the van. She supposed, though, that was he focused first on getting victims to safety, and there was little safety in a crumpled vehicle.

"Walk!"

The voice was male, with a Hispanic accent. It seemed an odd demand.

"Walk!" The order came again, and she forced her eyes to open slightly. The sight was horrific. Skulls danced before her—a sphere of bloody, massacred heads. And in the middle, eyes as evil as any she had ever seen.

The shock brought her back to consciousness quickly, and she realized that she was looking into the eyes of Vincente Carpio. She felt something hard and sharp pressing into her abdomen and she looked down to see a gun jabbed under her rib cage.

"The water!" Carpio said. "We are going to the water! If you move or you scream, you die." He was half pushing, half carrying her down Courthouse Way, toward the harbor. There was a small pier just off the edge of the seawall less than fifty yards away. None of it made any sense. Was he planning on jumping into the harbor? Was he planning on drowning them both?

Steele's feet slipped beneath her, but Carpio kept her upright. Around them, people were shouting and running in different directions. It seemed as though no one was in charge. Worse still, it was as though no one could see them. She looked at Carpio and saw that he was still in his orange prisoner's jumpsuit, and yet no one was stopping them as they hurried away from the smoldering courthouse.

She was thinking that she was possibly dead and in some nightmare of an afterlife—but then a BPD officer shouted at them. "Hey! What the fuck are you doing?" He approached them. He looked like he was in his fifties, heavyset, with dark circles under his eyes. Judging from his age, he probably spent nearly all of his time in some administrative role, and had only been pulled out onto the street because of the extra manpower requested to deal with the planned attack. She opened her mouth to talk, but her tongue wasn't ready to function.

"She is hurt," she heard Carpio say. "I am helping her."

The officer was confused by the answer. He was standing right in front of them now, blocking their way. He had a hand up, making clear that he didn't intend to let them pass—as though his hand could stop a madman. "You're a prisoner!" he said.

"She's hurt," Carpio repeated. Steele could feel the policeman looking at her, and yet she still wasn't physically able to speak—to warn him that he was about to be killed, and that she would soon follow. Carpio kept one arm around her waist, keeping her moving. He pulled the gun out of her abdomen, though, and shoved it into the officer's prodigious gut. He fired three times, and the policeman's eyes went wide as the bullets tore his insides apart. He went down like a sack.

The man's belly had muffled the sound of the shots somewhat, but after the earlier explosions, everyone in the area was sensitive to anything that sounded like any sort of attack. All of a sudden, dozens of law enforcement personnel turned their attention to Carpio and Steele. "Stop!" they shouted. "They're getting away!"

None of them, though, was between them and the pier. Carpio pulled her along at a near sprint as the gunfire started behind them. She assumed that they would hit the seawall and he would drag her into the water. That was fine with her. At least he'd be dead, and if she had to sacrifice herself to make sure that Vincente Carpio never hurt anyone else, she was happy to do it.

As they came to the seawall, though, she looked down the narrow ramp to the small pier and saw the two boats waiting there. They were both military vessels with guns mounted fore and aft, both with three armed men on board. They were shouting to Carpio, urging him on.

It was at that moment that she knew T'phong Soh had lied to her. The attack on Northern Avenue had been a diversion to keep the law enforcement forces at the front of the courthouse and leave the waterfront unguarded. She'd been an idiot, and Carpio's escape was her fault. Any further brutality that Vincente Carpio would carry out in his lifetime was on her head.

Cormack was only a hundred yards from the courthouse when he saw Vincente Carpio appear at the edge of the shore. He had what looked like a hostage, and it took only a moment for him to realize that he was dragging Kit Steele with him as he hurried down onto the ramp to the small pier. The two heavily armed boats were pulled up to the edge of the pier, and they looked poised to speed away as soon as Carpio was on board.

"What are you going to do?" Cicero called to him.

"We can't let them get away from the shoreline!" Cormack called back. "If they get out onto the harbor with all this traffic, there's no way to know where they'll disappear to!"

"They've got machine guns," Cicero responded. "We've got peashooters. How are we going to keep them from getting away?"

"Only one option! Hold on!" Cormack floored the engine and crouched down behind the center console as he sped straight at the two boats.

Cicero rolled his eyes and got down low next to him, pointing a gun up ahead, but waiting to fire until he had a realistic chance of hitting anything. "This is stupid," he muttered under his breath.

Javier Carpio's attention was focused on the shore. He was gratified to see his brother had made it to the edge of the harbor, but he knew that the mission wasn't over yet. Several of the police and federal officers now realized what had happened, and they were giving chase. They were shooting down at the boats from the shore, but were easily dispersed with volleys of machine-gun fire.

Javier was far less gratified to see that his brother was bringing a hostage with him. Hostages, in his view, were often more trouble than they were worth, and in this case it was clear that the presence of the woman was not preventing the police from firing their weapons. She was also slowing Vincente down, and speed was of the essence if they were to get away. The increased traffic on the water would make it possible for them to disappear and get on another boat undetected, but only if they could get away from the shore before the police could get a boat on the water.

"Vincente! *Vamos!*" Javier called to his brother.

More gunfire rained down from the seawall, and Javier directed one of his men manning the forward machine gun to return fire.

Vincente and the woman he was dragging with him were almost at the boat, and Javier could almost taste the sweetness of a successful mission when he heard more gunfire. He looked up at the shoreline to find the source, but there was no one visible—it seemed that they had been chased away, and yet someone was shooting. The gunfire came again, and one of the men on the second boat screamed out in agony and fell into the water. Still, though, Javier could see no one firing from the shore.

"Over there!" one of his men yelled.

At that moment, Javier realized that the gunfire wasn't coming from the shore—it was coming from the water behind them. He turned to see a boat headed toward them at full speed. There were two men on board, and one of them was firing an assault rifle as they bore down on Javier's men.

"Shoot!" Javier screamed at his men, directing them to fire the mounted machine guns at the unanticipated attackers. The machine guns, though, were bulky, and turning them was difficult. Vincente was almost at the boat, but it wasn't clear whether he would be able to get on board in time for them to get away. "Get in, Vincente!" he called.

Vincente and the woman stumbled on board just as the oncoming boat slammed into the port side of Javier's vessel, and Javier heard the hull split. One of his men was thrown overboard, and the machine gun he'd been trying to swing around at the attackers fired into the air. Freezing water started to flow in through the split. The boat that had rammed them was caught on the hull, and it, too, was taking on water. "Onto the other boat!" Javier shouted. It pulled alongside, and Javier jumped onto it.

Vincente was still holding the woman, and he tried to pull her with him onto the second boat, but she was too strong, and she fought him. He'd wanted to take his time with her. He'd wanted to enjoy the experience of watching her scream as he cut her to pieces—savor the delight in witnessing her agony and holding her gaze as the life faded from her eyes. It wasn't to be, but he could still take some small joy from her death.

He pulled her close and whispered into her ear, "You will not be the last," he said to her. Then he pushed the gun under her protective vest and fired four times, just under her ribs. He kept his hand there so he could feel the warmth of her blood as it spilled out.

He stepped back and looked her in the eyes as she felt the pain. She was strong, there was no doubt. She fought death as she looked at him, but they both knew death would win—and quickly.

"Vincente, now!" Javier yelled. The police and marshals were back on the seawall, firing down, and there was now only one machine gun firing back, so they were harder to disperse.

"You will not be the last!" Vincente yelled into Kit's face. Then he let her go and moved quickly to jump into the other boat.

SEVENTY-TWO

T'phong Soh was moving as fast as he could away from the courthouse. He held O'Connell's daughter by the hair at the back of her head with one hand, and a knife to her stomach with the other. She'd struggled at first, but when he showed her the knife and held it against her she'd become more cooperative. He kept the knife low, against her belly, to avoid anyone noticing. It seemed unlikely that anyone would pay any attention to the two of them as they hurried away from the site of the attack. The entire area was in chaos.

He'd seen her run past him, and was shocked that she was there. That meant that Juan Suarez had failed in his mission, and it meant that Soh would have one card fewer to play against O'Connell when the day was over.

He would kill her as soon as he was sure that he could get away undetected. He would have preferred to take her hostage, but it wasn't practical under the circumstances. At least her death would send a final message to Cormack before Soh took over the harbor. If he was confronted by the police before he could get away, though, a hostage would come in handy.

As they ran up Bond Drive toward Marina Park Drive, he saw several police officers running toward them. He couldn't tell whether they were running specifically toward him, or whether they were just running toward the courthouse generally, but he couldn't take a chance. There was a construction site on the water just off Fan Pier Boulevard. He veered east and ducked through a loose gate, dragging O'Connell's daughter with him.

Once through the fence, he held the knife to the girl's throat, looking at the gap in the fence, waiting for the site to be rushed by the police. Nothing happened. He held his breath, listening as the footsteps rushed past the fence and continued on toward the mayhem at the courthouse. He waited for a minute or two, and then looked out. There was no one there. It appeared that the path for his escape was as clear as it would ever be.

He threw the girl against the fence and raised his knife. He was looking forward to the sensation of spilling her blood.

Diamond had been thrown to the sidewalk before the missiles struck the courthouse. She'd felt the earth move under her as she lay there, but because she was already braced against the ground, she'd avoided further injury.

When she'd picked her head up, the first thing she saw was Buddy lying on the street. He wasn't moving, and she was terrified that he might be dead. She had no idea what had happened, but it seemed as though some sort of a real war had come to Boston. There were bloodied people everywhere, and the screaming was deafening.

She'd gotten to her feet and started toward Buddy's motionless body, but before she could take more than a couple of steps, T'phong Soh had grabbed her by the hair. "Come, now!" he hissed at her. She tried to punch at him, but he yanked hard on her hair and threw her off balance. Then she'd felt the knife at her abdomen. "I will split you open," he said in his high voice. The horror of having a knife so close to the baby she was carrying was too much to bear. She'd nodded. "OK," she said. "Just don't hurt me!"

He'd dragged her down the street, and when she saw the policemen running toward them, she'd thought she might be saved. He'd pulled her into the construction site, though, and held the knife to her throat. She prayed that the police would find them, but they didn't. And then, when he threw her against the fence, she knew that he was going to kill her.

As he raised the knife, all she could focus on was the possibility that he was going to split open her belly and her tiny child would spill out onto the ground. That terrifying notion touched something primal within her, and as his hand was raised, she shot her delicate hand out and connected with his windpipe. She wasn't large, and there wasn't much power behind the blow, but it was well placed, and she could see the momentary panic on his face as he struggled to breathe. He would recover soon, she knew, so she barreled past him and ran to the gap in the fence.

She could hear him right behind her, still choking, but determined as the air forced its way through his windpipe. She was just through the fence when she felt his hand on her back, and she knew the knife would come next. At least, she thought, it wouldn't be in her belly.

Buddy was dazed for a moment, and all he could do was call out her name. Under any other circumstances, others on the street would have stopped to help him, but there were so many dead and wounded, and so many others calling out for people who'd been lost, the world seemed to pass him by.

He didn't know where to go, so he stumbled in the direction he'd last seen Diamond and Soh. He was headed away from the courthouse and all the death and destruction there. That seemed to make sense in his temporarily addled brain. There seemed no reason why Soh would go back toward the courthouse. He looked down and saw, to his surprise, that he was still carrying his gun.

He was on the corner of Bond and Fan Pier Boulevard when he saw her dart out from one of the nearby construction sites. "Diamond!" he shouted as he ran to her.

He was nearly there when he saw Soh reaching out for her. Buddy raised his gun, but his eyesight and his hand were still unsteady from hitting the pavement, and he was afraid of hitting Diamond. Instead he lowered his shoulder and drove himself into Soh's chest with all the power he could.

Soh was just bringing his knife down in a looping arc to stab Diamond, and as he was carried back into the fence, his arm's momentum continued and the knife sank into Buddy's back. The two of them careened off the fence, and Buddy fell to the ground. He was still dazed, and he could feel the blood running down his back. The focus in his vision was coming back to him, but slowly. He looked up at Soh as the smaller man came toward him, knife raised again. Buddy raised his gun and fired. He still couldn't aim very well, but at least Diamond was no longer in the line of fire.

The shot hit Soh in the shoulder, and knocked him back. The knife went skittering along the street. Rage flashed in his eyes, and for a moment Buddy thought he was going to retrieve the knife and come back to finish him off. In a flash, though, the rage seemed to ebb. He looked around and seemed to realize where he was. He put his hand up to his shoulder and felt the blood. Then he turned and ran toward Northern Avenue. Buddy watched as he disappeared into the crowd fleeing the chaos.

"Buddy!" Diamond was at his side now. "Let me see, roll over!" He did as he was told. "It's bleeding, but it doesn't look too deep," she said. "We need to get you to a hospital."

He was looking around, still shocked by the madness. "I'm not the only one," he said.

"What happened?" She was looking around too, now, taking in the carnage.

"I don't know," Buddy replied. "Your father said it was an escape attempt, but I wasn't expecting anything like this. Looks like no one was. Jesus Christ."

"Can you walk?"

"Yeah," he said. "I can walk. Are you OK? Did he hurt you? Did he hurt the baby?"

She put a hand to her abdomen. She had no way to know for sure, but everything felt OK. She shook her head. "I think we're both fine."

SEVENTY-THREE

Kit knew she was going to die. That didn't concern her. The only thing she could focus on was Vincente Carpio's words.

You will not be the last.

She'd failed. She'd spent years fighting to protect those who couldn't protect themselves. She'd devoted herself to keeping predators like Vincente Carpio off the street, but it was pointless. She'd caught the man who'd killed Ollie and now he was going to escape. She looked down at the blood pouring out of her and felt more lost than ever before. There would always be evil in the world, and there was nothing she had been able to do about it.

She couldn't accept that. She wouldn't accept that. She fought back against the agony ripping through her body and forced air into her lungs. As Vincente Carpio turned to leap onto the other boat, she threw herself at him, wrapping her arms around him and burning through the last of her life's energy as she pushed her legs forward and the two of them toppled into the harbor.

She heard him scream as they hit the water, and she felt a wave of pleasure at his shock and surprise. The water enveloped them, and the cold burned through her. Carpio fought to free himself, but she clung to him as they sank. Her lungs were no longer working, and the feeling in her extremities started to fade. Her eyes were closed, and she kept all of her focus on holding tight to Carpio as he thrashed and hit and kicked out at her. She could no longer feel anything, and she wasn't sure whether he was still in her grasp. She was aware that she was sinking, deeper and deeper into the harbor. It was done. She no longer needed to fight. The blood from her wounds mixed with the water. She no longer cared—she'd done what she could, and now it was time to rest.

* * *

She woke on the shore of Nantasket beach. The water was summer-warm, and the sun was shining down on her face as she pulled herself off the sand. A light, warm breeze blew off the sea, and she breathed the scent of the water deep into her lungs.

She saw Dillon. He was walking to her with that smile he had that melted her heart the first time she'd seen him. It was filled with warmth and love and desire.

She ran to him and threw her arms around his body, hugging him so tightly she thought she might hurt him. He hugged her back, almost as tightly, as she sobbed joyously into his chest. After a moment, she tilted her head up and her lips found his. It was at once familiar and new. She felt nearly complete and she melted into him and let herself believe it was real.

She couldn't remember the kiss ending, but her head was now on his shoulder, and she was looking down the beach. She could see a small figure in the distance, playing in the shallow water, splashing with a joy that only a six-year-old can exude on a summer day at the beach—as though every grain of sand was placed there specifically for his enjoyment.

She gasped and pulled away from Dillon, looking at him for reassurance, afraid that it was an illusion. He nodded at her. "He's been waiting for you," he said.

Her first steps toward him were cautious. She kept waiting for her feet to falter or slip. She felt certain that he would run away or disappear somehow. He didn't, though. He continued splashing in the warm water, his laughter washing over her the way it had so long ago. With each step she became more hopeful, and more confident, until she was running at a full sprint.

He saw her as she neared, and he opened his arms to her, a look of pure love in his eyes and in his smile. "Mommy!" he called out to her.

She swept him up, still running, and he threw his arms around her neck and kissed her cheek. He was clinging so tightly to her neck that she found it hard to breathe, but she didn't care. He was there. He was really there, and he wasn't fading into a pile of dust. She knew that she was with him again, at last.

She knew in her heart that, this time, it wasn't a dream.

SEVENTY-FOUR

Cormack saw Kit go into the water with Vincente Carpio. The MEP boat he'd driven into Javier Carpio's craft was taking on water, but it didn't seem as though it would sink immediately. He and Cicero Andolini were shooting at Javier Carpio and the men on the second boat. It was an even fight until Steele and Vincente went into the water. Javier Carpio lost his focus as he rushed to the side of the boat to try to retrieve his brother, and a fresh volley of gunfire from the shore hit him in the head and took out two of his last men.

Cormack dove over the side of the boat, swimming down furiously to save Kit. He could see nothing underwater, and he had only a rough idea of where they had gone in. He came up twice for a breath, and then dove down one last time.

He could barely feel his fingers anymore, but just as he was about to come up for air again, he thought he felt something like fabric brush up against his hand. He churned his arms, and felt a wrist. Grabbing hold of it, he kicked to the surface, fighting the need to take a breath until his head broke the surface. He was right next to the pier, and a dozen law enforcement officers were leaning over him, reaching down. He looked at his hand, still grasping the arm, and saw the orange jumpsuit.

He let out an angry scream. "Goddammit!" Cicero Andolini was on the pier, too, and Cormack, out of breath and frozen, looked at him. "She's still down there!" he shouted. He was trying to force air into his lungs, but hypothermia was setting in, and his muscles weren't functioning properly anymore.

"She is," Cicero agreed. "She's gone, Cormack. And you will be, too, if you don't get out of the water."

Cormack knew he was right, but he couldn't bring himself to climb onto the pier. Two BPD officers reached down and hauled him up. There were emergency crews on the scene still trying to cope with the dead and injured from the attack on the courthouse, and one of them put a blanket over Cormack's shoulders.

At the edge of the pier, two paramedics were frantically trying to bring Vincente Carpio back to life. They were breathing into his mouth and pumping his chest, but there didn't seem to be any chance that they would be successful. Then, just as it looked like they were going to give up, Carpio's body convulsed, and he spat up what seemed like a gallon of water.

Cicero shook his head. "God has an ironic notion of justice," he said.

Cormack was tempted to grab a gun and shoot Carpio, but he held his temper. Besides, he still couldn't feel his fingers, and he wasn't sure he could hold a gun. "Let's go," Cormack responded. "There's nothing left for us to do here."

They started walking up the ramp, off the pier. "You can't leave," one of the cops nearby said.

"You gonna arrest us?" Cormack asked.

"We need to interview you," the cop said. The confidence in his voice was wavering.

"OK," Cormack said. "Call my lawyer and make an appointment. In the meantime, I have a harbor to run."

Kit's body washed up onshore three days later. She was found by a fisherman, lying facedown on the rocks at the end of Hull, only two miles from where she and Dillon and Ollie had spent their summers frolicking in the surf on Nantasket beach.

The funeral was a somber, quiet affair. She had no family and few friends. The FBI sent an official contingent, but none of the senior brass attended. Some of the local agents and cops who had worked with her over the years made appearances, but there was no talk of her wit or her warmth or her heart. All of that had been taken from her before any of those there knew her. They knew a different Kit Steele than the one that existed before her husband and son were murdered.

Cormack didn't go to the funeral. His presence there would have drawn stares and raised questions that were not in anyone's interest to have asked. Besides, he preferred to remember Kit as she was the last time they were together.

In all, not including the perpetrators, thirty-two people were killed in the attack on the John Joseph Moakley Federal Courthouse—ten of whom were law enforcement officers. Another two hundred people were badly injured. The funerals stretched out for two weeks, and the BOSTON STRONG signs once again were ubiquitous, not only in Massachusetts, but around the country.

Federal district court proceedings were moved to the old federal courthouse at Post Office Square for the four months that it would take to fix the damage done by Javier Carpio and his men, but Vincente Carpio was arraigned in F. Barton Baylor's courtroom in the courthouse by the water, even as it was undergoing repairs. It would be the only hearing held in the building before the grand reopening. Baylor assured Carpio that he would be given all the protections of the United States judicial system as he was charged with thirty-two counts of capital murder. The United States Attorney's Office refused to discuss a plea bargain, and no one really doubted that he would ultimately be strapped to a table and injected with a lethal combination of sodium thiopental, pancuronium bromide, and potassium chloride.

That winter would go down in the books as the coldest in Boston's history—a record that would stand for more than a hundred years. Those who lived through it would talk of it in the mythic tones that only true New Englanders could carry. Eventually the city returned to normal, and all that remained were the smattering of new monuments to those who gave their lives on one fateful day in February when the cold snap finally broke and for one brief moment the city seemed to explode.

SEVENTY-FIVE

Friday, February 15

Cormack agreed to the terms of the meeting. At some level it was crazy, he knew—anything could happen when you were on the enemy's turf. And yet he had to have closure. He wouldn't live his life wondering when the other shoe was going to drop.

He went alone to the Colombian restaurant in East Boston, unarmed and unprotected. He walked in the front door and didn't wait to be escorted to the back. He'd been to the restaurant before, and he saw no reason to wait.

There were three armed men in the back room, all looking twitchy, with automatic weapons slung across their shoulders. Cormack couldn't blame them. After the turmoil of the past few days, everyone in the city seemed twitchy.

There was a table set up in the middle of the room with chairs placed at opposite sides. Cormack sat in one, leaning back in the seat as though he was the only one in the place with nothing to worry about. He had to sit there for a few minutes by himself. That was fine with him. Even without any men or weapons, Cormack felt confident that he had the upper hand.

T'phong Soh entered the room in a whirl, the door at the far end of the room swinging on its hinges as he strode toward Cormack with what appeared to be impatience and anger. The events of the past few days had unnerved him most of all. One arm was in a sling. "You have put limits on my business in the past," he said, his tone accusatory.

"I have," Cormack conceded. "We all have to have limits."

Soh shook his head. "No," he said. "I decide what business I will do. No one else. That is the way it must be going forward. Is that understood?"

Cormack looked at the men with the automatic weapons. "I understand that that's the way you feel," he said. "But that's not the way it is ever going to be."

Soh slammed his fist down on the table. His face had turned bright red. "No!" he shouted. "It will be that way, or you will die!"

"You asked me here under a flag of truce," Cormack said. "I accepted your invitation. And now you threaten me?"

"You will die! And I will kill your daughter as well!"

Cormack could feel the anger burn within him, but he fought back against it. Now was not the time for him to lose control. He leaned back even farther in his chair. "Have you checked with your superiors about this?" he asked.

"I have no superiors!" Soh shouted, and for a moment, Cormack thought the small man was going to lunge across the table at him.

The door behind Cormack opened, and five men walked in. All of them were heavily tattooed, and four of them were heavily armed. The other one was a man of enormous girth. He was not quite six feet tall, but he was well over four hundred pounds, and his presence seemed to crowd out everything in the room.

The impact of the enormous man's presence was clear on the faces and in the demeanor of Soh and the men behind him. Soh's face went white, and the men behind him eased back, lowering their guns.

The man moved slowly, and without a word. He reached over and pulled a chair that was leaning against the wall over to the table. As he sat down, everyone in the room held their breath, wondering whether the chair would take his weight. It groaned and sagged, but managed not to collapse.

He folded his arms on the table and took a deep breath. When he spoke, his voice was so low and soft that Cormack had to strain to hear him.

"It surprises me to hear that you have no superiors," he said with a tone of disappointment.

"Pineda, I didn't mean—"

The huge man waved at Soh to cut him off. "It is too late for that, my friend," he said. "Juan Suarez is dead. Most of your people are dead." Soh's face went whiter still and he started to try to talk, but Pineda held a hand up to silence him. "I recruited Suarez in El Salvador, and brought him to this country. You were doing good business out here, but there were rumors that you were no longer loyal. There were rumors that you were no longer paying your tributes in full. There was a rumor that you were building an army for yourself. I sent Suarez out here to look into that. I thought he would likely kill you in a matter of weeks, and that would have been fine with me."

Pineda shifted his weight, and the chair gave a loud shriek.

"He didn't, though. Instead, he fell under your spell, and pledged his allegiance to you." Pineda drummed his fat fingers on the table, and it was like each tap was the pounding of a great bass drum. "Do you think you can cast the same spell on me?" He looked sideways at Soh, the way a giant lizard might look at its prey.

He shook his head slowly. "Juan Suarez received his fate. Will you accept your fate as well?"

Soh looked around the room, and Cormack could see the panic in his eyes. All at once, he leaped from his chair and shouted orders at the three men standing behind him. They reacted, but not in the way that he anticipated. One of them drove the butt of his gun into Soh's stomach, and the other two fell upon him to restrain him.

"Bring him to the car," Pineda said. "And bring the machetes."

He stood up, and the chair breathed a sigh of relief. He looked at Cormack. "It was dangerous of you to contact me."

"I didn't think I had a choice. And I knew my counterpart in Los Angeles would know how to reach you."

"How?"

Cormack shrugged. "It's the job of the head of the harbor union to know everything that happens in his harbor. I just figured . . ."

"Thank you for the information," Pineda said.

Cormack stood. "I thought you should know."

"I will make sure that whoever takes over here will obey your rules."

Cormack knew that that was a lie, but there seemed little advantage in pointing that out at the moment. He just nodded and walked to the door.

Behind him, he could hear Soh shout his name, but he was immediately silenced, as the three men he had thought were loyal to him pummeled him into the cement floor.

Cormack walked out without looking back.

SEVENTY-SIX

Friday, September 6

Diamond bore the labor bravely, particularly given its duration. Twenty-seven hours wasn't a record on the maternity ward, but it was enough to draw the admiration of the nurses who spent their lives ushering souls into the world.

It was worth it, in the end. Everyone agreed that they had never seen a more beautiful baby. Buddy, who had stayed by her side all through the labor and looked almost as tired as she did, beamed nonetheless as he held his son.

Mack Cavanaugh.

It was an oddly mature name for a newborn, and yet somehow it seemed to fit. The boy hardly cried, and there was a strange self-assurance about him as he lay comfortably in his mother's arms. It was almost as though the peace that generations had sought found purchase in the baby boy.

The boy's grandfather, for whom the boy was named, was the first one in the room once it was acceptable. He brought cigars that couldn't be lit, and pride that couldn't be extinguished. And as the commotion of the delivery died down, the baby was left alone with the only three members of his family.

"What now?" she asked.

"Now, you get some rest," the boy's father responded.

"No, I mean for us."

"Now, we get back to normal," her father said.

"What's normal for us?"

He shrugged. "Fall is here, and winter won't be far behind. The harbor is running smoothly again, thanks to Buddy. He's a natural at scheduling and making sure everything is accounted for . . . and everyone is accounting."

"I enjoy it," the younger man said.

"Good," the new grandfather said. "I'm getting older. And if it's possible, I'd like to keep this a family business."

She looked down at her newborn and smiled. "What do you think, Mack?" she asked. "Would you be OK if we built this together as a family."

The baby looked up at her and gurgled amicably.

"Good," she said. "Then it's settled."